THE DARK SIDE OF THE BALCONY

THE DARK SIDE
OF THE BALCONY

Patrick Gooch

Book Guild Publishing
Sussex, England

First published in Great Britain in 2007 by
The Book Guild Ltd
Pavilion View
19 New Road
Brighton, BN1 1UF

Typesetting in Baskerville by
SetSystems Ltd, Saffron Walden, Essex

Printed in Great Britain by
CPI Antony Rowe

A catalogue record for this book is
available from the British Library

ISBN 978 1 84624 085 0

To Gwen –
committed researcher,
invaluable reader, and
keen-eyed critic

Prologue

Archival document from the church of San Luca, Cremona

Como gli altri, presto passerò a miglior vita.

Temo che sofferenza e disperazione mi

abbiano colto in un momento in cui ho ancora

molto da offrire.

Raggiungerò I miei pari prima del tempo e,

per tale motivo, mi sentirò per sempre

inappagato e a loro inferiore.

Perchè, e chi ha fatto questo a me?

Firmato il 17 settembre 1747

Carlo Bergonzi

Costruttore di strumenti a corda

Like the others, I am soon to depart this world.
I fear my affliction, and despair it has caught me at a
moment when I have still much to offer.

I shall join my peers long before my time is due, and
because of this, will stand unfulfilled and ever
in their shadows.

Why, and who has done this to me?

Signed this day – 17th September 1747

Carlo Bergonzi
Instrument Maker

Chapter One

Swinging onto the Autostrada del Sole, he veered across the carriageway, accelerating hard, driving with an urgency at times verging on the reckless. Taking the superstrada at Orte, he kept up the same relentless pace, often closing rapidly on slower vehicles in the outside lane, with heart-stopping use of the brakes. The displeasure of other drivers was proclaimed by their blaring horns and flashing lights. He covered the hundred and fifty kilometres in just over the hour, bringing the car to rest on the side of the mountain road. The cooling tick of the engine was the only sound breaking the silence. No birdsong. No wind rustling in the trees. None of the traffic noise which had enveloped him since leaving Rome. Slowly, he eased his tall frame from the car, and walked towards the barrier. Far below, the Tiber twisted and turned through the countryside.

The barrier had not been there in 1947. Although metalled, the road had been pitted and uneven, often wreathed in mists – unpredictable when the rains ran off the heights and flowed down the track from the hillside village.

His shins pressed hard against the deep ribs of the Armco railing. Peering down the tree-covered slopes, he turned slowly to survey the upward tilt of the roadway, shifting his gaze to plot the imaginary course across the stony verge, and out beyond the edge.

It was still difficult to come to terms with the incident: over half a century ago, his grandfather had driven down the hill, ignored the bend, and plummeted three hundred metres into the valley below. His father was often given to describing it in detail. It had been raining, heavily at times, water gushing off the mountainside. But driving would not have been especially hazardous – not for someone, his father would stoutly declare, accustomed to such conditions.

He leaned against a tree, a cigarette in his lips, trying to make sense of it. Then, abruptly stubbing it out, he strode towards the car. Today, more than at any other time, he felt the loss of his grandfather keenly.

The summons had come from the administrator. Going to the third floor, he had waited the customary twenty minutes before being ushered into the room. Standing before the large, ornate desk he had been given his instructions. Detailed and exacting, they had taken almost an hour to impart. Yet, within the first few minutes his attention had been dragged elsewhere. Walking away afterwards, he had made a conscious effort to pull himself together, to grasp the essentials. No notes were kept. Written records were forbidden.

The assignment was to commence the following day. In twenty-four hours' time he would receive flight tickets, a fresh passport, the necessary funds and, of course, the package.

All he could think of was to turn for home, the urge to discover what had happened in the past, irresistible – for this was a most bizarre circumstance. Unknown to his masters, after an interval of almost seventy-five years, he was now the second member of his family to be allotted the identical task!

As he drove up the mountainside, flashes of past conversations intruded, especially when his father had revealed more than he should about his grandfather. It had been at a village wedding. The occasion had been joyous: laughter, gaiety, music, and copious amounts of wine.

His mind fixed on the moment his father and he had sat together, companionably, in the olive grove. How papa had found out he never knew. In 1929, his grandfather had received an important commission. He was to approach a certain individual, gain his commitment, and act as the go-between. Six months later, grandfather had been involved in some vast cover-up. His father was unaware of the details, but from that moment *il nonno* had been a troubled man.

He recalled his father's words. 'I was young, very young, but even I noticed the changes in him. Looking back, it was as though his very beliefs had been undermined.'

He recollected other snatches of the unexpectedly frank tête-à-tête.

'He served another fifteen years, undertaking modest assignments, nothing of consequence. At the first opportunity, when the Armistice was signed in 1945, your grandfather retired to spend the rest of his days here, above the Vale Tiberina, in his beloved Umbria.'

He had made one other significant comment: 'By then, I too had entered their service. A bishop, a kindly soul, called me to his office to tell me my father was dead. His car had run off the road in a storm. But, he knew that road. Knew it well! Anyway, coming from the village, it would have toppled towards the poplars . . .'

'Toppled towards the poplars!' – the phrase kept echoing in his mind.

He came to a halt outside the rambling farmhouse, home to his family for more than a century. His mind was in turmoil: anxious to bombard his father with questions, yet reluctant to disregard the most basic of all the tenets of 'I Messagieri': '*Tutto quello che sai morrira con me!*' – 'My lips are sealed forever!'

How could he presume *il papa* might cast aside this most fervently-held of all obligations? The only hope, he realised, was to make him aware that he, too, was about to take on the rôle once expected of his own father.

Making his way up the path to the front door, another thought struck him. Was it really unforeseen to have been chosen for the mission? The Rules of Patrimony dictate that son follows father. There were never more than twelve Messengers. Few, very few outsiders, were ever co-opted to their ranks.

Was it so extraordinary, bearing in mind he was the seventh generation in a service committed to discharging the discreet, very private work of the Curia?

Chapter Two

Perched on the western bank of the Tiber, occupying forty-five hectares within the centre of Rome, lies the Vatican. A tiny theocracy, independent of Italian rule, guardedly neutral in both Roman and national politics.

On the north side of the Piazza San Pietro, behind the colonnade which almost encircles the square, are the principal offices of the Curia, the administrative arm of the Papacy.

More than three thousand people are in its employ, working in a bewildering number of departments spread throughout the walled enclave and beyond into the city itself. But the heartbeat of the organisation is to be found in the building adjoining the Apostolic Palace.

As might be expected of any bureaucracy, more so in an environment shut to public gaze, cabals will form, stratagems are plotted. Factions will polarise to consider topics of concern – often for the common good; just as often, to counter encroachment upon personal domains.

So it was that a meeting in an elegant salon on the third floor, observed by the staff at the end of the working day, did not seem out of place. After all, three distinguished cardinals were present. As the corridors emptied and the noises of the building slowly subsided, six men seated themselves in a ring of ornate, gilt chairs.

'Unfortunately, Cardinal Carzinsky will not be with us,' intoned the prelate in whose rooms they had gathered. 'However, on this occasion, it is of little consequence. Although he has long been retired, I hope he will recover sufficiently to attend in the future.'

The statement was uttered by a man who typified the higher ranks of the Church. Statesmanlike in manner, a persona cultivated to his office, Cardinal Marchetti reflected the image many would expect of an eminent ecclesiastic: tall in stature, smooth, grey hair

4

carefully brushed back from a prominent forehead; strong features, marred only slightly by the somewhat hooked nose that, at times, suggested a bird of prey. An impression reinforced by piercing eyes.

'Will he ever recover? His age surely weighs against him,' commented a senior cleric, resplendent in the silk robes allowed the Pontifical Family. 'After all, he must be in his late eighties.'

'In fact, he is ninety-one,' corrected the cardinal. 'Fortunately, he is still in command of his faculties – which is highly beneficial. As a close aide, he has recall of all that Pope Pius XII explained to him of the event. His contribution will be invaluable.'

'When was it? Remind me,' prompted a cardinal to his left.

'In 1929,' interjected another, seated opposite. 'Pius, or Monsignor Eugenio Pacelli as he was then, drafted the Lateran Treaty, which our beloved Duce signed.'

'In fact,' added Cardinal Marchetti, rising to his feet, 'Carzinsky also held a high-ranking post in the Administration of the Patrimony of the Holy See. He was in charge of investments before outsiders were brought in to perform such tasks.'

'Pity we didn't keep that side of affairs to ourselves,' sighed one of the intimate group. 'Perhaps we wouldn't be in this situation now.'

'We have ever been in this 'situation', as you put it, Your Eminence,' snapped Marchetti. 'That's why our predecessors took action. That's why we must do so now!' He looked at those seated before him. 'My friends, this is the moment to resurrect the Plan. The last seventy-five years, or so, have brought about any number of changes to Italian politics. And, as you are all aware, constitutional memories are short.' He paused momentarily.

'Also, to put your minds at rest, the last remaining records in the parliamentary archives relating to 1929 have been destroyed. You can take my word, we are the only ones who know what actually happened.'

The expressions of concern on several faces visibly eased. Marchetti went on.

'I can also confirm that every aspect of the Plan is in place. Everything is in readiness. There remain just one or two minor details to deal with before we set it finally in motion.'

'I'm sure I speak for everyone in this room, Your Eminence, when I say that any way we can improve our finances is welcome,' acknowledged Cardinal Temple, the prelate from Connecticut. 'However,' he added bleakly, 'if, for any reason, the project comes back to haunt us, I would not wish to suffer the same fate as my fellow-American, Archbishop Paul Marcinkus.'

'The Marcinkus affair was quite different!' the cardinal responded, testily. 'Thanks to his dealings, we had to pay out two hundred million Euros to the creditors of the Banco Ambrosiano!'

He stared at Temple, then added in a steely tone. 'As you know that crisis led to an unbroken run of twenty-three budget deficits. Thankfully, we now have a positive balance – just – bearing in mind that it costs us one hundred and sixty-five million Euros a year to run the Holy See.'

The cardinal shifted his gaze, looking searchingly into each of their faces.

'I would emphasise, nothing can go wrong with the Plan! Importantly, we stand to make a substantial amount of money for the Church, with no one the wiser as to our involvement.'

No one uttered a word.

He continued. 'As I said a moment ago, there are still a few issues to be resolved. Nothing of consequence. Allow me forty-eight hours then we should meet again to approve its commencement.'

Ushering them from the salon, the cardinal displayed supreme confidence. However, he was troubled. For the past two months he had been searching for the right person for the Cremonese mission – a key part of the Plan. A number of people had been considered. For one reason or another each had been discounted: too prominent in their field, not conversant with the language, or carrying the baggage of extensive family ties. Now a name had come forward, someone who met all the criteria – particularly, the last. The cardinal would soon learn if he were the right choice.

There was also another aspect: the opening gambit. It had been carefully orchestrated, but he wanted to review it yet again – to make one tiny, critical adjustment. Even as the last of the group was making his way through the outer office, the cardinal was reaching for the telephone.

Two of them walked together down the long, carpeted corridor. The elder glanced towards his companion.

'Tell me, Giovanni, what are your thoughts on a successor?'

'Do you mean to the Holy Father? But he has just been elected.'

'Are you not aware there is already talk of succession? The Pontiff is not a young man. The feeling is that we shall have to endure another election in three or four years' time – less, if we have to invoke the adjustment agreed at the last gathering of the College. If he becomes *non compos mentis.*'

A measured silence. The cardinal continued.

'If there were an election in the near future, the Austrian is the clear favourite. Cardinal Goehr has many supporters, and they are growing. At the moment, I would say he has many more than Cardinal Serafini or Cardinal Montanini, and any of the other likely contenders.'

'Unless there is a concerted effort to blacken his reputation. In this house such things are ever possible!'

'The point is, Giovanni, if our little ploy succeeds it could swing the vote in favour of one of our own countrymen.'

'Which prompts the comment . . .?'

'I was wondering,' said the cleric in a low voice, 'perhaps Cardinal Marchetti, could himself emerge triumphant.'

'But no one will learn of the Plan!'

'That is what he says. But Monsignor Pacelli's tactics came to light. Look what he achieved.'

His companion stopped and turned towards him.

'All I hope is that what we are doing never comes to light.'

'*Nos miseri homines et egeni!*'

'Indeed, we are most miserable, but needy.'

Chapter Three

The wind tore at his coat, cracking it like an unfurled sail. It teased his hair, wrenching it into random partings. The autumn leaves, one moment swirling around his ankles, were swept up and hurled provocatively into his face. But Marcus Danby was oblivious to the elements.

Even the clamminess of the rain went unnoticed. Another gust threw itself upon him. Instinctively, he leaned into the stiffening breeze, thrusting his hands deeper into the coat pockets. Few were abroad on such a wretched night – except, perhaps for the suggestion of a dark figure keeping pace with the solitary walker.

Then he was there, at the entrance to the studio. It was a moment before he thought to insert the key. As he freed the lock, an impulsive draught wrenched the handle from his grasp and threw the heavy, oak door violently against the inner wall. The boom startled Danby into abrupt awareness of his surroundings. Motionless in the doorway, he took in what had been his sanctuary these past six years.

Even in half-darkness, he knew every inch of the cavernous room: benches set against the walls; a small dais, partially enclosed by tall acoustic panels; the heavy, much-marked table around which the four of them sat, often companionably, occasionally in argument.

Marcus made his way to the far end. Slumping onto a stool, he put his head in his hands, breathing deeply to dispel the lightheadedness threatening to cloud his mind.

At dinner he had consumed two glasses of red wine, the same as the others. Later, in the confines of his room, he had drunk one bottle of passably good wine, and then most of another. He shook his head irritably, upsetting an already uncertain balance, and reached out hurriedly for support.

He sat there for nearly an hour, gathering his wits. Finally, summoning up some small resolve, he turned on the overhead light to illumine his station. Removing the protective cloth, Marcus stared at the instrument before him. Despite his dependence on alcohol, it was a singular achievement. They all said so. The violin was fast becoming a thing of beauty; when finished it would rank highly among the instruments for which the Bellman Studio had gained its reputation.

He flexed his long, narrow hands a gesture so typical of the performer, which he had once believed it was his destiny to become. Yet, graduating from the London School of Music, with the musical world at his feet, he had chosen a quite different path. At twenty-two, Marcus had joined the Teaching Order of St Francis Xavier.

Picking up the carcass of the instrument, he readied himself for the next stage: fitting the inset trim around the top and bottom plates. Brother Marcus was now thirty-seven. Tall, narrow-framed, with a self-effacing demeanour, it was his face that spoke of hidden depths. Below the blond hair, now streaked with strands of grey, were clear, blue eyes that reflected deeper passions. When the nostrils flared, his aquiline nose added intensity to his gaze. He had a mobile mouth; the soft lines etched into the corners suggested humour, although a recently acquired compression of the lips indicated a brooding dissatisfaction.

He took up the purfling tool. Carefully inserting it in the lightly scored line, he worked the narrow-bladed chisel, opening a slender channel round the edge of the top plate. Marcus concentrated – silence absolute, just the slow ticking companionship of a distant clock.

When Marcus had first met Geri Bellman a decade ago, an affinity had quickly developed between them. Geri, outgoing, cheerful, had soon come to know the religious. It was not long before he was privy to his innermost feelings, particularly the anguish about his vocation.

Thus, when time permitted, Marcus had been invited to work in the studio, to learn the art of making violas, violins and cellos. Surprising even himself, he had progressed rapidly. Five years on, he could produce an instrument in its entirety; soon after, he attained recognition as an accomplished luthier.

He had discovered a measure of contentment in his new-found

abilities. That is, until the next torment had emerged. Not only was there no longer a school at which he might teach, the latest proposal was that he and his remaining colleagues in the Order transfer to America, to take up posts in Danver, Massachusetts, the town once infamously known as Salem.

Since the school had closed, Marcus and the remaining Xaverian brothers had been living an uncertain existence in a large Victorian house on the outskirts of Mayfield, a village in the heart of East Sussex. It was during this limbo of an existence that Marcus had taken to drinking. Thus far, it had not affected his work, though Geri was well aware of the growing habit. To hide it from others Marcus kept irregular hours, often coming to the studio late at night.

Absorbed in his work, his head clearing, Marcus laboured on the bee-stings – the intricate mitres tapering into the corners of the instrument. Applying the hot glue with a small brush, he pressed the thin, delicate sandwich of black dyed pearwood and white poplar into the groove, finally tapping home the inlay to achieve a perfect fit.

It was almost two in the morning when he set it down. Too tired to start on the back plate, he sat at the bench surveying his workmanship. When given to such application, the mind has little chance to brood on inner conflicts but, as he dwelt there, so the spectres rose to haunt him. Should he admit the ill-wisdom of his choice and leave the Order?

Beset by such thoughts, he failed to hear the soft opening and closing of the outer door; or notice the heavy curtain in the doorway shudder in the draught. The shadows took on firmer shape, coalescing into the figure of a man, who remained still for some moments, gauging Marcus' awareness. Swathed in a long cloak, his features masked by a wide-brimmed hat, his appearance was menacing.

The figure made its silent way forward and stood just beyond the cone of light which encircled the bench. It remained there, looking down upon the instrument maker, whose head was lowered over the bench in miserable contemplation.

'Good morning, Brother Marcus.'

The voice betrayed its Italian birthright.

'My God! Who the devil are you?'

Grabbing the chisel, Marcus rose to his feet in a single motion. Tall as he was, the figure before him stood several inches higher.

'Don't come any closer!'

His voice cracked as he thrust the purfling tool before him.

'Calm yourself, brother, I mean you no harm,' said the new-comer quietly.

Marcus stared at him, trying to distinguish his features, but the face was deep in shadow.

'I have come a long way to speak with you, Brother Marcus. Be generous enough to listen to what I have to say.'

'How do you know my name?'

'We know much about you, signore. We have knowledge of your musical background, which you forsook to join the Xaverian Order. Your creative talents are also known to us.' The head inclined to the half-finished violin on the bench. 'We are also well aware of your increasing disaffection. Now the school is closed, we are informed of your impending transfer to the United States. We are mindful, even, of your fondness for drink.'

Marcus lowered himself onto the stool, his hand still clutching the chisel.

'How do you know so much about me?'

'Signore, we have many sources by which we gain information.'

A thought struck him. 'Are you here to encourage me to go to the States?'

'Brother Marcus, your future is in your own hands – although we shall be most interested in the outcome.'

'We? Who are "we"?'

'Let me explain. But, before I do so, answer first this question. Please be so kind as to tell me something of *this*.'

From beneath the folds of the loose-fitting garment, he withdrew a violin and brought it forward into the bright light over the bench. Hesitatingly, Marcus took hold of the instrument, which shone with a rich luminescence. Again, his head bowed, this time not in despair but in wonderment. Turning the violin, he let out a slow breath.

Holding it lengthwise he examined the arching, the geometry of the top plate; he studied the bottom plate, the choice of woods, the depth of finish. Then he laid it, almost reverentially, on the bench beside his more modest effort. Marcus sat still for several minutes; only the languidly ticking clock disturbed the silence.

'I do not know who you are, sir, but I can tell you this is a "del Gesù", made in Cremona in the early 1700s by Giuseppe Guarneri. I am privileged to hold it.'

For a moment he was lost for words. Then, conscious that this was the strangest of situations, he asked, 'What do you want coming here? Who are you?'

'It is of little consequence, Brother Marcus,' the voice declared softly. 'I am the Messenger. My reason for coming to you is simple. We have a task we wish you to perform. If you are successful the violin will be yours.'

Chapter Four

On the second storey of the building housing the Curia, the rooms are similar in size to those on the floor above. But the differences are soon apparent. The décor is noticeably less impressive; the walls plainer, adorned by fewer pictures; the furniture less ornate; the floors simply-carpeted without the splendour of richly-coloured rugs and tapestries. Nevertheless, the low tones of some conversations can be equally significant.

The quiet voice of the cleric leading the discussion carried to those seated on the two facing sofas. Modulated and precise, its message encompassed the room, commanding their attention.

'My Lord Bishop is probably right, but . . .' The soft declaration presaged an amendment. 'If we ignore the situation, and for some reason the extent of their involvement is made known, it would jeopardise his chances.'

The speaker looked into each of their faces.

'So I would urge you to consider the problem most carefully. Doing nothing will not guarantee the status quo. Doing something positive, as has been shown in the past, will ensure the secret remains buried.'

The five prelates glanced nervously at each other. Recognised for favouring the Austrian, professing a readiness to engineer his success in a future papal election, they were now confronting a bleak step into the dark. Or were they? Perhaps there had been a misunderstanding? Here was a cardinal from the third floor and, oblique observations or not, his allegiance was not in doubt. For the first time, one of them spoke out, hesitantly.

'I cannot answer for the others, Your Eminence. However, I'm a committed Hapsburgian.' He paused briefly. 'I am also Viennese, which, if anything, confirms my loyalty to the ancient monarchy. It is a thousand pities that it will never be restored.' He drew a

13

laboured breath. 'I must tell you, there are still many adherents to the royalist cause, even after it was extinguished in 1918. For me and for many others the *AEIOU* lives on in our hearts.'

The elderly Monsignor rose awkwardly. Looking down at the others he recited in a tremulous voice: '*Austria est imperare Orbi Universo!*'

It was a powerful, moving display, all the more telling in the surroundings and before those present. The cardinal saw that he had caught their imagination. He rose swiftly and embraced the venerable cleric.

'Who can forget the dictum of the Hapsburgs? *It is given to Austria to rule the world!*' he declared in ringing tones. 'Monsignor, you have uttered the clarion call. We shall be delighted to stand behind your flag in the name of the Church and the unquenched flame of the Monarchy. We will not falter in protecting their reputation, or their past actions.'

They all rose to their feet, united, shaking hands, committed to the cause . . . whatever that might be. Monsignor Keppel knew he had said something profound and stirring. He was a little puzzled by its effect, and uncertain to what he had committed himself. But, Cardinal Grossmann was content. That was a valuable outcome.

Chapter Five

Marcus awoke long before breakfast. He had slept fitfully, his mind gripped by what the stranger had asked of him. On the face of it, it was quite straightforward. But, were things ever as they seemed? He questioned why the Messenger could not have made his own enquiries.

Then the thoughts of owning a Guarneri flooded in – even to resurrecting his career. But, as he conceived the idea, so it was dismissed. It was too late. The demands on a soloist are continuous from one's early teens – practice, practice, and yet more practice. Marcus looked down at his hands. Years of physical toil, time spent in the workshop had taken their toll. Of course, he could play again for his own pleasure. He had shunned any form of musicianship from the day of joining the Order. Even in the studio, others played the instruments he made. In all those fifteen years never once had he tucked a violin into his neck. All that had been expunged with the first vows of his novitiate.

Then the excitement gripped him. His features brightened into a grin – the temptation of owning a Guarneri could well reverse the pledge made so long ago. At the same time came the realisation that the decision had been made for him. If he took up the Messenger's commission, he could refuse the command to transfer to Massachusetts. More momentously, he could leave the Order.

Last night's visitor had given Marcus time to consider his proposal, promising to return for an answer at the same hour the following day. Lying in his bed, Marcus knew the choice was determined: he would take up the Messenger's assignment.

Chapter Six

The air-conditioning on the third floor was a mere whisper, as discreet as the machinations of its inhabitants. When the cardinals from Bolzano and Turin passed each other in the corridor, courtesies prevailed.

'Your Eminence!'

'Your Eminence!'

Smiles were exchanged, heads graciously inclined. Doors then shut on their personal fiefdoms.

Few outside these portals are aware that, within, numerous causes are espoused, and intrigues abound. On the rare occasions when such happenings become public knowledge, the conspirators are seldom seen to condemn their opponents, or to reveal their identities. For all embrace the belief that their clandestine works are, ultimately, for the greater good of the Holy See. Were this belief in the moral worth of their designs to be undermined it would rend large holes in the very fabric of the Curia.

Cardinal Gustav Grossmann was seventy-seven that very day. Not that anyone knew. Certainly, not within his immediate circle, for Grossmann was a very private individual.

Born in Bolzano into a privileged Austrian family, his antecedents had been courtiers to the Hapsburgs. Even though the region had been ceded back to Italy after the First World War, the young man had enjoyed a comfortable upbringing. He had been ten years old at the time of the *Anschluss* – when Germany had annexed Austria – and the Grossmann family had taken the fateful decision to re-affirm their citizenship by moving to Vienna.

In 1941, caught up in the fervour of the war, young Gustav had joined the Hitler Youth Movement. It was then he found himself at odds with his parents. Though ardent Austrians, they retained their monarchist stance, and were increasingly concerned about the rumours of the extremes perpetuated by the Nazi régime.

Undeterred, he had dressed in the uniform and strutted with others of his age. Eventually, susceptible to the torrent of propaganda, he had revealed his parents' conflicting attitude to the authorities. Retribution had been swift. Within the hour they had been taken into custody. Too late Gustav Grossmann realised the enormity of his action. Even worse, he learned, some years later, that they had been transported to Dachau and interned in the infamous camp, twenty kilometres north of Munich. He had never seen them again.

Before the hostilities had ended, Grossmann had fled Vienna and returned to Bolzano, where childhood recollections were of much happier times. Moreover, he involved himself in the Church. With the same commitment that he had exhibited when joining the Youth Movement, he rose steadily through the ecclesiastical ranks. In his early forties he was called to serve the Holy Father in Rome. By then he had acquired all the convictions of his parents and, being a convert, had transformed them into passions.

Now, sitting at his desk, the aged prelate was feeling his years. It was hard to concentrate on what he was about to do. He had their declared support. Even if they did not comprehend the extent of their allegiance, they had accepted his guidance. Now he must turn honeyed words into actions, the first step being to advise the people in Mittenwald that it was starting again, that they must be prepared to take the same steps as in the past. He could ill-afford to convey his comments electronically, or by mail. He rang the bell that connected with his secretary, an oblate of the Franciscan Order.

'Your Eminence?'

The man stood uncertainly in the doorway.

'Brother Giuseppe, arrange for a Messenger to come to my office.'

Cardinal Marchetti had been born in Turin sixty-six years earlier. The fifth child of an immigrant family from Albania which had entered Italy illegally, he had lived on his wits from childhood. The local catholic church had frequently offered crumbs of comfort when he was small; and, during his teens, had become a sanctuary for Angelo Marchetti, in the mediaeval sense of the word – when his rivals were keen to let a little blood.

His faith, which he admitted only to himself, was discovered when he found himself spending rather too much time hiding away from the vicious street life that was his existence. The priest had been concise and to the point.

'If you don't mend your ways, Angelo, find a way to earn a living without fearing for your life, you'll be dead within the year!'

Marchetti was intelligent. Earn high rewards with an uncertain future, or choose a career that provided a modest living but, the gods willing, ensured a greater chance of longevity? He looked at the priest enquiringly.

'I don't suppose you make much money, do you, father?'

Nevertheless, he foresaw opportunities. From that moment, he embraced the ideals of the Church with fervour. He achieved high office, accepting its abundant trappings without a thought of his turbulent past – except, perhaps, when his native cunning was called into play. This was such an occasion.

His tall frame was loosely draped over the comfortable chair behind the desk. His hawk-like features were exaggerated as his eyes assumed a half-hooded stare. He was thinking deeply about what was to happen. Every step passed through his mind, as he searched for problems or possible weaknesses. There was none. The only uncertainty was the work about to be undertaken in Cremona. Brother Marcus Danby, the Englishman, should do the job adequately, but a little direction might be necessary.

He rang a bell.

'Your Eminence?'

'Felipé, I want you to send for a Messenger. Make sure it's the one who went to England recently. Then go to the offices on this list and ask them all to join me.'

The cardinal wrote six names on a sheet of hand-made paper.

Chapter Seven

At Bilbao airport Marcus suspected it was the roman collar that helped obtain a sizeable discount on his hire car. He was still reluctant to divest himself of all religious trappings, even though he had sent the letter, irrevocably stating his intention, to the Order's headquarters in Baltimore.

He had not received a reply when he had explained his intentions to Geri Bellman. The Messenger had insisted on secrecy, so his comments were guarded. Geri had simply smiled.

'There's more to it, isn't there Marcus? But I won't press you!'

Nor had a response arrived when he spent the last morning in prayer with the five remaining brothers. Thereafter, events moved swiftly. Marcus had packed his few personal possessions, leaving the double-breasted and single-breasted cassocks, the black shirts with the fly fronts, his lace cotta, scapula and plain preaching scarf all neatly folded on the bed. After a moment's thought, he had put the grey tunic shirts and collars in his case.

Geri had been generous. On the day of departure he had pressed an envelope containing £500 into Marcus' unwilling hands.

'Pay me when you come back,' Bellman had said, clasping him by the shoulders. 'After all, someone has to take over from me soon! I'm not getting any younger!'

Marcus had stared at the man who had befriended him, for the first time realising that the short, round figure, always good-humoured and considerate of others, was now showing his years.

'I shall be back soon, Geri!' he had declared, hugging him fiercely.

The memory of that moment was still with him as he drove the small Seat towards Pamplona. He was heading for Sanguesa, another thirty kilometres to the south-east. From there it was but a short distance to Javier – Xavier in the Basque language – the

19

birthplace of St. Francis. Although the teaching Order had been founded in 1839 by the Dutchman, Theodore Ryken, Marcus was anxious to visit the site where the beatified cleric had been born. For some indefinable reason he felt compelled to explain himself to the memory of the man whose Order, in name, he was now forsaking.

He had stayed overnight in an hosteleria on the outskirts of the town, where he had slept badly. It was nearly eleven o'clock when he arrived in the village of Xavier.

At the church, he anointed himself with holy water as he entered its cool interior. Suddenly overwhelmed, he fell to his knees. He had seen others cast off their calling without any qualm, but shedding his vocation was for him an emotional trauma. Although it was clear he could not have carried on, the catalyst to pursue a different path had been missing – until the arrival of the Messenger.

Nevertheless, having set aside fifteen years of his life, it would take time, and moments of anguish such as this, before he could come to terms with his loss. Two hours passed before Marcus retraced his steps to the car parked in the town square. From Xavier, he drove eastwards. In the late evening, he booked into a hotel in the market town of Lerida.

He arrived in Barcelona just before lunch the next day, returned the hire car and took the first available flight to Milan. At Linate, he was once again asked only a modest hire charge for the Alfa-Romeo. Taking the ring road, he picked up the autostrada going south. At five o'clock in the evening he passed through Piacenza. Thirty minutes later, he drove into the historic town of Cremona, on the northern shore of the River Po.

Chapter Eight

'Signor Lambertini, Your Eminence.'

The secretary stood to one side and ushered in the young man. Cardinal Marchetti looked up and smiled a greeting. Then he glanced towards the door.

'It's late, Brother Felipé. I suggest you leave anything outstanding until the morning!'

Dismissed, he withdrew, silently closing the tall, double doors.

Sitting behind his desk, the cardinal watched the visitor stride across the thick-piled carpet and seat himself in one of the elegant chairs.

'Signor Lambertini, I am glad you were able to come at such short notice.'

'It's my pleasure, Your Grace.'

'You betray your roots, Mister Lambert,' the prelate replied mockingly. 'Only the British refer to a cardinal as "Your Grace."'

He smiled once more, though no hint of humour reached his eyes, then leaned forward, businesslike, elbows on the desk, the fingers of both hands steepled beneath his chin.

'Signore, I have to tell you that we are ready. There is but one last hurdle. I must ensure we are in complete accord. Please be so kind as to go over your part once more.'

Michelo Lambertini injected the appropriate level of gravitas into his voice.

'I shall be speaking with contacts in the Ministries of The Interior, Foreign Affairs, Finance, Foreign Trade, and Communications. Then, I shall be in touch with the Prime Minister's Office, the Tourist Board and the Mayor's office. Since we first spoke on the matter, I have held back approaches on behalf of a number of clients, so that I shall have legitimate cause to be in touch with each of the administrations. Only at the end of each conversation shall I, fleetingly, touch upon the so-called rumour.'

The cardinal nodded.

'Excellent! However, I want to make one slight amendment. I now suggest you speak *first* with the Mayor's office. This is important. Then, allow twenty-four hours before continuing with the rest of the schedule. Is that understood?'

'As you wish, Your Eminence,' responded the man on the other side of the desk.

Beneath his acquiescent exterior was a smouldering anger. Consummate professional that he was, he knew how to present himself to others, sublimate his personal beliefs and, importantly, be extremely influential in his dealings. The son of an Italian mother and a British father, his good fortune had been to acquire the notable genes of both parents. Intelligent, speaking several languages fluently, Michelo Lambertini had sculptured good looks that were commanding more than eye-catching. A singular feature were his light blue eyes which, set against a dark, Mediterranean complexion, were immediately charismatic. His thick, wavy hair was neatly cut, though perhaps a shade long. A smile came easily to his lips, revealing strong, even teeth. However, what was soon apparent was his quick mind and ready wit. He was ideal for his profession as a parliamentary lobbyist. He executed his job well. As a consequence, at the age of thirty-five, he was extremely wealthy, and very discriminating in his choice of commissions.

Unfortunately, he had been given little choice when he had received that first phone call. It had emanated from the very room in which the discussion was now taking place. A number of veiled references had been made to his father: his questionable business ventures, his more dubious partners. Hints had been dropped that such revelations made public might have a deleterious effect on Signor Lambertini's career. No further persuasion was needed. Lambertini had been briefed, instructed to prepare his approach, and await a call. That moment had arrived.

'And so, my friend, the next phase. Be so kind as to tell me how you will proceed!'

'A week later, I shall be in touch with business connections in the key associations, particularly in travel and tourism, to ensure they question the authorities, to establish whether there is any validity in the rumour, and what they are going to do to deny it!'

The cardinal nodded.

'Good. When these two phases have been completed, we will meet again to discuss the next step.'

'A consideration, Your Eminence. If there are questions, I may, perhaps, need to elaborate on my remarks. Can I assume that the engineers' reports are positive, that the architects and surveyors have completed their part in the venture?'

Cardinal Marchetti was given to smiling at questions to which he knew the answers. 'Signore, you need have no concerns. We have been planning this for years. The many services on which we are calling have been as eager as yourself to participate.' He smiled again. 'Indeed, they are very committed, and they, like yourself, are receiving notice that the Plan is about to be implemented. We have even appointed someone to undertake the Cremonese mission. If I judge correctly, he should be arriving in Lombardy as we speak.'

Chapter Nine

His memory had not failed him. The badly-painted sign still hung over the entrance door. He had discovered the pensione above a restaurant sixteen years earlier when attending the Milan Academy of Music. During his year-long scholarship, he had been drawn like a pilgrim to Cremona, frequently taking the bus to the small town ninety kilometres to the east.

Climbing the stairs to the reception, he smiled at the sight of the carpeting, still unchanged from his student days. He signed in, remembering to ask for room eleven, opposite a bathroom on the top floor.

Marcus had taken the room for a week. The money given him by Geri Bellman had been supplemented by his savings from what he had earned in the studio. However, almost half the amount had been spent reaching his destination. The Messenger had mentioned that expenses would be paid, but had failed to say when. Marcus would need more funds if he were to stay beyond the coming weekend.

As he lay on the narrow bed, his thoughts turned to the assignment. The Messenger had been quite specific. Amass all the pertinent details relating to the instrument makers of Cremona during their golden period, then produce a detailed proposal on how the knowledge and expertise of Amati, Stradivari, the Guarneri family and all the famous luthiers could be revived.

Since accepting the commission, Marcus had devised several courses of action. One had been to make a close study of the store of documents in the Vatican Library. The eighteenth-century archivists of the Holy See had been zealous in gathering records from cities and townships. But a call from the airport in Milan had established that, until early September, their doors were closed to all seeking access to their records.

The other had been to pursue the project by a scientific route, to render an appraisal of the technical aspects covering the techniques of the Cremonese in precise, objective terms. Any number of studies had been conducted in recent years – notions conceived, theories broached – on how they had gone about the creation of their instruments. However, whilst he might accept that their craft could be calculated in some formal dimension, Marcus was nervous that the measure of their skills might be beyond his humble abilities as a luthier and his past talent as a musician.

'Si, signore, cosa desidera mangiare? Posso suggerire alcuni piatti locali non compresi nel menu.'

The waiter in the restaurant below the pensione was keen to please.

'Vorrei avere il bollito di misto, con mostarda di Cremona, per favore!'

He ordered the local dish of boiled meats, and a mustard in which were suspended chopped pears, cherries and apple, a favourite from his early student days. He also found his command of the language returning, and even a suggestion of a local accent. It caught the waiter's notice; he smiled.

'Certamente, signore, e da bere?'

He ordered the house red.

He had intended to limit himself to one bottle. However, when he rose from the table, having enjoyed a second, and then two glasses of passito, he found that a brief, perhaps unsteady, stroll was required to settle an uncertain stomach.

It was not late. At eleven o'clock he found himself in the Piazza di Stradivari, close to the Terrazzo, the tallest campanile in Italy. The four-hundred-year-old astronomical clock bathed the street below in a mellow, golden light. Marcus breathed deeply. He could not recall when he had last felt such peace of mind. He had taken a major step in renouncing his vocation. No doubt he would suffer guilt for some time to come, but the inner contentment could not be ignored. It must have been beckoning for a long, long time.

Across the square, in the Via ala Panzone, he looked up at a row of opaque windows that housed the town's musical treasures. They

25

gave little indication of the heritage that lay behind them. Tomorrow, he thought, I shall attempt to unravel their mysteries.

Collecting the room key from the portiere, he climbed to the second floor and made his way along the corridor. There were automatic light switches every ten metres, but the lights extinguished themselves long before Marcus had walked to the next. Reaching his room, he was again plunged into darkness. Fumbling for the lock, Marcus finally inserted the key and pushed open the door.

'*Buona sera, Signor Danby*', whispered a voice. 'I trust you ate well.'

'Why do you keep doing this to me?' Marcus hissed, angrily. 'You appear when least expected. Then you have the gall to believe that you are welcome.'

'My apologies, signore, it was not my intention to disconcert you,' murmured the Messenger. 'I shall draw the curtains, then we can talk more openly?'

'If you must,' replied Marcus, irritation in his voice.

The bedside lamp relieved the obscurity. It outlined the visitor, though failed to illuminate his features.

'Did you enjoy your journey to Cremona?'

Marcus slumped on the bed. 'If you must know, I went first to the Basque country. I have been travelling for forty-eight hours and I'm exhausted!'

'I am aware of your detour, signore. But now to business. First, the funds I promised.'

The Messenger placed an envelope containing banknotes on a small table.

'I've yet to prepare a summary of expenses,' said Marcus abruptly, his eyes on the package. 'Allow me to write the details, and you can give me what is due tomorrow.'

'Signor Danby – I shall not refer to you as Brother Marcus, now you have submitted your letter of renouncement – Signor Danby, there are no demands upon you to give me a list of your expenditures. Firstly, we know in broad terms what they will be, and secondly, we have no need for written records.'

The figure moved closer to the bed, into even deeper shadow.

'The main purpose of this visit is to ensure you want for nothing.

That tomorrow you will commence your work. Do I presume correctly that nothing stands in your way? For now the task must be completed within the next four weeks. Certain factors have arisen, and you must submit the report my masters require sooner than expected. Is that understood?'

In those few words, the tone of his voice had taken on a more emphatic note, one that clearly announced no allowance would be made for delay or time-wasting.

'I understand you perfectly, my friend!' Danby was suddenly tired of the melodramatic appearances, and of the way the Messenger was making his demands. 'Let me say two things. I dislike, intensely, your manner – as though you have bought my soul as well as my services. Secondly, this sudden time constraint – you are asking too much, too soon. I want to know why the people you represent could not conduct this assessment themselves. Most of the technical details are available to anyone with a modicum of researching ability. Why employ an outsider?'

The visitor took a step towards Marcus – a rather frightening step.

'Signore, do you wish to withdraw from the project?'

It was said with such menace that Marcus hesitated.

'What I'm saying is,' he murmured, dry-mouthed, 'why call upon someone like myself, when so much has already been produced by others?'

'Let me explain. But first, do not ignore the fact that in accepting our agreement, eight nights ago, you bound yourself to a contract. A contract that can only be broken at my choosing. Do you understand?'

His attitude made Marcus apprehensive.

'I agree, much information is available – but from a wide number of sources. My masters perceive the report as a singular account, covering all the key aspects of how the luthiers perfected their craft.' The Messenger's voice took on a firmer note. 'It can fall to only one person, an individual who can unravel the intricacies of their talents as well as the scientific data. It must identify exactly how the skills of the Cremonese can be harnessed, to bring about another renaissance! To create, once more, the fame and artistry of the instrument makers of the eighteenth century. That responsibility, Signor Danby, falls to you.'

Chapter Ten

'My friends, thank you for coming at such short notice. I can now confirm that everything is in place, and we have reached the moment to take action. Again, I would emphasise, there is little chance of exposure.'

Cardinal Marchetti made his comments confidently, merely awaiting their unanimous agreement. But this time, aware of the enormity of their decision, concern was again evident in five pairs of eyes. Another's were cast downwards.

'Like yourself, Your Eminence, I can visualise the benefits,' opined Cardinal Temple. 'I can also see any number of pitfalls. Particularly, if they call our hand.' He noticed one or two uncertain nods. 'I can appreciate the general thrust of the scheme, and the required result. Forgive me, Your Eminence, I have never completely understood what you call the history of the Plan or its mechanics. If I am about to commit my name and my resources, kindly indulge me by reviewing these aspects again.'

Marchetti stared at him in silence. Why, he wondered, do I have to deal with such people? I've explained it endlessly. It should be plain enough for them to understand. However, I have to carry them with me, and Temple clearly represents their anxieties. His support, as well as their commitment, are essential. He smiled – a mirthless contortion of the lips.

'Very well. But before I do so, I think you should appreciate how critical is the need for an injection of funds. As a consequence, I have asked My Lord Bishop, Pietro Marsini, to join us. I have made him party to all our previous deliberations. Working in the Administration of the Patrimony, he has a first-hand knowledge of our finances. My Lord Bishop.'

Marsini was a small man, almost lost within the depths of the chair. It was not just his size that made him inconspicuous, it was also his demeanour. Balding, with a slightly puckish face that betrayed little emotion, he had sat, thus far, looking down at his hands. Although he had been in the room, within this intimate group, since the beginning of the meeting, no one had thought to remark on his presence. Now everyone's gaze was upon him. He moved forward to the edge of the seat, and began to speak in a high, falsetto voice, making his comments as though itemising a balance sheet.

'On paper, we show a positive position,' he declared. 'But, analysing the present sources of revenue, we could well see a different picture emerging in the medium-term. The "Peter Pence" is declining year by year as numbers professing the faith fall by the wayside, and their contributions diminish. We now estimate the universal congregation to be under one billion. At the current rate we shall run into a negative situation from this side of our income within the next decade!'

Although delivered in a monotone, its import was compelling.

'I would point out that our investments look healthy. These days, we are spreading our portfolio, attempting to minimise risk.'

He looked questioningly at those around him, nodded, and continued.

'No longer are we putting funds into derivatives, high risk bonds, or playing the markets. Nor is the Vatican Bank financing dubious, possibly illegal, enterprises.' For some reason, Marsini smiled. 'Nowadays, we are far more circumspect. But, I have to tell you that we are about to suffer the sins of our fathers. Quite literally! We are talking of the priests who have indulged in paedophilia, and other similar pastimes – and the hierarchy which covered up their misdeeds. The lid is coming off.'

He paused to sip a glass of water.

'In the United States we have already paid out six hundred and fifty million dollars in compensation – and it won't end there! One diocese in Portland has filed for Chapter Eleven, which is protection from the demands of its creditors. Quite frankly, if we do not take drastic steps to refill our coffers, the Holy See could well be bankrupt by 2020!'

There was a stunned silence. Even Cardinal Temple said nothing.

'Thank you, My Lord Bishop. You summarise it painfully, but well,' commented Cardinal Marchetti.

He rose and walked to his desk to collect a leather-bound file. He put the document case on the seat and stood behind the chair with his hands resting on the carved scrolling of its back. From this vantage point, looking down on his audience, his presence was all the more imposing.

'First of all, my friends, you are well aware of the aim of the Plan.'

Expectant eyes focused intently upon him.

'It is to relocate the Vatican City in its entirety. To move it, stone by stone, brick by brick, from the centre of Rome!' He looked briefly at the file. 'To remove the Basilica of St. Peter, the Apostolic Palace, the churches, residences, museums, all the key buildings, even the tiles of the piazzas, to a setting on the banks of the Po river, between Cremona and Mantua.'

The cardinal paused and sipped from a glass of water on a nearby table.

'The site, of more than one hundred hectares, was gifted to the Holy See by the Hapsburg monarch, Joseph II, when the Austro-Hungarian Empire encompassed the Lombardy region. I can only believe it was a gesture of contrition for his attempt to reform The Church when he was Holy Roman Emperor.' He glanced again at the file. 'On a number of occasions during the last two hundred years the Papacy has considered moving from the capital. But the Italian Government of the times has, invariably, persuaded us to remain in Rome.' He smiled his cheerless smile. 'As you've heard, the stakes are even higher since the last time, seventy-six years ago. On that occasion, it was put to Mussolini by Monsignor Pacelli himself, our late Pope Pius XII, that if the "Roman Question" was not reconciled, we would provide the solution ourselves. We would vacate the walled city, and re-establish the Holy See away from Rome.'

The cardinal stopped briefly, letting his words sink in.

'The Lateran Accord, signed in 1929, was influenced by Pacelli's comments. The city stood to lose the major part of its attraction. So, whilst the Accord recognised the Papacy's sovereignity, an agreement was also signed whereby the Government paid out almost one billion lire, ostensibly for the loss of the Papal States. In reality, it was a payment for the Vatican to remain exactly where it is.'

Marchetti paused, awaiting comment. There was none. Clearing his throat, he continued.

'After three-quarters of a century, no record relating to the issue of those monies survives in the official archives. Most documents were destroyed by the civil servants of the time. Those that escaped their searches have since been removed by devotees to our cause.'

The cardinal from Connecticut finally leaned forward, surveying those seated around him.

'Thank you, Your Eminence, and Lord Bishop Marsini. A disturbing summary of our finances, and a concise résumé of the past. Now, tell me, what and who are involved this time round?'

No-one else said a word. Stunned by the revelations of the Papacy's financial position, they were hardly likely to question the cardinal's subsequent remarks. But Marchetti was forgetting Cardinal Temple's tenacity.

'One thing I want made clear,' declared the American. 'Are you in favour of relocation, or are you set on blackmailing the Italian Government?'

The cardinal's eyelids drooped in their predatory fashion.

'The economics of moving to a new site would be as beneficial as staying in Rome, Your Eminence!' he replied, evenly.

'How can that be? Surely it would cost a vast sum of money to move everything 400 kilometres and resurrect the Vatican City. It would certainly take time to re-establish the whole fabric of the Holy See.'

'If this were 1929, I would agree. Costs would far outweigh the benefits. Today, it is quite different. Civil engineers, structural engineers, surveyors, town planners, architects and community developers have each contributed to the grand design. They estimate that we could have a walled city, complete with all the existing buildings, plus many more, erected and occupied within five years. Moreover, our new city would have ready access to all the major road networks that cross Europe. It would be equidistant between Milan and Mantua and their airports, and it would be able to accommodate and feed many times the numbers of tourists that currently visit us in Rome.'

Temple stood his ground. 'How could we possibly afford it?'

'My friend,' the cardinal remarked, unctuously, 'do not forget the Papacy owns, outright, forty-five hectares of prime Roman real estate. The returns from that sale alone would more than pay for the relocation. Indeed, a considerable amount would be left over!'

'What happens during the interim?'

The cardinal could see he was gaining ground. Silence the American, and the day would be won.

'The transfer to the new city would be accomplished in stages. We would negotiate sales of the building sites within the Vatican on a piecemeal basis. We would not want to offer the whole forty-five hectares – that would reduce prices. Selling each building or plot separately would maintain values. At the same time, it would allow us to transfer staff over a period of time. They would stay in the hotels we would build first until accommodated elsewhere. It's a straightforward, logistical project. One our experts have already worked out.'

'You still haven't answered my question. Where do *you* stand? What is the proposition to the Government?'

'Simply this. We believe it is appropriate to consider separating the Vatican City, an autonomous and independent state, from the capital of Italy.'

'Meaning?'

Marchetti was getting angry. 'Surely, it's quite clear, Your Eminence. Would Rome countenance the schism between itself and the Papacy? They would weigh up the loss in revenue if Rome no longer held the same attraction for tourists and adherents to the faith. Then, they would try to persuade us to stay. In my opinion, it would be worth ten billion Euros for us to do so.'

There were audible gasps at the magnitude of the sum.

'That's blackmail, Your Eminence!'

'It's business, Cardinal Temple. It may appear extreme, but do not forget the Church is in an extreme position. After all, with thirty million visitors coming to Rome annually, all we are seeking is less than four years' income. I prefer to see it as a choice they have to make. After all, why shouldn't the Vatican get a share of the tourist trade? It's what people come to Rome for.'

Temple was flagging, his powder running dry.

'It's still sordid commercialism – Holding the city of Rome to ransom! I thought we were above all that.'

'Let me answer your original question. I am in favour of establishing the Holy See on the banks of the Po. Not only would it be aiding our finances . . .' He nodded in the direction of Bishop Marsini. '. . . our aim would also be to re-create the cultural strengths of that part of Lombardy. As you know, Cremona was long the centre of the world's finest instrument makers. I want to see the Church nurture the heights achieved by Amati, Stradivari, Guarneri, Ruggieri, and all the others.'

He could see that the artistic aspect was reaching out to them. Their faces reflected growing interest in this more profound aspect. Here was something that fired their high-minded imagination.

'I would like to see our ties and investment in the region bringing the old skills to light. That in itself would almost justify the relocation!'

'How would you go about it?'

Someone else had taken up the baton from Temple.

'I have already started. A highly-trained instrument maker and skilled musician has arrived in Cremona to investigate the secrets of the masters, to determine what made them truly great. He will assess how we can replicate the materials, conditions and, importantly, the necessary skills to bring about the re-birth of our most famous heritage.'

Ringing words. Everyone nodded – even Temple.

Marchetti had their support. Moreover, it seemed he was not going to be pressed into revealing the more questionable features of the Plan. Neither would he need to bring up the contingency plans, which ensured that no one inveigled into taking part would ever reveal the mammoth undertaking about to begin.

Chapter Eleven

Monsignor Keppel was worried. If he had understood Grossmann correctly, he was now party to some sort of 'defensive action'. When he and his compatriots had first rallied together, Grossmann had openly encouraged them. Now, it would appear, he had taken their zeal a step further, setting in motion something which, if one stripped away the veneer of pious phrases, was tantamount to an act of aggression. Grossmann had not said as much: he was the master of circumlocution. It was only when leaving his office that Keppel had realised what the cardinal had done – '. . . *for the good of Goehr's legitimate claim to the Papacy, and our beloved Austria*!' Would it be churlish to oppose the cardinal? Should he reveal his concerns to the others? Keppel hesitated. A Prince of the Church would be unlikely to resort to violence. Surely he must have misinterpreted his remarks. In any event, as the acknowledged leader of those espousing the Hapsburg cause, was it not for Keppel to decide the course of action? He had everyone's support. Archbishop Szabo from Hungary had called several times to applaud his idealism and to pledge backing. A tiny flame flickered. He must take a firmer stand against Cardinal Grossmann's dictates. First though, he must attend morning service.

The flame died: the decision was deferred. It was understandable. A man such as Monsignor Keppel, wrapped in the Church's protective layers, sheltered from life's realities, lacked the tenacity for open confrontation – for the moment.

He carried the single case lightly in one hand as he threaded his way through the knots of passengers wearily struggling along the platform towards the distant barrier.

He moved easily. The observant might have thought the athleticism of the cleric was at odds with his calling. But, at this hour, senses were dulled and much went unnoticed.

He had joined the afternoon train in Munich, knowing that his night-time arrival in Verona would be unlikely to excite attention. During the journey, attendants in their cursory promenades through the train would have seen only an inoffensive priest talking with fellow-travellers.

It had been decided that he should go by rail.

The car had dropped him at the hauptbanhof before taking the others to the airport. They would not have been able to carry the tools of their trade, so their needs were now safely stowed in the priest's hand luggage as he strolled the short distance from station to hotel.

Tonight, Father Schmidt would stay at The Firenze, on the Corso Porta Nuova. Large, impersonal and crowded, it would allow him to emerge the following morning as Herr Schmidt, a well-dressed businessman about to board the local train from Villafranca station to Cremona.

The house was in the suburb of San Felice, two kilometres from the town centre, close to the autostrada. He had watched it since dusk. There had been little sign of occupation.

Arriving in Cremona in the late morning to familiarise himself, Schmidt had walked all four points of the town. After lunch he had hired a small, nondescript car. Then, he had criss-crossed the township within a five kilometre radius, noting the road intersections and key landmarks.

It was dark when he made his way inconspicuously towards the house, set back from the road amidst a thin stand of trees. Schmidt was the planner. Alert to any contingency, he foresaw problems before they arose. There was no reason why anyone should be interested in the house taken on a short-term let. Yet his inner caution stayed him from marching up to the front door. Even in the darkness, he had determined a clear path to the car three hundred metres away, its ignition key located on the nearside front wheel in readiness.

Satisfied, but still wary, he edged round to the rear and found a window which would provide safe entry. Easing it gently open, he raised himself lightly and perched on the sill until his sight adjusted to the gloom. Thirty seconds elapsed before he dropped silently to the floor. Moving to the far corner, he gently turned the handle, and looked out onto an unlit hall.

A glimmer of light showed beneath a door, from behind which came the muffled sound of a television. Silently he padded the short distance and placed an ear to the woodwork. Taking the compact P99 from an inner pocket, he quietly turned the doorknob.

'*Guten abend, Meine Freunde. Sie sind beide tot!*'

Neither of the two men moved.

'Come in, Jozsef. We've been expecting you,' said one, not taking his gaze from the small screen.

'Did you find the window we prepared for you?' asked the other, raising a lager can to his lips.

'One of these days, you will welcome the trouble I take. It could save your lives,' responded Schmidt, humourlessly.

'For God's sake! Who will be checking on us when we have done nothing to draw attention?' said the short figure lounging on a sofa. 'Perhaps, in a few days' time, but not when we have just arrived.'

'You can never be too careful.'

'Right,' said the taller of the two non-commitally. He was seated on an upright chair, an elbow on the sturdy table which held the remains of a pack of beer cans.

'And tidy this place up! This is not an opportunity to party,' added Schmidt irritably.

Both men looked at each other.

'Right again, Herr Schmidt,' replied the man at the table. This time the laconic tone was missing; there was a steely glint in his eye.

'Jozsef, tell me,' asked the other. 'Do you honestly believe this is a serious operation? What sort of opposition will one man provide? A man of the cloth, accustomed to the soft life.'

Chapter Twelve

Marcus sat at the pavement-side table. Before him, a large expresso, rolls, and a copy of the *Corriere delle Alpi*. He glanced at the local newspaper, but the headlines failed to register. Still on his mind was last night's conversation with the Messenger. He had slept fitfully after the encounter, risen at five o'clock that morning, and begun making notes on how best to tackle the task that lay ahead. Taking the notebook from his pocket, he turned to his scribbled first thoughts.

Logically, he would have to start with Nicolo Amati – the acknowledged father of the Cremona School of instrument makers: the man who had taught both Antonio Stradivari and Andrea Guarneri. Marcus would have to assess how and what he had passed on, for the secrets of their success could well derive from his teachings. So the first step was to understand how Amati used his apprentices, and most of that information was to be found in the town records. Once this aspect was fully covered, he could then widen his researches, looking at methods of production, the materials they used, and the significant differences in interpretation and style. This would involve travelling to other centres to review the makers' sources of supply, and their materials. These investigations would take time. In addition to chronicling the Amati and Stradivari households, to obtain a rounded picture of the Guarneri family of instrument-makers, he would have to include the elder Pietro, who had opened a studio in Mantua, and his nephew, also called Pietro, who had moved to Venice.

As he drank his coffee, Marcus idly thought of the possible influence David Tecchler, the Austrian, might have had on the Venetian Guarneri. Tecchler, he recalled, had left Venice rather hurriedly upon encountering a few difficulties with the mayor – or, rather, his wife. He had moved on to Rome.

There were so many strands to the appraisal, it would be difficult to know what to ignore, where to draw the line. He was fast realising that the new time constraint imposed by the Messenger might not allow him to be as detailed as he would have wished. On another sheet Marcus began making notes on what he should learn about the current practitioners in Cremona. Collating all the details and writing the final report would take at least four or five days. In total, the project would occupy his time for at least four weeks. Moreover, there was little room for the unforeseen built into the schedule. To submit the complete document by the required date would be nigh on impossible. His thoughts turned, fleetingly, to Geri Bellman. Perhaps he should invite him to Italy to conduct the assessment of the current instrument makers. One thing was obvious. He must find a store selling IT equipment and purchase a computer. He would need to log a wealth of data as well as compile and produce his findings.

It had cost over 2000 Euros. The salesman assured him that it was fast, it would connect him quickly to anyone and any web resource in the world, and that its hard drive had an extraordinary capacity. Relieved, and a little uncertain of what he actually had in the black, leather case, Marcus also bought several reams of paper, and a pocket-sized recorder. The sales assistant assured him that the small machine would be ideal for verbal notes, and sensitive to the softest voice in interview.

On his way back to the pensione to stow his purchases, Marcus stopped outside an inconspicuous bookshop. The jangling bell echoed as he stepped inside, and descended a narrow step. Appearances are deceptive. The interior was as wide as the frontage, but surprisingly long, with rows of shelves disappearing into the depths. Just inside the entrance, against the right-hand wall, was a desk where, surrounded by piles of books sat the bent figure of an elderly man.

As Marcus walked towards him the bookseller looked up and smiled in welcome. He had a kindly face, thick glasses perched on a snub nose and the remains of his white hair somewhat awry.

'*Buon giorno, signore. Posso esserle utile?*'

'*Avete, per caso, una copia del libro* I Segreti di Stradivari *da Simone Sacconi?*'

'*Ma certo, signore. quale edizione?*'

Sacconi's book, with its wealth of detail on the production of stringed instruments, concentrating on the various styles Stradivari had adopted during his lifetime, was the *vade mecum* for students of the maestro. However, even in a town such as Cremona, its appeal would be limited, and he little expected the bookshop to hold a copy. Yet, the bookseller was actually asking which edition he wanted. He acquired a 1972 second-hand copy, slightly worn, but clearly treated with respect by its former owner.

'Are you interested in the art of instrument making, signore?' enquired the bookseller. 'If so, I have many books on the subject.'

Marcus nodded, and asked, 'Do you have Hill's *The Violin Makers of The Guarneri Family*, and perhaps a copy of *The Violin Masterpieces of Guarneri del Gesù?*'

The old bookseller's face broke into a smile. 'Naturally, signore.'

Marcus felt obliged to comment on his presence in Cremona.

'I am undertaking a research commission on the skills and techniques of the old masters.'

The bookseller nodded.

With the books wrapped in an old-fashioned brown paper parcel, Marcus handed over 350 Euros. His eyes widened slightly as he realised that in one morning he had spent almost 3000 Euros.

The elderly bookseller noted his dismay. He said gently. 'I also have a copy of Stewart Pollens' *The Art Forms of Antonio Stradivari,* and the Chiesa work, *Giuseppe Guarneri del Gesù.* It's the leather-bound edition.'

'Thank you, signore. Unfortunately, my resources do not allow me to purchase either.'

'No, signore, you misunderstand. You do not have to buy them. When you need, come in and read them at your leisure,' said the old man, benignly. 'Many of my customers are like yourself. Why should I deprive them of the enjoyment of learning?'

He was taken aback by the bookseller's kindness.

'That's most generous. My name is Marcus Danby. May I ask, is that your name above the shop window?'

'Si, I am Roberto Marciano.'

'Signor Marciano, I may well take up your offer.'

After an early lunch, Marcus made his way to the Civic Museum. As a student he had frequently visited the salon of musical instruments. Assimilating the creative beauty on display would get him into the right mindset.

An hour later, he set out towards the Records Office. Time to tackle the opening part of the project: assessing the conditions in which the masters worked in the late seventeenth and early eighteenth centuries; learning about their workshops, how they gained their knowledge and skills, how they imparted their craft to others – to get beneath the skin of the Cremonese instrument makers. Getting the background fixed would allow Marcus to understand the many other facets of their work. The visit to the archives was the critical first step.

The archivist was an earnest, be-spectacled young man, whose response to his request for sight of certain files, was to declare officiously, 'Impossible! I cannot allow it!'

Marcus was perplexed. 'This is the Records Office, is it not?'

'*Si!*'

'The public has right of access to the records?'

'*Si!*'

'Then can you explain why I am being prevented access to this material?'

'Because, signore, someone else has called for those files! The guidelines clearly stipulate that only one person at a time shall have the right to examine our records.'

Here was an individual whose central purpose in life was to live by rote and regulation. Marcus restrained his irritation.

'Then, can you tell me when they will be available?'

'Come tomorrow, and I will tell you tomorrow.'

Fuming, Marcus retraced his steps. To avoid any similar situations he vowed the next day he would be at the Records Office when it opened.

On this occasion he had brought his laptop and a digital camera, in case he was unable to have documents copied. He mounted the steps as the bell finished ringing across the piazza, and walked towards the archivist's desk.

'Good morning, I would like to examine the records of the Amati Family from 1600 to 1650, please?'

'I'm afraid that's impossible.'

Marcus took a deep breath. The man before him was poles apart from Signor Marciano, the bookseller.

'Then, I would like the files for 1650 to 1700.'

'That, too, is impossible.'

Why, for heaven's sake?'

'Someone else is already using these files. I told you yesterday that they can only be provided to one person. That person was waiting for us to open this morning, and laid immediate claim to all the volumes you have requested.'

His anger flared. In fluent Italian he castigated the system, the archivist's petty-fogging application of what he termed 'guidelines'. They were not even rules. He should be there to encourage the search for knowledge, not to be obstructive. Ending the tirade he stomped out, realising as he did so he might well have barred himself from admittance to the records of the Cremonese luthiers altogether. He went to the next source, the Stradivari Museum in the Via Palestro.

Had he heard something? Was it a dream or his imagination? There it was again. A soft tapping at the door. Climbing from his bed, Marcus peered through the inset spy-hole. The dim light in the corridor identified a grey shape wearing a wide-brimmed hat. Opening the door cautiously, he stepped aside for the Messenger to enter.

'Well, at least this time you didn't make a spectral appearance!'

Under the hat, Marcus caught the gleam in an eye.

'I have to ask you, Signor Danby, are you making progress?' There was a hint of acerbity in the Messenger's voice.

'As it happens, I'm not,' responded Marcus, sharply. 'I have been unable to get into the Records Office for the past two days. Some small-minded official keeps barring my way. I've been to the Stradivari Museum, but that's a mere gloss. I need access to the archives as my starting point.'

The Messenger stood there for a moment.

'Signor Danby, present yourself at the Records Office at nine o'clock tomorrow morning. There will be no further hindrance to your quest!'

'No? Then thank you.'

The figure made for the door, opened it in one swift movement and disappeared, leaving it to swing back silently on its return spring. It clicked shut.

In the small reading room he had been shown to a desk on which sat a microfilm reader. Original documents were sacred, rarely available for actual inspection, and never touched by hand.

The archivist had welcomed him with deference; almost syco-phantic in his attempts to please. Within minutes of his arrival a cup of coffee had been placed at his elbow. By ten o'clock, he was steadily compiling notes, typing at his computer and selecting documents to be copied. Engrossed, he did not immediately regis-ter the first sounds of the uproar in the reception area. However, as they became louder and more insistent, Marcus could pick out actual words. The female voice was strident and unrelenting.

'I have been reading these files for the last three days. How dare you stop me now!'

Although the reply was indistinct, it was obvious the archivist was trying desperately to placate her. She was indifferent to his platitudes.

'I want to speak with your director – and I want to speak with him *now*!'

The low voice of the archivist took on a whining tone.

'Why should I come back again when the files are free? I am not prepared to wait. My editor won't accept that I missed the sub-mission date because some civil servant was being deliberately unhelpful.'

Marcus recognised that here was someone who refused to yield. He, on the other hand, had had to call up help. He left his chair and quietly made his way to a small, glass window set in the door. From there he had a glimpse of an auburn-haired woman who, by every gesture of her slim frame and the piercing tones of her voice, was causing the archivist to ring his hands in anguish.

'But, you do not understand, signora. I had no choice. I was told to allocate the reading room and the files to someone else.'

'We'll see about that!'

She turned abruptly on her heel, her hefty shoulder bag catch-ing the archivist a glancing blow, and marched from the building, high heels clacking furiously on the marbled floor.

Marcus returned to the microfilm viewer, intrigued that the Messenger had such influence. He thought upon the redhead's words, and formed the opinion she was a journalist. From the little he could see of her she was attractive, even when angry. He smiled and continued his searches.

He worked on until two o'clock, enjoying the frequent cups of coffee which were provided. At last he told one of the assistants that he would soon be going to lunch, and asked if he might leave his notes and computer in the room.

'Of course, signore. We shall lock the door until your return.'

He strolled through the carefree and contented crowds in the piazza. Marcus had had a good morning. Whilst his principal interest lay with the golden period, he had gone back almost a hundred years to Andrea Amati, considered by many to be the father of the violin. He had revelled in the documents, fascinated by the minutiae relating to the three generations of the Amati dynasty. Interestingly, he had not appreciated that when plague, then famine, had struck the region in 1630, the Cremonese school had hung by a thread with only one master remaining, Nicolo Amati. Marcus suddenly realised that if Amati had been taken by either epidemic, there would have been no Strads, no Guarneris – none of the finest instruments would have been made available to the world.

He had also traced the original locations of the Cremonese workshops, long since destroyed when, in 1920, the site around the piazza of San Domenico had been razed by an unfeeling bureaucrat. Marcus had pored over documents that gave chapter and verse on the style and set-up of their workshops, the tasks to which their apprentices were set, and their daily work routine. Already the essential information was starting to come together. He was creating a foundation on which he could develop his thoughts and subsequent proposals.

Turning into the Via Gaetano Tibaldi, Marcus walked as far as the Via Albertoni, then hesitated, steeling himself for disappointment. When a student, a feature of his visits to Cremona had been dining at The Napoli. It had been run by the Brughieris, an elderly couple with the ability to make everyone feel they were guests. Importantly, at the time, it had not been expensive. The Brughieris had come from Naples as newlyweds and opened the restaurant within a few years of their arrival. It had become Marcus' haven when he was thinking seriously of giving up a musical career in favour of the Church. On one occasion he had even confessed his intentions to Signor Brughieri. Fifteen years later, here he was again, this time in the throes of surrendering his vocation. An odd reversal, Marcus thought wryly. Obviously, it would have new owners, he told himself. The Brughieris had been in their late sixties. He stopped, momentarily, on the corner, before turning into the narrow side street.

It had not changed. The restaurant front was still a faded maroon, the linen on the tables the same cream fabric. Buoyed by a frisson of nostalgia, he took a seat under the awning, midway between the pavement-side tables and the interior.

'*Si, Padre?*'

The smiling waiter at his elbow took his order for saltimbocca.

When the waiter was setting the plate before him, Marcus asked, 'Tell me, is the restaurant still owned by Signor Brughieri?'

'*Si, signore. Signor Lauro Brughieri*'

'Antonio's son?'

'Did you know old Antonio Brughieri, signore?'

'*Si*, I used to come here often as a student.'

So the restaurant was still in the family.

When Marcus mentioned his earlier visits, the waiter grinned, and called over his shoulder, '*Lauro, c'è qualcuno che desidera vederti.*'

A man in his forties shouted back from the depths of the restaurant. As he threaded his way through the tables, wiping his hands on a long maroon-coloured apron, Marcus was taken aback. The owner was the living image of his father.

'*Si, Padre?*'

'I was explaining to the cameriere that I used to come here years ago, and knew your father.'

The man nodded. Moustached, slightly overweight, he even had his father's rolling gait.

'Unfortunately, he died about six years ago, and I took over the business. But my mother still lives. Tell me, signore, can I get you something to drink?'

The restaurateur even had the same mannerisms.

'Not for the moment, thank you, Signor Brughieri,' he smiled. 'When I was a student, I passed many happy moments here. Perhaps, some time, I may be permitted to pay my respects to your mother?'

'But of course, signore. She usually comes to the restaurant in the evening – to check up on me,' he declared, looking at his waiter, who grinned, and raised his shoulders, knowingly. 'I'm sure she would be delighted. But, I have to warn you, my mother's memory is not what it was. After so long, she may not remember.'

'I understand,' said Marcus, rising to his feet to shake the proprietor's hand.

During the meal other tables started emptying as lunchtime diners returned to their workplaces. It was when he ordered coffee that he noticed the striking, auburn-haired woman from the Records Office seated at a table by the kerbside.

Do I say anything? considered Marcus. Do I apologise, explain that I have a tight schedule, or simply ignore her?

Somehow, the quiet elation that had welled up when he found the restaurant as he remembered carried him forward. What am I doing he thought to himself as he rose and walked over to her table.

'*Scusi, signora.*'

The woman looked up perplexed. Then, seeing his roman collar, she relaxed.

'*Si, Padre?*'

Suddenly, he was hesitant, recalling her anger and loud voice when berating the archivist.

'I should explain . . . I was the person who was in the reading room, this morning.' It sounded like an apology. Wrong approach, he realised. Too ingratiating. 'What I mean to say is, I have an important mission to accomplish, and needed urgent access to particular archives.'

Now it was too emphatic.

She stared up at him coolly. 'Strings were pulled, eh? I might have guessed.'

Finding it hard to suppress his irritation, he commented. 'I shan't be very long – no more than two days.'

'So I've been bumped because a member of the club expects special treatment. What is it with you guys?'

Exasperated, he said, 'Do you think the Church gets preferential treatment whenever it has a mind?'

'In Italy . . . all the time!'

'Arrant nonsense!'

45

'Listen, my reverend friend. Wearing that gear, you've got all the authority you want in this country.'

Marcus unconsciously chewed his lip. There was a strong American intonation to her Italian. He reverted to English.

'This is not some commercial venture for which I'm being paid. What I'm doing is important.'

'Well, well, a Brit! You must have some clout.' Her eyes were starting to flash. 'And I am merely a creature of the fourth estate, with no rights!'

Her voice was hardening.

Until that moment, neither had been conscious of people around them turning their heads in their direction. Several waiters were looking on apprehensively. Some common signal had alerted them. Marcus reddened, and sat down hurriedly.

'Perhaps, we can sort this out, amicably,' he said in a hushed voice.

'Who asked you to sit at my table?' she responded, her mouth a tight line. Marcus drew a deep breath. 'Can I, at least, make some amends? Can I buy you a drink? Then we can discuss it like adults.'

'Don't you patronise me,' she muttered in a loud whisper. 'It would take more than a drink to placate me.' She looked down at the table. 'But, here – if you want, you can pay my coffee bill!'

She pushed it across the table, rose abruptly, gathered her shoulder bag and strode away.

At four-thirty Marcus was reminded that the Records Office was closing. He saved the data on his computer, and paid for the document copies.

As he strolled back to the pensione, his mind turned to the notes he was compiling. With many of the instrument makers in a family having the same Christian name, epithets were often used to distinguish individual members. In the Amati dynasty, for example, there had been two named Girolamo – the younger being known as Hieronymus. Among the Guarneris, there had been two Pietros and two Giuseppes. Pietro, the brother of Giuseppe, had moved to Mantua, and became known as 'Pietro of Mantua'. Giuseppe had two sons, one called Pietro, the other bearing the same name as his father. To avoid confusion, the younger son had been referred to as 'Pietro of Venice'.

Working side-by-side in the same studio as his father, the other Giuseppe acquired the appellation, 'del Gesù', derived from the cross and the initials 'IHS' – *Jesus Hominum Salvator* – he featured on his labels. Many believed that, because of his close association with the Jesuits, he was a man of exceptional piety. In truth, he had been a roustabout and often drunk. Legend had it he once killed a man and was imprisoned, where he spent much of his sentence making violins.

Crossing the piazza, Marcus turned on a whim in the direction of the bookshop he had visited the previous day. He would take up the offer to check a reference on Nicolo Amati.

He was in luck. The book shop in the Via Ferante was still open.

'Signor Danby, back so soon?' greeted Marciano, coming from behind the cluttered desk. Noticing his collar, he hesitated. 'I'm sorry, I did not realise you were a cleric.'

Marcus shrugged, as though it was of little importance.

'Signore, you mentioned yesterday that I might refer to one or two of your books.'

'But, of course. Seek whatever you need from my shelves.'

A disembodied voice declared, stridently, 'I thought it was you. You seem to take advantage of people wherever you go!'

Grimfaced, the redhead appeared from behind a line of shelves.

Marciano smiled. 'Do you know each other? This gentleman bought a number of books yesterday, but could not purchase all he wanted. I suggested he called in to refer to others. The same offer I made to you, cara.'

'You don't know what this man did to me.'

The bookseller turned questioningly to Marcus, who reddened. He hastily stammered. 'I beat her to the Records Office this morning, and she will not forgive me.'

'It was the way it was done,' she replied, tartly. 'The bureaucratic nonentity in charge told me he had been ordered to give access to this jumped-up priest.'

She was bristling again.

'Cara, you should show a little respect for our town's esteemed archivist,' smiled Marciano. 'Even if he is a small-minded idiot with little sense and poor judgement! What do you expect of an unfrocked priest?'

'Is he now?' Her irritation was turning to curiosity. 'How did he get the job?'

'My dear, he has relatives in the Town Hall. *Il nepotismo!*'

'So, even when you're outside the club, you're looked after.'

Her nose twitched; she was still prickly.

'Look, the offer of a truce is still there,' Marcus said, ignoring the intended slight. 'Spare me a moment to explain.'

'There's nothing to explain. Perhaps I should wear a collar and look ineffably pious. I might get treated as well as you, if I looked the part.'

Marcus reined in his irritation with difficulty, more out of respect for the bookseller. He breathed out slowly.

'I am trying to be polite. Signor Marciano, perhaps it would be better if I returned another time.'

Suddenly, her indignation was spent. The bookseller glanced at her, then said. 'What are the terms of the truce, father?'

'Opposite sides of a table where they serve the best zabaglione in Lombardy. Then we can discuss how best to resolve our differences.'

Marciano turned, and grinned at her. Her eye caught his amusement, and she stifled a half-formed retort. She took a deep breath, exhaled, and nodded her acceptance.

Signor Marciano opened the door of his shop for the two of them to pass through. In silence they returned to The Napoli. As she walked towards a table she said, over her shoulder, 'How do you know it's the best?'

'As a student I used to order it whenever I visited Cremona.'

He caught the eye of an anxious waiter, who came forward uncertainly to take their order.

'It's all right, there'll be no raised voices,' Marcus assured him.

Turning back, he leant on the table. 'What part of the States are you from?'

'Chicago. And you?'

'Originally, London. But, I've moved around.'

She placed her shoulder bag at her feet, then, almost resignedly, offered her right hand over the table.

'I'm Lisa. Mrs Lisa Robards. As you might suspect, my family are Italian. My maiden name was Monticelli, an old family from Trieste.'

'Marcus Danby. A brother in the Order of St Francis Xavier.'

She nodded. 'I know of the Order. You've got a Theological Community in Chicago. I've met Father Bongiovanni who runs it.'

'The Order is well established in America. Unfortunately, it is failing dismally in the UK.' The sadness in his voice was all too evident.

'What does that mean?'

'It means the remaining brothers in Britain are waiting to be shipped to Massachusetts.'

'Ouch! That's tough!'

'I guess it is. But, that's another story. So, tell me, how do you know Signor Marciano?'

'He is my godfather. A wonderful man! I love him dearly.'

The coffee and dessert arrived. For a while the conversation lapsed.

'You're right! This really is very good!' exclaimed Lisa, looking up.

Green eyes peered at him. She had a strong, full mouth, and a pointed chin which, at that moment, was not thrust out in gladiatorial manner.

'OK, let's hear it. What's so mightily important that you can't wait till I've finished?' the woman enquired.

He was slightly uncomfortable, and it showed in the formality of his reply.

'I have been commissioned to produce a report in just a few weeks about the Cremonese. To pick out their abilities, what sets them apart from all others.'

'And no one has done this before?' she said disingenuously. 'If you went to any of the libraries in your home town, you'd find the information is there on tap.'

'Not in the form or the depth required.'

'But, you're not quite sure, are you? And why choose a Brit? Surely an Italian could do the job more easily.'

'I have a clear cut idea of what is required, what is available from general resources, and what I need to discover by personal investigation.'

Unexpectedly repentant, the woman opposite said. 'Look, I didn't mean to rile you. You could say I'm here for the same purpose. I want to find out more about Stradivarius, not regurgitate age-old material.' She picked up her cup and held it in both hands. 'I have been asked by *Andante*, an on-line music journal, to write a meaningful piece on his life and works.'

'I know it well.'

Marcus was silent for a moment as an idea formed. She had a thrusting manner, which he lacked. She was also an attractive woman; her looks might unlock doors he would find difficult to open. And she was a writer. Her facility for words could well be of benefit. He looked up.

'I've been thinking. We're pursuing a similar quest, you and I. Why don't we both use the reading room?'

Lisa Robards raised a cynical eyebrow.

'What about our friendly archivist?'

He smiled across at her. 'Perhaps, I could pull a few of those strings.'

Chapter Thirteen

It took him by surprise. It was out of character. He bowed his head in case those in the Janiculum Gardens witnessed a religious with an irrepressible smile.

He had dined well. They had been affable and warm-hearted, encouraging him to try the fish, which had been superb, and then the veal. Each course accompanied by a particularly fine wine – now, he realised, a little too much wine. Not that he had revealed much. No more than His Eminence had suggested if approached. Or had he? For a moment his step faltered. Cardinal Marchetti believed he was unacquainted with all the details of the project, but snatches of conversations, occasional raised voices, deliberate eavesdropping, had contributed to his fund of knowledge. It was much more fulsome than His Eminence was aware. Dangerously so! A slight sweat touched his brow at the thought that he might have gone a little too far.

At the top of the Janiculum he paused to take in the view. Although not counted among the seven hills, it was the highest point in Rome and provided an awe-inspiring view of the sculptured steeples, rotundas, and rooftops. They shimmered in the bright sunlight. Then, his tonsure of St. Peter lowered to mask features now prey to merriment, Brother Felipé made his way towards the Vatican. He cut across the Via di Conciliazione and into the Borgo Pio, a narrow street leading to a small, discreet gate in the City wall. Designed long ago as an emergency exit for the Pontiff if the Vatican were under siege, it was used nowadays, by those who knew of its existence, as a short cut to the offices of the Curia.

He wondered if he could summarise how the chance meeting had occurred and give the gist of the conversation over the lunch table. It had taken longer than he realised. It was already three o'clock.

51

Three hours earlier he had slipped away from his desk for a brief lunch. Strolling across the Piazza in front of the Basilica, he had heard his name called by two approaching figures.

'Brother Felipé, I thought it was you!' called the taller of the pair. It was Signor Pantoni of the Mayor's Office, at his shoulder Giancarlo Rondesi, one of the Mayor's assistant directors.

Felipé Mendoza hesitated. They hurried forward and stood either side of him.

'We were just on our way to lunch. Would you care to join us?' proffered Rondesi.

'Thank you. Unfortunately I have very little time to spare.'

'Is Cardinal Marchetti keeping you so busy?' smiled Pantoni. 'Surely, a quick meal with us would be in order. We don't have much time either, but one must eat?'

'Well, I suppose something light and quick would be all right,' said Mendoza, 'but I must be back at my desk by one o'clock.'

They had hailed a taxi in the Porta Angelica, which whisked them up the Janiculum to the Piazza San Cosimato. Stepping from the vehicle, Mendoza was almost hustled into the restaurant. It dawned on him that the casual invitation had been planned. They had been taken to a small private room, a waiter immediately on hand to take their drinks order. The two civil servants had sat with their backs to the window, the light falling on the hapless Franciscan, whilst they were in shadow.

'So, Felipé, you are busy, you say,' said Rondesi, smiling towards his companion. 'What is so important that prevents you from taking so little time to eat?'

'Nothing of great consequence. Leastways nothing out of the ordinary,' replied the cardinal's secretary. 'As you will appreciate, ensuring the best financial returns for the benefit of the Church is uppermost in our minds. When investment opportunities arise we have to make sure the funds are available. That demands our full commitment.'

'Of course,' nodded Rondesi. 'And you are showing a profit?'

'Our advisers tell us that our finances are quite satisfactory,' he replied, a little smugly.

'Good, good!' smiled Pantoni, topping up the glasses.

'How much is invested in stocks and shares, Felipé, and how

much in real estate these days?' asked the assistant director, taking a long draught.

'It's hard to say,' said the cardinal's man, pondering the question. 'It was almost one hundred per cent in land before the authorities of the time expropriated the Papal States more than century ago. It has risen over the intervening years, but it's probably no more than ten per cent on current values. The rest is in stocks, shares and bonds.'

'Does that take into account the territory in Lombardy?' queried Pantoni.

Mendoza was now sure the Mayor's two representatives had worked out a strategy to steer the conversation in a particular direction.

'Yes. And in Le Marche, and Tuscany.'

'Exactly how much do you hold in Lombardy? It's near Cremona is it not?' This time the question had come from Rondesi.

'As I understand, it's about a hundred hectares, close to the river, about ten kilometres from Cremona. Why do you ask?'

Pantoni ignored the question. Instead he continued, 'Is it farmed? Are there buildings on the site?'

'To my knowledge, there are a few buildings. Mostly barns, sheds, with several large dwellings, as I recall. It's largely grazing land, at the moment.'

Mendoza was warming to their game. He drank a good measure of the wine and allowed Pantoni to re-fill his glass.

'What do you mean "at the moment"?' asked Rondesi. He called for another bottle.

'Well, it could be sold to bring in income. It was bequeathed to the Church by the Hapsburgs. Since then it's been leased out to a local farmer. But the present tenant has just died, and we are considering the best use to make of it. Why? Does the Mayor's Department want to buy it?' he smiled archly.

Pantoni looked up, and his eyebrows rose. Rondesi's eyes glistened.

The table was cleared, and readied for the next course. Rondesi ordered another wine, making a show of his knowledge.

'I think we'll go for the Barolo from Monforte d'Alba. The 1990 will do nicely,' he told the wine-waiter. Turning to Mendoza, he said, 'I find that if you drink a good Barolo under ten years old the tannins are still ready to fight back. I'm sure you will find this to your liking.'

The bottle was opened, the cork sniffed, the wine allowed to stand.

'Coming back to this parcel of land in Lombardy. What would you get if you sold it?' Rondesi inquired, swirling his glass.

'We have not really considered its commercial value. I suppose, as farming land, it would fetch close to five million Euros.'

'But you don't want to sell, I've heard,' added Pantoni. The comment seemed a little premature for Rondesi's liking, judging by the look he gave his junior companion.

Mendoza saw an opportunity. 'What prompts that statement, signore?' Slightly turning his shoulder towards Pantoni, he contrived to create a one-to-one situation.

'Well . . . I've heard rumours . . .'

Suddenly, he was on the back foot, and glancing at Rondesi to extricate him.

'What my colleague means is that such a site, distant from the heart of Italy, offering little in terms of access or facilities, where communications are virtually non-existent, would provide little advantage to city people who might be contemplating a rural retreat. It would be far better to retain your status as an absentee landlord,' answered Rondesi, smiling at the Franciscan. 'Don't you agree?'

'It's not for me to say, Signor Rondesi,' replied Mendoza, courteously.

'No, of course not,' the official acknowledged. 'But, theoretically, would members of the Curia encourage a move to the wilderness?'

'It might be aired as a proposal,' nodded Mendoza, appearing to give it thought. 'But, you know how Curialists work. Everything is a deep secret – which everyone knows about. Tensions mount, an announcement is imminent. But the real secret, the best one, is that the idea has been dropped. Another project has captured their imagination!'

Wine was poured into three glasses; they were raised; a triple clink, and each of the diners was left, briefly, to his own thoughts.

'So, the odd little rumour I've heard is untrue?' commented Rondesi.

'What rumour would that be, signore?'

'Come, you have no need to be coy with us, Brother Mendoza,' said Pantoni.

But, before he could continue, Rondesi interjected, 'What my friend has heard is the unlikely report that the Church's administration is thinking of relocating. We were aware that you hold several parcels of land and, if there were any credibility in the rumour, the Curia might occupy one of these. Frankly, we give no credence to the suggestion. The Curia would be isolated from the Holy Father, and it simply would not work. Don't you agree?'

'It is only a personal opinion, you understand,' commented Mendoza, leaning forward conspiratorially, 'but you are right. The Holy See could not operate effectively if there were any distance between itself and the Curia.'

'You see, Rondesi,' said Pantoni abruptly. 'I was right. They could not exist independently. It's a wild, misleading rumour.'

The other man frowned. Pantoni had gone a little too far. The topic was hurriedly changed and the conversation became more desultory as the diners enjoyed their meal. Soon it was evident that the Mayor's envoys were wishing to bring it to a close.

'So, Brother Mendoza, I am glad all is well with the cardinal. I particularly hope his money-making projects are productive. Please pass on the Mayor's best wishes to him,' said Rondesi, crumpling his napkin, and setting it down on the table.

Pantoni, taking the signal, made to rise. Halfway from his seat he looked down at the Franciscan and said, sealing the reason for the tête-á-tête, 'So, your people will not be moving from the walled city, brother?'

'I did not say that, Signor Pantoni. All I said was that I agree with you. We could not work properly in isolation. If any such move were contemplated, both the Palace and the Curia would have to move as one. Now, who is to say that is not a possibility?'

'Thank you, Felipé. That sounds quite satisfactory,' said Cardinal Marchetti, nodding to his secretary. 'Now, be so kind as to get Signor Lambertini for me.'

Moments later the telephone rang.

'Signor Lambertini, it would appear the Mayor has risen to the bait, albeit at an exploratory level. They have been quizzing my secretary . . .'

The cardinal responded to a comment from the lobbyist.

'Well, I had briefed him. Not disclosing much, you understand, but enough to provoke their interest and, doubtless, further concerns.'

Something else was said.

'No, we do nothing, pending contact from the Minister. I'll let you know when that occurs, then we'll implement the next stage. Arriverderlo!'

Mendoza had been unwilling to intercept the call for fear of detection. So it was, by pressing his ear to the door, he heard but one side of the conversation.

Chapter Fourteen

Marcus collected Lisa Robards from her hotel, the Ibis Cremona on the Via Mantova.

He had contacted the Messenger the previous evening, and arranged a rendezvous. As usual, his arrival was announced only by a gentle tapping on his hotel door. Marcus had sat on the narrow bed. The Messenger had stood in the shadow cast by a tall clothes cupboard and listened to his request for Mrs Robards to work with him in the reading room. Then, he had braced himself to put forward his other suggestion. If they could work together in the Records Office, he had thought to invite Lisa Robards to join him in his research – two people could work faster, make certain relevant facts were not ignored, exchange opinions, ensure a truer perspective was reached.

But the enthusiasm to involve Mrs Robards was lessening now. He questioned whether she might be the right person. Perhaps she was too volatile. Progress hindered by argument. Worse, they could have such strong differences of opinion nothing might be achieved. Nevertheless, having requested the meeting, Marcus felt obliged to put the proposal to the Messenger.

The tall figure listened without interruption. Then he had uttered one word: 'No!'

Such an adamant denial of his request annoyed Marcus, despite the fact that he was having second thoughts.

'I'm sorry?'

'Signor Danby, it's quite simple. I cannot allow it.'

'Really? So you think I'm going to be able to run all over Italy, checking every source, noting every fact, every piece of fiction, sift through their relevance, and write a detailed report on which your principals can act in just days? The undertaking is hardly feasible for two people, yet you want me to do it on my own!'

Marcus was angry – as much with himself for agreeing to the ridiculous timetable, as with the person standing before him, denying him additional help.

'OK. Forget the whole thing,' he had shouted. 'The contract is off. Finished! I quit!'

'Signor Danby,' the controlled voice had replied. 'Let me remind you of my words. If anyone is going to cancel our agreement, it will be I, not you. You have no say in the matter.'

The Messenger stood over him.

'Let me explain for your own good: whether I like it or not, others now know of your commission. There could be . . . difficulties.'

'What do you mean?'

'At this point you can trust no one.'

He had stepped back, allowing the words to sink in.

'This lady you have met – she may well be a bona-fide journalist, writing for an American magazine. Her assistance may, indeed, be welcome. But, now your quest is known to others, she could well be working for them.'

'If, as you say, the work I am doing is known to "others", then it stands to reason the quicker I complete the project the more readily you can take advantage of its findings.'

They walked along the marbled corridor, the archivist saying little. He led them to the small reading room where the viewer was on the table, turned on his heel marched out.

'Whoever organises your string-pulling is no slouch. He, or she, must have got our friend out of bed to make sure we were both welcome.'

Marcus looked up from his laptop. 'I didn't get the impression we were exactly welcome! Over-riding his precious regulations must have been more than he could bear. I'll bet he is having apoplexy right now somewhere in the building!'

'You're probably right,' she said, taking a chair alongside him. 'OK, now to business. I'll show you what I've got; you show me what you've got.'

For the next hour, the pair discussed their notes and the approach each had adopted. Marcus took a copy of his outline plan and passed it to her.

'This is deep,' she commented, absorbing the detail. 'Much more into it than mine.'

'Well, my aim is to dig well below the surface. And I'm not just researching Stradivari, but all his contemporaries. I've got to come up with the results they are looking for.'

Lisa Robards, turned towards him. 'Who are this mysterious "they"?'

'I don't know,' confided Marcus. He saw her scepticism. 'I don't really! Everything is being conducted through a third party.'

'An agent?'

'More an intermediary.'

'OK. If you want to keep it under wraps, that's fine by me.'

Marcus changed the subject.

'Tell me, do you make a worthwhile living writing about music?'

'Not really. It gives me freedom to do my own thing – to travel, to meet interesting people, to immerse myself in a subject I love. No, I don't make much money. Fortunately, I have a small inheritance which keeps the wolf from the door.'

'What have you written lately?'

'I have spent the last six weeks in Austria, compiling a lengthy piece on the Strauss family. I came across one or two nuggets that have not been aired before, and *Andante* snapped it up. On the basis of that they commissioned me to write on Stradivari.'

The door opened and the woman who had looked after Marcus the previous day set a tray of coffee on the table. However, on this occasion, there was no friendly smile.

'If looks could kill!' commented Lisa.

'Do you play an instrument?'

'Not well. I once had ambitions to play the cello in Carnegie Hall, but never made the grade. You?'

'The violin, many years ago.' He paused, then came to a decision. 'Look, I was thinking. If we were both to seek out this level of detail, get under the skins of the real Cremonese, wouldn't that give you the platform for a good, in-depth piece on Stradivari?' He was about to ignore the Messenger.

She thought about it. 'Are you saying I help you research all the others, and for that I get to use the plum bits in my article?'

'Why not? You may pick up some nuggets of information that would lift it above anything else that has been written, thus far.'

'No strings?'

'None. I'm not writing for publication.'

'Well, my ecclesiastical friend, let's set to.'

Marcus appraised the woman sitting opposite. She wasted little time in weighing things up before coming to a decision. He realised they were quite different in temperament.

'So, how far have you got on their workshop practices?' she began.

'I have been concentrating on the Amatis, though at the moment I'm just scratching the surface, especially as the first two generations flourished before the plague struck this area in the mid 1600s. I've found more about Nicolo, who taught Antonio Stradivari and Andrea Guarneri. I've got some solid material on his working life and, more importantly, his methods of teaching his apprentices. This will help when I study the later Guarneris and the Stradivari family. You can already see the effects his tuition had on their development.'

Marcus was animated. Lisa listened carefully. Although each was seeking a different reward, at that moment they were united in wanting to unearth every detail of the world and times of the instrument makers. Marcus' enthusiasm was mirrored in Lisa's eyes. He grinned at her. The Messenger's forbidding words were forgotten.

Chapter Fifteen

'I am sorry, the reading room is not available at present,' declared the archivist's assistant.

'Can you tell me when it will be?' asked the man in clerical habit, clutching at his broad-rimmed hat. 'I desperately need access to certain records.'

He was clearly agitated. She had turned away several people seeking access to information during the past few days, but the disquiet of this member of the clergy touched her.

'What records in particular are you seeking?'

The handsome cleric leaned forward. His age was indefinable – somewhere in his thirties, possibly. His pale, blue eyes were fixed on the assistant with a look of pleading and concern, yet something more. She was entranced, like a hare caught in the headlights of a car.

'I need to read about the famine and the outbreak of the plague in Cremona in 1630.'

There was a disturbing sexuality about this priest. A faint blush touched her cheeks.

'I believe those records are being used at the moment. But let me see when they will be available.'

She rose, stepped round the reception desk, and with a shy smile walked down the corridor. Moments later she returned.

'I understand they will be ready tomorrow. The records of that event are quite sketchy and comprise just one file. As the reading room is occupied, if you wish, you can read it in my office.'

'That is most generous of you, signora. Or is it signorina? I shall look forward to meeting you again tomorrow.' His eyes took on a different quality. 'I had thought to review the archives for the early years of the eighteenth century. Are they also available, by chance?'

'I can tell you they are not. And it seems likely they will be in use for some days yet,' the assistant replied. 'Whoever is using the reading room at present seems to have unlimited access to most of the archives, especially those covering the period 1700 to 1750.'

'Powerful people, signorina.'

'Influential, signore. Our chief archivist is falling over himself to accede to their wishes.'

'Will you go back tomorrow?'

'But, of course! I may be able to get closer to them, to pick up something that gives us a clearer guide to their intentions. And, more importantly, learn what they have discovered so far.'

'You'd better phone in and report what we are doing.'

Chapter Sixteen

'I am disappointed in you, Signor Danby. I specifically told you not to involve the woman. You have defied me. I shall give you one more chance to tell her she is not welcome. If you do not, I shall take matters into my own hands.'

'Listen to me, Messenger. I am still committed to this project. Perhaps more so than you! You want the report in twenty-one days' time – then you shall have it. But if that means calling on an extra pair of hands then that's the way it will be!'

After a tiring day of researching, and making copious notes, he had returned to the pensione for a shower before meeting Mrs Robards to discuss their findings over dinner. The Messenger had been there in his room. Taken off guard, Marcus had reacted belligerently.

The taciturn figure seemed unperturbed by Marcus' tirade. After a few minutes he had spoken, a hint of apology in his voice.

'I have learned, Signor Danby, that someone is likely to hinder your research. I do not know how, but presumably they will be obstructive – aggressive even – in attempting to dissuade you from pursuing your work.'

'Are you saying I'm in some sort of danger? Surely, someone hasn't taken offence at what I'm doing? I'm not posing any threat.' Marcus was silent for a moment, digesting the Messenger's words. 'You should have mentioned this when you came to me in England. I would certainly have thought twice about accepting.'

'I was not at liberty to do so,' the Messenger said quietly.

'Do your principals always get what they want?' snapped Marcus. 'Well, do you realise, Messenger, or whatever your name is, that Mrs Robards has been in my company? If they – whoever they are – are alive to my presence, they're fully aware of my association with the lady. Even if you don't want her involved, she could

63

well be, because you didn't warn me about the likelihood of reprisal.'

Marcus realised his voice was raised.

'So, what do you suggest?' he demanded in a more measured tone. 'If you want me to complete the task you've set, I need extra help. Otherwise it won't be finished in the time. So what's it to be?'

Eventually, the Messenger conceded the project was first priority and gave grudging approval to Lisa's involvement. Significantly, he agreed to provide protection for the two of them. However, his parting comment was disconcerting.

'Signor Danby, you must inform her of the situation. If, as you declare, you need her help, you must also tell her of the dangers. It would not surprise me if she departs immediately for the United States! Whatever the outcome, I want that report on time.'

Marcus was quiet over dinner. Lisa did not notice, for she did most of the talking.

'Do you realise that with the three days we have spent in those archives and the time I was there on my own, I have been closeted in that room for almost a week,' she declared, taking a mouthful of lasagna.

Marcus nodded, preoccupied. I've got to tell her, he thought. I cannot let her continue without some sort of explanation.

'Lisa,' Marcus cleared his throat. 'There's something I have discovered that is important. You should know, because . . .' He hesitated. 'Because the consequences could be unpleasant!'

Marcus was surprised. Firstly, at her inner calm. He fully expected her to rant when the news sank in. To exhibit that fearsome temper he had witnessed on several previous occasions.

'When you say obstructive, what are we talking about? Being bloody-minded and interfering, or a more physical deterrent?'

'I honestly don't know,' replied Marcus. 'But the Messenger did say he would provide protection.'

'When did you first find out?' she asked quietly.

'Last night, when I returned to my room.'

'Are you saying you had no idea this could happen before you accepted the assignment?'

'None at all. I thought it was a simple case, albeit a hurried one, of researching and reporting.' Marcus gazed at her across the table. 'I've been thinking, if you pulled out now, you would be rid of me – the whole business.'

'What about my article for *Andante*?'

'Lisa, your safety comes before meeting the deadline of a musical publication. You could do what you suggested to me. Go to your local library for material. I could send you my notes.'

Lisa Robards snorted. 'Tell me, who is this Messenger guy?'

'I don't know. Or, shall I say, I don't know who his principals are.'

'But, surely, they are going to pay you for the work?'

'Yes, in kind,' replied Marcus, suddenly embarrassed to tell her of the bait that had been dangled before him.

'Well?'

'Actually, it was a Guarneri violin.'

'Actually, it was a Guarneri violin,' she mimicked in a flat English voice. 'Pull the other one, Marcus!' Red spots appeared on her cheeks. 'A Guarneri is worth thousands of dollars. Who, in their right mind, would pay you that much for four weeks' work?'

'It's a "del Gesù",' he remarked hesitantly, appreciating for the first time his naïvety. How readily he had responded to the inducement without weighing up the reality.

'That's worth more than a million dollars! Honestly, Marcus, how could you be so gullible?'

'Well, that's my problem,' he said irritably. 'As far as you are concerned, you are going back to your hotel, packing, and taking the first plane out of Milan.'

'Who says?' she flared. 'Who the hell do you think you are, telling me what to do?'

'Don't argue! It's for the best. I don't want anything to happen to you.'

'But you want my help. Make up your goddam' mind!'

'Forget it. I want you to go home.'

Marcus' voice was rising. Other diners were looking towards their table.

'I feel it's for the best, that's all,' he finished lamely.

She stared at him, then moved her chair round the table to sit alongside him.

'Listen, Marcus. I can't believe I'm saying this. Oddly enough, I'm enjoying the work. I feel that the project could open minds to the real Cremonese – perhaps, for the first time, to tell it as it was, warts and all. That, in my view, would be a wonderful thing.' Lisa looked down at the table. 'For my part, I think the piece on Stradivari I was going to write would not have been much better than all the others, no matter how much I delude myself. You've given me a fresh insight. I'm getting to understand the real person. That has to be a good thing.'

'What are you saying, Lisa?'

'You're sure the Messenger will protect both of us, right?'

'Yes . . .'

'Then, Marcus, I appreciate your concerns, but I'm staying.'

Chapter Seventeen

Monsignor Keppel leaned on his stick. Cardinal Grossmann's secretary had offered him a seat but he had declined.

Now, twenty minutes later, he was in two minds: ease his bones by sitting down, or let growing discomfort fuel his indignation. Suddenly, both doors were flung open.

'Monsignor! Forgive me for keeping you waiting. Come in. Come in.'

He was ushered into the cardinal's inner sanctum.

'So, my friend, what can I do for you?' smiled Grossmann, when Keppel was seated.

The monsignor placed two arthritic hands on the handle of the walking stick poised in front of him and stared directly at Grossmann.

'In all conscience, I cannot allow what you are doing to continue. I must insist you stop immediately,' he declared.

The cardinal's eyes narrowed.

'And, pray, what am I doing that so upsets you?'

'Don't play word games with me!' exploded the aged prelate. 'You are encouraging your friends in Austria to . . . to . . .'

He could not say it. Doing so would make him party to Grossmann's actions.

'To what?' asked the cardinal, harshly. 'What am I doing that you cannot speak of?'

'You know, Grossmann. For all your fine words, you are concerned that Marchetti will uncover something that will hinder Goehr's chances. What you really meant was not hiding or removing evidence, but removing the people involved in his investigation.'

'Who told you that?'

'Your Eminence, I too have friends in my homeland,' said

Keppel, now levering himself slowly from the chair. 'You may think that you have fooled the others with your anodyne words, but I have found out. And I'm going to tell them. Then we shall publicly declare what you are up to!'

'Don't forget, monsignor,' said the cardinal icily, 'we made a pact in your office. Perhaps you have forgotten. Let me remind you what was said.'

From a drawer in the elegant desk he withdrew a small device. He pressed a button and the tinny, clear voices agreeing to Keppel's ringing words of support for the ancient house of the Hapsburgs, and a stand against those who dared undermine the Austrian, Cardinal Goehr, rang around the room.

'I would have a care, monsignor. It is evident that it was you who fired our zeal. Perhaps you should review your position?'

The cleric looked at him with contempt. Then, turning on his heel, he slowly made his way from the cardinal's rooms.

His fellow-conspirators would be reluctant to oppose a cardinal; once they learned of the recording, they would shrink even further from a bruising encounter with Grossmann. He was on his own. Or was he?

Perhaps a word with Cardinal Marchetti? A severe reprimand; perhaps some form of sanction, possibly demotion. That would still be better than being party to . . . to . . .

He still could not bring his mind to contemplate what the likely outcome for the hapless researcher of the Cremonese might be.

'I believe we may have a slight problem . . . No, I prefer not to deal with it! That's why I am phoning . . . No, it cannot be traced! . . . Yes, someone should come to Rome, straightaway! . . . Good! When can I expect him? . . . Well, the sooner the better . . . If he flies into Fiumincino, tell him to meet me at the usual place in Ostia Antica on Wednesday evening.'

Chapter Eighteen

'That's it, I'm bushed!'

Lisa pushed back her chair, and stood up.

Marcus looked up. 'I think I'll work on for another hour or so. Then I'll put what I've got today in some semblance of order.'

'I'm going to have a long soak and prepare myself for this evening. I'm meeting an old friend for dinner'.

'Er . . . do you know where you are going?' enquired Marcus.

'Don't worry. I'll be quite safe. We are eating in the hotel.'

'Well, if you do decide to go out, give me a ring on my mobile.'

The Messenger had provided him with a mobile phone and several numbers where he could be reached. As yet, other than testing its camera qualities, he had neither made nor received a call.

Lisa gathered up her things. They agreed to meet in the reading room early the next morning.

Marcus was making progress. His appraisal of workshop practices was coming together nicely. Already he had uncovered more detail than could be found in many published works on the subject. He had spent time in Signor Marciano's bookshop reviewing numerous texts and, surprisingly, had found them wanting.

Yesterday, he had come across some papers relating to Nicolo Amati's studio. They had covered the manner in which he had developed the skills of his apprentices by making them accountable for specific aspects of the week. Every two years during their twelve year apprenticeship, each had been allocated a new responsibilty. These had embraced the creation of moulds and patterns, the art of carving, the acquisition of ingredients, the preparation of glues and varnishes, and drying and finishing.

During their final periods, for example, Amati's son – also Nicolo – had been responsible for the tools, Antonio Stradivari had been in charge off selecting the various woods, and Andrea Guarneri the finishing materials.

Such detailed information was not to be found in reference books. Yet here was an aspect of their tuition which was, undoubtedly, of great significance, and which would have had a profound effect on their later lives. This method of teaching will feature prominently in the final report, thought Marcus.

As the afternoon drew to a close and he was typing up the last of his notes, there was a tap at the door.

'*Entri!*'

It was the archivist. He noticed that Marcus was alone.

'*Pax vobiscum.*'

'*Et cum spirito tuo,*' responded Marcus automatically.

'So, they are going well, your researches?' enquired the young man, rubbing his hands together.

'Thank you, very well. Thanks to your welcome support.'

'We must work for each other, brother. Is that not our maxim?'

Marcus was puzzled. 'I suppose it is, yes.'

The archivist beamed. 'So, is there anything more I can do to help?'

He was about to say 'no', when he remembered something.

'I have been checking on the household of Nicolo Amati and can find no reference to his apprentices. Surely they would be listed with other members of his family? Stradivari, Guarneri and others spent years in his studio, but nowhere are they mentioned by name. Do you have any other records showing when they were living in his house during the late seventeenth century?'

'What we have has been made available to you,' replied the archivist. He removed his glasses and massaged the bridge of his nose. Then he added, 'Of course, you could always check the *Stati dell'Anime.*'

'What are they?'

'Each year the priests used to check on "the state of the souls" in their parishes,' explained the archivist. 'Like an early form of census. They used to conduct it every Easter. Everyone in a household had to be listed – largely, I suspect, to ensure there was no shortage in church income.'

'Do these records still exist?'

'Naturally, brother. Many are in the Town Hall Records Office, though the majority are now lodged in the main archives in Milan.'

'What time does the Town Hall close?'

'Not for another hour. If you wish, I'll phone and ask that the Amati file is made ready for you.'

Marcus hurriedly scooped up the last of his belongings, thinking as he did so of the change in the chief archivist's manner. The Messenger must be either a close friend or have some hold over the official. Either way, it was working to his advantage.

The woman in charge of the records was welcoming.

'Don't worry, padre,' she responded to Marcus' concern about the time. 'I have the key, so I decide when we shall close.'

She led him to a small room. The records Marcus was seeking were in a box file already on the desk.

'Do you know of the *Stati dell'Anime*, padre?' she asked, as Marcus took off his jacket. 'They were like an annual census conducted by the Church. They give the names and ages of those living in a household, as well as identifying relationships with the owner of the property.'

She was a well-rounded woman, in her fifties, with a ready smile and an obvious knowledge of her subject. She sat on the only other chair in the room and made no comment while Marcus began his searches. However, after half an hour, he had still not come across any of the names he was seeking.

'Signora,' he remarked. 'These are very detailed, but seemingly incomplete. Nicolo Amati had numerous apprentices but, other than a few luthiers I recognise, there is no mention of when Antonio Stradivari and Andrea Guarneri were apprenticed to him. Why would that be?'

'Probably because they did not live in, padre,' she replied. 'Like so many of Cremona's instrument makers they lived in the parish of San Domenico. In fact, close to each other around the piazza. So most of them would have gone home each day'.

'As simple as that. Why didn't I think of it? Thank you, signora.'

He continued staring at the three hundred year old document held in his white-gloved hands.

'Amati seemed to have had a great many young women living in his household. Were they all family?'

She took the sheet from him, then smiled slowly. 'Many were, padre. The rest were, how shall I put it, trainees, perhaps.'

71

'Trainees?'

With that she laughed loudly.

'Padre, women in many walks of life have always been used for the more delicate work. They have dexterous fingers, an eye for detail.'

'But, instrument making was always regarded as men's work. Women were not allowed in the workshop.'

'In those days, what was allowed, and what actually happened were two different things. In Cremona it was never spoken of, but it was common knowledge that women did many of the intricate jobs. Antonio Stradivari lived until he was ninety-three, but it would have been impossible for him to make all the instruments for which he is famed without help – and not just from his apprentices.'

Marcus had not contemplated this aspect of the luthier's work rate before, nor supposed that the maestros were ever assisted other than by their male apprentices. Yet another facet to be taken into account.

'Can I take copies of some of these documents, signora?'

Exhilarated by his discovery, on his way back to the pensione Marcus stopped off in a bar to celebrate. He ordered a decent Barolo and took the bottle of red wine to a corner table to contemplate the progress of the mission.

His early fears about working closely with Lisa Robards had been dispelled, although he still could not come to terms with the manner in which she worked. Each morning, she would distinguish clearly what she wished to achieve by the day's end. Yet within minutes of starting she would often go off at a tangent as either the document she was studying, or a stray thought, prompted another avenue of research. Marcus, by contrast, was methodical and committed to the pursuit of each objective. Each method yielded success in its own way, as they discovered when they got together to discuss their notes and summarise the results.

He was keen to see her face when he told her about the women in Stradivari's life. It was then he noticed that the bottle was empty. He waved to the cameriere to bring another to his table.

*

Someone was banging on his head. Marcus rolled away to avoid the blows, but they persisted. Opening his eyes to glimpse his attacker, he peered over the bedclothes. The knocking on the door became more intense.

'Marcus! Are you in there? Dammit, where are you?'

Slowly he eased himself upright and shuffled across the room, slipped the lock and opened the door.

'What the hell are you doing in bed at this hour? We agreed to meet at nine. God! This room is the pits! I'm going to suffocate!'

Marcus stood there as she marched over to the window and threw it open. She turned.

'Well? You've got a hangover! What sort of a guy are you?' She peered at him. 'Are you a closet drinker?'

An hour later they were seated at a pavement-side table.

'I got worried when you weren't there. I thought they'd got to you. Come on, drink another cup.'

'Do I have to? I've got a headache.'

She ignored him and signalled to the waiter.

'So what prompted this little episode? Or do you often drink yourself silly?'

Marcus shrugged his shoulders.

'What sort of an answer is that?'

He drew in a deep breath. 'I haven't had a serious drink for weeks. I haven't needed to. In fact, I have not even thought about it. Last night, would you believe, was a small celebration that got out of hand.'

'Celebration? For what?'

'After you had gone, the archivist suggested I check the records they hold in the Town Hall'.

Lisa frowned. 'Why?'

'You know I was trying to find out why the names of Amati's apprentices did not show up among those in his household? Well, our previously obstructive friend directed me to the *Stati dell'Anime.*'

'What are they?'

'I hadn't heard of them either. But they cast a new light on the subject. They will be extremely interesting for you – for your piece on Stradivari.'

'In what way?'

Lisa leaned forward, Marcus' drinking forgotten while he explained their relevance.

'A very helpful woman in the Town Hall showed me the actual documents. Here, read my notes; look at the copies I made.'

He took the material from a folder and passed it to Lisa. The third coffee came, but she did not look up.

'This is fascinating, Marcus. They were residents until their late teens. If they were family, they were not just visiting.'

Finally, she lifted her gaze.

'The use of women in the workshop could also have applied to Stradivari. Did you manage to view his *Stati dell'Anime*?'

'No. Apparently, his records are stored in the State Archives in Milan, in the Sala Quarter,' responded Marcus. 'If his returns also show an abundance of females in his household, it would confirm what the woman in charge of the records said. Even if he'd lived to a ripe old age his output would have had to have been in excess of twenty instruments a year. Yet we know he never made more than fourteen hundred under his own label. Even with a few apprentices he would have been hard-pressed to keep up the pace of one a fortnight for nigh on seventy years of his working life!'

Marcus was silent for a moment.

'According to Hills, and other sources, he rarely took on apprentices. So, bearing in mind the complexity of work, using women in his studio for the more dexterous jobs would have been the obvious answer.'

Lisa's mouth set in a determined fashion. 'Right, I'm off to Milan. I need to see those records.'

'Not before I inform the Messenger.'

'There's no time. Anyway, I'll be quite safe. I'll go by train.'

'Well, if you are going to Milan, I'm going to Verona. I have to visit the Dendrology Institute there some time. I might as well go while you're away. In fact, if someone is after us, my trip eastwards will probably draw them away from you.'

Chapter Nineteen

Michelo Lambertini shut the door of his Maranello. The front-engined Ferrari suited his persona. Its classic shape was eye-catching, but not so head-turning as many other models. For him, it was the ideal vehicle.

The gatekeeper hastened to raise the barrier. He knew Michelo by sight – and by the banknotes he discreetly passed over. Earlier in the day, a brief phone call had ensured Lambertini was allocated a prime parking spot in the congested Tourist Board's car park. He waved his thanks to the uniformed official and turned towards the Viale Pretoriano. It had been a satisfactory meeting on both counts. Michelo had put the case for his client in a measured way, and he could tell that his comments had made the right impression. He felt confident of the outcome.

It was as he was being escorted to the door by the Director in charge of Administration, Heritage and General Affairs that he had casually remarked, 'When are you going to quash the rumour?'

'And what rumour would that be, Michelo?'

'Have you not heard? Everyone is talking about the wild idea that the Vatican is moving from the city. Nonsense of course! Fortunately, the city and the tourists have not got wind of it.'

The director stared at him, trying to gauge how much he knew.

'Yes, there is nothing of substance in the rumour, but it is annoying,' he replied, his eyes hardening. 'The problem is we cannot openly refute the notion, for then we would have to admit that there was something to deny in the first place. Tell me, what have you heard?'

'If, like yourself, I were sure it was a reckless comment, from someone who is either a fool or, worse, is deliberately trying to foment trouble, I would call in the press, tell them it is a nonsensical idea, and say that to print one word of such a misleading story would expose them to ridicule.'

'Hmm . . . perhaps, Michelo.'

They shook hands at the door and Lambertini was escorted out of the building. Now on his way to the Ministry of Productive Activities, a knowing smile creased the corners of his lips. His contribution to the project was developing nicely.

'You have heard it as well?'

The Minister's chief aide had his back to Lambertini, as he topped up their glasses.

'Apparently, they are talking of nothing else at the State Tourist Board.'

'Someone from the Mayor's office mentioned it to me,' remarked the official. His manner was quite sanguine. 'I cannot think it is more than a wild comment made at a party. I wouldn't give it any more credence than that.'

'I'm sure you're right.' Lambertini took the proffered glass.

'What are they going to do about it?'

'Nothing, and rightly so. But they are keen to run the source to ground.'

The aide sat up. 'For such a bizarre rumour as that?'

'Perhaps they think there is more to it than just rumour,' commented Lambertini gravely.

Suddenly, the aide was preoccupied with his own thoughts.

'Michelo, you will have to excuse me. I must see the Minister.'

He was heading towards the Town Hall on the Campidoglio, but not to visit any of the officials this time. Lambertini was going to catch the receptionist when she left the building. He knew that after work she always went to a small café in one of the back streets. A chance meeting would not seem out the ordinary.

He had been delayed at the Ministry of Cultural Assets. One of the directors had quizzed him at length about the reactions to the 'latest gossip', as he had termed it. He hurried along the street. Entering the café, his first thought was that he had missed her. People milling around the counter, the noise of the coffee machine, the hubbub of conversation combined to obscure her presence. Then he noticed her, alone at a small table at the back.

Carrying an expresso, he made his way down the crowded room.

'Angelina! How are you? May I join you?'

The woman, neatly but not attractively dressed, looked up. She was in her mid-forties; her features, sharp and inquisitive, registered irritation. She had been reading a magazine. Then the face softened.

'Of course, Signor Lambertini. Please do.'

He eased himself into the narrow space occupied by the second chair.

'I didn't know you came in here,' she remarked.

'They make good coffee.' He grinned at her. 'And not many others from the Town Hall know of its existence.'

'Have you just come from a meeting, signore?'

'Yes, it has just finished.'

'That's odd. I don't remember seeing anything in the visitors' log, or a badge issued in your name.'

'It would not have been, Angelina.' He leaned forward conspiratorially. 'It was a very discreet gathering.'

'I didn't see you arrive!'

'You would't have done. There are more entrances to the Palazzo Senatorio than through the main door.'

Her eyes widened. 'I am supposed to keep a strict record of everyone's comings and goings. How can I do my job when you and others bypass the system?'

'Perhaps you should take that up with the mayor, Angelina!' Lambertini appeared to hesitate, then added, 'Perhaps you had better not. For then he would know someone had told you, and I could get into trouble.'

'So what was so important that they saw fit not to tell me?' she enquired huffily.

'I can't tell you, I'm afraid. But it's to do with the rumour going the rounds at present.'

'What rumour?'

'That the Vatican City is moving from Rome.'

His voice was guileless. Angelina was shocked.

'Surely, that can't be true?' she whispered.

'Of course not. It has to be stopped before it gets out of hand.'

'What are they going to do?'

'Frankly, no one knows what to do. Probably, it will just die away like so many others. I should not tell anyone about it, Angelina. The less people talk about it, the quicker it will disappear.'

Her face was alight with anticipation.

'Of course, Signor Lambertini. Of course.'

She was already rising to her feet, collecting her bag and magazine.

'I must go. Otherwise I shall miss my bus.'

'Remember! Not a word.'

But she was already threading her way through the tables.

Michelo Lambertini exhaled slowly. Of all the conversations he had had during the day this could be the most telling. Signorina Angelina Scacchi was good at her job; many said she was the most efficient receptionist they had ever had in the Town Hall. She remembered faces, recalled names, and was always welcoming. However, they would also tell you her one failing was a wayward tongue. On too many occasions unwelcome revelations had been traced back to the reception desk in the front lobby.

The next day, the staff in most government offices would be taking an extra day off, prior to the public holiday, celebrating the Assumption of the Blessed Virgin – she would not be back at the Town Hall until Monday, in four days' time. But *then* she would be in her element as the purveyor of gossip. It would be only a matter of time before everyone entering and leaving the city's administration would know about the rumour. Coming from Angelina, it would be recounted as fact.

Chapter Twenty

Marcus checked his mirror. There were several cars trailing him –
a Fiat, a Mercedes and a Japanese four-by-four. Which of them was
the Messenger? If he were there at all. After all, I only have *his*
word that there are people out to do us down. It's probably a ploy
to keep me in check. Lisa has already seen through it.

He was on his way to Verona. Lisa had slipped away last night
to catch the last train to Milan. Although she had insisted contemptuously that it was quite unnecessary, he had walked two
hundred or so metres behind her to check if she were being
followed. At the station, Marcus had closed the distance and lin-
gered in the shadows, watching other passengers. But he had seen
nothing suspicious. Finally, he had watched the train ease its way
along the platform, and gather speed on its non-stop journey to
Milan.

She answered on the first ring.

'Marcus?'

'Lisa, you're quite safe? No one followed you?'

'I didn't expect anyone to do so!'

'Don't forget, phone me at any time, day or night!'

A brief silence, then: 'Thank you. All being well, I'll be back
Thursday lunchtime. When are you off to Verona?'

'Tomorrow morning. The Messenger thinks we are travelling
there together.'

'Is he in for a surprise!'

Now he was on the outskirts of the town, looking for signs to the
Dendrology Institute. He had spoken with Professor Roberts to
arrange the appointment. The academic was from Bristol, and had
arrived at the Institute six years ago via The Sorbonne and
Heidelberg.

Briefly distracted, he somehow missed the route Roberts had

given him to avoid the one-way system and found himself crossing a bridge heading south. Suddenly, he caught sight of a board proclaiming '*Instituto Italiano di Dendrocronologica – 400 metres*'.

He yanked the wheel to the right glancing in the mirror to check if any other vehicles had also made the turn. None. Where was the Messenger? Suddenly, Marcus felt vulnerable. He was glad to see the welcoming entrance to the Institute.

'Mr Danby, you found us.'

A bustling figure appeared – a short, stocky man in his middle years. As he came closer, Marcus was drawn to the cheery smile above a well-trimmed greying beard. Roberts pumped his hand energetically. 'So you are researching the woods used by the Cremonese, Mr Danby. Well, you have come to the right place.'

Moments later Marcus found himself in a small, but remarkably tidy, glass-walled office, beyond which was a large laboratory occupied by white-coated technicians.

'Now tell me, what exactly are you seeking? There is so much data here, we could be in danger of not seeing the woods for the trees!' Roberts grinned. 'A poor joke but mine own. Forgive me, Mr Danby, I can't often use that one. It doesn't have the same irony in Italian.'

'What I am doing, Professor Roberts, is reviewing the factors that contributed to the skills of the instrument makers of eighteenth century Cremona. Thus far, I have a fair appreciation of how their workshops operated – their methods, approach, how they undertook their commissions, and so on. What I now need to establish is the relevance of their selection of the woods they used: the characteristics they sought, how long they were left to dry before being worked. In short, how the maestros treated the materials they had at their disposal.'

'That's a tall order. How long have you got?'

'I know this subject alone would fill numerous shelves in a library. I suppose what I am seeking is the essence of all the data you possess. Let me explain a little more.' Marcus leaned across the desk. 'Before I begin, Professor Roberts, may I request that this conversation remains strictly between the two of us?'

'I am the depository of many confidences, Mr Danby,' responded the professor, his face unsmiling. 'You can be assured I can accept another, which will remain here . . .' he tapped the side of his head, 'until you release me from that obligation.'

'I have been commissioned, professor . . .'

'Call me "Adam". It's shorter and easier.'

'I am Marcus, Adam. My principals have asked that I assess the skills of the Cremonese, and determine if their abilities can be replicated to the same standards today. Key, obviously, are the woods they used. When I leave here I want to know all about the spruce, sycamore, maple and willow incorporated in their instruments. Critically, whether we can source wood of the same quality and temper as in the eighteenth century.'

Roberts nodded. 'As I said, a tall order. Strictly speaking, as the name of the Institute suggests, we are much more involved in age, weather conditions and growth patterns. But, with our links to the Museum of Natural History, and being in this part of Italy, we have a particular interest in the timbers used in instrument making. I would suggest we spend the rest of the day and, if you are free, some of tomorrow attempting to satisfy your request. You will be bombarded with facts. Can you write quickly, Marcus?'

'Would you mind if I recorded our conversations as well as making notes?'

'Not at all.' The scholar was preparing himself. Sitting back in his chair, his hands came together, his eyes focused on the ceiling.

'Do you know about the construction of wooden instruments, Marcus?'

'I am a trained instrument maker.'

'Splendid!' he replied, his seat tilting backwards at an even sharper angle as he marshalled his thoughts. 'Of course the early Brescians used poplar, lime, even cedar, for the top plates, and cut the wood in the slab, from the outer edge to the centre. But, as you rightly say, the Cremonese dealt specifically with three types of wood: spruce, maple and sycamore. The trees were felled on the heights of Paneveggio, and floated down to Venice. Originally destined for shipbuilding, the area soon became known as "the forest of the violins". The instrument makers used to gather in Trento and inspect the trees as they were felled. Venice also served as the incoming port for some of the more exotic woods from Croatia, Turkey, and Africa.'

Roberts halted and rose to his feet. Going across the room to a bookcase, he withdrew a much-thumbed work of reference and leafed through several sections.

'Yes . . . as I thought. An interesting point: Stradivari appeared to prefer wood from trees which had lain for a time in the Bay of Venice. He thought it improved the resonance. Perhaps he was right. Nowadays, we know it would have slowed water loss from the cell cavities. There is also the suggestion that the organisms in the bay might have contributed something as well.'

'I'm not sure one could replicate that,' remarked Marcus. Another morsel for Lisa, he thought.

Roberts resumed his chair.

'Tell me, Marcus, have you heard of the "Maunder Effect"?'

'No. What's that?'

'Rather, what *was* that! It was a climatic condition that existed between 1645 and 1715, a phase of reduced solar activity which resulted in lower temperatures. It slowed tree growth. In areas where the elevation and soils were right, such as in Eastern Trentino, it produced higher-quality sounding boards.'

'Has this condition occurred since?'

'No, not since the golden period of the Cremonese.'

'Are there any other regions in Europe where conditions have encouraged the slow, even growth of spruce and maple?'

Roberts reached for another tome and spent some minutes poring over its text.

'Well, there are virgin forests of these woods in Hungary. But certainly the spruce at the higher elevations in the Karkonsze Mountains, bordering the Czech Republic and Poland, could provide the timber you are seeking. Even the maple on the lower slopes should be a particularly good source. I believe you could find what you want there.'

The academic plunged into the bio-chemistry of tree cell structure and the intricacies of fibre saturation and equilibrium moisture content, then onto readying the wood for use in the workshop.

'Normally the trees were cut into rounds, slightly longer than needed for the finished pieces, then left to season for up to ten years. Before they were cut, some makers would insist on the trees being stacked vertically for a time to ensure the drying process was effective. This was after the bark was removed and the trunks coated with borax to kill off any resident bugs or latent fungal spores. Interestingly, when the infestation of wood-boring insects died out in the early seventeen-hundreds, they stopped using borax. In my view, it had a notable influence on tonal quality. We've discovered that borax acts as a "cross-linker". It binds different molecules together as it enters the pores of the wood, making it harder and stronger. At the time, the instrument makers weren't aware of its other properties.'

So the afternoon passed. In addition to writing notes, Marcus made full use of his recorder, for which, thankfully, he had brought a good supply of tapes. He had filled several spiral-bound books by the time Adam Roberts glanced at his watch and declared he would have to call it a day.

Marcus was surprised to see it had gone seven o'clock. He was apologetic.

'My friend, I would have been quite content to continue, but my wife has a dinner party arranged for this evening,' explained the professor. 'We can start early tomorrow if you wish. In fact, come to my house for breakfast – I want to show you something.'

He had found a modest hotel for the night and eaten sparingly in a nearby restaurant. Back in his room, Marcus reviewed the tapes and his notes. They comprised a mass of priceless material, information that would make a major contribution to his report. By the time they had finished, Roberts' office had been strewn with reference books, research data, reviews yet to see the light of day, and numerous theses. The professor had been a gold-mine of facts, figures and statistics. He now had solid evidence of the manner in which the luthiers had selected, stored, pre-pared and utilised the various woods, one of the remarkable facts being the dedication of 'del Gesù' – Giuseppe Guarneri the sec-ond – to work from just one tree for the whole of his productive life.

Tomorrow promised to be equally rewarding. Although outside the remit of the Institute, Professor Roberts was going to cover methods of construction. He had been captivated by the techniques of the masters and, over the years, had amassed a wealth of photographs and fragments of instruments.

Just after eight o'clock the following morning Marcus drew up outside a house set back from the road behind a screen of trees. Appropriate, he thought.

He was welcomed into the dining room and the two chatted amiably over the meal, the professor talking in general terms about his work at the Institute, Marcus commenting on his role as a Xaverian brother, though failing to add that he had recently withdrawn from the Order. Eventually, Roberts led him along the hallway and into a room that was clearly his study, as neat as his office at the Institute. Marcus' eyes were drawn to the displays mounted on one of the walls. From floor to ceiling were glazed boxes, in which Marcus identified fragments of violins, violas and cellos, every one of them clearly labelled.

'This is amazing, Adam,' he said, reading the inscriptions.

'More to the point, Marcus, as you've probably noticed, they are all labelled by maker and relate to specific features in the construction of their instruments,' said Roberts, a note of pride in his voice. 'For instance,' he continued, taking an item from the wall. 'This is the neck junction of an early Strad. See the three nail holes he used to secure it into the block. The nails were no more than twenty millimetres long, so they only penetrated six millimetres into the neck. Had he mortised the base of the neck, he could have avoided nailing altogether. The first to do it were the French in the early years of the nineteenth century.'

He chose another.

'This is one of his bass bars.' He removed the slender piece of pine from its box and handed it to Marcus. 'Look how small Stradivari made them compared with modern makers.'

For the next five hours they discussed the Cremonese's methods, Roberts citing many examples of their particular style not evident in other schools: how their edgework, arching, and chamfers were created; how they constructed their purfling, using poplar for the white centre inlays, whilst the Venetians use beech, and the Germans, maple. Each time, he was able to demonstrate his observations from the many sections of violin, viola and cello on display, even to the extent of how each of the noted luthiers made their own adjustments to the norm – if there were such a thing!

They stopped briefly for a snack. During the conversation, Marcus happened to mention that a colleague was following up the suggestion that women might have been regularly employed by the maestros, despite the generally-held view that they had no place in their workshops. Roberts considered this.

'You could well be right. It has often puzzled me that although Stradivari took on few apprentices his output was formidable. That might well explain how, in 1715, when he was seventy-one, he undertook a commission from the King of Poland to produce twelve violins. Did you know he completed the order in just three months? The cunning old fox! That could well be the answer: Antonio did it with the help of his women.'

Later, Adam Roberts showed Marcus his collection of instrument labels. The majority were photocopies. However, he did have a number of originals, notably of the Guarneri family, showing their individuality and the various changes they had introduced during their lifetimes. Marcus was particularly drawn to the ornate labels of Pietro of Venice.

They continued well into the evening, and it was close to eight o'clock when Roberts' wife, a woman similar in stature and temperament to her husband, appeared in his study. They urged him to stay for dinner but, suddenly aware how late it was, Marcus declined the offer.

As he saw him to his car, Roberts asked, 'What's the next step, Marcus?'

'Now, I have to learn more about glues and varnishes.'

'Well, the universities are good sources, especially Parma – although, for my money, I would opt for the Department of Chemical Sciences for Conservation and Restoration at Ca' Foscari.'

Marcus looked perplexed.

'Sorry. The University of Venice,' Roberts qualified. 'You will find Doctor Granadigli a fount of information. Wait a moment. I'll get his telephone number.'

Chapter Twenty-One

'In view of our recent discussions, I thought it appropriate we met to consider what had best be done.'

They were gathered in Cardinal Grossmann's suite on the third floor.

The mood was sombre. An air of uncertainty prevailed. Monsignor Keppel, though elderly and wracked by infirmities, had instilled a spirit of commitment in his colleagues. He had given the project an impetus, which now was suddenly lacking.

'I knew he was not well. But, I was not prepared for him to go so quickly,' commented one of the group, a bishop from the Congregation of the Clergy. 'When I saw him yesterday, he seemed pre-occupied, but not ailing. In fact, he particularly wanted to discuss something with me in my office this afternoon, but he did not appear. Now I know why.'

'How did he die?' asked another.

'It would seem he had a heart attack,' declared the cardinal.

'Crossing the bridge on his way to the Piazza della Cancellaria,' commented the bishop attached to the Supreme Tribunal of the Apostolic Signatura. 'Apparently, he also wanted to see me about a matter. Now we shall never know what was on his mind.'

'The point is,' interrupted Grossmann, 'he was the driving force. I do not see how we can continue without someone as committed as he to our ideals.'

'Surely, Your Eminence, we all have the same zeal. We can be the rallying point for the Goehr campaign. Do we need a leader?' asked a cardinal-deacon.

'With your indulgence, Your Eminence, when the occasion demands might we not meet, as we are this morning, in your rooms?'

'Most certainly, my lord bishop,' responded Grossmann. 'I have no objection to my offices being used for the cause, although I believe we should apply some discretion. Cardinal Goehr is regarded as a worthy, and likely, successor, but we have a long road ahead of us before declaring in favour of our candidate.'

He looked into each of the faces around him. 'At the moment, suppressing adverse criticism still remains our priority. We must contain any source of ill-comment either from factions or individuals. As we agreed earlier, it is our sovereign duty to limit the harm undesirable revelations about our former royals and the Cremonese might provoke.'

'You have evidence of such a conspiracy, Your Eminence?' asked the bishop, hesitantly.

'As I explained at an earlier meeting, Ricardo,' said Grossmann imperiously, 'it is beyond doubt that my colleague along the hall has a scheme afoot that could upset our hopes and aspirations. It is in everyone's interests, and for the greater benefit of the Holy See, that his project is confounded. Surely, we are as one on this?'

There was an uncertain chorus of agreement.

'Good. So, if we are in unison, what should be our next step? I should advise that our friends in Austria have been alerted to the cardinal's little venture – particularly, that part of it that directly affects them.'

There was a silence. No one in the room proffered a suggestion.

'Well, do I take it that, for the moment, we just keep them informed of developments and let them take any necessary steps?'

There was a moment's hesitation, but the nods of affirmation which followed were unanimous.

The limousine drove the short journey back to the Vatican. On the rear seat the Vatican's prime minister, the Cardinal Secretary of State, reviewed the brief meeting – more particularly, the parting comment.

The venue for the monthly meetings alternated. This one had been held at the Ministry of the Interior on the Piazzale del Viminale. The usual delegates had been present: the Minister of State, the Mayor of Rome, and a clutch of advisers.

With the presence of an autonomous city in the heart of the nation's capital, the purpose of such gatherings was the maintenance of harmony and equilibrium between the two. In reality, other than brief exchanges concerning criminal activities, utility services, disruptions caused by road repairs, or agreement on building works, there was little to disturb the tenor of co-existence. Over the years, the meetings had taken on the characteristics of social events at which good wines were enjoyed and gossip exchanged.

There had been nothing raised during the short, formal part of the meeting. It was later, when they were readying themselves to depart, that the mayor, walking alongside the Cardinal Secretary of State down the marble staircase, had said casually, 'An item of gossip I did not raise earlier, Your Eminence, was this far-fetched rumour about the Vatican. When one of my people told me, I dismissed it immediately as absurd. Honestly, what will people dream up next?'

'What was that, Giovanni?'

'Surely you must be aware of it?'

The prelate smiled to himself. The mayor was known for his humour. At times, one never knew if he were being serious or constructing some elaborate joke.

'No. I am not aware of it,' he responded, keeping a straight face.

'Why, the tale about the Vatican moving out of Rome!'

At that, the Secretary of State had burst into laughter. The mayor, who had been watching him intently, now grinned hesitantly.

'Someone in your office tells a good story, Giovanni.'

'That's what I thought, Your Eminence. But you know how idle comment can be exaggerated and grow out of all proportion . . .' And he turned back, exchanging glances with one of his advisers.

Now, in the confines of the vehicle, the Cardinal Secretary pondered on what had been said. It struck him as odd that, despite the mayor's bluff exterior, the rumour had clearly touched a nerve. He would have to raise the subject with his deputy, Cardinal Marchetti, to discover if he had any knowledge of it.

Chapter Twenty-Two

Marcus turned off the Autostrada della Serenissima onto the A21 motorway to Cremona. Another fifty kilometres and he would be back in his room at the pensione. He was tired. Although only ten o'clock, he had had an exhausting two days digesting all Professor Roberts had thrown at him. It had, however, been extremely rewarding, and would add much to the material he was slowly compiling. He yawned, and shook his head to avoid the drowsiness, then pressed the button to lower the driver's window, hoping the breeze might clear his head.

Where was the Messenger? he thought idly. I haven't been aware of him at all during this trip. There had been lights trailing him, but whenever he had slowed the vehicles behind had overtaken. Nothing was to be seen in the mirror, except a pair of bright headlamps in the far distance.

Marcus also thought about Lisa and her quest. In fact, she had been on his mind frequently. I must call her on the mobile directly I reach Cremona, he decided.

The lights were much closer the next time he looked.

At Persichello, five kilometres from Cremona, he wondered briefly if he should take the road directly into the north of the city. But tiredness and the straight road ahead encouraged him to continue.

The lights of the vehicle were now shining into the rear view mirror. Idiot driver, thought Marcus, no consideration! He slowed to let it pass. As it overtook him, he saw it was a tow-truck, the type used on motoways to move heavy vehicles, set high above the ground on six pairs of wide tyres, its hoisting arm and carrying cradle stowed on the massive steel body behind the driver's cab. The truck pulled in front of him into the nearside lane.

Marcus saw the sign for the Via Mantova, his route in towards the town centre. At five hundred metres he slowed the Alfa and changed into third gear, then fumbled for the money for the toll. It was at that moment that blinding lights pierced his windscreen and he lost all vision. The impact was sickening. Despite heavy braking the car was still travelling at fifty kilometres an hour. There was a brief sensation of pain and Marcus lost consciousness.

To reach the change in his left trouser pocket he had unlocked the safety belt. Instinct had taken over. He had turned the wheel automatically to the right to avoid the oncoming vehicle. The driver's door had burst open and Marcus had been thrown clear, tumbling across the grass verge. Some moments later, the petrol tank exploded and the Alfa-Romeo had burst into flame.

The doctor in the hospital's emergency department was satisfied, apart from a few bruises, Marcus was unhurt. He had been lucky.

'So tell me again, signore, what you think happened?' asked the taller of the two policemen.

'I was slowing, about to turn off the autostrada when car head-lights blinded me. The next thing was waking up in here. That's all I can remember,' he told them for the fourth time.

'The fire officer did suggest there was damage to the offside front wing of the car. But, it is difficult to tell as it was contorted by the fire.' He looked at his companion. 'Fortunately, the test confirms you were not under the influence of alcohol, Signor Danby. Otherwise we would have looked at the incident quite differently!' He lowered his voice. 'Were you taking anything at the time?'

'If you believe I was using drugs, officer, you are very much mistaken,' declared Marcus, indignantly. 'I am returning to my hotel. If you need me further you can contact me there.'

The policeman shrugged. 'I was wondering more if you were taking any medication. You must understand, Signor Danby, that despite your story, no other vehicle was found in the vicinity. And there was no evidence of a collision, only the debris from your car.'

Marcus looked up in surprise.

'I should add, signore, that you were found on the verge, some distance from the incident – without even the restraining marks of the seat belt on your body. So what should we think, eh?'

'I just cannot explain it, officer,' said Marcus, now completely bewildered.

'All I can say, Signor Danby, is that it looks highly suspicious,' opined the other policeman, who had thus far remained silent. 'However, as no one else was involved and no one was hurt, we shall not proceed further with the matter. But how you explain yourself to the hire company is going to a problem. They do not appreciate their cars mysteriously bursting into flame.'

Marcus slipped on his shoes. He had not been wearing his clerical clothes on the trip to Verona; for that he was thankful. The police would undoubtedly have spokent with the authorities if they thought a religious were acting strangely. Pulling aside the curtain, he saw the examining medic approaching.

'My thanks, doctor!'

'It is my job, signore. I heard your explanation to the two policemen. If it happened as you say, then you were extremely lucky. Tell me, why were there no strap marks?'

'I didn't mention it to the police, but I was searching for coins in my trouser pockets, and undid the belt. It was then I braked hard and hit whatever it was.'

'Then this was one occasion that the gods smiled upon you, signore. If you had been wearing the seat belt, you would have been incinerated.'

Marcus took a deep breath. 'I had not thought of that. So how did I get onto the verge?'

'You have heavy bruising to your right side. You won't feel it until tomorrow morning, but it was not from a head-on collision,' the doctor conjectured. 'It was more consistent with being thrown from your car.'

Marcus made his way to the entrance doors, intending to take a taxi to the pensione. It was then he realised, as he checked in his jacket for his wallet, that he did not have the leather case in which the computer, the recorder, mobile phone and crucially, his notes were stored: all his work on the project to date. It had been lying on the front passenger seat beside him when the crash had occurred. Everything was lost.

He sank into a chair, and put his head in his hands. There was no way he could start again and go over the ground he had covered in such detail. It would be impossible to search through all the archives, list every piece of information, recapture all that lost data.

'Signor Danby! Are you all right?'

Marcus looked up. It was the doctor who had attended him.

'I was hoping to catch you. I presume this is your case? It was brought in with you when you arrived.'

Relief flooded through him. Gasping his thanks, he stuttered, 'How could this be? It was on the passenger seat.'

The doctor handed it to him.

'It must have been thrown from the car as well, signore.'

He climbed slowly up the stairs and along the dark corridor to his room. It was late. Almost three o'clock in the morning. Locking the door, he removed his jacket and eased himself onto the bed. The doctor was right – the pain in his side was growing. It was difficult to find a comfortable position.

At first he did not hear it, but its insistent ringing finally broke into his dreamless sleep. With a start he came to. The noise was coming from his carrying case. It was the mobile phone, its tone now strident as he removed it from the outer pocket.

'Hello?'

'Marcus! Where have you been? I've been trying to contact you all evening. Where were you when I wanted you?'

It was Lisa, her voice tremulous, close to tears.

'I've just got back to my room, Lisa. Where are you?'

'At the Ibis hotel. The police went ages ago.'

Suddenly, he was wide awake.

'The police! Have they been troubling you about me?'

'I've been mugged, Marcus. They've taken my computer with all my material on it.'

Room service had brought coffee and sandwiches. He had recommended she drink nothing alcoholic. He had been sitting beside her on the edge of the bed for almost an hour whilst she talked of the experience.

'I arrived at the station, and all the cabs were taken. But then someone said there was a cab in a side street. Apparently it had just dropped him.'

Lisa was screwing her handkerchief in her hands as she related the event.

'Well, I rushed over and jumped in. The Ibis is too far to walk at that time of night. As I told the driver where I wanted to go, suddenly, the other door opened and the man who had pointed it out to me got in. Then the cab drove off.' Her eyes filled. 'I shouted for the driver to stop, but he wouldn't listen! Then it dawned on me I had been set up. I was petrified!'

Instinctively, Marcus put his arm around her shoulder. She leaned against him.

'They didn't say a word. The cab just careered through the streets. I didn't know where I was. Then it halted by some waste ground, and the other guy said very quietly, "Give me your bag!" I said, "No way!" Then he hit me!'

She burst into tears, and he pulled her to him in a gentle, compassionate hug, until she continued in a quavering voice.

'He hit me again and simply pulled it from my hands. Then he got out, came round to my side, opened the door and threw me out. I managed to walk to a garage and use their phone to call the police. I still can't stop shaking.'

'At what time did it happen?'

'Around ten thirty, I guess.'

About the time of my accident, thought Marcus.

'So, all your notes, all the work you've been doing has gone?' enquired Marcus.

'Fortunately, I always back up what I've written. A lesson learned the hard way some years ago.' She reached for her shoulder bag and took a disk from an inner pocket. 'At least I've got that – though I lost my PC . . . and my self-control!' she added, her eyes misty.

'Come on, try to get some sleep. I'll sit in the chair and keep you company. It's almost light, but you can rest for a few hours.'

'There's no way I shall sleep now. I'm too wound up. I'll just lie here for a short while.'

However, the incident had taken its toll of her emotions. Within minutes, she was asleep and breathing lightly. Marcus turned off the various lights and sat gingerly back in an armchair. The curtains were open, and he looked at her in the soft glow of the dawn. What he saw in the gradually strenghtening light was a very vulnerable young woman.

*

93

It was close to lunchtime when Marcus returned to the pensione, his mind occupied by the attacks on Lisa and himself. Had they been orchestrated? Timed to occur at broadly the same moment? If so, there was more than one person ranged against them. And where had the Messenger been in all this? He was supposed to protect them. He'd been nowhere in sight. OK, he had not mentioned Lisa's visit to Milan, but it had seemed safe to travel by train and away from Cremona. That had clearly been a false premise. And what about his accident? The Messenger should have been on hand to stop that. It was high time to have it out with him.

'Shut the door, quickly!'

Marcus was unprepared for the command, or for his presence by the window but his anger was quick to rise.

'Where the hell were you when I needed you?' he hissed to the tall figure coming towards him.

'Signor Danby, if you had been trapped in the car we would have saved you. We were close by. But I'm afraid we could not prevent the crash from happening. It was quick, efficient and effective.'

'That's not good enough! You warned me to expect some form of reprisal, but not attempted murder,' he shouted. 'How could they have got to me so easily?'

'The tow-truck that overtook you just stopped dead, then turned on its rear recovery lights. You were meant to believe it was an oncoming vehicle. You smashed into the back of the truck. It wasn't damaged, of course; they are built to withstand heavy contact. After the crash it simply drove off.'

'Well, I was lucky. I was thrown out onto the grass. And my case with me, thank goodness!'

'Actually, I retrieved it from the car and put it beside you,' commented the Messenger. 'I checked, and found you were only knocked unconscious. I waited at a distance until the ambulance arrived and watched it take you and your bag to hospital.'

'Well, you didn't do a very good job for Mrs Robards,' exploded Marcus, forgetting, for the moment, that the Messenger had not been warned of her trip.

'What are you saying, signore?'

'I thought Mrs Robards would be safe going to Milan. On her return this evening, she was mugged and abandoned on the outskirts of town.'

'You did not advise me of her trip, Signor Danby! I hope that will be a lesson for you both. Now, perhaps, you will heed my advice. Stay together and you will both be protected – at least, as far as we are able. You must appreciate that, from now on, neither of you will be completely safe.'

Chapter Twenty-Three

'*Jawohl*, you could say we have made our presence felt, Herr Schumann.' He laughed, and nodded to his companions. '*Ja . . . Ja . . . Auf Wiedersehen, Mein Herr, ich werde Sie auf dem Laufenden halten!*'

'So you'll keep him informed, will you?' smiled Heinz, the largest of the trio.

He had a bull neck and immense arms, though with his height of more than two metres everything was in proportion. Not a person one would wish to encounter on a dark night – as Lisa Robards could confirm.

'So, what is the next step?' he asked. 'Do we bring it to a conclusion or wait for them to get a little closer?'

'We wait. Perhaps yesterday's encounter will prove sufficient deterrent. We shall keep them under observation and report back,' responded Jozsef, their leader and sometime priest.

'I cannot understand why we need to prolong the inevitable,' declared Franz. A short, weasel-faced man in his thirties, he was more suited to the use of guile and agility than muscle. His only significant feature was the shock of pure white hair that, even cut *en brosse*, stood out like a beacon against his swarthy skin. The third member of the team, he was their acknowledged expert in explosives and other murderous devices.

'We shall abide by our master's wishes. You are being well paid for this little venture, so we shall follow demands to the letter. Do you understand?' said Jozsef, pointedly.

The little man shrugged. It was all the same to him.

Heinz turned off the television set. 'I repeat, what is the plan? Do I sit here whilst you and Franz follow them? I would be a little more conspicuous than you two. And she has seen me.'

'Only an impression in the dark, Heinz. But you are right, it would be best if you stay in the background for the moment. However, as our man of the cloth is the key, it is he who will dictate our moves. I want you to take a room in a boarding house across the street from where he is staying, Heinz, and tell us immediately he is on the move and the direction he is taking.' He turned to their smaller companion. 'I have the feeling they will travel together from now on. But, just in case, Franz, hire another car and be ready to act if the woman goes in a separate direction.'

'Heinz!'

'It's nine thirty. Any sign of movement?

'None so far!'

'Are you sure he is in his room?'

'Why shouldn't he be? He left hospital gone midnight, and with the battering he took I doubt he can get out of bed!'

'But do you know for sure?'

'No!'

'Then I suggest you find out. Ring the pensione and ask to speak to him.'

'Well if he's not there, he must be with the woman. Don't do anything! I'll contact the Ibis hotel.'

Eating a late breakfast in Lisa's room, he had overheard her conversation with the policeman and noted, with an inward smile, her unwillingness to confirm his presence, and the glow on her cheeks when she put down the phone.

'It seems the police were worried about your absence from the pensione. Why do they want to know your whereabouts, Marcus?'

He drew in a deep breath. 'I was involved in a little accident last night, on the way back from Verona.'

'You didn't tell me. And there's me crying on your shoulder. Are you all right? Did you hurt yourself?'

Not wishing to add to her anxieties, Marcus was reluctant to tell her much of what had occurred.

'What do you mean you were hit from the front? How could that happen? Were you in the wrong lane?'

Then she chose another tack.

'You were drunk, weren't you? You can't stop yourself! What is with you? Can't you stay sober? No wonder the police are after you. Dammit, Marcus, this is second time you've been out of your skull in as many days! Don't you have any control?'

He was stung. She had jumped completely to the wrong conclusion.

'Listen! I didn't want to tell you. You weren't mugged – it was a warning. The same happened to me, but worse. Look!'

He undid the buttons of his shirt, and turned his right side towards her. From the shoulder to below his waist was a wide, continuous pattern of bruising.

'My God!'

'That's the result of being thrown from the car when a tow-truck deliberately reversed into me. The car burst into flame. I wasn't drunk. I haven't touched a drop since you came to my room the other morning.'

Her eyes dropped. 'There I was, feeling sorry for myself and all that time you were injured.' She sniffed and tried to hide a tear. 'It has started, hasn't it? They are after us already. We didn't tell him I was going to Milan, but I thought the Messenger was looking after *you*. Where was he?'

'All he can do is his best. Last night he was there to pull me out of the wreckage if I had not been thrown clear. But, even if he is close by, I'm afraid he may not always be able to protect us. So it's back to the States whilst you are still in one piece.'

'There's no way you're getting me on a plane. I'm not going to be hustled out of the country by these sons of bitches. I'm staying. I have to, to get my goddam story . . . And to protect you!'

'Heinz, she answered the phone. I told her it was the *inspettore di polizia* and I was trying to reach Signor Danby. After some hesitation, she confessed he was in her room . . . No, don't stay there, go back to the house. I'll join you. Franz can tell us if he leaves.'

*

98

To restore some semblance of normality they discussed their efforts in Milan and Verona. Lisa recounted how she had gained access to the parish records, despite the obstructive attitude of the curator.

'I went to the city hall's public relations department,' she said, 'and mentioned that I was writing a piece on how the major municipalities began documenting their inhabitants. I was particularly interested in the Church's attempts, the *Stati dell'Anime,* and hoped to feature Milan prominently in the article which would be syndicated world-wide. But, if they didn't want to cooperate . . .' She smiled for the first time that day. 'Would you believe it? In minutes I had complete access to any of the records I wanted. The curator was put out and showed it – a bit like our friend the archivist here in town.'

She paused for a moment and added reflectively, 'I wonder why his manner changed so radically? The Messenger must have had a word with him; his whole demeanour altered towards us.' Lisa stood up. 'I'm thirsty, can I get you anything from the mini-bar?'

'Nothing alcoholic. Anyway, it wouldn't mix well with the pain-killers I'm taking. Just sparkling water for me, please.'

Lisa had the grace to look contrite. Returning to her chair, she continued. 'The nub of it was I found there were any number of women staying under the Stradivari's roof from 1680 onwards. Supposedly distant relatives, in both senses of the word! Most of them seemed to come from Mantua. There was nothing I could find about them in Milan, so I want to visit Mantua as soon as I can. I hope to find something about the women of the Camilli family in their local archives.'

Marcus reviewed his time in Verona – the wealth of material he had gathered, what it would contribute to his summary. Parma or Venice would be the next stop, in order to learn more about the glues and varnishes used by the Cremonese.

The phone rang again.

'*Pronto!* Emilio, how nice to hear from you! Yes, I called your office from Milan. I was hoping you might be free sometime so we could meet . . . This evening?' She glanced towards Marcus. 'Well, yes, I could make it. Would it be OK if I bring a friend? . . . Good. At the Barca Orientale at eight thirty . . . I look forward to seeing you again. *Ciao.*'

She put down the receiver and sat on the bed.

'That was a family friend who moved to Cremona some years ago. He has asked us to dine with him tonight. What do you say?'

'Fine by me. A family friend, you say?'

'He's a lecturer at Pavia University, though the department he is in is based here, in Cremona. I phoned when I first arrived, but he has been away.'

'I'll have to go back and change. I heard you say La Barca Orientale. Is that near the river?'

She nodded.

'What if I pick you up at eight? I'll have a cab and we can go on from here.'

'Jozsef, our mark has just come out the hotel entrance. He is taking a taxi. I'm in the car, so I'll follow him. I'm putting down the phone, but keep on the line. I should know where he is going in a few minutes.'

Jozsef stood with the phone to his ear, staring out of the window. A minute passed.

'Jozsef, he is on his way back to the town centre – presumably to where he is staying. When he enters the building I'll come back.'

The line closed.

Flipping his mobile shut, he turned to the big man watching television. Heinz was absorbed in a French cartoon. Unable to understand the language, he was laughing at the characters' exaggerated antics.

'Our friend is returning to the pensione. I suggest you go back to the room opposite and keep an eye on him.'

'I'll just see the end of this.'

'Perhaps you didn't hear me, Heinz. Back to the boarding house. Now!'

Heinz's tone was sullen but his comments were concise.

'He is on the move, again. He has taken a taxi, licence number AR 2059KE heading north on the Via Palestrano – no doubt towards the Via Mantova. I expect he is on his way to her hotel. Over and out.'

Franz quickly picked out the vehicle. He followed, keeping two or three cars between the taxi and himself. It was unhurried progress. The vehicle pulled into the forecourt of the Ibis Hotel.

Ten minutes later it came back out, carrying two passengers. It threaded its way around the outskirts of the city before pulling up at a restaurant overlooking the river.

Franz waited a quarter of an hour, then made his way through the door and asked for a menu to take away. He was able to glimpse the pair seated at a table with another couple. They were talking and smiling – a social gathering he surmised. He would relay the information to their leader.

Chapter Twenty-Four

He closed his mobile with a snap. It had been good to talk with Geri Bellman; to speak of commonplace things; to ignore, albeit briefly, the incidents that had occurred since his arrival. They were hard-pressed in the studio to fulfil the commissions steadily coming in, yet Geri had heard him out and agreed to the request.

He sipped his coffee at a table in the roadside café, reflecting on the dinner with Lisa's friends the previous evening. He had been reluctant to go, but felt obliged to accompany her. With an old acquaintance, he thought, there is always much to talk about – Lisa and Emilio Puigi would be busy exchanging family news and gossip.

But Puigi had brought his wife, a tall elegant woman, younger than her husband, and extremely vivacious. Not much older than Lisa, she used her dark, long hair and flashing smile to devastating effect. Marcus recognised after a time that, whilst she was not beautiful in the classical sense, she had an attraction which, combined with her outgoing personality, captivated those around her.

By contrast, Dr Emilio Puigi was bald, short and rounded. But he too was effervescent and decidedly extrovert. They made an entertaining couple. In a matter of minutes the conversation became animated. Marcus soon found himself immersed in discussion, putting forward opinions, laughing at humorous comment, thoroughly enjoying himself.

Moreover, Puigi's work was fascinating. He was a leading light in the Department of Musical Paleology and Philology.

'I am attached to Pavia, Marcus – a hundred kilometres away! Why they put me here, I don't know. Perhaps I should belong to Brescia University; it's closer and easier to get to!'

'Emilio,' said Marta Puigi mischievously, 'it's because you are a damn nuisance!' She turned to the others. 'He likes things to be

102

just so. Everything organised, on time, and in the right order!' She leaned towards her husband. 'Caro, that's not the Italian way. I can't think where you get such ideas.'

He grinned.

'True. I do annoy the fraternity in Pavia with my demands. Actually, being in Cremona suits me. The students enjoy it, and it's a wonderful source of material for a project I am working on.'

'What would that be?' Marcus had asked.

'Well, in addition to getting into the mindset of Europe's mediaeval composers, studying and deciphering their works, which is the main preoccupation of my department, I am also working on transcribing a number of early Italian works into modern notation.'

Marcus had found this fascinating. But perhaps more interesting had been where Puigi was gathering his research material.

'As you would expect, Marcus, some of my sources are most unlikely. Would you believe, many of the small parish churches still have manuscripts and documents hidden away – those that are left. Many were destroyed in the cause of development. Even in earlier times there were people ready to create bigger, taller, fancier structures, in the process razing buildings that were symbols of our heritage.'

Marcus' association with Lisa had been quickly dealt with: they were both involved in a research project on the Cremonese, had met by chance and had joined forces.

'When she phoned to say you would be joining us, I didn't realise that Marcus was a man of the cloth, Lisa,' said Marta, raising an eyebrow quizzically. 'From what I recall, you have never had much time for religion, or its followers.'

'Don't get the wrong idea. I haven't been converted. It's just an arrangement that, for the moment, is mutually beneficial.'

'Yes, I can see why,' Marta teased.

'Marcus, you speak good Italian,' said Emilio, changing the subject. 'Where did you learn?'

'In Milan, when I attended the International School of Music.'

'Did you now?' replied Emilio, thoughtfully. 'What did you study?'

'The violin.'

'Lisa studied the cello like Emilio,' remarked Marta. 'I play the piano. Whenever she stays with us we often have musical evenings. We could extend our repertoire with a violin.'

She looked expectantly at him.

'That was many years ago. I don't play any more.' said Marcus, flatly

'You must have been good to have got a scholarship to the School,' Emilio commented. 'Did your vocation replace your musical career?'

Marcus had felt uncomfortable at the academic's gentle probing, but just then Lisa had intervened.

'I know Stradivari has long been of interest to you, Emilio, but, talking of unlikely sources, I found something very interesting about the maestro for this article I'm writing. It is my . . . no, *our* . . . belief – for Marcus put me on this particular track – that young women were employed in his workshop, *not* as apprentices. I'm convinced they fulfilled a role in producing not just Stradivaris, but many of the instruments made by the Cremonese.'

Puigi's interest had been fired. For some time the topic dominated the conversation. It was only when they had made their farewells and were travelling back to the Ibis in a taxi, that Marcus had remarked they might have been a little too free in revealing their researches.

'Do you really think he would take advantage of our efforts to claim a first for himself?' retorted Lisa, the telltale signs of her rising anger flashing in the half-light.

'No. I was just thinking that our conversation was a bit too public. It could easily have been overheard. That might also make them vulnerable.'

Professor Robert had left a message on his mobile.

'Marcus, I was thinking about your searches into the old glues and varnishes when a name came to mind – an instrument maker in Venice. His great, great . . . whatever . . . grandfather, was an apprentice to Antonio Stradivari. So all the family's succeeding generations have perpetuated the maestro's style, using the same templates, methods and finishing materials. I think you will find him a fount of information. His studio is by the Ponte delle Guglie, close to the Jewish Quarter. His name is Tomasina.'

So the decision was made. Not Parma, but Venice.

Chapter Twenty-Five

'Gentlemen, thank you for coming so promptly. As I said to each of you on the phone, it is time we met to discuss our mutual problem.'

All in their sixties, they were seated around a circular table. The eldest had made the opening remark. He was Martin Goehr, the president of Instrumente Tiroler Gmbh, a company renowned for the quality of a range of stringed instruments. It was one of five founded in 1747, all had achieved world-wide reputations.

They nodded silently in agreement.

It was a large room, tastefully furnished. The light panelled walls added dignity without making it sombre. Oriental carpets were strewn across a pale, wooden floor. Predictably, being a male domain, the furnishings were leather, but fashionable, in character with the rest of the décor. Around three of the walls were carefully-lit modern paintings, on the fourth a record of the family's history, from paintings of the founders to photographs of more recent generations. The principal window overlooked the low buildings comprising the production facility. A century ago they had been housed in an unappealing three-storey edifice, until the chief executive, a would-be aesthete, had demolished the structure and provided himself with a panoramic view of the valley and the Arnspitze mountain which dominated the township of Mittenwald.

Even now, having occupied the seat for the past twenty-five years, Martin's gaze was drawn to the scene filling the floor-to-ceiling window. Slowly, turning his head away, he smiled thinly at his compatriots.

'I have advised you of the preliminary steps I have taken. So far, they have been largely surveillance – keeping watch on the two people concerned. However, I want to inform you that two days ago I requested the application of mild deterrents to dissuade the couple from continuing their quest.'

He looked into their faces.

'I have learned that the measure taken against Brother Danby was, perhaps, a little extreme. Nevertheless, the point has been made. Now he will more readily comprehend the message when it is delivered.'

Another voice. 'Which will be when?'

He looked at his wrist watch. 'I would judge in three hours' time, Sigmund.'

Someone else commented, 'For their sake, I hope they take notice of Martin's warning.'

The man at the head of the table stared at him. 'It is not *my* warning, Doctor Felzmann. We are all party to preventing the slightest chance of exposure. There is no other course. It could have monumental consequences for us all.'

'But, surely, the likelihood of uncovering something that happened three hundred years ago is remote in the extreme,' said a cadaverous-looking man, seated at the end of the table. 'No links can possibly exist that would tie us to that episode in our past.'

Goehr's tone grew harsher. 'I believe that was also the opinion of your grandfather on the last occasion, Guido. But even he changed his mind. The point I'm making is that we simply do not know. Therefore, we have to presume that somewhere a document, an old record, survives which might disclose what happened. So I say it again: what choice do we have? Our forebears committed us and, whether we like it or not, there is no shying away from their legacy.'

He was silent for a moment. When he resumed, his voice had moderated.

'Gentlemen, our children are heirs not only to the fruits of successful businesses, they will also inherit this added burden. As we ourselves have found, the two are indivisible.'

Martin Goehr had a commanding presence. Short, slight of build, with a nondescript countenance below a shock of iron-grey hair, his telling feature was a pair of piercing blue eyes, slightly magnified by square, rimless glasses. What chiefly set him apart was his brevity of speech, a decisive manner, and – usually – his quietness of voice. He continued.

'My elder son already knows what is expected of him. I hope you are preparing your successors. However, for the moment, it is our duty to safeguard the past so that we may guarantee their future. Does anyone disagree?'

Not one of the four executives of Europe's leading instrument makers uttered a word. It had always been like this. The companies had been founded in Mittenwald in the eighteenth century, when the town was then located on the edge of the Austrian Empire. The Goehr manufactory had been the first, and from that moment had dominated all the collective decisions ever taken. Even when several of the companies had moved to Füssen, and another to Markneukirchen on the Czech border, they had always remained in thrall to the Goehr dynasty. Now, when their self-appointed leader and his family had the most to lose, they acquiesced to his demands.

'Good. I take it then there will be no dissenters to what I am about to recommend. As I said earlier, Danby will receive a firm warning. If he does not respond accordingly – which means he and the woman leave Italy immediately – then, gentlemen, we shall be compelled to move to the next phase.'

Chapter Twenty-Six

The atmosphere was tense. After her outburst at the hotel, Lisa had said little, other than to give the briefest of directions on their way to Venice.

'Come off the freeway at the Miranese exit. It will bring us straight into San Giuliano,' she said tersely. 'I presume you've booked a slot?'

Marcus ignored the jibe and once more glanced in the mirror. A car had been following them since Cremona; its indicator was also flashing to take the slip road. He hoped it was the Messenger.

They had decided to leave the car in Mestre, the mainland district of the city, and take the train across the lagoon. From Santa Lucia station it was a short water taxi ride to their hotel, where they had reservations.

She was probably right to be irritated, thought Marcus, though I am damned if I'm going to apologise – especially after that flare-up. Lisa had suggested that before starting out they had an early breakfast at her hotel. Marcus had parked the new hire car and entered the foyer just as a short, round figure emerged from the lift.

'Marcus! A friendly face. How are you?'

Geri Bellman walked across the marble floor towards him, grinning hugely. Marcus opened his arms and hugged him warmly.

'Did you have a good trip? When did you arrive?'

'About ten o'clock last night. There was a slight delay, nothing of any consequence, but the queue for cars was horrendous. It took me three-quarters of an hour to get the keys.'

'I hope the room is all right. It was the first hotel I could think of. Have you had breakfast?' Marcus enquired.

'Not yet. I was going for a short walk, but I can do that later. Shall we eat together?'

Marcus hesitated. He had promised Lisa he would wait in the lobby for her.

'Yes, if we take a seat near the door so that I can watch out for a friend.'

They were shown to a table.

'So, who is this friend?' asked Geri.

'Look, I believe I should explain,' said Marcus hurriedly. 'She is a journalist. This has become more of a joint project. She is writing an article on Stradivari, and we have combined forces.'

'Really?' grinned Geri, raising an eyebrow.

'Absolutely,' protested Marcus. 'I can assure you it is merely a convenient way for us both to extract what we want from the research! I am not even staying in this hotel!'

'I believe you, Marcus,' commented Geri, his grin growing broader. 'Many wouldn't!'

'Marcus! There you are!' Suddenly, Lisa was standing at the table.

'Sorry, Lisa. I meant to watch out for you, but got caught up in conversation,' he said rising to greet her.

Geri stood and smiled politely.

'Lisa, let me introduce a good friend of mine, Geri Bellman. Geri, Mrs Lisa Robards.'

They shook hands, and Bellman helped Lisa to her seat.

'So what brings you to Cremona, Mr Bellman?' Lisa asked with her customary directness.

'Geri, please.' He looked uncertainly at Marcus, who nodded. 'Marcus asked me if I could help him with some work he is doing.'

'I've asked him to conduct an assessment of the current instrument makers in Cremona, Brescia and Mantua,' explained Marcus. 'I cannot do it on my own and it seemed a logical solution.'

'I see,' she responded, her earlier warmth congealing to frost. 'I don't recall you mentioning it, Marcus. After all, I am involved as well.'

'Do you want me to take another table, Marcus?' enquired Geri.

'Mr Bellman, don't get me wrong. I am not put out by your presence.' Lisa looked at him across the table. 'It's just that Marcus lacks the common courtesies – like keeping the people he is working with informed of what is happening.'

With that she had pushed back her chair and walked to the serving section to select her breakfast.

'Sorry, Geri. She has a sharp tongue.'

'I have the feeling she is right, Marcus. You should have told her I was coming,' he said quietly.

They ate, for the most part, in silence. Marcus attempted to lift the mood with light-hearted comments, but soon gave up. It was when they were finishing coffee that Geri remarked he had recently acquired several antique bows at a local auction. Though he awaited confirmation, he felt certain they were French, conceivably the work of Charles Bazin.

Lisa looked up. 'That sounds like a good find, Mr Bellman. That is if they were not too expensive.'

'I paid four hundred pounds for the two. One is for a violin, the other, for a cello. I didn't think that was too bad.'

'Especially, when you can pay anything between five and ten thousand dollars for a good example,' said Lisa, looking knowingly at Geri. 'Do you often come across finds like that?'

'Not often, Mrs Robards. I was in the right place at the right time.'

By the time they rose from the table, they were on first name terms and the exchanges between Lisa Robards and Geri Bellman were good-natured and friendly. She was interested in his observations on the many variations of instrument bows. He was delighted to meet the author of notable articles appearing in music magazines. However, Marcus knew the matter would not rest there.

They were given directions by a clutch of students, and made their way towards the building.

'Look, I'm sorry Lisa. I should have discussed it with you!'

Marcus suddenly found himself apologising, though all his instincts had been against it. What am I saying? he thought as the words came forth. Lisa stopped and faced him.

'I was angry for several reasons, Marcus. You should have let me know your intentions. After all, who is this man you say is your friend? Out of the blue I find somebody telling me he is also involved in the project. For all I know, he could just as easily be one of the people we are up against.'

'Impossible. He is someone I've known for years.' His face was going white with annoyance.

'Then, if he is such a friend, are you wise to expose him to danger?'

This was something Marcus had not considered. He fell back to mumbling, 'I would trust him with my life.'

As they approached the entrance Lisa murmured 'You may well have to.'

Adam Roberts had half-prepared Marcus for Doctor Granadigli. As they waited in the secretary's office of the Department of Organic and Industrial Chemistry, he recalled the professor's comment.

'In many ways, shall I say, he is larger than life. You will certainly find him entertaining as well as knowledgeable. I won't say more. I don't want to spoil your enjoyment of meeting him.'

Just then the door burst open. Marcus raised his eyes expectantly to catch a glimpse of the face, then had rapidly to adjust his gaze. The figure that swept in was fifteen to twenty centimetres below average height.

Doctor Granadigli was very short, his rounded physique topped by an outsize head. What immediately caught the attention were the flashing eyes, and the wide, bright smile sited between an ornate moustache and well-tended goatee beard. He was dressed impeccably in a dark suit with a waistcoat. In his button-hole was a bright red rose, complementing an extravagant tie of the same hue. His entrance was almost theatrical.

'I am aware of you, sir,' said the chemist, turning to pump Marcus' hand energetically. 'But who is this delightful creature?'

He pirouetted, bowed deeply, and kissed Lisa's hand.

She was captivated, her earlier irritation forgotten.

'How do you do, doctor. My name is Lisa Robards.'

'Brother Danby told me he would be accompanied. But he failed miserably to tell me by whom.'

She glanced across at Marcus. 'He has this facility for being economical with the truth.'

Granadigli looked up, a grin lighting up his whole face. 'So . . . you want to know all about the maestros' finishing techniques, eh? Well, you have come to the right person.' He seemed to swell in stature. 'I am the acknowledged expert in such things. You need go no further.'

111

He opened his arms in an expansive gesture. They could not help being swept along by his manner.

'Come! Come! First, we shall have coffee in the refectory. We can discuss precisely what you have in mind.'

With a flourish, he opened the door to Lisa, bowing as she passed him, then raised an eyebrow for Marcus to follow.

'You will find it is surprisingly good, *miei amici.* Better than we make in the laboratories!'

They sat apart from the smattering of mid-morning visitors in the dining hall, close to an expanse of windows overlooking the canals.

'So how is my good friend, Professor Roberts? He is well I trust?' asked Granadigli, at the same time turning to wave a greeting to a colleague.

'Very well, doctor. He sends his best regards.'

'I must visit him soon. The things his wife does with mascarpone cheese . . . outstanding!' Granadigli grinned. 'For a foreigner, that is!'

His face seems perpetually wreathed in grimaces and smiles, thought Lisa. Even his eyebrows have a will of their own.

'So, where shall we begin?' Suddenly he was serious. 'Glues, grounds and varnishes are each monumental subjects. I have been studying them for years.'

'What we are attempting to search out, Doctor Granadigli, are what materials the Cremonese were using during their golden period at the beginning of the eighteenth century,' explained Marcus, glancing at Lisa. 'We need to understand why they selected certain items, discarded others, where they got their ingredients, whether such materials are still available from the same sources, and if there are more suitable modern-day substitutes.'

'My young friends, what you are seeking cannot be covered in a few words, or in a brief moment. Whilst I am happy to answer your questions, you must realise it will take time.'

'How long, doctor?'

'To do the subject justice at least two full days. And bearing in mind that I have a lecture to give tomorrow morning I cannot see you leaving Venice before Thursday. Even then we shall have only taken a broad sweep across *l'arte dei maestri.*'

He sat back and looked at them intently.

'So, what is it to be? Do you want to leave now and read a book or two, or are you prepared to spend time delving into the subject?'

There was no uncertainty.

'I am delighted. But, first, let us clear the way. Call me Alfredo, not Doctor Granadigli. It is far too stilted. And it would get worse if we are going to spend time together. Are we agreed? I shall call you Lisa and Marcus.'

They both nodded their acquiescence. Granadigli looked up and raised an arm. Two young students immediately detached themselves from a group and came to his side.

He said, through a broad smile, 'I am having an important discussion with these two good people, Antonio. Here's ten Euros. Get me three coffees and one for yourself. And while you are at it, buy your companion, Francisco, a coffee as well.'

Clearly, Granadigli was a popular member of the faculty. In minutes both had returned, depositing beakers and the requisite change. He dismissed them with smiles and a wave.

'Let us start with the glues used by the Cremonese. This is the first step, and the easiest to deal with.'

'Can I record your comments, Alfredo?' asked Marcus.

'There is no need for the moment, Marcus. I am just making general observations. You can use your machine when we get to the laboratories.' He continued. 'Everyone in Cremona used hide glue. In fact, even today, it's unbeatable. Stronger than most modern glues. You see, it's the strength of the protein bonds which has been used for centuries in works of art – the egg in tempera, the casein in milk, and the animal protein in hide glue.'

He slurped his coffee. 'The other advantage is that it is water-soluble, making it ideal for repairs, when you have to reverse the process. Hide glue works in two stages. First when it cools and gels, making a good, initial adhesion. Then, as the water evaporates, it creates a durable bond. This two-step process allows for an "open time" in which the pieces of wood can be repositioned if necessary.'

Granadigli rose from the bench.

'Shall we continue this in more comfortable surroundings?'

As he led them down a corridor, he half-turned his head. 'Do either of you know much about the construction of stringed instruments?'

Before Marcus could answer, Lisa declared, 'I know the rudimentary aspects – what is involved and the factors that go into their making – but Marcus is a qualified luthier.'

'Good. Tell me, just to satisfy my curiosity, why are you both researching the subject?'

This time Marcus answered.

'Lisa is writing an article for a music journal and I am doing a project comparing the techniques of the maestros with their modern-day counterparts.'

They stopped and Granadigli pushed open a half-glazed door into his personal domain. They followed him across the expanse of a well-equipped laboratory where all the stations were in use. They passed several rooms, one a library, another a large lecture salon, before entering an outer office in which a woman was answering the telephone. She waved and smiled. Granadigli mouthed 'My secretary' as they passed through into his office.

Marcus' initial reaction was that they had entered a picture gallery. Oils, watercolours, drawings, ink sketches adorned every wall, save one. Around the lone window of the room were photographs. They depicted sections of instruments, close-ups of their construction and a host of electron microscope details of woods and finishing agents. There was no desk.

'Ah, I see you have noticed, Marcus.'

Lisa glanced towards him.

'I have no use for a desk, signora. When I work, I stand at the table in front of the window or I sit in that casual chair – Yes, the flattened one – and work at the coffee table. I deplore the need for a barrier between myself and my guests. Please, make yourselves comfortable.'

They sat together on the large sofa, Granadigli taking up residence in his favourite chair.

'So where was I? Yes, glues. Do you want to set up your recorder, Marcus?'

With an effort Granadigli crossed his short legs and sat back, patting his various pockets. He eventually withdrew a battered cigarette packet, extracted a cigarette and made great show of lighting it, drawing on it to such an extent that his cheeks were briefly concave, while Marcus removed the machine from its travelling case.

'Right, Alfredo, let's pick up on your remarks concerning glues.'

For the next four hours, Alfredo Granadigli dealt with aspects the Cremonese would have experienced in the preparation of their bonding agents. Lisa was clearly troubled by the cigarette smoke and whenever the packet appeared she made some pretence to leave the room, at one point going off with Alfredo's secretary to acquire sandwiches and a bottle of wine for their lunch. When she returned the chemist was in full flow.

'They would measure the amount of crystals they needed for the following day, put them in a pot and cover them with water. The next day they would be soft and gelatinous. Pouring off the excess water they would heat the pot, *bain-marie* style in a larger pot of water, checking the consistency by frequently dipping a piece of wood. If the glue ran off smoothly, they had got it right. If it was too thick, they added a little water. And they always used the glue when it was hot.'

Towards the end of the discussion, Marcus asked, 'What about the ready-made hide glues you can buy today?'

'The additives they use to keep the glue liquid make it more sensitive to water, and thereby weaker. In my opinion, hide glue has to be made up fresh for each application, using crystals or pellets in a double boiler.'

'So, even today, you would still use hide glue?'

'Yes! Of course, there are many variations in its composition. There always have been. But there is no need for change for the sake of change.' He reflected for a moment. 'I would use exactly the same as they did three hundred years ago – except perhaps that I would employ the finest grade you can buy. I'm not always certain they used the best. I know they purchased many of their materials here in Venice. I often wonder if they could not have obtained better quality elsewhere.'

'What would you recommend?' asked Lisa

'Always stipulate the weight needed to indent a gelled cube of glue. It's calibrated in Bloomgrams – a funny name. Anyway, never buy anything less than 240 Bloomgrams; it's the ideal grade for woodworking!'

A half an hour later Marcus noticed Granadigli discreetly looking at his watch.

'Well, thank you for your time, Alfredo,' he said, standing up.

Lisa, who had been writing in her notebook, looked up questioningly, but stirred from the sofa when the chemist also got to his feet.

'Forgive me, my friends,' he said, 'I always try to be home to see my children to bed. If you wish we could continue this conversation over dinner, perhaps?'

'Only if you join us as our guest?' declared Lisa. 'We'll book a table at my favourite restaurant, The Gam Gam. You may know it?'

'By the Ponte delle Guglie? The bridge of needles. I know it well.'

'Excellent! Shall we say eight thirty?'

Marcus knocked on Lisa's door at eight fifteen.

'Come in, Marcus.'

She was peering into a mirror, intent on fixing her earrings. Marcus noted the strong profile, the brow slightly furrowed as she concentrated on the task. She had a pleasing figure, curvaceous without undue emphasis in any of the principal areas – certainly arresting. He suddenly realised he was in the presence of a very attractive woman.

'There! I always have trouble with the right ear. How's that?'

She looked towards him, then turned a full circle.

'Delightful!' he offered hesitantly. Then, boldly, 'No, much more. Beautiful!'

Lisa laughed at his pink cheeks.

'Don't worry! I'm not trying to seduce a man of the cloth.'

She gazed at him intently.

'You look different tonight. I can see you are wearing a suit, but something is different.'

Then her eyes opened wide.

'You're not wearing your clerical collar! You look normal, Marcus.' Her hand went to her mouth. 'Ouch! I didn't mean that. What I meant was . . .'

'I know what you meant.' He laughed. 'I thought it would be better to leave it off tonight.'

Lisa laughed too. They left the room and walked arm-in-arm to the lift.

'I didn't realise this was a Jewish restaurant, Lisa,' he commented, as they sipped their drinks while waiting for Granadigli.

'Does that concern you?' she enquired, looking up from the menu. 'Is it against your belief?'

'Not at all! Why should it be?'

116

'I'm sure you will like the food. Being Jewish, whenever I'm travelling, I try to find a restaurant that does it well.'

'Is that why we are staying at that hotel in the Ghetto?'

'When in Venice I always try to book into the Locanda sull'Isola. I'm not sure if it's my upbringing, or because the quarter has such strong historical undertones. Did you know this was the world's first ghetto? The word is actually Old Venetian for "throw", a term used in iron smelting. Apparently they had foundries in the Cannaregio district centuries ago.'

She turned back to the menu.

An interesting combination, mused Marcus: a failed Catholic brother and an unorthodox Jewess.

The door burst open and Granadigli made a predictably dramatic entrance.

'Signora! Bellisima! I hope I have not kept you.'

He bowed low and kissed her hand. Marcus grinned, amused by the extravagant gesture that again had Lisa blushing prettily.

'Come! Tonight, we shall enjoy ourselves.'

Granadigli was already masterminding proceedings. The headwaiter was immediately attentive and led them to their table.

Much of the evening was taken up with the chemist's whimsical account of his involvement in his chosen profession.

'My father wanted me to be a doctor of medicine, like himself. But who, in their right mind, would wish to spend a lifetime peering up or down human orifices?'

Granadigli had warmed to the subject as he consumed more than his share of the wine.

'I studied chemistry in Milan. Then lectured in Rome, Paris and Vienna, before settling in Venice. It was here that I developed an interest in conservation and restoration.' He looked bemusedly into his glass, then asked Lisa, 'So, my beloved young lady, what paths have you trodden to bring you to this restaurant, on this very night, with a drunken academic and a man of the Church?'

Bearing in mind Lisa's scathing remarks about his earlier drinking, Marcus had been deliberately abstemious. Consequently, Lisa had enjoyed a goodly share of the bottles brought to the table. She pondered Granadigli's question.

'I have always been interested in music. When I was old enough

I attended a conservatoire in Chicago.' She smiled wistfully. 'Living in Italy for a couple of years, I went to the Academy in Cremona. They recognised it before I did. I was never going to be good enough to play the cello as a soloist. The impetuosity of youth! If I couldn't play on the concert platform, I was certainly not going to sit with others in an orchestra! So I became a music critic and joined the staff of a newspaper in Rockford, a hundred miles or more from the windy city.' She drank deeply, and put the glass carefully on the table. 'From there I went to California to work on the *LA Times*, doing music reviews. At the paper I interviewed the man who later became my husband. In those days he was writing for the screen.' She wrapped her arms around herself. 'Later, I began freelance writing for music magazines. As I mentioned earlier, I'm doing a commission on Stradivari. That's how I find myself sitting here.'

She shivered, and broke free of her memories, turning to smile at Granadigli.

'How did you meet up with our churchman here?' continued the academic.

'Oh, that was something else,' responded Lisa brightly, proceeding to tell him, rather elaborately, how she had been ousted from the Records Office in Cremona, then how Marcus had attempted to appease her with the offer of a coffee.

'So, how do you say it? You have now buried the hammer and have combined forces?'

'Actually, Alfredo, it's hatchet,' corrected Marcus.

Lisa emptied her glass. 'Don't be stuffy, Marcus. Hammer, hatchet, hardware – who cares?'

She was a little tipsy. Even Granadigli was grinning inanely.

'I think we should be making a move, Lisa. We have a busy day tomorrow, and we don't want to keep Alfredo out all night.'

Suddenly her gaze was sharp and clear as she looked down at her watch.

'I'm sorry, Alfredo. It is later than I thought. I've got to be with it in the morning.'

They saw Alfredo into a water taxi and strolled back through the old part of the ghetto towards the hotel on its tiny island surrounded by canals.

'It was a great evening, Marcus. Alfredo is a roly-poly man who really enjoys life. I wonder what his wife and children are like?'

'I imagine the same as he is. Carefree and contented. He seems to have what so many people are searching for.'

Lisa stopped. 'That sounded wistful. Almost as though you could swap places with him.'

'No, I suppose I'm happy too, in my way.' He grinned. 'I hope I'm not becoming maudlin.'

She gripped his arm. 'Being here will work wonders.' She stopped, abruptly, glancing over her shoulder. 'As long as the Messenger is close by.'

Chapter Twenty-Seven

Both double doors were opened by a Franciscan brother, who inclined his head respectfully.

'Come in, Angelo . . . take a seat.'

He moved to a chair by the window. Crossing his legs, the cardinal placed his elbows squarely on the armrests.

'You wanted to see me, Your Eminence?'

'Yes, Angelo. You may be able to help me with a problem.'

The Cardinal Secretary of State rose from behind his desk and took a chair facing Cardinal Marchetti.

'As you know, Angelo, in addition to overseeing the administration of the Holy See, one of the principal duties of this office is to act as the eyes, heart and arm of His Holiness.' He gave a wan smile. 'In truth, there is much that escapes my attention. But, when I have such capable men as yourself providing support, resolute in maintaining order and respect and, most importantly, keeping us solvent, I am confident that any unreported happenings will be of minor significance.'

The Secretary of State rose again and walked over to an elegant Tuscan console. From an ornate Brandimarte wine cooler he took a bottle of Tocai Friulano and poured two glasses.

He handed one to Marchetti. 'I would say this is my favourite wine. Slightly aromatic, you can pick out the hint of bitter almonds, don't you agree?'

Marchetti nodded dutifully. In truth, the wine held little appeal for him. He much preferred the reds of Piedmont.

'I attended my usual monthly meeting with the government and city authorities, yesterday,' the Cardinal Secretary continued. 'Nothing untoward came of the meeting, as you might imagine. That is, until matters were being concluded. As we descended the steps, the mayor asked if there were truth in the rumour.'

He took a lingering sip of the wine.

'Do you know we shall soon have to drop the word "Tocai", and just call it "Friulano"? Apparently, according to Brussels, the word conflicts with the Hungarian Tokaj, and they have the prior claim. What nonsense! Where was I?' The Secretary of State fixed his gaze on Marchetti. 'Yes, this rumour. It would appear that the Vatican is about to move its domain from Rome to the outskirts of Cremona. Gibberish! Have you heard about this so-called transfer, Angelo? I told him it was stuff and nonsense.'

'What did the mayor say to that?' asked Cardinal Marchetti, neutrally.

'What do you mean?'

'When you said there was no truth in the rumour, what was his reaction?'

The Secretary of State stared at the cardinal.

'You do know something about it, don't you?' he said softly.

'I have heard the rumour, yes. But, for the moment, I would be inclined to do little about it,' Marchetti declared. He had expected this conversation to arise and had carefully prepared his response.

'Nonsense, Angelo! If we don't do something immediately it could cause bad blood between the Church and the State. That is something I would definitely not relish.'

Marchetti allowed a moment of silence. Then he commenced the reply which, in his mind, he had rehearsed many times.

'I understand your concern, Your Eminence. But let us view the situation from another quarter. Let us ignore the source, whoever that may be; let us look at what we might derive from it.'

'All we would derive would be obstruction, non-cooperation and setbacks to any proposals we might submit to the city authorities. An untenable position! I want you to do something to counter any misunderstandings now.'

Marchetti sipped his wine.

'Naturally, we do not want to incur the wrath of the mayor's department, nor, for that matter, any of the government offices. But I have been thinking about the substance of the rumour since it was told to me. If it is without foundation it will mutate, take on a different slant each time it is relayed. At the moment, I have heard that the Pope is thinking of spending more time at his summer palace at Castel Gandolfo. As a consequence, he will move the Curia, its Colleges, Congregations and Departments, all to a new site by Lake Albano.'

The Secretary of State peered at him intently.

'Hmm . . . I was told something different.'

'There you are! It proves my point. Such rumours often spiral wildly, becoming more and more distorted until they simply perish through lack of credibility.'

He continued to stare at Marchetti.

'You could be right. Would you believe, the mayor whispered to me that we were intent on selling the forty-five hectares of the land we occupy, and establishing a new enclave in Lombardy, on the banks of the River Po.'

Marchetti snorted derisively.

'If it progresses at this rate the rumour will expire in matter of days. Frankly, I would just ignore it until that time comes. In the meantime, surely it would do little harm for the government and city authorities to believe something is afoot. If they actually fear that the Holy See might leave Rome, they might be persuaded to improve services and charge us less for the privilege.'

The Secretary of State smiled.

'Ever the opportunist, Angelo. But I take your point. The rumour need neither be denied nor confirmed. Eventually it will die away of its own accord. Meanwhile, if it unsettles them enough to improve our bargaining position, so be it.'

'I think that would be the appropriate way to deal with the situation, Your Eminence.'

'Thank you for your advice, Angelo.'

But, as the tall figure of the cardinal rose and made his departure, the Secretary experienced a moment of unease. He sensed he had been out-manoeuvred in some way. Even though he had advanced a reasoned argument to do nothing, he sensed that Marchetti was weaving an elaborate web of deception to which he and others were unwitting contributors.

Chapter Twenty-Eight

When they arrived at the university Granadigli was working in the laboratory.

'Good! Good! How are you both today?' He came bustling towards them. 'I've given my lecture, so the rest of the day is entirely free!'

He led them into his office. Once more they occupied the sofa, the academic his battered chair.

'So. Grounds and varnishes. Monumental topics, eh!' He smiled broadly at Lisa and Marcus. 'Let us begin with the unadorned instrument.'

Granadigli rose and picked up a viola from a shelf. Plain and unvarnished, it looked naked in its natural state.

'The moment of truth, my friends. What I do now will make or mar all my efforts. If I put too heavy a ground into the pores of the wood the tone will be lost. If the coating of vernica blanca is misapplied it will sound like a gypsy fiddle. If the top varnish is too thick every note will be dulled.'

He sat down again, and put the instrument on the coffee table.

'Let us start with the ground: the filler which erases all the gouges, scores and woodworking marks, and seals the pores of the wood. Look at this, signora – it's beauty lies dormant. The swan has yet to emerge.'

She took the instrument and ran her hands over the carcass. Now she could feel the many slight indentations and grooves.

'Not significant in its present state but, if a varnish were applied at this point, those marks would show up like a ploughed field. Our famous luthiers had to smooth them out, and in the eighteenth century they used all manner of filling materials.'

Granadigli was enjoying himself. He was performing before an audience also engrossed in his favourite topic.

'However, even before they did that, they would have exposed this to the sun for a week or so to take away its whiteness. The ultraviolet rays literally suntan the wood. Some modern-day luthiers even put their instruments on a sun bed!'

The chemist returned the viola to a shelf and picked up another.

'So, to the ground or filler. This was done much in the same way that painters of old prepared their canvases. The ground coating not only enhances the beauty of the wood by accentuating its depth, it also penetrates and adds strength. Come into the laboratory for a moment and you will see what I mean by the variations in the basic coating the masters applied.'

They followed him to a station where a wall-screen stood above an array of instrumentation. Granadigli busied himself for a minute or two, then pressed a switch. A bizarre landscape was revealed on the screen.

'Isn't technology wonderful? We have managed to obtain instrument fragments of the maestros and subjected them to the EDAX Spectrum.'

He turned and laughed at their perplexed looks.

'EDAX stands for Energy Dispersive Analysis by X-ray. We take selected areas of the samples and position them under an electron microscope. These are the results. Amazing, aren't they!'

Lisa and Marcus looked at each other.

'My friends. Let me explain,' declared Granadigli, moving closer to the screen. 'What we have here is a splinter of a violin made by Stradivari. You can see the three layers quite distinctly.' He raised his arm and pointed to the lines of demarcation. 'A thicker particulate layer which is the ground, the intermediate varnish, and the finishing varnish. What is significant is the mineral rich mixture of the ground layer. It is high in numerous chemical additives.'

'What is that thick line running across the top?' asked Lisa, fascinated by the image.

'That's a brush hair that Antonio lost when applying the top coat,' replied Granadigli. He pointed to another section. 'That's a chunk of silica.' He moved his finger. 'And that's alumina. I'm told they even included realgar and the old Arabic version of sandarac.'

'Have you identified all the substances in the grounds and varnishes?' queried Lisa, her eyes still fixed on the screen.

'Most of them, signora. Now, let me show you a fragment of a violin by Nicolo Amati. This was made about 1685.'

This time the image was markedly different. The base layer contained fewer additives and was thinner than those used by his famed apprentice.

For the next hour, the chemist showed them a number of magnified photographs of instruments made by the Cremonese during their golden period, and compared the varying ways they created their finishes.

'But, it is evident,' he said, clarifying each image in detail, 'that, though they adjusted the strength and mixes of their grounds and varnishes, in their heyday they all used the same range of chemical additives.'

'I suppose they all came from the same source,' commented Marcus.

'Yes, from the local apothecary.'

After a light lunch, the chemist continued his presentation. Marcus made full use of his tape recorder. In the afternoon they discussed the characteristics of the varnishes and the methods of creating the striking colour tones.

'Like the paintings of yester-year, they would have been brighter, more blatant than they are now, after three hundred years of exposure and useage,' intoned Granadigli, explaining how the instrument makers used the hot dry climate of Lombardy, and the care and time they took to complete the finishing stages of their creations.

'As I said earlier, you must be a master craftsman to produce the structure, and an artist to bring out all the beauty and tonal qualities of the wood.'

Inevitably, towards the end of the afternoon Marcus asked the key question.

'Tell me, Alfredo, could one replicate the techniques of the maestros today?'

Granadigli laughed. 'Of course, Marcus – if we knew exactly what they were! I can show you in great detail what they used. Even how they applied their finishing materials. But I would not know how they mixed them exactly, at what temperatures, how long were the intervals between the various stages . . . I am a simple chemist – all I can do is guess.' He rose from his chair and went to a bookcase. 'However, I want you to meet a friend of mine. We have countless discussions on this subject. I've got his telephone number here somewhere.'

He spent a few minutes opening various books before a piece of paper fell from one and fluttered to the floor.

'Here it is! His name is Tomasina. He has a studio by the Ponte delle Guglie, not far from your hotel.'

They found the street, Calle del Forno, and headed south. A three minute phone call the previous evening had secured the appointment. Signor Tomasina would be delighted to welcome them at ten thirty. He had told them his workshop was just up from the Cannaregio canal, and to look out for the sign of the violin.

Opening the door activated a solemn ring of a bell, Not tingling and light, but a sonorous, single chime. They mounted three steps and stood peering uncertainly into the depths of the building. Stepping from bright sunlight into the gloom of an unlit expanse their eyes took a moment to adjust before their surroundings came into sharper focus.

Lisa and Marcus found themselves in a simple reception area comprising comfortable seats and small tables. On the walls were photographs of cellos and violins, the contented faces of artistes holding, no doubt, instruments made by Tomasina; below these, angled shelves displayed a number of well-presented violins and bows.

They heard the unhurried descent of feet on stairs, which, eventually, preceded the gradual appearance of the rest of an elderly figure.

'You are Brother Marcus, are you not? Few clerics come through our doors.'

Marcus nodded slightly. 'Signor Tomasina, may I introduce my companion? Mrs Lisa Robards.'

Taking Lisa's hand he bowed and drew it close to his lips. 'Honoured, my dear lady.'

The gentleman must be in his late seventies or early eighties, thought Marcus. He was similar in height to himself, though slightly stooped with age. Narrow features, almost vulpine, were accentuated by long white hair swept straight back from his forehead. His rheumy eyes were a watery blue, but they seemed to take in everything around him.

'Come! Let us find somewhere more comfortable.'

They followed him back up the stairs to a workshop, not dissimilar to that in Mayfield, though there were more benches, and all were occupied. The trio walked half the length of the workroom, then ascended another flight to the floor above.

'This is my personal sanctuary,' said Tomasina, holding on to a post, and trying discreetly to recover his breath. After a slight pause, he said, 'Please, sit down. May I get you some coffee?'

As though she had been listening at the door, a young woman entered the room.

'*Nonno*, let me bring coffee for your guests.'

She was in her early twenties and tall, like her grandfather. She smiled at Lisa and Marcus, and asked what they preferred.

When she had gone, the elderly man remarked, with a mixture of pride and disquiet in his voice, 'She is my son's only child, and she is not interested in instrument making. All she does is study the violin.' He sat down carefully in a chair with stout armrests. 'But her teachers at the Music Academy believe she has a promising future, so I should not be too concerned. Perhaps, eventually, one of her children will carry on the tradition.'

'Have your family been long in this business, Signor Tomasina?' asked Lisa.

He leaned forward. 'Cara, for more than three hundred years. We have occupied these same premises since 1685. My great, great, great, great grandfather was apprenticed to Stradivari.'

'Really! I'd very much like to hear about him, Signor Tomasina.'

'Mrs Robards is writing an article on Stradivari for an American magazine,' explained Marcus.

'I see. Well, his presence is here in this very room, my dear. He resides in a box behind you. Come, let me show you.'

Lisa looked inquiringly at Marcus as they rose to follow the gaunt figure, Marcus noting that the salon was furnished with a wealth of antique furniture and expensive carpets and rugs. Tomasina caught his appraising glances.

'What you see, Fra' Danby, are the acquisitions of the past three centuries. There are other such pieces on the two floors above. I feel privileged to pass my time amongst them.' He stopped, and for a moment he was lost to them. Then he continued, 'Soon, they will be in the safe keeping of the next generation.'

They stood before an exquisitely carved Tuscan buffet, on which stood a box matching the walnut sideboard in its styling and finish. Marcus leaned forward to read a small metal plaque.

'Giovanni Tomasina. Born 1713, died 1797. May God rest his soul.'

'I didn't think cremation was allowed in those days, Signor Tomasina,' commented Lisa.

'It wasn't. He was buried on the island of San Michele, the city's cemetery. But it has been full for many, many years. Nowadays, the authorities bury our dead on the mainland. The few who are interred on the island are dug up after ten years and taken to an ossuary in Mestre.' He put his hand on the box as though comforting his long-gone relative. 'They started to remove bodies back in the 1800s. When informed of the transfer, one of the family brought back the bone fragments of our noted forebear, and placed them in this casket. Now, he is with us forever.'

They returned to their seats as Tomasina's grand-daughter entered with a tray of coffee and Amaretto biscuits.

'Grandfather's favourites,' she said, setting it down.

'So, my young friends, tell me how I can be of assistance?'

Marcus, now well-versed in the explanation, or those aspects of it he felt able to reveal, provided the background to their research.

'So, you have visited Professor Roberts, and spent time with our exuberant Doctor Granadigli. As you might expect, I know them both well.'

'Yes, Alfredo Granadigli was extremely obliging. He gave us a considerable amount of his time explaining how the masters finished their instruments,' said Marcus. 'It was when I asked if their techniques could be replicated that he suggested we spoke with you, signore.'

'Did he actually tell you what we do here, brother?'

Marcus shook his head, then, before the old man could launch into an explanation, asked, 'Would you mind if I use my tape recorder, Signor Tomasina?'

The elderly gentleman, in typical latin style, shrugged and raised his hands in agreement. 'My forebear, Giovanni, who is still with us in spirit, was apprenticed to Stradivari from 1725 to 1737. Whilst he helped produce cellos, violas and violins to the master's designs, Giovanni always favoured the violin, in particular the "long pattern" made prior to 1700. It had flatter, narrower bouts, a darker tone, stronger arches in the front and back and a longer than usual body length. He was convinced the sound quality was superior to those even of the Golden Period. When he returned to Venice he set about producing violins to this original pattern.'

He took a sip of coffee, holding the cup in his two hands.

'This has been maintained throughout the ages. Clearly, if someone is quite specific in their commissions we meet their wishes. But the practice, until now, has been to encourage a demand for the older style of violin.'

He returned the cup to its saucer.

'Now we get to the reason why Granadigli sent you. Not only do we reproduce violins to a format created three hundred and ten years ago, we also produce all the other stringed instruments. What is more, we use the same materials and methods. We can do this because Giovanni told us precisely how to do so.'

Marcus had been leaning forward to catch every softly-spoken word. He noticed a contradiction. 'Have you told Alfredo of this?'

'Many times, young man. And he has tried to replicate Giovanni's instructions in his glass-walled domain, Among his test-tubes, microscopes and other fanciful paraphernalia.' The luthier's eyes glinted. 'Would you believe, he never can get it quite right! So he distrusts the evidence we produce in our workshop. We argue constantly.'

Tomasina chuckled at the thought.

'Surely you can't access the wood the Cremonese used in the eighteenth century?' queried Lisa, looking up from her notebook.

'Cara, long ago we discovered a source for maple and spruce that is very, very close to what they used. That is a closely guarded secret, you understand. We even have suppliers in Saudi and other areas in the Middle-East, providing us with all the old-style grounds, and all the many ingredients and additives used by the masters. No doubt, Alfredo would have told you what they were – the minerals, the semi-precious gemstones, the little oddities that were included in their fillers, white varnishes and colour top layers.'

'Do you reproduce only Stradivari's instruments?' questioned Lisa.

Tomasina gazed at her searchingly.

'Why do you ask, my dear?'

'It would be wonderful to know that the instruments made by Bergonzi, Guarneri and the others were also not lost to the world.'

'Well, Carlo Bergonzi was an apprentice to Stradivari like Giovanni. And even though he moved back to Venice they kept in close contact. So the answer to your question is yes. We have a record of his methods.'

'And the others, Signor Tomasina? The Guarneris, for example?'

For some reason he looked slightly abashed.

'Perhaps we have some note of their methods, But I could not immediately lay my hands on it. Come, I think it is time to venture into our workshop.'

He rose hurriedly, and led them to the staircase, which they descended to the workshop below. This was familiar territory to Marcus. But then he began noticing subtle differences. Two luthiers constructing violins were not using moulds to shape the ribs. Stradivari produced moulds for each original pattern, but often introduced marginal differences. In the workshop he found their use too restricting. Another was carving the edge groove in the completed instrument, a method also used by Marcus, but the modern-day practice was to insert the purfling around the top and bottom plates before assembly. Another was working the ground into a cello. As he neared the bench, he detected a distinctive, sweet smell he could not place.

'What is the filler he is using, Signor Tomasina?'

'Propolis, Brother Marcus. Bees produce it to insulate and fill the gaps in their hives. The Cremonese found it an ideal ground. The only trouble is it can be a major irritant to the skin, creating red, sore patches that swell and weep. That's why we always wear rubber gloves when applying it. Unfortunately, the maestros did not have that luxury.'

For Lisa this was a foreign world. Interesting, but it did not capture her imagination as much as it enthralled Marcus. He was still hovering over the workshop benches when Tomasina suggested they enjoy a light lunch.

'Sorry, I got carried away, Lisa' he muttered contritely as they sat in a nearby trattoria.

He turned to Tomasina, sitting benignly opposite.

'I did notice that you have lengthened the bass bar, signore'

'In some respects, you have to adapt to the times, Brother Marcus. The longer bar gives greater resonance. You may have noticed we have also updated the fixing of the neck. We now secure it with three screws to cope with the added tension needed for concert hall instruments. But, other than the use of electric drills in the workshop, much of our work practices are unchanged.'

They returned to Ca' Tomasina in the mid-afternoon and spent much of the remaining time discussing the ingredients of the varnishes.

'One of the big influences on finishing was the growing popularity of Japan lacquers,' explained the studio proprietor. 'In the late 1600s Europe was enamoured of the high gloss finish, a fashion that brought about the growing interest in spirit varnishes for all manner of woodwork finishes, and the almost frantic search for new ingredients to add to the oil-based varnishes used by the Cremonese. You would be surprised at the lengths they went to bring out the colour and create a hard, bright finish.'

'Granadigli showed us a number of photos of the microscopic detail of the layers applied by the maestros. The comparison with photos of earlier Amati instruments was incredible,' declared Marcus.

'Yes, they experimented with all sorts of additives, minerals as well as ground gemstones – especially, in the final layers. They were looking for materials that would maintain the translucency of the varnish, allowing the natural woods to show through, yet contained crystalline particles suspended in the coatings to refract the light.'

'So what did Stradivari use during the Golden Period?' asked Lisa, keen to extract as much information as possible about the maestro.

'Antonio and his sons were probably more enthusiastic than most to come up with ingredients that would give them an edge. They were the first to use organic pigments. In fact, they created dichroism, a varnish characteristic that shows two colours: a golden thin layer, and a thicker layer which would have had reddish tints. But, to a large extent, whilst they kept their recipes secret from each other, they all used the same ingredients, just varying the proportions.'

'Doctor Granadigli mentioned that the Cremonese bought their materials from the apothecary in San Domenico,' said Lisa, looking up from her notebook in which she had been scribbling furiously.

'Yes, they would have done. That is until they began obtaining their supplies direct from Venice. The supplier was able to offer them a wider range. Many of these ingredients had been used for years by artists. The Venetian painters have long been noted for the brighter, more intense colours in their works of art.'

'It would appear the masters were occupied with a range of substances we would not use today, Signor Tomasina. In a number of Alfredo's photos they even indicated the presence of light metals,' observed Marcus.

'They mixed many things in their finishing varnishes, Brother Marcus, some of which might not have shown up under his microscope, from the exotic to such extremes as realgar and orpiment.'

'Doctor Granadigli mentioned the use of those yesterday,' said Lisa, thoughtfully. 'What are they, exactly?'

'Cara, they are highly dangerous substances.'

Chapter Twenty-Nine

The door was ajar. Peering in, he saw that Lisa was near the window speaking on the phone. She turned to beckon him in, mouthing the word 'publisher'.

'The draft should be with you in a week to ten days . . . No, I've got some new stuff which will make him happy . . . Yes . . . OK, I'll email it to you . . .'bye for now.'

She closed the mobile and put it in her bag.

'The magazine editor has left several messages, the last telling me he would ring about now, so I left the door open.'

She was wearing a dark emerald dress, which highlighted her auburn hair and accentuated the green of her eyes. For the past ten days she had dressed in trousers and shapeless casual tops. Her make-up had been minimal and her hair had often been scraped back or hidden beneath a headscarf. Her steadfastness to the project, her forthright – at times, abrasive – manner had obscured the fact that Lisa was an extremely attractive woman. She slipped stockinged feet into high-heeled shoes.

'Right, I'm ready. Where are we going?'

He had booked at a restaurant recommended by the portiere.

'It's called La Casa Rossa, along the canal at the back of the hotel. We can walk there quite easily.'

It was a warm, inviting evening, with a gentle breeze barely making its presence felt. Turning northwards they crossed the bridge onto the Fondamenta dei Ormesimi and strolled along the canal bank.

'What a wonderful night!' murmured Lisa. 'I felt quite drained after our day with Signor Tomasina. I didn't think I would be up to it but it's surprising how a good soak can perk you up, especially if you are hungry.'

'We certainly crammed a lot in,' admitted Marcus. 'I still haven't had time to absorb it all. He gave us any amount of valuable information.'

At the restaurant they were shown to a table in a corner that afforded a view of the dining area.

'What a delightful choice, Marcus!' exclaimed Lisa. Clearly the food was good, for the restaurant was filled with Venetians.

They ordered from an attentive waiter, and each sat back contentedly, enjoying a glass of the local white wine.

'I overheard you remark that you hoped to submit a draft shortly. Did you get much from today?' enquired Marcus.

'Not so much specific to Stradivari, but that doesn't matter. I'm going to include much more about the techniques of the Cremonese – thanks to you,' replied Lisa. She leaned forward and the sparkle in her eyes was intensified by the light of the candle.

'Do you know, I think this is going to be really something. There will be so much original material going into this article it will make my name as a journalist in music circles. That is . . .' She looked contrite. 'That is if you allow me to use the information. By rights, you have first call on it for your report.'

'Don't worry. As I said earlier, what I'm doing is not for publication. Anyway the report will be submitted long before your article appears.'

He gazed at her across the table – and, in that moment, he was caught like a moth in a flame.

'What?' she enquired. 'Is something wrong? You were staring at me.'

Marcus blushed.

'Sorry. No, nothing is wrong.'

He turned away quickly, caught the waiter's attention and ordered a bottle of their best red wine.

'So, what did you think of our interviews in Venice?' Lisa asked, after the antipasta had arrived.

Marcus added a little olive oil to his dish.

'You know how your mind absorbs facts and files them away, then unconsciously sifts through them and pulls out the anomalies. Well, mine's working like that at the moment. The trouble is it hasn't come up with what they are yet.'

Lisa took a sip of wine.

'I must say applying propolis as a filler is a new one on me.' She dabbed her mouth with the napkin. 'Though I suppose it's logical. If bees use it to construct their hives, a resinous substance mixed with beeswax would have worked well – and it became transparent under the varnish so that the wood grain shone through.'

'Yes, the masters were always experimenting. Signor Tomasina confirmed Sacconi's assertion that they incorporated a variety of materials in their grounds and varnishes.'

'I didn't realise that, until Granadigli showed us those images taken by the electron microscope. That was really fascinating.'

'And they included ground-up semi-precious stones,' added Marcus. 'It was remarkable to see the ground, the white varnish and the inclusions in the colour varnish showing up so clearly.'

He tasted the red wine and nodded to the waiter, who poured it into their glasses.

'Tomasina said the maestros never revealed their secrets. Even their apprentices were not trusted with the formulae of the varnishes they used,' he continued.

'He also said that the instrument makers might not have known the actual composition of their varnishes, but relied on the apothecary's expertise,' she commented thoughtfully.

'Yes. A contradiction perhaps? I wonder if my subconscious picked that up?'

'He did refer to some manuscript that indicated they all went to the local drugstore and obtained a varnish suited to their needs. Even Antonio Stradivari, the great man himself, would carry his bottle to be refilled by the druggist. "To make sure I'm not being served from the bottom of the pot!" Great stuff, eh?'

'What caught my attention was Granadigli's comment about their varnishes being oil-based. That means, logically, they should not be alcohol-soluble. But they were. How does one explain that?'

When their main courses arrived at the table they were still engrossed in discussing the key points that had emerged during the two days in the university. Neither wanted a dessert, so they decided on another bottle of wine. This was followed by coffee and several glasses of amaretto Villa Luisa. By this time the conversation had become more personal.

'Does your husband still write for films?' asked Marcus, casually, leaning both elbows on the table.

Lisa looked wistful. 'No, he has moved on. He directs them!'

135

There was a companionable silence.

'What about you? Come on, tell me! What prompted you to give up the world and wear sandals?' asked Lisa.

He shrugged. 'At the time, I was mesmerised by the Church. I was almost twenty-two, impressionable, and enchanted by the notion that I could pursue a religious life and be involved with music. Joining an Order such as the Xaverians seemed the answer to my needs.'

'Does it still?'

'The truth is . . .' Marcus took a deep breath. 'No . . . Not any more. At the moment I am in the wilderness. You see before you a man who gave up what might have been a promising career as a soloist and now finds himself lost, within and without.'

She stretched out a hand and held his, which had, without his knowledge, been clenching the table.

'I'm sorry. I didn't mean to sadden you. Now I've spoilt the evening!'

'Of course you haven't! I just had a momentary lapse into self-pity. In truth, there is much to look forward to.'

They rose together. Lisa waited on the canal bank while he paid the bill. Neither said anything as they strolled along to the stray sounds of music and the water lapping by their side. Marcus sensed before it happened that her hand would seek out his. When it did her touch was tentative, uncertain.

'I've never held a cleric's hand this way before,' she said.

He held it briefly, then let it go and put his arm round her shoulder. Lisa shivered, though not from the cooling breeze, and leaned against him.

They reached the bridge leading to the ghetto. Senses dulled by alcohol, entranced by Lisa's closeness, the softness of her hair, the beguiling waft of perfume, Marcus fleetingly forgot himself. He turned his head to kiss her cheek. She gasped softly, raised her face to his and kissed him on the lips. There was no awkwardness. He hugged her briefly and they continued towards the hotel. They collected their keys at reception, she preceding him in to the lift. When it stopped at the top floor, he trailed her along the corridor until they came to a halt before her door.

'Thank you for a wonderful evening, Marcus.' She took his hand. 'I'm pleased we talked.'

She gathered him suddenly in a fierce hug. Startled, it took a moment for Marcus to respond but, encircling her in his arms, eyes closed, he was quickly overwhelmed by the strongest of desires. Conscious of its physical effect, he tried to ease himself away, but she pressed closer. Then, stretching out a hand, she turned the handle and pushed open the door. Stepping back, Lisa held him fast, and led him into her room. The door closed slowly on its hinges and clicked shut.

He awoke with a start. Lisa was asleep next to him. Marcus listened to the soft rhythm of her breathing, then eased himself from under the thin coverlet and retrieved his clothes, strewn alongside Lisa's in an unsteady line from the door. He dressed quickly and quietly, then tip-toed to the door carrying his shoes and jacket. Lisa lay there, peacefully asleep. In the corridor he glanced at his watch. It was a quarter past three.

Quietly unlocking the door to his room he clicked on the light switch – nothing happened. The room remained in darkness.

He was feeling his way towards the lamp on the chest of drawers when they rushed him. Each arm was grabbed by a figure and he was propelled towards the balcony. The double doors were wide open – there was nothing he could do. As he toppled over the narrow railing he uttered only one short cry, more of despair than terror.

Chapter Thirty

'Signor Lambertini, Your Eminence.'

This time the cardinal rose and came round his desk to greet him.

'Signore, I am delighted to see you. Come, take a comfortable seat. Can I offer some refreshment?'

'Thank you, no, Your Eminence.'

They moved to a large, leather sofa.

'I must congratulate you,' declared the cardinal. 'The pace is quickening. At their monthly meeting the mayor told our Secretary of State of the rumour.'

'Is that a difficulty?' enquired Lambertini. 'Does he know who is behind it?'

'I'm sure he has his suspicions.' Marchetti smiled, bleakly. 'There was always the possibility the Secretary would hear of it. When he probed its origin I was ready with a plausible answer, which will suffice for the moment. Now, let us move on. I need to learn of your contacts' responses and discuss the next stage.'

Lambertini reviewed what he had done so far. At the end of meetings, or apparently casual encounters with personnel from the city's administration and government departments, he had raised the possibility of the Church's departure from Rome.

'Even if they try to stifle it, I have also passed on the rumour to certain individuals.'

'I hope you have not been too enthusiastic, Michelo,' said the cardinal, now gazing at Lambertini intently. 'When you and I discussed our ploy I was quite specific about the people and the organisations you should approach. Whoever you told would be as ardent as ourselves in ensuring not a word reached the ears of the media. Were they to hear of it, they would also want to know the outcome. The resolution would be on public record. That, I have emphasised, time and time again, must not happen. Do you understand?'

'Naturally, Your Eminence. No one I have spoken to would consider talking with the press.'

'I repeat, Signor Lambertini . . .' Marchetti's voice took on an intimidating edge. 'I hope you are right.' He stared at him a moment longer. 'Let us move on. This is what I want you to undertake.'

Lambertini picked up the important aspects of the cardinal's demands. Beneath his suave exterior he was distracted. Perhaps he had gone too far. He had passed on the rumour to Angelina Scacchi, the receptionist at the Campidoglio. Known widely as '*la voce de un angelo*' – the voice of an angel – she would broadcast the rumour to everyone entering the Town Hall. Before Monday, when she returned for work, he would have to ensure what had been said in the café was suppressed.

'Brother Danby is no longer a threat, you say? . . . When did that happen? . . . I see . . . No, leave the woman. She can't do much without the cleric . . . What was that? . . . This man, Bellman? . . . Again, do nothing. Just go back to Cremona and await my instructions.'

The line from Germany was abruptly terminated.

He replaced the receiver and thought about Bellman. He had been assessing the capabilities of the present-day instrument makers and, according to the report, had thus far called upon five workshops. He wondered when word would reach him of Danby's demise. At first he thought of leaving a message at his hotel but, on reflection, realised it might be prudent for events to take their natural course.

Instead he picked up the phone to contact his associates in Mittelwald and the others in Füssen, Vils and Markneukirchen.

They approached the villa on the outskirts of Cremona with caution. Jozsef led them through the trees, coming to a halt in the undergrowth a short distance from the back door.

139

'Why must we always play this game?' said Heinz in his deep growl of a voice.

Jozsef waved his arm to ensure silence.

Franz turned to the bear of a man beside him and shrugged his shoulders. He, for one, was not going to go against their leader's wishes.

'We wait,' whispered Jozsef, 'until I say it's clear. Always check. Always have an alternative escape route. And, above all, keep silent!'

He glared at Heinz in the failing light. They stood in the bushes for a further ten minutes.

'Right, Heinz, you open the door.' He gave him the key. 'When you do so, turn on the kitchen light. But don't go in. I repeat, do not enter! Franz and I will check the windows for any signs of movement.'

'What a waste of time. Good drinking time, as well,' muttered Heinz in exasperation as he moved towards the door.

Suddenly, the lights blazed on. The other two skipped towards the windows, quickly checking that all was clear. Predictably, no one had been near the house. Heinz was already at the refrigerator when they joined him in the kitchen.

'Beer, Franz?' he called to his diminutive companion, and tossed a can in his direction.

In one stride Jozsef had caught it and hurled it back with force, hitting the big man on the cheek. For a moment he was dazed. Then he turned, eyes blazing with fury, and bent his knees ready to launch himself in retaliation. But the anger drained from his features. He rose to full height and stood still. Jozsef had adopted the characteristic pose of the professional, his Walther automatic firmly clenched in both hands and pointing at the other man. He spoke quietly, but they could hear every word.

'When I give an order, it is meant to be obeyed. Without question, without the slightest hint of protest! If you do not say now that you will obey me, whatever order I give, I will shoot you on the spot. What is it to be?'

To emphasise his words he released the safety catch and marginally increased the pressure on the trigger. Heinz saw the whitening of his knuckles. Seconds passed in silence. Then Heinz bowed his head. 'OK! OK! You're the boss. I'll do what you say.'

The gun stayed trained on him for a long moment. Then Jozsef slowly pointed the weapon towards the ground and flicked on the safety catch.

'Do not forget that, Heinz. I shall be ever-watchful.'

He walked from the room.

'One of these days, someone will get that bastard,' muttered Heinz.

Chapter Thirty-One

At first he could hear voices. They were distant and echoing. He tried to shut them out. He hoped the noise would go away so he could lapse again into unconsciousness. But someone was persistent. The tone was shrill and demanding.

'*Fra' Danby! Fra' Danby! Svegliarsi!*'

I don't want to wake up, he thought. I'm tired. Just leave me alone.

Then his heart lurched and his memory suddenly returned. His eyes opened wide with shock to focus slowly on the figure standing at his side. She was holding his hand and smiling.

'Good! You are back with us. Not for the first time we thought we had lost you.'

Someone behind her was tidying a trolley carrying equipment and wires connected to round cup-like handles. Marcus stared around. There were other people hesitantly making their way towards the door, as though, at any moment, they might be called back to minister to him.

'It's OK, Marcello, Anna! I don't think we shall need to call on you again!'

She looked down at Marcus. 'I can tell by your eyes that you are going to be all right. And I am never wrong. Well . . . almost never!'

He was in hospital, lying on a bed covered by a thin sheet.

The nurse moved to a side table to pour water from a carafe into a glass. With her back to him she asked, 'Can you remember what happened, Brother Danby? How you sustained those injuries?'

Until that moment Marcus had not appreciated he had suffered injury. Panic seized him. Am I in a bad way? Will I be able to walk, move my arms, neck, or head? Will I be a permanent invalid? The questions crowded in. He gasped, afraid to test any part of his body. Stretched out, he lay rigid with fear, his heartbeat erratic, out of control.

The nurse took her time. She walked back to the bedside and tried to raise his head.

'Relax, brother, for goodness' sake! You have suffered severe bruising to your back and thighs, presumably when you hit shutters before toppling into the rio. But you have no broken bones. The main concern was that you almost drowned. You were not breathing when they brought you in, and your heart had stopped beating. But we managed to revive you,' she added cheerfully.

To Marcus, it sounded serious. However, gradually the tension eased and the nurse, cradling his neck, lifted his head sufficiently for him to drink. Only then did Marcus realise how thirsty he was; he gulped down the remainder.

'Where am I?' he croaked, his voice sounding strained and unnatural.

'You are in the hospital of the Fatebene-Fratelli! You were brought here in a water ambulance with the porter who saved you. Fortunately, you went in the water only several hundred metres away. Any greater distance and I doubt you would have made it.'

When she had left he took note of his surroundings. He lay in a small, neat room, the drawn window blinds obscuring the light and casting much around him in shadow. Being thrown bodily from the balcony, that much he remembered. The nurse had said he had fallen into a narrow canal. Presumably, his attackers had not been aware that his hotel room overlooked the Rio San Girolamo. No doubt expecting his body to be dashed on the unyielding surfaces of the piazza.

Comforted by the nurse's comment that he had not sustained irreparable damage, Marcus began making his own assessment. First moving his arms, then bending and twisting his elbows, wrists, and fingers. However, when he moved his legs he gasped as sharp, shooting pains travelled through his lower back. He lay there breathing deeply until they subsided.

'I can't seem to move my legs, nurse,' he said anxiously when she came back into his room.

'I don't suppose you can, brother. As I said, when you fell you suffered intensive bruising from crashing into obstacles before hitting the water. The doctors did a thorough check on you while you were unconscious. Though nothing is broken, it does mean you will not be able to move freely for a while.'

Left alone, Marcus relived the savage attack. They must have been lying in wait for some time. He could recall the main light not working, and edging towards the bedside as his eyes slowly adjusted to the dark. He sensed, rather than heard, his attackers. They must have been standing either side of the door. Each had taken an arm and quietly, efficiently, hurled him through the open, full-length windows. The most frightening part was that the attack had been carried out in complete silence. His mouth went dry at the remembrance.

He eased himself down the bed, gasping at the pains in his lower body. Pulling up the sheet, he closed his eyes and recalled what had taken place earlier. The image, still vivid, of Lisa's soft auburn hair enveloping him as she moved above him.

Suddenly, the sound of raised voices reached his ears. They got louder and were accompanied by the sharp clack of high heels on the tiled corridor floor. He grimaced, not from pain, but with the thought of how he must dissuade her from staying by his side. The door burst open.

'Do you know they actually tried to stop me coming in to see you!'

Lisa rushed to the bed, and put out her arms. Then, seeing his unsmiling face, she hesitated. Hers was crushed with concern.

'Are you alright, Marcus? God! I didn't know until this morning! I went down to breakfast and someone told me you had been rushed to hospital.'

She bit at her lip.

'What happened? How did you get like this? Did you have too much wine?'

Should he tell her the truth, that he had been thrown from his balcony? Frighten her, then leave her without protection.

'I think perhaps I did, Lisa.'

'Do you remember anything of last night?'

'At the moment my mind is blank. I can recall us having dinner . . . then waking up in here.'

'Nothing at all?'

'No! Why?'

Once more, she chewed her lip.

'Are you sure?'

'Lisa, I've been concussed. My injuries are killing me!'

Her face changed again.

'Jeez! I'm sorry. Are you badly hurt?'

'I was fortunate, so I'm told. I fell into the canal. I must have opened the window for some fresh air and toppled over the railing.' He averted his face from Lisa's scrutiny. 'Anyway, I haven't broken anything, but my legs and back are severely bruised.'

'Thank God for that! Is there anything I can do for you?' she enquired, unconsciously wringing her hands.

'It seems I'll be in here for a few days. Would you mind bringing in my computer and tape recorder? When I've recovered a little more I can at least do some reading and put my notes in order.'

'I'll bring them in this evening.'

With that she picked up his hand and squeezed it fondly, then blushed.

'You don't recollect anything about last night?'

Marcus felt guilty. The time he had spent with Lisa had been sublime. It seemed she had thought so, too. But now he was desperately concerned for her well-being. If she stayed by him she would be in appalling danger. And, clearly, the Messenger would be of little help, judging by his efforts to date. He must get her away as soon as possible. Aware of Lisa's tenacity if he told her the truth, he decided the only certain way was to discount any awareness of what had taken place between them, deny any feelings for her, and demonstrate his steadfastness to the Church.

'Why should I? We had a pleasant meal together, and then I wind up in a hospital bed! As far as I'm concerned, everything about last night is best forgotten!'

With the last of these words, he stared directly into her face.

It was a while before she spoke.

'I'll . . . I'll bring in the items later.'

Lisa closed the door behind her. This time the receding beat of her shoes in the corridor was slow and uneven.

He had been ready for him when the Messenger had slipped unheralded into the room. On this occasion, probably because his normal appearance would have been thought sinister, and certainly unwelcome, he was dressed in a plain dark suit.

For the first time Marcus was able to take a close look at him. In his late forties, he stood almost two metres in his black shoes. His angular face was clean-shaven, and tanned, displaying a conventional mouth, straight nose and bright, alert, brown eyes. His hair was cut neatly and swept back, without a parting, off the brow. Other than his height, one would have been hard-pressed to pick out a single, outstanding feature. He stood with his back to the window.

'Where were you when I needed you?' said Marcus angrily. 'I was almost killed last night! This is the second time it has happened. What were you doing?'

'Signor Danby, I made it quite clear that your assignment might be obstructed. Perhaps even I did not realise how resolute they might be in hindering your progress.'

'Hinder my progress! Whoever it was tried to *kill* me! You were going to protect me. Remember?'

The Messenger nodded. 'You will recall I said I would do my best.'

'Well, your best wasn't good enough, was it? Supposing they had succeeded. Who would you get to do your work then, eh?'

The tall figure sank into a nearby chair.

'Since we last met I have received some disturbing news.' He looked across at Marcus. 'I think it's important I explain something to you, Signor Danby. It would appear this is not the first time this project has been undertaken. There have been four previous occasions when people, such as yourself, have conducted similar missions.' He sat silent for some moments. 'I have to tell you two have died performing the task. Another simply disappeared.'

Marcus was deflated. He lay back on the bed and closed his eyes.

After a lengthy interval in which neither man uttered a word, he broke the silence.

'Mrs Robards doesn't know yet how dangerous it has become. It's more than stealing computers, isn't it? She could be seriously hurt.' He was becoming agitated. 'I don't want Mrs Robards harmed in any way. I must persuade her to leave me, abandon this mission . . . leave Italy. When she comes tonight I'll do my damnedest to make sure she goes home to Chicago.'

'And you?'

146

'If you can guarantee round-the-clock protection, I want to complete the project.'

She couldn't understand why. There was an even greater gulf between them that night. Lisa had brought in his computer and recorder, and thought to bring in the notebooks and mobile telephone. But he had appeared pre-occupied and distant. She had bustled around, plumping his pillows, making small talk, asking if he wanted anything further. Marcus had been non-committal.

Exasperated, convinced that he had remembered every detail of the previous night, Lisa experienced a sensation she had not encountered in years. She was close to tears. She had enjoyed men's company and been gratified in moments of intimacy, but any dalliance had been fleeting, and she had remained unaffected emotionally by such pleasurable encounters.

She was unsettled by this man – this self-possessed cleric, who had spent the night with her. His calling would not be lightly cast aside for a few hours of passion, yet he seemed determined to erase it from his mind, as if refusing to acknowledge it would mean it had not happened.

'Lisa,' he began, hesitantly. 'Lisa, I've been thinking. You probably have enough material for your article. I can't think there is much more you can add . . .'

He is trying to get rid of me, she thought.

'Yes. There are just one or two items I need to research. In particular, the women who were listed in the Stati dell'Anime for the Stradivari household. The majority came from the same family. They originated in Mantua. I must go there.'

'Well, after that, I think it would be for the best if you went back to Chicago. Take the car. I can't drive. I'll make my way back to Cremona by train.'

Abruptly, she swept up her things and walked towards the door. There were tears in her eyes, but she was not going to let him see them.

'Goodbye, Marcus,' she said in a small voice.

*

147

'She is going back to the States?'

'I believe that's for the best. She will be safe there.'

Marcus looked down at the computer screen. He had been working when the door had opened to admit the Messenger. For a moment his heart had lurched, thinking Lisa had returned.

'She is driving to Mantua to fill in some missing details for her article. Then she will be flying home.'

The Messenger sat in a side chair.

'So, Signor Danby, where are we going next?'

'I've been out of bed,' replied Marcus. 'I'm hellishly stiff and uncomfortable, and I can't drive. But I need to get back to Cremona. All the masters lived around the piazza fronting the Church of San Domenico. According to a reference I've found, all their records were stored in the crypt. Apparently, there was not enough room in their workshops; the conditions were better anyway. They were moved when the church was demolished in 1869. I want to find out where they are now.'

'How will that help?'

'I'm interested in their old purchasing orders and invoices. I want to find out more about their suppliers.'

What Marcus did not add was that he had been reading through his files stored on the computer and the jottings in his notebooks. After Lisa had gone the evening before, he had needed to occupy his mind. Looking back over the ten days he had been in her company he now realised how much he missed her presence. She was forthright, whilst he was diffident. Her temperament was mercurial, he was even-tempered – except, perhaps, when he had been drinking. Not that he had thought much about alcohol since meeting her, although it had been partly responsible for what had taken place the other evening.

'I said, how soon can you leave?' asked the Messenger.

'Sorry! I was thinking of something else. What about this afternoon? With a little help I could make it down the stairs.'

'Signor Danby, we should take precautions. If they believe you are alive, your attackers could be watching the hospital. We shall leave this evening, when it's dark. It would also be easier to slip away without the staff being aware of your departure.'

'No. Let us go this afternoon. I want to get back as soon as possible.'

Suddenly, the need to see Lisa was overwhelming. Even if she were married, even if she were unattainable, he did not want her to go without knowing how much she meant to him.

'That is not wise, Signor Danby. We should not jeopardise our safety for a matter of a few hours. No, be ready when I come to your room at eight this evening. I shall have clothes for you, and a water taxi waiting at the entrance to the Rio dei Zecchini. It will take us across to the mainland.'

Chapter Thirty-Two

Lisa pulled into the space and switched off the engine. She had found a parking spot in the Piazza Anconetta, only five hundred metres from the Historical Archives Centre. En route to Mantua she had phoned Emilio Puigi and he had advised her of the likely source.

'If they can't help, you could also try the State Archives in the Via Ardigó.'

She had been fortunate. An hour later she was immersed in the family records of the early eighteenth century. The trouble was her mind kept wandering. As she drove from Venice, every kilometre marker had impressed upon her the increasing distance between herself and Marcus. But there was no going back. There was no point. Better to cut her losses now, forget he existed, get on with her life. But what life? She was leaving behind a man wrapped up in his vocation. He had been too many years in an ordered, almost monastic, existence. He wouldn't, couldn't, shake free from that. In any case, he had made it plain they should go their separate ways. No doubt, he would return to England, immerse himself in his studies, make instruments for his friend, Geri. There would be no room for her in his life.

She found the name, Camilli, and the three sisters – Maria, Robina and Lucia – missing from the household over a seven year period, ostensibly enjoying extended visits to Cremona, in reality working in the maestro's studio. They reappeared in the census records for Mantua in 1738. Lisa also traced their marriages, noting that all died in their thirties, without bearing children.

Having obtained copies of the documents, she left the Archives Office and returned to the car. On the outskirts of Cremona she stopped briefly for petrol and a coffee and made two phone calls, the first, and most pressing, to Alitalia to book a direct flight to Chicago.

'The lady is back in Cremona. I have discovered she has booked a flight to the States on Friday. Two days' time.'

'Good! Make sure she is on it.'

'Nothing else? We take no further action?'

'No, it's not necessary to impede her exit.'

'From what I have seen, she appears upset and distracted.'

'To be expected, surely?'

'Well, her making the reservation confirms all went according to plan in Venice.'

'I would have expected nothing less. Just make sure you see her go into the departure lounge, then wait until her flight takes off. After that, the three of you make your way back here. Is that understood?'

He sat back in his chair. Another crisis averted. His brother would never know the support he was providing – nor should he. Like Caesar's wife, he must be above suspicion. He thought of the many times he had come to Vincent's unknowing aid. When they were children in Innsbruck, Martin Goehr had always protected his younger brother, from schoolboy fights and scrapes, to being caught up in the price riots in Munich in the 1950s. When Vincent had been herded like so many other young radicals into a pen, it was Martin, in close pursuit, who had used wire cutters to free him. Then, there was the period when Vincent had gone to the university in Stuttgart and become an acolyte of 'Joshka' Fischer. From vehement socialist to revolutionary Marxist, then to the Green Party's most flamboyant politician – at each turn Fischer had found an ardent disciple in Vincent. The younger Goehr was always at his side in the politico's early wayward years. Each time Martin had been in the background to extricate his brother when difficulties arose. Vincent Goehr was never truly aware what Martin had done for him.

Now, like Fischer, he had experienced a change of social and spiritual direction. Opting for the Church, he had made his way unerringly to the top, to the Vatican itself, and was now on the

151

threshold of absolute power. Yet, Martin recognized, his sibling was still an innocent, detached from reality, from the strife and turmoil that was an essential part of life. He processed with his bishops and priests – as he had done throughout his days with gangs of radical youths – bent on putting the world to rights, but with no true appreciation of the chaos it could bring. Even now, Martin was his shadow, carefully orchestrating his path, brushing aside unwelcome problems, ensuring that he would lead an untroubled existence. The irony was that not for a minute did Vincent doubt he had attained his position by his own merit and application.

Martin smiled wearily to himself. One day he would stop being his 'brother's keeper' and concentrate on the company, try to emulate the success of his father and his forebears. He had been brought up an Austrian living in Innsbruck, as had all the earlier generations of the Goehr family. Even when his ancestors, encouraged first by the Emperor Charles VI, then the Empress Maria Theresa three centuries ago, had moved their workshops to the border town of Mittenwald, they had retained the home in Innsbruck.

In those days, Mittenwald, straddling the border between the mighty Austrian Empire and the tiny German province of Werdensfels, was much in the administrative thrall of its larger neighbour. Here, in this small community, they had joined with the celebrated instrument makers, Matthias and Sebastian Klotz, and with others, to establish the centre for Tyrolean instrument makers. In later years it had become known as 'The Village of a Thousand Violins'.

Nowadays, Martin Goehr chose to spend the working week close to the factory site, living several kilometres away on the outskirts of Klais. Trade was not so easy; the influx of cheaper instruments from Asia affected European markets. Now that Vincent was once again secure he would have to dedicate far more time to ensuring the continued profitability of the family business.

He had been sitting in his Ferrari for almost an hour. Earlier he had managed to wheedle her address from one of the other receptionists, and from that it had been a simple matter to obtain her phone number. But each time he had rung he had got the answerphone. In exasperation, Lambertini had taken up station outside the block of apartments where she lived.

Now he was getting anxious. Supposing Angelina Scacchi had gone away for a long weekend – gone on holiday with a boyfriend, gone to stay with her parents, gone without leaving word . . . only to return on Monday morning and head straight into work at the Town Hall. It could jeopardise the Plan – or so the cardinal had said. But how could it? Too many people knew about the cleverly-planted rumour; anyone of them could leak it to the press.

Then another thought struck him: he did not know who else was in the cardinal's employ. Those, like himself, who had been inveigled to take part in the scheme – for their greater good – would, doubtless, whoever they were, report any deviation or irresponsible act. Loose talk by Angelina would soon be noted and conveyed to Marchetti, the spider in the centre of the web.

No, he had to deal with the problem, and quickly.

Parked in such a nondescript area, his Ferrari was drawing attention. Reluctantly, he started the engine, vowing to return later.

Chapter Thirty-Three

Marcus lay along the seat of the water taxi, his back and legs complaining vigorously each time the boat hit the swell in the lagoon. Opposite him sat the Messenger.

After lunch the nurse attending him had opened the door to his room and enquired if he were well enough to receive a visitor. Before he could reply, a dark-suited man had pushed past her and walked to his bedside.

'*Buon' giorno, Fra' Danby,*' he had said in a guttural tone. 'My name is Marconi ... Paolo Marconi. I am the police officer investigating the incident the other night. Are you able to give me your version of what happened?'

He had taken out a notebook and pulled the chair close to the bed. Half an hour later he had risen to his feet.

'Thank you. That seems to tally with other reports. I shall have a word with the hotel – the balcony rails might be a danger to others, if they have had a few too many drinks.'

With that, he had nodded and left the room.

Marcus had pondered on the conversation. The officer had confirmed that a night porter, passing one of the rear windows, had seen Marcus fall. Instinctively, he had thrown open the window and jumped into the canal to save him. He regretted that he would be leaving before he could adequately thank him. However, Marcus consoled himself with the thought that if the earlier telephone conversation he had had with Signor Tomasina, and the points raised during the brief visit of Alfredo Granadigli were to be resolved, he would soon be returning.

In Mestre, he had sat uncomfortably on a bench while the Messenger collected his car. Ten minutes later they picked up the Autostrada skirting Padua and headed west.

Little was said, the Messenger being content to drive in silence.

Canting back the passenger seat eased the pressure on his back and allowed Marcus to relax. He closed his eyes, but knew sleep would elude him. He was too fretful, restless to catch up with Lisa. Earlier that day he had tried to reach her on her mobile but without success. The thought flashed through his mind that she might already have caught a flight and be on her way home. Common sense intervened, reminding Marcus that it would take time for her to drive back to Cremona, make the reservation and pack her cases – though she might conceivably have arranged an early morning departure. He stopped himself from urging the Messenger to go faster.

His thoughts turned to what he might say when he saw her. 'Don't go!', 'I need you here!', 'I love you!'. The last surprised him. Did he love her, or was it merely infatuation? It had been a long time since he had been in bed with a woman. The intimacy he and Lisa had shared had been heady, but Marcus was sure it was more than physical attraction – certainly on his part. He realised how much he had come to enjoy her company, her humour, her high-spirited reactions. Marcus *knew* he did not want to lose her.

As they neared Cremona, Marcus broke the silence.

'I want you to drop me at the Ibis Hotel.'

'That's where Signora Robards is staying. I thought you had finished with her – or was I mistaken?'

The Messenger glanced sideways at Marcus.

'So did I. Now, I'm not so sure. Anyway, I do not want to part with her thinking badly of me. I need to speak to her again.'

The Messenger shrugged. 'You know the situation, Signor Danby. Please do not make it hard for yourself, or dangerous for her.'

At the hotel, it took several minutes for Marcus to extricate himself from the passenger seat. He was helped into the foyer. On the point of leaving the Messenger muttered darkly, 'I hope that you will not be persuaded to go with her, Signor Danby. If that were to happen you might not make it to the airport!'

However, Lisa was not there. In fact, the receptionist, recognising him from previous occasions, declared she had not yet returned from a brief trip. 'But she left Venice this morning. She was stopping briefly in Mantua, but it wouldn't take that long. Could you please phone her room for me?'

There was no reply to the receptionist's call.

'I'm sorry, sir!'

With a detached smile she turned to attend to someone else.

He wandered towards the entrance, trying to think where she might be. Had Lisa been abducted? Had they succeeded with her, having botched the attempt to do away with him? The painkillers the hospital had prescribed made his head feel as though it were stuffed with cotton wool. Rational thought eluded him. Outside he hailed a taxi to take him to the pensione.

It had taken considerable willpower and time to climb the stairs. Now, lying on the bed, Marcus ignored the pain in his back and legs. If this were the price for a clear mind, so be it.

Lisa would surely have gone straight to the hotel, packed, made a reservation, called home, spoken to her editor. Unless . . . she had stayed overnight in Mantua. She had found the information she wanted about the women staying at the home of Stradivari, but too late to drive on to Cremona. Yes, that was it! First thing in the morning she would be back at her hotel.

He picked up his mobile and phoned the reception desk at the Ibis. Introducing himself to the young woman to whom he had spoken earlier, he asked that immediately Mrs Robards arrived she be told it was vital that she speak with Marcus Danby.

'Do you understand? It is very important.'

He lay back on the bed, trying to relax. But it was nigh on impossible. Now his thoughts were on all the other possibilities that might have befallen Lisa.

Could she have broken down? They hadn't passed a car on the hard shoulder of the Autostrada. Perhaps it had happened elsewhere and she was stranded. Again the irrational thought crept in that they, whoever they were, may have killed or kidnapped Lisa by way of reprisal. Marcus shook his head. No! No! They were only after him. If the aim was to silence both of them, they would have gone to her room last night and thrown her from the balcony as well.

Could she have visited a friend? He glanced down at his watch. It was close to one o'clock in the morning. Too late to phone anyone, and whom would he contact anyway? She probably had so many friends and acquaintances in the town he wouldn't know where to begin.

A second thought: he could try the Puigis – or Signor Marciano, the bookseller. He had the Puigis' home number somewhere, and the shop number would be on a receipt. But what if they had caught her on the way back to Cremona, and she was now lying in some out-of-the-way spot, never to be found?

Eventually, at five o'clock he fell into a fitful doze.

The shrill ring of the phone brought him back to reality.

'*Pronto!* Lisa?' he shouted into the receiver.

'Good morning, Signor Danby. I trust you slept well.'

It was the Messenger.

'For your sake, I am glad to note that you are still here.'

'She was not at her hotel last night. What are you going to do about it?' snapped Marcus. 'I'm worried, and you ask if I slept well. Of course I didn't sleep well.'

There was a studied silence. Then the line disconnected. Five minutes later it rang again.

'You are right. She was not there last night. Mrs Robards did not return. I'll contact you later.'

Again he was left holding the phone, the dialling tone buzzing in his ear.

At eight o'clock he phoned the number for Marta and Emilio Puigi. He let it ring until the automatic messaging system interrupted, then replaced the receiver.

A few minutes after nine he phoned Signor Marciano, who was immediately welcoming. But Marcus interrupted his good-natured effusiveness by asking if he had seen Lisa within the past twelve hours. The concern in his voice conveyed itself to the elderly bookshop owner, who became anxious, and the conversation ended with Marcus attempting to calm him, declaring that Lisa had probably forgotten to keep in touch, nothing more. As soon as she did so he would let Roberto Marciano know.

It was then he remembered that Emilio Puigi worked at the University of Pavia, but his department, Musical Paleology and Philology was located in Cremona. Luckily, there was a local telephone directory in the bedside cupboard. He found the number and was put through to the department.

'*Signor Puigi, per favore?*'

'*No, penso che ci sia! Momento, per favore.*'

Whoever had answered didn't think he was there. Marcus waited impatiently.

'*Sì?*'

'Signor Puigi?'

'Yes!'

The gods be praised.

'It's Marcus Danby. Tell me, have you seen Lisa?'

'Hello, Marcus. Yes, she stayed with us last night. Why?'

'Emilio, I desperately need to see her. It's vital! Is she all right?'

'Well, she seemed upset when she arrived. She spent a lot of time with Marta. This morning Marta took her into town. She wanted to visit the Music Academy where she was a student, before flying home.'

'Where is the Academy?' fretted Marcus.

'Why it's here, Marcus.'

He was almost beside himself.

'OK, Emilio – where is here?'

'In the Corso Garibaldi. Paleology amd Philology is located with the Violinmaking School in the Palazzo Raimondi. The Academy is next door.'

'Thank you.'

Marcus shuffled out the room and down the two flights of stairs. It was only eight hundred metres away, but beyond him physically. Fortunately, he was able to hail a taxi, though the driver was disgruntled at having a fare for such a short distance.

Inside the building there was no one to ask about former pupils, but Marcus did not even stop to ponder if she were there. He had to find her.

Past a grand staircase, through swing doors, he hobbled along a wide corridor. The first door on the left he threw open and surveyed the room. A small group was clustered around a piano; the pianist, no doubt the tutor, looked up as Marcus surveyed the room.

'*Mi dispiace!*'

Marcus shut the door. He opened the next more cautiously. It was empty – just music stands and chairs casually forsaken.

He lurched on down the corridor. He could hear voices; the sound of violins further on. Again he turned a door handle and peered round. Several heads twisted but the teacher was unmoved. Not wishing to interrupt, he quickly shut the door. The next two rooms were devoid of occupants.

Marcus retraced his steps to the entrance hall and began a slow climb up the stairs. Perhaps she had already been to the Academy and left. She could be at the hotel, or even now on her way to the airport.

Reaching the next floor, he stumbled into the corridor and entered the first room. It was spacious, folding doors opening onto another salon. He stood there among stands and chairs recently occupied, music sheets were still open and instruments lay abandoned on the seats.

Through the gap Marcus could see a group of young musicians and teachers at the far end. They were clustered around someone playing the cello. It was a slow, melancholy piece. Whoever was playing this Mozart adagio had an easy mastery of the difficult passages. One of the group shifted – no more than from one leg to the other; someone else moved their head; and there was Lisa, seated on a chair, deep in concentration, playing with immense feeling.

His heart leapt and his eyes closed in silent thanksgiving. He wanted to rush forward, ignoring everyone, and gather her in his arms. Instead, he walked over to a chair and picked up a violin. The awareness and feel of the instrument as he placed his chin on the rest sent a shiver down his spine. He picked up the bow and, returning to the opening between the full-length doors, waited for the passage to end.

The students applauded. One of the teachers came forward to speak with Lisa. It was at that moment that Marcus, edging his way into the next salon, commenced the opening movement of the Divertimento.

Lisa's head snapped up. Her audience turned to the new player. To Marcus' ears his playing was ragged, his fingering clumsy. Not surprising after so many years. But an inner compulsion drove him on.

Then the mellow, richer sounds of the cello married with the violin until both were singing in parallel sixths. The voices alternated, creating constant variations in texture, combining with the most intense counterpoint.

The movement ended. The room erupted.

Oblivious of the applause, or the people, he fastened his gaze on Lisa and walked slowly towards her. She was transfixed to her chair, her eyes damp with unshed tears. Marcus lifted her to her feet.

'I remembered every wondrous moment, Lisa. I don't want it to end.'

Chapter Thirty-Four

He had almost given up. For the past two days he had patrolled the area, often spending long hours gazing up at her apartment windows. There had been no sign of her and he had eventually come to the unwelcome conclusion she would not be returning during the weekend.

He had left the car at home – it was far too conspicuous, especially parked for long periods in a side street with someone sitting at the wheel. Having arrived, he went about on foot, occasionally entering a nearby bar for refreshment or to use the men's room.

Now it was almost eight o'clock on a Sunday evening. Standing in a shop doorway, on the point of calling it a day, Lambertini was pivoting on his heel when a flash of light caught his eye. He stared up intently, trying to glimpse the occupant. Yes, he was sure – at long last, Angelina Scacchi had come home.

Michelo Lambertini waited another ten minutes, then crossed the road to the apartment block.

The table was set for two the meal was to be both private and inquisitorial, he realised. He had not appreciated that possibility when accepting the invitation, which had come in the form of a phone call intimating most strongly that it would be in everyone's interest to have 'a little get-together'.

'Your Eminence, take a seat, please. I thought that it might be prudent if you and I ate alone so that we can discuss the current problem.'

'I am not conscious of any problem, Mr Mayor.'

The mayor nodded affably, though his lips narrowed. They were served the first course, and a white wine was poured. The doors closed.

'We shall not be interrupted until I ring, so what I have to say will not be overheard.'

The mayor picked up his glass and gazed reflectively at the contents.

'I wish to consult with you about the rumour that the Holy See is contemplating a move from Rome.' He looked up and stared directly at Cardinal Marchetti. 'From time to time, there have been ill-informed comments about the differences between this city's administration and the Vatican. They pop up now and then, and just as soon disappear. But this present item of gossip shows little sign of fading. If anything, it is growing stronger. It is still confined to those who would see no merit in broadcasting such a tale, But I am anxious to bring it to a halt before it reaches the press. Were it to do so, it could be damaging for both parties. It would certainly hinder our relationship.'

The implication was obvious: the Vatican was responsible for the rumour; it must do something about it.

'Mr Mayor, are you suggesting that we had a hand in promulgating such an entertaining notion? I'm surprised. No one in the Vatican has such a sense of humour!' Marchetti took up his glass.

'Are you aware, Your Eminence, that the heads of all the key departments – those occupied in the running of the capital, involved in maintaining its attraction to tourists – ' he caught Marchetti's eye. ' . . . and those publicising the splendours of the Vatican – know of it?'

He paused before continuing.

'The point I'm making is this: the message has not changed. Inevitably, a fanciful tale becomes distorted, often to the point where it bears no relation to the original. This time the rumour has been constant. That I find disturbing.'

'The Secretary of State told me of your comment to him, Mr Mayor,' remarked the cardinal. 'I told him the very same thing. Invariably, hearsay mutates like a virus. I'm amazed it has not done so. But the question is what do you want me to do about it?'

'Before I answer that, Your Eminence, let us rid ourselves of these plates.'

The bell was rung. Doors opened, two waiters entered, and the

161

remains of the first course were cleared away. Soon after, they were served the main course with a choice of wines.

'Knowing your enthusiasm for a good Barbaresco, Angelo, I think you will enjoy this.' The mayor swirled his glass and tasted its contents. He nodded in approval. 'Yes, I'm sure it will be to your liking.'

The cardinal made appreciative noises and both diners concentrated on the food before them. The mayor was first to break the silence.

'You asked me what you can do about it,' he said, wiping his mouth on his napkin. He looked directly into the eyes of the cleric. 'I am convinced the rumour started inside the walls. Don't get me wrong – it may have been an inadvertent remark, a throw-away comment about some petty difference of opinion between us. But the fact is it has percolated to the outside – or to outsiders. It may be that someone overheard the comment and is now bent on provoking strife between us. Could it have happened that way, do you think?'

The cardinal appeared to be considering the suggestion. He picked up the glass.

'You are right. This is most enjoyable.' He met the mayor's searching gaze. 'That is entirely possible, Luigi. Who can say? However, I am intrigued that you are so certain the rumour emanated from within our city. If you are right, I repeat: what do you want me to do?'

'Angelo, we have known each other a long time. I am aware you cannot talk about matters relating to the Holy See, or about its inmates, but I want you to promise me you will search out the source and discover how it got out. I want to know who is airing this vicious rumour, and why.'

The mayor stood, retrieved the wine bottle, and refilled the cardinal's glass.

'I am convinced, Angelo, that there is more to this than an ill-intentioned prank. There is some deeper motive, and I mean to find out – with, I hope, your help.'

'If you are right, Luigi, what possible reason could anyone in the Pontifical Family have for creating dissension?'

'Forgive me, Angelo, but in the breeding ground of the Borgias, anything is possible!'

162

'I have a feeling I should take exception to that remark!' smiled the cardinal silkily.

'Let me put it to you another way, Angelo.' The mayor resumed his seat. 'You know well the minds of those most likely to foment discontent between us. Can you think of any reason why they would wish to do such a thing? What can they hope to gain? More significantly, what would the Vatican stand to achieve?' He watched the prelate intently, then added, 'It wouldn't be for themselves – or even for himself, if it is a single person behind it all.'

'The Messenger is here, Your Eminence.'

The cardinal was at a side table pouring himself coffee. The tall presence was ushered into the inner sanctum by Brother Felipé, who withdrew, leaving the merest crack in the door. The cardinal smiled inwardly and shook his head.

'Before you begin, kindly shut the door – firmly.'

The Messenger pushed it to with a satisfying click.

'Good! Come, stand by me. What is the latest news?'

Tonelessly, the Messenger relayed all that had happened during the past three days. The stakes had been raised. Danby had been attacked, with the clear intention of killing him. Fortunately, he had survived and had been persuaded to carry on, but only in the certain knowledge that he would be fully protected. Mrs Lisa Robards was preparing to return to the United States. That, at least, would ease the situation.

'What about this man, Bellman? Is he also a possible target?

'I don't believe so, Your Eminence. He has had only the briefest contact with Danby and his activities have not drawn attention.'

'Why we got involved with him I fail to understand. I expressly forbade this research being made known to all and sundry.'

'Because, Your Eminence, it would have been impossible for one man to complete the task in the time you set.'

Cardinal Marchetti grunted disconsolately, not a little surprised that the Messenger had seen fit to respond in such a manner.

'So when will Danby be able to resume his work?'

'Probably tomorrow, Your Eminence.'

'Good. Well, you'd best return so that you can be close to him.'

'Of course – though as I promised him complete protection I

shall need more people, Your Eminence. That was the additional purpose of my request for an audience.'

'We have no-one to spare – no-one whom I wish to be involved. I have emphasised the need for secrecy; that has meant telling only those who *need* to know of our activities. I'm sorry . . . Danby will have to rely solely on you.'

'The Messenger has returned, Your Eminence!'

The Franciscan stood aside to admit a man, in his forties, soberly dressed, his mien cultivated to draw the minimum of attention.

'Good! What have you got for me?'

A sealed envelope was passed to the cardinal, who opened it with a silver paper-knife and read the contents carefully.

'Thank you. That will be all.'

The Messenger withdrew, softly closing the double doors.

Cardinal Grossmann sat in quiet contemplation. He had suspected something was wrong when Goehr had requested a Messenger be sent to him immediately. It had to be of considerable import, something that could not be transmitted by any other means.

The letter was brief. No signature – none was needed. No formal address, just a bald statement:

Despite our efforts, the target, though damaged, has re-appeared. I was led to believe the issue had been satisfactorily resolved. Unfortunately, it was premature. My apologies for misleading you.

Naturally, I shall attend to the matter. However, it would also be appropriate if, within your domain, you can devise a means of wrecking Marchetti's grand scheme. That would also ensure the Cremonese mission is brought to a halt.

Please keep me advised.

Chapter Thirty-Five

'You bastard! You should have told me. You made me cry in front of the whole school.'

Marcus was contrite, but quietly elated. I don't care, he thought. She is holding my arm tightly. That's all that matters.

My face is a mess! Give me a few moments,' Lisa said. She strode off towards the ladies' room, calling over her shoulder, 'And don't move a muscle until I'm back.'

When the door closed behind her, a predictable wave of guilt engulfed him. Not only have I forsaken my vocation, he thought I am delighting in the company of a married woman. More than that, I want her physically! What has happened to me in these past two weeks?

Several minutes later she rejoined him, once more taking his arm.

'Let's find somewhere to have lunch, Lisa. There are a number of things I want to tell you.'

They walked south towards the Via Albertoni and the trattoria of the Brughieris. It was early, there were few diners, and it was Signor Brughieri himself who led them to a table at the back of the restaurant. Marcus noticed he wore a puzzled expression, particularly when they were seated and Lisa covered his hand with hers. He thinks I'm still a cleric, Marcus realised.

'*Si Padre, desidera vedere il menu?*'

'Yes, please.'

He began hesitantly. 'Lisa, I don't want you to go home, but for your own safety I think it would be for the best.'

Her face clouded. 'So you still want to get rid of me.'

'Before you jump to conclusions, let me explain. I was not drunk the other night.' He squeezed her hand. 'At least, not intoxicated

165

by alcohol. When I went back to my room in the early hours, two men jumped me and threw me out of the window.'

Lisa's face crumpled. 'My God!'

'I was concerned for your safety. I wanted you out of harm's way. If you were back in Chicago, you'd be safe.'

'You should have told me. I might have flown home thinking I'd made a big mistake. I could have regretted it all my life!'

Her voice had risen. Fortunately, no one was in earshot, except the waiter who had served them that first day. He began to wring his hands, his eyes searching for Signor Brughieri. Marcus observed his disquiet.

'It's alright. We are really good friends!'

He leaned across the table.

'Shsssh! Keep your voice down. You're disturbing people.'

Her voice went an octave higher.

'Who the hell gave you the right to tell me what to do? A violinist, too afraid to perform in public! A Xaverian brother who is being shipped out because he has lost his pupils! Damn you, Marcus! I would have stayed, whatever!' She rose to her feet. 'I'm going to get that plane. Not because I'm frightened for myself, but because you didn't have the consideration to ask me what I wanted.'

Marcus stood up too. 'Good!' he shouted. 'Haven't you the slightest notion that I *care* for you? I didn't want you to suffer on my account. I would have come to the States to look for you when this was all finished!'

'Yer! En route to hiding away with your fraternity in New England! Ignore your musicianship. Escape from life for all I care.'

He gripped the edge of the table. 'I'm not going anywhere – certainly not to America. I have resigned from the Order.'

Suddenly deflated, Lisa sat down.

The waiter had been joined by a colleague. Alongside them stood Signor Brughieri.

'Are you saying you are no longer a Xaverian? You're out of it?' She began to stretch out her hand to him, then withdrew it. 'Why the hell didn't you tell me before? I've suffered no end of guilt. You really are the pits, Marcus!'

Once more, her voice was growing in volume.

'It doesn't matter, does it? You are not a free agent. I may have

166

forsaken my vocation, but how could I hope to be with you when you're a married woman?'

Signor Brughieri stepped forward. Friend of his parents or not, it was not seemly for a full-blown row to be taking place in his restaurant.

'*Fra' Danby, devo chiederle di andarsene!*'

'But I'm not married. I've been divorced for nearly six years.'

He pushed back his chair, ignoring Brughieri's instruction for them to leave, stepped round the table and, pulling Lisa to her feet, held her tightly.

The restaurant owner was nonplussed. One moment they were arguing, the next they were embracing – and he was a man of the cloth. Brughieri looked across at his waiters, opened his hands and lifted his shoulders in an exaggerated shrug. Shaking his head, he walked away.

Marcus and Lisa stood transfixed for several minutes. Then he pulled up her chair and sat down opposite.

'So, what now?' she asked, beaming.

'Nothing. I'm enjoying the moment.'

'You know what I mean. I'm not going home, and that's definite!'

'Lisa, we are both in danger. Whoever is trying to stop us will resort to murder.'

'But you are willing to expose yourself to danger!'

'The Messenger has promised to guard me night and day. I'll be all right, as long as he keeps his word.'

'Didn't you say he would also protect me, when we were together?'

'Yes, but that was different then. The opposition is far more committed.'

'Well,' she replied, determinedly, 'the best way to be safe is for all of us to be together. Let's go back to my hotel. I'll cancel my flight reservation, and ask for a suite – with three bedrooms.'

'Marcus, I didn't mean that about being scared to perform in public.'

'Do you know, I really think you did!'

'You have a gift. How could you throw it away like that?'

'Coming to Italy, away from my previous existence has, in a way, been cathartic. I've been able to rationalise my thoughts. At the time I joined the Order I believed I was responding to a long-held vocation.' He smiled ruefully. 'Perhaps, in truth, it was a way of not having to submit myself to public gaze, not having to be compared with others of greater talent – an escape route.'

They were sitting on the sofa in the suite Lisa had arranged for them at the Ibis.

'I've been able to see things much more clearly,' he said simply. 'I'm not saying the time has been wasted. Far from it. I enjoyed teaching. When that was denied me, that's when I started to question what I really wanted out of life.'

Marcus put his arm round her.

'Now, I know I have what I want.'

Lisa kissed him on the cheek.

'When will you get your things from the pensione?'

'I'll wait for the Messenger to arrive and he can accompany me. I don't think either of us should leave the hotel beforehand.'

'When will he put in an appearance?'

'He said he would be out of reach for twenty-four hours but would phone immediately he was back in Cremona. He should be in contact any time now.'

Lisa shivered. 'I'll feel safer when he's here. Let's call room service and eat in.'

'Good idea. We can talk through the crazy thoughts I had in Venice. When I was in the hospital I had the chance to go over my notes and recordings. Several things struck me as odd. They may be the idle thoughts of an idle person, but I want to get your opinion.'

The waiter removed the food trolley and they settled again on the sofa with the remaining wine. Ten minutes passed. They sat close, each comfortable in the silence. Then Marcus went to his bedroom and fetched a folder.

'In here is a distillation of my notes thus far. Eventually, they will form the basis of my report.'

He resumed his seat and opened the folder on the coffee table.

'In the cold light of day I'm wondering if some of the conclusions I reached are too far-fetched!'

Lisa took his arm. 'I like off-the-wall comments. They're stimulating.'

'Well, you can decide if the concussion has addled my brain!'

Marcus pulled the writing pad onto his lap.

'What we have been doing is looking at each of the Cremonese, from Nicolo Amati, the father of the instrument making school, to Carlo Bergonzi, reputedly an apprentice of Antonio Stradivari. We've looked into their workshop practices, methods of construction, their selection of woods, and the finishing materials they used.'

He looked up; Lisa was listening attentively.

'In a short space of time I believe we've got to know them quite intimately – even to the composition of their households. No one, to my knowledge, has come up with the notion that they actually used women in their studios before. We are acquainted with how they fashioned their instruments, how they chose, stored and prepared the timber. We know their techniques when sawing, chiselling, carving; the variations they introduced; even the methods of drying the white wood prior to finishing. We are also aware of the fact that, for many years, they bought their glues, grounds and varnishes from the local apothecary.'

'Where's this leading, Marcus?'

'I'm not sure – but bear with me. I now want to run over the things we *don't* know about . . . yet!'

Marcus got to his feet and began pacing the floor.

'As I said, although the finishing techniques were secret – they even tried to hide their methods from their apprentices – the maestros bought their materials from the same source in Cremona . . . until they started buying them from Venice, this being the main arrival port from Arabia – as it was then – for gums, resins and minerals used by both artists and instrument makers. Thus, fact number one: the supplier of their finishing ingredients changed.'

'Right. Is it important?'

'I don't know. It seemed clearer lying in a hospital bed. More so after I had spoken with Signor Tomasina and Alfredo. Anyway, I'll move on. You can demolish my theory later.'

She sat forward, her arms around her knees. Marcus resumed his pacing.

'During our visit to the Department of Conservation and Resto-

169

ration at Ca' Foscari, Granadigli went into some detail about the grounds the Cremonese were using. Propolis, the material created by bees, was used to smooth the surfaces of their instruments. By its very nature, propolis is harmful to the skin. It causes oedemas, dermatitis and other hypersensitive reactions. It used to affect the hands of the instrument makers, even their faces, probably, when they wiped the sweat from their brows.

'Now, according to Alfredo, the ground coming from Venice was excellent for the wood, but not so good for the luthiers. It gave them even worse skin problems. At times, their hands must have been red raw!'

Marcus paused and sat down abruptly.

'This is where it becomes slightly fanciful. Our chemist also told us of the additives the Cremonese used. Do you remember the photographs he showed us of the various layers applied to their instruments? How they introduced dyes and colours in their varnishes by using powdered metals and other such chemicals? Just like the Venetian painters of the times. He even referred to the fact that the artists from Venice had long been renowned for their vibrant colour tones. This was because they had ready access to all the many minerals and ores coming in from the East, and they had been using such materials for over two hundred years. By comparison, the Cremonese were just starting.'

Marcus picked up his glass of wine and drank deeply. Lisa sat in silence.

'So, fact number two: the maestros become adventurous in their finishes. As you know, in this so-called golden period Stradivari opted for a deep red finish to his instruments; the Guarneris preferred one more amber-orange. When we studied the spectrographic prints you could make out how they got their individual finishes, they were the result of the additives they used. Now, remember, this was new territory for them. As Alfredo said, they added metals to their varnishes, notably silica and aluminium – aluminum to you – and even orpiment.'

'What's orpiment?'

'Orpiment, my dear Lisa, was well-known to Venetian painters. Tomasina was right when he said it was a dangerous substance, which they treated with respect. The ore, when ground, provided them with the brightest yellow. In fact, they called it 'King's Yellow'. It had a mica-like sparkle, ideal for luthiers creating a two-tone finish. It is also known as 'realgar', and even as 'sandarac'. You often see the last as an ingredient in instrument varnishes. Perhaps that's why violinists even today suffer from skin allergies on the neck. But I digress. The ore is dangerous because it is highly toxic. It's more common name is . . . arsenic disulfide.'

'Do you mean the Cremonese were buying poisons? Surely many of the materials they used would have been toxic in some way or other!' exclaimed Lisa. 'I'm still not sure of the point of all this.'

'OK, let me spell it out. One, the Cremonese change the supplier of their finishing materials. Two, the ground they begin using is highly effective, but causes increased skin problems. Then, they add all sorts of constituents to their varnishes: organic and inorganic compounds to improve the lustre and colour of their finishes. Whilst they may have been known to painters, who would have taken the greatest care, a number of these substances were toxic; one in particular, arsenic disulfide, was deadly.'

Lisa eyes narrowed. 'My God!'

'You're there, aren't you? The Cremonese line of instrument makers came to an abrupt halt in 1747. In just a decade, all the principal luthiers were dead: the three Stradivaris, the two Guarneris, the last of the Amatis and, finally, Carlo Bergonzi. In just ten years they had all gone. I believe they were all deliberately poisoned!'

Chapter Thirty-Six

Every Sunday Martin Goehr and his wife would walk from the house in Hötting, the old residential district, cross the river by the Innsbrucke – the bridge over the River Inn – and on to the Domplatz where they would worship at the Cathedral of St James. After mass, they would meet with their married children, return to the family home near the zoo for morning coffee and then sit down to lunch. It was a ritual that Martin had performed with his parents, and it had become a Goehr tradition.

This Sunday, the convention was to be broken – at least, the first part. For Martin had an appointment. As his wife and children walked away, he turned in the direction of the taxi rank in the Kaiserjaegerstrasse.

Ten minutes later, he arrived at the Altenburg Hotel in Mutters, just south of the city. The man was already there, drinking a beer in the comfortable, wood-panelled stube. Martin ordered a glass of Rheinriesling, and took a seat beside him. He said nothing until the waiter had brought his glass.

'You failed,' he observed with quiet menace. 'What is more, I was told by someone else. *You* didn't have the courage to let me know.'

'Herr Goehr, we believed he was dead. His woman friend was making plans to leave. Everything indicated that we had succeeded.'

'But you didn't check, did you? You took the word of your two henchmen – for all *that's* worth!'

Goehr took up his glass, and drank.

'You have embarrassed me,' he hissed. 'I do not forgive that. You no longer work for me.'

Suddenly, Jozsef was fearful. Once excluded from Goehr's employ his life would be in jeopardy. The man opposite had a reputation for never leaving loose ends.

'I need one more opportunity, Herr Goehr. Please allow me that! This time I will not let you down, I promise!'

Beads of sweat broke out on his brow. He was pleading for his very existence.

Goehr sat there impassively for some minutes.

'If I did, what would be the outcome?'

'What do you mean?' asked Jozsef anxiously.

'As I see it, you now have to rid me of four people: the cleric, this woman Robards, and your two so-called companions. They are now a liability. If you want to work for me, they must go. And I mean permanently!'

Jozsef chewed his lip. Until the task was accomplished he would need their help. He couldn't do it on his own. Once they were finished, however, he would do what Herr Goehr wished.

'OK – but after the job is done. It's too late to get anyone else, and I will need support. Until then, they will work under the closest supervision.'

Goehr scrutinised him closely, then finished his glass of wine. Getting to his feet, he looked down on the hapless figure.

In a low voice he said, 'My friend, you know the price of failure. For your sake, I trust it will not happen again. This time you will have to be more cunning. I will not accept the slightest suspicion being laid at my door. Do I make myself clear?'

The man nodded.

Goehr went out to the waiting taxi, and gave an address off the Höttinger Au. With luck, he would be in good time to enjoy the rest of the day with his family.

Chapter Thirty-Seven

It was as they were processing from Benediction that Cardinal Grossmann chose his moment. He blocked a fellow prelate, stepped quickly into the aisle and genuflected. Rising to his feet he turned to partner the Secretary of State.

'Are you well, Gustav,' murmured the Cardinal Secretary.

'Apart from the toll on my bones from the passage of time, Silvestre.'

His senior nodded to someone in the congregation.

'Tell me,' he enquired, in a low voice, 'have you heard of this nonsensical rumour that is circulating among government departments? Another misleading impression which will upset our relationship with the city.'

The opportunity had come sooner than expected. He had not even had to raise it himself.

'Yes. But this is different from the usual tittle-tattle. Usually it's about the taxes they are going to levy, or the likelihood of our imposing swingeing charges on visitors to the Vatican.'

'So what do you make of it?'

Grossmann considered his reply. 'I mean no disrespect, Your Eminence, but I was of the opinion it emanated from your office.'

The Secretary's brow furrowed. He looked questioningly at his companion.

'Why do you think that? Do others hold a similar view?'

'Few, if any, in the Curia know about it, Silvestre. I happened to learn it from someone in the Town Hall. I was there recently, on a charity matter.'

'I repeat, Gustav, why do you believe I was responsible?'

'Not you, Your Eminence, Cardinal Marchetti! Obviously a ploy, though I am not aware of his motive.'

The Cardinal Secretary said nothing – enough had been said already.

'*Pronto!*'
'Michelo?'
'Yes. Who is that?'
'It's Angelina. From the Town Hall.'
'Is there something I can do for you, Angelina? As I said earlier, I'll get the money just as soon as the banks open.'
'Well, yes. It's to do with our little arrangement. I've been thinking.' She was suddenly hesitant. Lambertini recognised it in her manner.
'Yes, Angelina?'
'I suppose what you asked me to do, or not to do, must be important. Otherwise you wouldn't be paying me.'
There was a protracted silence.
'Then I began to wonder how important. If you are prepared to pay that much for my silence, it must be worth more. Much more. Like 10,000 Euros!'
'Are you serious? Do you think I'm made of money! It's worth only 2000 Euros to me to suppress the rumour. That's all! It could compromise a deal I'm setting up. I'm not interested in paying that sort of figure.'
'Don't try to kid me, Michelo. Knowing you, and the sort of business you're in, it must be worth far more. I'm not going to settle for less than 10,000. I'll bet the press would be interested. I know someone working for *La Repubblica*. I'll see what that newspaper will pay.'
La voce de un angelo was living up to her name!
'Don't do anything rash. I tell you what, why don't I come round? We could discuss it.'
Angelina Scacchi suddenly foresaw opportunities.
'Why don't you come round *now*?'

'Come in, Angelo. Take a seat.'
Marchetti could not think why the Cardinal Secretary should call for him so early on a Monday morning. Surely, nothing of any consequence could have prompted this summons after a weekend

of attending divine service and prayer. He was totally unprepared for the question when it came.

'Tell me straight. Are you the instigator of this malicious rumour?'

Marchetti was dumbfounded. How could he have found out? There must be spies within the group. However, it was a mark of the man that his face and demeanour reflected little of his inner concerns. He moved towards a chair, beckoning the Secretary of State to do the same.

'As your deputy, Your Eminence, I appreciate that, since you are at the heart of the Curia, the Holy Father relies upon you to keep him abreast of every deed, every action, committed in the name of His Ministry.' Marchetti paused. 'And, of course, any injury or harmful act that might touch upon His Church.'

He looked earnestly into the Cardinal Secretary's face.

'Before he was elevated, he was aware of the devastating charges against our clergy in the United States. We shall have to pay out millions of dollars in compensation to satisfy public opinion. That is bad enough.'

Marchetti leaned forward. 'No doubt, our Archibishop in charge of Foreign Affairs has kept you fully informed of the incidents in Paraguay, Venezuela and Guatemala. I foresee all the elements of a disaster that will cost us way beyond what many will seek from us in the USA. Have you told Him?'

He watched the Cardinal Secretary intently. It was as he thought; he could see it in his eyes. The Holy Father's right-hand man had not mentioned any of these recent scandals.

'Occasionally, as your *sostituto*, I also take upon myself certain responsibilities. I act both in your interest and, most decidedly, in the interests of the Church. I could tell you, but then you would have to wrestle with your conscience as to whether or not to pass it on to the Pontiff – as in the cases I have just cited.'

Cardinal Marchetti rose to his feet. He looked down on the Secretary of State staring sightlessly at the opposite wall.

'So, Silvestre, the answer to your question is "yes". I did instigate the rumour. But, unless you press me, I shall refuse to say why.'

He paused, judging the moment. 'It is neither an illegal, nor an immoral act. If anything, it is born of despair. If you insist on knowing the detail you would most certainly have to pass it on.

The consequence could be the loss of millions of Euros at a time when the Church is desperately short of funds!'

Now, thought Marchetti, what is he going to do? If he calls my hand the Plan is lost. So much effort, time and expense . . . all for nothing.

'You say what you are doing in no way contravenes ecclesiastical or common law? Everything is within the bounds of good order? There'll be no unwelcome disclosures which could cause embarrassment?' asked the other uncertainly.

'You have my word!'

He stood up suddenly. Pulling back the edge of the heavy, brocade curtain, the Cardinal Secretary stared out of the window of the Apostolic Palace.

'Angelo, this meeting has not taken place.'

It was Pantoni, in the Mayor's office, who made the remark. Responsible for the staffing and security of the building, he was expressing annoyance that there was only one receptionist on duty. After all, Mondays were always busy. The ratepayers have the weekend to dwell on the administration's shortcomings, and when the Town Hall reopens they are more than ready to air their grievances.

'Well, she damned well should be here! If she is ill, she should have let us know. It's not good enough. Tell Angelina to see me the minute she arrives.'

Chapter Thirty-Eight

'Why can't they use the same materials?'

Marcus and Lisa looked at each other.

'Because a number of them would not be available,' declared Marcus. 'Their use may have given the Cremonese an edge and added to their creations but, in the end, it killed them.'

'What do you mean by that?' asked the Messenger.

'Marcus has this notion,' said Lisa, 'that someone poisoned the instrument makers by spiking their varnishes. They all died within a ten year period.'

'Surely that was just misfortune? An odd set of circumstances?'

'Perhaps,' said Marcus. 'But when you are talking of the seven best instrument makers in the world and the laws of probability, to my way of thinking it is more than just coincidence.'

'Who would do such a thing? Who would gain by it?'

'No one knows,' replied Marcus. 'But another factor is the absence of their work books, studio records, drawings, notes, the written requests for instruments by their patrons, even the formulae for finishing their instruments. Little has come to light of their techniques or practices. Most of the works written about them are based primarily on the jottings of apprentices, journeymen and suppliers.'

'Are you still suffering the effects of the concussion, Signor Danby.'

'Look, I'm not trying to solve a three hundred year old crime. I want to discover if the materials they used can cause fatalities. Are the substitutes adequate? If your masters want me to provide a sound basis for the future, we need to know. In the process we might even come across their missing documents and learn more about the chemicals and ingredients they used. They had secrets. Supposing those secrets are the key to their very success, what then? Do we ignore them?'

'Signor Danby, your hypothesis is tenuous. It is based on the slightest of evidence, namely the toxic nature of the materials they used . . .' The Messenger rose and went to the table to pour himself another drink. 'But you could be right. For the moment I can think of no other explanation why you have been run down on the autostrada and then thrown from a window. It could explain the reason why others have been "removed" from the project. Why you are in danger. Perhaps the opposition – whoever they are – are motivated by the need to cover up seven deaths that took place three centuries ago.'

Lisa and Marcus were silent. The Messenger seemed to have taken a leap too far.

'What do you mean?' Marcus asked huskily.

'Signore, like you, I cannot be sure. It may all be conjecture. But the closer you have come to uncovering details about the maestros, the more vicious the assaults. What conclusions would you draw?'

'I think we must get to the bottom of it,' declared Lisa.

'You may have no other choice,' the Messenger said flatly. 'Although still not enough . . . you may now know too much. My need is for you to finish the report; time is running out. But, for your own safety . . .' He looked across at the couple on the sofa. 'I agree – you need to find out what really took place in that fateful decade.'

'Then we must return to Venice,' said Marcus.

'Can you guard us?' Lisa asked. 'Or do we hire protection?'

'I have all the necessary resources,' responded the Messenger.

For the first time Marcus noted the hint of a smile.

It took no more than an hour. He had told the driver to remain while he packed and settled the bill then he hobbled out to the Messenger and the waiting taxi. They had impressed upon Lisa that she must not venture from the hotel. She must pack what things she needed for two days, and be ready to leave as soon as they returned.

When it pulled into the hotel forecourt, Marcus paid the taxi, telling the Messenger, 'I'll put my suitcase in the car. It will save carrying it down again.'

As he started towards the car park, Lisa came out of the entrance and waved to them. At that moment Marcus saw a car speeding

179

towards the entrance. A rear door was flung open and a man stepped forward and hurled Lisa onto the back seat. The vehicle's acceleration slammed the door shut. Tyres squealed on the tarmac as it turned towards the exit.

Everything was happening in slow motion. Marcus was running, the pains in his legs and back excruciating, but his strides were laboured and slow. The case fell from his hand, clothes spilling behind him. He was shouting, but the sound was stretched out and distorted. The Messenger had pivoted round and waved. No one else was even moving.

Just as suddenly everything changed. As the car neared the exit, another drove straight across its path. The screeching sound of tyres filled the air. The escaping vehicle slewed sideways into the bushes, coming to an abrupt halt. The doors flew open. Three men jumped out and fled up the Via Mantova. It had been quick, well-planned, and would have succeeded but for the blockade.

Marcus, reached the abandoned car and got in. Lisa was sitting there trembling.

After a few moments he said, 'Are you able to get out?'

She nodded. Standing by the door was the Messenger.

'My God, that was fortunate – that car pulling in front of them like that!'

'No, Signor Danby. That was prepared. Those obstructing the exit work for me.'

'Let us get Signora Robards up to the room.'

Lisa held on to Marcus' arm as they walked along the corridor. Ushering her into the suite, he stooped gingerly to pick up a note that had been slipped under the door.

'You were wise not to involve the polizia, Signor Danby,' commented the Messenger, 'even though the hotel manager was insistent. It would have delayed us. Anyway, they would never have apprehended Signora Robard's attackers.'

Marcus helped Lisa to her bedroom.

'Lie down for a while. I'll get you a glass of water – or would you like anything stronger?'

'No, water's fine. I'll be alright in a minute, Marcus. Just let me rest.'

In the sitting room the Messenger was finishing a conversation on his mobile phone. He snapped it shut as Marcus walked to the mini-bar.

'Phoning your masters?'

'No, I was speaking with my people thanking them for their rapid response.'

'Well, they certainly have my gratitude,' said Marcus. He removed a bottle of water and poured the contents into a glass. 'Are they people your principals normally provide?'

'Signor Danby, never before have I had to resort to such actions. My principals, as you call them, could make no such provision. They are my cousins. When I was returning to Cremona I stopped by my village and asked for their help.'

Marcus took the Messenger by the hand. 'My heartfelt thanks!'

The tall man bowed in acknowledgement.

Marcus picked up the glass and walked towards the bedroom. At the door he looked over his shoulder. 'Tell me, do you have the violin with you?'

A short time later, the Messenger went off to retrieve an overnight bag and the instrument case. Left by himself, Marcus remembered the note pushed under the door. He took the folded sheet of hotel writing paper out of his jacket.

Dear Marcus,

I've now called upon eleven of the studios in Cremona. To gain the fullest impression, I believe there are another eight I should visit. After that, it may be sensible to extend the appraisal to Brescia and Mantua, so I expect to be occupied on my quest for at least another week.

Does this fit in with your plans? How would you like me to submit my findings?

When you have a moment, please phone me on my mobile.

All the best,

Geri

He tapped his teeth with the folded sheet. He had forgotten about Geri Bellman. Suddenly, he was concerned that he too might be in danger. He dialled his number, but got only the messaging service.

'Geri . . . your suggestion is fine. I think you are right to include Brescia and Mantua. Lisa and I are off to Venice shortly. I'll call you the moment we arrive.'

By mid-afternoon they had arrived at Mestre, and parked near the railway station. From there they had crossed the lagoon by train to the terminus of Santa Lucia and taken a water taxi to the hotel Al Ponte Antico on the Grand Canal.

Just after six o'clock Marcus came out and jumped into a water taxi, which turned in the direction of St Mark's Square. Passing under the Rialto bridge the boat turned quickly into the Rio San Salvador and coasted to a halt. Marcus ran up canal side steps into a waiting taxi which took him through Saint Bartholomew's Square back to the hotel.

Lisa and the Messenger were already in the water taxi when he joined them.

'I'm told a speed boat followed you up the rio,' smiled the Messenger.

Twenty minutes later they were ushered along silent corridors, through the now quiet laboratories, to Doctor Granadigli's office at Ca' Foscari University.

'Signora, signore, I'm delighted to see you both again! An intriguing telephone call.' The chemist peered at the Messenger. 'We haven't met, signore. My name is Alfredo Granadigli.'

The Messenger shook his hand But made no attempt to introduce himself.

'This gentleman,' said Marcus hastily, 'is both our protector and the provider of the instrument in question. It was made by Bartolomeo Giuseppe Guarneri in 1740. I have assured him it will be in safe hands and that the removal of a minute sliver of the surface material will be virtually unnoticeable.'

'Absolutely, signore! I can assure you, you will not be able to see where it has been removed,' said Granadigli.

The Messenger opened the instrument case. There lay the Guarneri del Gesù.

'I can understand why you were hooked when you saw that, Marcus!' exclaimed Lisa.

'What precisely do you want me to test for?' asked the chemist.

'Alfredo, in the electron microscope images of the Cremonese instruments you identified base metals, strange additives, even glass in their coatings. But I need you to test for arsenical compounds and, if possible, the amounts present. Can you do such a thing?'

Marcus was suddenly uncertain. Was it a wild goose chase? Would the tests show anything? Could they even be done?

'Well, we could have a problem.'

Marcus' heart sank.

'I will not be able to do it, or get the results for at least two days.'

'But such a thing is possible, Alfredo?'

'Naturally. We can easily perform spectrographic analysis to achieve what you want. But the equipment is in use at the moment, and I can't interrupt the schedule. Whilst I'm waiting, however, I could do an electron scan, which might be useful.'

'Can I presume the violin will be secure?' asked the Messenger. 'Or do we need to guard it?'

'I'll put it in the safe now. Don't worry I am here throughout the day, and when we leave this office it will be fully alarmed.'

Chapter Thirty-Nine

He had expected it. When Danby came out he had told Heinz and Franz to follow. They had not returned when, a short time later, the three of them departed the hotel by water taxi. Unfortunately, he had lost them near the Accademia. Mooring further down the Grand Canal, he had walked the streets near the bridge. Nothing – not a sign of their presence in any of the restaurants or bars.

That morning they had returned to the villa and he had checked the recording machine, then the radio scanner.

'It would seem we are in the clear.'

Jozsef had shut down the equipment and slumped into an easy chair.

'No one has contacted the police from the hotel. I think we can safely assume there will be no record of the incident. No thanks to you, Heinz! You should have reversed, swung the car round and gone out of the entrance. You've done the course. What is the first thing you do when there's a road block and the way back is clear?'

Heinz had said nothing, his anger slowly mounting at the relentless, verbal attack. Franz had got up to help himself to a beer.

'It also applies to you, Franz. You were sitting next to him. Why didn't you tell him what to do if he can't think for himself?'

Jozsef pulled himself out the chair.

'I'm going for a walk. Be ready to leave for Venice when I get back!'

Ever since then, they had hardly spoken.

It was lucky for him that Herr Goehr would not hear of the abortive attempt to kidnap the woman. It had seemed such an elementary plan. Remove one of the key players, force the others to drive out of Cremona on the autostrada and arrange for the

184

truck to take them out. Then do away with the woman. Simple. Except that he was blessed with incompetents!

It could not go on. When he had left the villa for a walk he had spoken on his mobile to a contact in Munich and organised a replacement for Heinz. He would be arriving at the hotel in the morning. Tonight, he would dispense with Heinz's services – permanently.

Chapter Forty

Marcus awoke with a start. He was trapped. There was a dull ache in the muscles of his lower back. He tried to turn, and then realised Lisa was lying tight against him, her head on his shoulder. He eased his arm away, and stretched out. Lisa murmured, but slept on.

Marcus had crept into her bed in the early hours. Not to make love. With the Messenger occupying a room in the suite it would not have been fitting. In any event, his injuries would have rebelled at the exertion. It was more for mutual comfort. He had been warmly welcomed.

As he lay there, his mind turned to the meeting with Alfredo Granadigli. He recalled the look on his face when he had halted in the foyer of the university building.

'You do know, Marcus, that the compound you are looking for is highly toxic! I can't think any luthier would be working with that sort of material. They could easily finish up dead if they didn't know what they were doing.'

'Exactly Alfredo!'

'My God, Marcus!' Lisa had exclaimed, as they walked away. 'I've just thought of something. If they were poisoned, so were their apprentices. Men and women.'

Putting his arms behind his neck, Marcus pondered on whether they should wait in Venice for the results, or return to Cremona. If they stayed and the tests were negative he would have wasted two days. Time he could ill-afford. As it was, the document was going to take four or five days to draft and edit before being handed to the Messenger. And he still had to incorporate Geri Bellman's assessment. As he lay there he had a fleeting impression that he had missed something relating to Geri. Perhaps it would come to him later.

But what if the tests were positive? What would they do then? It would make for an interesting story. One that not only the music world, but the press worldwide, would feature prominently. Not that he would derive much from it, but it would certainly benefit Lisa, if she were named as the author of the discovery.

He looked at the recumbent figure beside him. What were his true feelings? He could not deny she occupied every moment of his waking thoughts. Each day, as his inhibitions crumbled, his passions rose. Lisa was the first woman he had come to know well. He was already thinking that a move to the United States might happen after all, only the reason and the circumstances would be different.

His mind turned again to the tests. It would be a significant step to prove arsenic had led to the maestros' demise. If it had been deliberate, who could have been the perpetrator? Was he interested in finding out? Yes . . . Even after all this time, he would be curious to know who and why. Anyway, Lisa would want to expose whoever had been behind the deed – and not just for her article. Of course, there was no point in searching for an answer if it was proved they were not poisoned. Every reason to do so, if they were!

Marcus came to a decision. While they were in Venice he would begin drafting his submission. He could also find out more, much more, about Pietro Guarneri, 'del Gesù's' brother, who had set up his workshop in Venice, well away from his family in Lombardy.

Chapter Forty-One

He took his accustomed seat, across from the ornate desk.

'Signor Lambertini, thank you for coming. I trust it was not too much of an imposition?'

In truth, it had been quite the reverse. He had had to hire a van, acquire a set of overalls and tools, and act the part of the handyman. He had visited the flat several times before he felt it wise to remove the body. Beforehand, he had taken her cat and dumped it on the streets some kilometres away.

When the time came he had bent the body double, tied the arms to the legs, then wrapped it in two dust sheets. With the load balanced precariously over one shoulder and a tin of paint in his hand, Lambertini had carried the corpse down the three flights of stairs.

He had encountered a number of passers-by when he was at the van, but nobody to connect him with the apartment block. The next question had been where to dump her? In the river? Even with weights, bodies had a habit of resurfacing, so somewhere deep in a wooded area, off the beaten track, would be the solution.

Driving out of the city, Lambertini had headed for the forest of Canale Monterano near Lake Bracciano. Forty minutes later, with dusk hiding his activities, he had, once more, hoisted the dust-sheeted corpse onto his shoulder and shuffled into the trees. After a short distance, he had left the track and searched for the spot chosen a few days earlier.

Half an hour later, he had driven back into the city, removed all signs of his use of the vehicle and returned it to the hire company. Finally, in the confines of his luxurious apartment in the old Monti district, he had thrown up in the bathroom.

'I am well aware that everything is going as planned. I have even persuaded the Secretary of State to let me progress the project,' purred Marchetti.

Lambertini shivered inwardly.

'In consequence, my young friend, I have another duty I would like you to perform.' Marchetti adopted the now familiar stance of resting his chin on his steepled fingers.

'I want you to follow someone. It will not be onerous – just note his final destination and phone me. The person will leave this building early tomorrow morning. I understand he will be going to Leonardo da Vinci airport. Unfortunately, I do not know his final destination. I shall rely on you to find that out, by whatever means you can.'

The cardinal paused and leaned forward.

'Michelo, this is important to me. You must do your best to discover where he goes. Be by the main entrance by seven o'clock in the morning and await a signal from Brother Felipé. He will indicate the man you must follow.'

Marchetti opened a drawer of his desk and passed Lambertini a slip of paper.

'Directly you have news, ring me on this number.'

'Yes, Your Eminence. However, you will appreciate that I am not skilled in shadowing people. Is there not someone else you could use?'

'My young friend, if there were, do you think I would have chosen you? By the way, wear something inconspicuous. One of the first rules is not to be obvious!'

It was raining – not heavily, but a wetting drizzle that showed little sign of easing. Once the man had been identified, Lambertini would take the waiting taxi to the airport. Getting there ahead of his quarry would give him the opportunity to follow closely and work out his flight and destination.

Another ten minutes passed. Even the overhang of the building offered little protection.

There he was. Brother Felipé was at the main door pointing discreetly at a tall man, dressed in a clerical coat. He wore glasses and had an incipient beard.

Lambertini strode quickly towards the Via della Conciliazone and jumped into the taxi. It pulled out immediately into the traffic and headed for the Fiumicino autostrada and the airport thirty kilometres away.

It was another twenty minutes before the man arrived. Carrying a small overnight bag, he turned in the direction of the Air Berlin desk in Terminal A. Lambertini fell in behind him in the line, straining to overhear the conversation.

'From Vienna, you are going on to Innsbruck by Austrian Airlines. Do you want me to check you through, sir?' The man nodded his head curtly, and Lambertini, pretending he had forgotten something, hurried away. At the ticket desk he bought a first-class open return to Innsbruck. By now he had shed his coat and hat. He purchased a morning paper and made his way casually through to departures, taking a seat on the far side of the lounge. Lambertini was one of the last to board the Fokker 100 bound for Vienna. There, after a lengthy wait, the passengers were transferred to the Austrian Airlines flight to Innsbruck. Sixty minutes later they touched down at Kranebitten airport.

He almost lost him. The man hurried through the concourse and took a waiting taxi. Lambertini was next in the queue, but the driver was out of his vehicle arguing with the dispatcher. Concerned he would lose his quarry, Lambertini demanded they leave immediately. His German was fluent and he employed a number of colloquial epithets.

'*Wo wollen Sie hin, Mein Herr?*'

'I want to go after the fellow who drove off in cab number thirty-four. He is a colleague and I've got his mobile phone. I need to give it back to him.'

'I can tell you where he is heading,' said the driver over his shoulder. 'For the railway station. I heard him tell the dispatcher.'

'Then get me there as soon as possible. Before he catches his train!'

Ten minutes later the taxi pulled up in front of the station. Lambertini rushed into the building and saw the tall figure striding towards an adjacent platform.

'Where is the next train going from there?' he questioned a porter.

'Munich, sir, in a few minutes' time.'

He had seconds to purchase a ticket to Munich. As he did so, he realised that the man would leave the train before it reached the Bavarian capital – otherwise he would have taken a direct flight.

Lambertini was beset with worry. The chase must surely be coming to an end. Having come this far, it would not be appreciated were he to lose him now.

When the train pulled into Mittenwald, Lambertini almost missed him again. As the whistle blew he glimpsed him moving rapidly towards the exit. Leaping from the train, he scurried after the disappearing figure. But the man was not taking a taxi, nor was there a vehicle to collect him. He was walking briskly into the town.

He was easy to follow: he never hesitated, looked over his shoulder, or stopped suddenly to check. After eight hundred metres the man came to a complex of buildings. He spoke briefly with the gateman. Lambertini watched as a woman came from the main building. She greeted him, then escorted the visitor across the forecourt, where they both disappeared from view through large glass doors. The name on the imposing fascia board read: *INSTRUMENTE TIROLER Gmbh*

So the company were instrument makers. His job was done. After phoning the cardinal, Lambertini would make his way back to Rome. He hoped he would not be called upon to undertake anything else.

Cardinal Grossmann accepted that his manoeuvre had failed. If his deputy could produce a substantial contribution to the Church's funds, the Secretary of State would do nothing. He had agreed to attempt to undermine the Plan – but if there were tacit acceptance by members of the Pontifical Family that the end justified the means, he would be hard pressed to force them into blocking Marchetti's scheme.

It was then he remembered Oreste Pacino. Their paths had crossed prior to an International Assembly held in the Vatican in 1999. Grossmann, representing the pontifical charity Cor Unum – 'One Heart' – had met with delegates of Caritas, the Italian arm of the charitable confederation, on a number of occasions. At the time, Pacino was running the Communication Department and Document Centre. Although there was a marked difference in their ages, both held similar views on the provision of relief aid. Subsequently, they found they agreed on a wide range of issues. Grossmann had lost touch with the younger man, but recalled he had seen reference to his appointment to the Prime Minister's Office when President Bush had visited Italy in 2001.

He rang the outer office for a telephone number. When it was relayed to him a few minutes later, he called the Director of Communications.

'Oreste, this is Cardinal Grossmann. We haven't spoken for a while; it seemed prudent to allow you to adjust to the demands of office. However, I am sure you now have everything in order and running well, so I thought I would ask if you would care to join me for dinner.'

Chapter Forty-Two

The Messenger walked beside him, ever-watchful – glancing left and right, checking passers-by, searching first-floor windows. The water taxi had dropped them close to the Campo dei Frari, only a short step to the Offices of the State Archives, but he was prepared for any measure that might be taken against his companion. He had seen no evidence yet that the opposition was in Venice, but he could not take the slightest chance. For that matter, he hadn't seen any of his support team either. Nevertheless, he was confident they were in place; he had briefed them earlier. Two members of his team had remained with Signora Robards. Wisely, she had decided not to venture from the hotel.

The pair entered the building, and he stepped forward to organise the needs of his researcher. The phone calls he had made earlier that morning had cleared the bureaucratic path, and they were led into one of the side rooms where the file relating to Pietro Guarneri had been placed on a table next to a computer terminal. As Marcus seated himself, the Messenger moved to the door, opened it, removed the key, and locked it from the inside.

'Is there anything you require, signore?'

'I don't think so.'

The title on the cover read: *Pietro Guarnerius, 1695–1762*. Inside were four CD-ROMs.

'So, everything they have has been transferred to disk. Convenient.'

The first revealed Guarneri's family life, from the time he moved to Venice in 1722 – his marriage to Angiola Maria Ferrari six years later and details of his ten children. The relevant documents – birth and death certificates, census forms, household composition returns and personal correspondence with family and friends – had all been copied. Marcus read quickly through the main items.

It was interesting to note that not one of his children had been trained as an instrument maker.

The second disk referred to activities in his studio. It included records of commissions, documents relating to his apprentices, drawings, dimension sheets and intricate detailing of scroll designs. Marcus noted several letters from grateful patrons. It was interesting to discover that he did not provide instruments for any of the major composers and players in residence in Venice at the time.

The third disk he inserted dealt with Guarneri's travels and his relationships with fellow instrument makers, like Gofriller, Tononi, Gobetti, Montagnana and Serafin. Written notes also showed he had spent time with David Tecchler before the luthier hurriedly departed for Rome.

The fourth disk was a revelation.

Numerous documents were listed, which Marcus found on opening illustrated Pietro Guarneri's extensive contact with many Venetian artists of the period. It appeared he was very friendly with Canaletto and Francesco Fontebasso. However, judging by the many exchanges of notes and letters, he and Giovanni Tiepolo were particularly close.

One letter caught Marcus' eye.

Pietro ~
I am still waiting for the materials ordered three weeks ago.
I have a mural to complete and desperately need them for the last
section.
Giovanni Tiepolo – 10 febbraio, 1735

He sat back and reflected on the note. Was Pietro Guarneri supplying painting materials as well as running a studio? He searched quickly through the files on the disk, but there were no other references.

After four hours Marcus had the details he wanted. He was collecting his things together when there was a knock on the door.

Instantly, the Messenger stood to one side and called, 'Who is it?'

'The Archivist,' came a woman's voice.

The door was unlocked.

'Have you finished with the files, gentlemen?' she enquired.

'Thank you, yes,' responded Marcus. Then, as an afterthought,

'Tell me, do you have any other material – papers, bills, documents – relating to Pietro Guarneri?'

She was hesitant.

'I believe so. There are some oddments in the basement. It would be hard to locate them and I could not bring them out of the storage room.'

'That's OK. I'll come down with you and help you search.'

It was said with authority. The woman was surprised. 'Wait here, while I return this to the archives.'

A few minutes later she was back and led them through the building, down three flights of stairs to a locked door. She entered the lock code, swung open the metal door and threw a switch that drenched the whole area in fluorescent light.

'I think the items would be over in this direction,' she said over her shoulder, walking between tall rows of shelves. 'Yes, here we are. Guarneri. I remember seeing them when I was searching for something else.'

She picked up three box files and marched to a table in the centre of the store. They were dusty and she wiped at a mark on her sleeve.

'There are gloves on the table, signore. Please put them on. I can give you fifteen minutes. Then, it's lunchtime, and I'm afraid you will have to go.'

Marcus expressed his thanks and sat down. On opening the first file, he found it contained household memorabilia. The contents of the second box held his attention. There were more notes from artists, the majority seeking delivery of the materials they had ordered. A number were actual detailed lists of their requirements. Right at the bottom of the file he found an envelope containing lists of the materials sought by the luthiers of Cremona. In the third box there were even more.

Marcus selected samples of the lists by makers' names for photocopying. What did it all mean? Was Guarneri the Venetian a supplier to the Cremonese? It made sense. He was based in Venice. Painters and luthiers use similar ingredients for their grounds and varnishes. With his involvement with the artists' community, it would have been a logical step to offer the materials to those in his home town. Marcus delayed the thought that Pietro had conceivably provided toxic compounds, or that he was aware of their potentially lethal effects.

He shut the files. Clutching the original documents he wanted copied, he and the Messenger retraced their steps to the ground floor.

The bell rang as they entered. As before, they were greeted by Signor Tomasina, on this occasion accompanied by Alfredo Granadigli.

'*Entri! Entri!* It's good to see you, my young friends.'

Lisa stepped forward and kissed them both. Upstairs, in the private rooms, refreshment was again provided by Tomasina's grand-daughter; then they settled to their discussion.

Marcus rose to his feet. Suddenly, he felt that what he was about to tell the two Venetians had to be done with a seriousness best conveyed when standing.

'Lisa and I, much appreciate the time you, Signor Tomasina, and you, Alfredo, are giving us.'

The studio owner interrupted. 'Tommaso, please!'

Marcus smiled and inclined his head.

'As you know . . .' he turned towards the Messenger. '. . . we were asked by my good friend . . .'

'My name is Leonardo,' the Messenger said simply.

'We were asked by Leonardo to investigate the backgrounds, abilities and techniques of the Cremonese. The people he represents seek to reproduce the long-forgotten skills of the famed instrument makers. During the past few weeks we have discovered a great deal about them. Much, to my certain knowledge, has never before come to light – including rather questionable facts relating to the finishing methods of the maestros, the details of which came largely from you, gentlemen.'

Marcus nodded at Tomasina and Granadigli.

'When we visited you, Alfredo, you told us of the many types of additives they included in their varnishes – all sorts of minerals and resins. What I didn't realise was what you meant by "Realgar and the old Arabic Sandarac". I played the tape of our discussion, and those were the very words you used. It wasn't until I was lying in the hospital that I found out what they were from the internet. Tommaso gave us a clue. He said they were highly dangerous. He was right. They are extremely toxic . . . their chemical name is arsenic disulfide.'

196

'But our painters have used them for centuries. In the right hands they are quite safe!' exclaimed Tomasina.

'True. But the Cremonese were inexperienced. Now, let me turn to the grounds they used. Tommaso referred to propolis, the material used by bees to fill the gaps in their hives. But he also told us that the substance was a skin irritant. That's why, today, they wear gloves.'

Marcus stopped to take a sip from his glass.

'So, these are the facts. The conclusions are, frankly, quite startling!'

Marcus listed the points, clasping separate fingers for emphasis.

'One, the instrument makers were using a filler material that caused the skin to erupt and weep excessively offering a ready path by which all manner of substances could enter the body. Two, unknowingly, they were including toxic chemicals in their finishing processes. A truly hazardous combination! Three, central to all of this was the fact that the source of these products was an importer in Venice. They were persuaded to change their supplier from the local apothecary in Cremona to a dealer in this city.'

Marcus paused and looked at his audience.

'I have uncovered proof that Pietro Guarneri, the brother of Giuseppe, was an importer and distributor of finishing materials to painters and artists in Venice and, from 1735 onwards, sold these items to the principal workshops in Cremona!'

There was an incredulous silence.

'Frankly, I don't doubt he knew what he was doing,' continued Marcus. 'Supplying a whole raft of oxides, mineral ores, and other compounds painters used for their grounds, colours and varnishes, demanded more than a casual understanding. We believe it was done deliberately!'

Signor Tomasina was the first to speak.

'I can't believe it! I know there was little love lost between the various members of the Guarneri household. Another Pietro, brother of Giuseppe senior, took off for Mantua. Apparently, he couldn't stand working in the family studio in Cremona either but . . .'

'It's a bit far-fetched, Marcus,' said Granadigli. 'There again, it was while he was working in Venice that his father and brother began to make names for themselves. That could have rankled with Pietro who, I have long believed, wanted to be acclaimed the

197

family's brightest star. He knew Antonio Vivaldi, but the composer never played any of his instruments, preferring those made by Amati or Stainer.'

'I think it was his close friendship with Giambattista Tiepolo that prompted his interest in supplying artists' materials,' added Marcus. 'And that would have been a short step to providing the same service for luthiers, though trading in such items was probably secondary to the work in his studio.'

At that point that Signor Tomasina excused himself from the room. When he returned some minutes later, he said, 'I've asked my grand-daughter for something to fortify us. I've also been checking some old family records. Your remarks rang a bell. Our ancestor, apprenticed to Antonio Stradivari, noted that Pietro made a number of visits to the family in Cremona during the autumn of 1734. It was the talk of the piazza. He doesn't say why, but some months later there is a reference to a whole host of items coming by cart from Venice.'

Once more, there was silence. It was interrupted by the appearance of fresh bottles of wine.

When everyone's glass was filled, Marcus said, 'If there were open sores on their hands from the propolis when they ground and mixed the ingredients for the varnish layers, it was only a matter of time before the poisons affected them. Being elderly, Antonio Stradivari died first, in 1737; Giuseppe Guarneri senior in 1739; Girolamo Amati in 1740; Omobono and Francesco Stradivari, Antonio's two sons, in 1742 and 1743; Giuseppe del Gesù in 1744; and, finally, Carlo Bergonzi in 1747. One by one, in just ten years. Then they were gone. The field was open to Pietro.'

Tomasina and Granadigli stared at him.

'I still find it fanciful in the extreme,' declared Alfredo, finding his voice.

'It just can't be true,' muttered the elderly studio owner, shaking his head.

But Marcus noticed he was less emphatic in his denial than the chemist.

Granadigli picked up on Tomasina's comment. 'My dear Marcus, I'm sorry I just cannot go along with it. Where is there one scintilla of proof for such an assertion?'

'Alfredo, it's here in this very room,' said Marcus quietly.

198

Chapter Forty-Three

They met in a room at the Duke Hotel, just north of the Villa Borghese, among the many embassies located in the Parioli district. In Rome, it was the nearest equivalent to a private club.

'I have ordered a simple meal, Your Eminence. I hope that is agreeable?'

'Signor Pacino, you are most kind. You should not have gone to any trouble. I just thought we should renew our acquaintance, take the opportunity to bring ourselves up to date with events. Nothing more.'

Oreste Pacino was not fooled. The elderly cleric wanted something from him. The question was, would it benefit him as well as the cardinal? Could he turn it to advantage?

'Come! Sit down. Let us have a drink before the first course arrives.'

The two men sat in comfortable, upright chairs either side of an ornate marble fireplace. The prelate had a copita of dry sherry on the small table beside him, the Prime Minister's man a glass of water. The lighting was soft, the atmosphere conducive to the exchange of secrets.

'So, Oreste, congratulations on the post you now enjoy. I presume it keeps you extremely busy?'

Pacino related the demands of his role and the sum of his activities, all the while taking note of the cardinal's level of interest. He is not taking it in, he thought. His mind is fixed on other things. Pacino asked him a similar question, a customary prelude to the main reason for the meeting.

'Oh, we have our problems. In many ways it's like the little boy and the dyke. Put one finger in here, and water comes through there. We often run out of fingers!'

199

The communications man smiled, amused by the cardinal's gentle wit.

Shortly afterwards, they sat at the table. It was not until the end of the main course that Grossmann got to the point.

'One of the problems we are facing at the moment is unity. There have always been differences of opinion within our community, as you know. But currently we have a strong-minded radical bent on disrupting the relationships we enjoy with the Rome administration. You may have heard about it?'

Pacino shook his head. Have we arrived, he wondered. Is he about to tell me what he wants?

'Have you not? Well, you have heard of Cardinal Marchetti, the Secretary of State's deputy, no doubt. It is he who is fomenting a monstrous plan to blackmail the city into giving the Vatican a huge sum of money. It even has the tacit approval of the Cardinal Secretary – although, I don't think he appreciates what his *sostituto* is up to.'

This is interesting, thought Pacino.

'Why are you telling me this, Your Eminence?'

'I want to ask something of you.'

For the next half an hour Grossmann told him how Marchetti was gradually bringing together his Grand Plan, of the people he was involving, and why he should be stopped. Pacino listened in silence; eventually he interrupted.

'The aim of which is what, exactly?'

The cardinal put down his knife and fork.

'He wants a huge sum of money. If not he proposes to move the Vatican in its entirety to another part of Italy!'

'He would not be able to do that, Your Eminence,' responded the Prime Minister's man. 'The Church does not have anywhere else to go. Besides, it's logistically impossible.'

'He believes it is not. And so do others. I'm told he even has a site earmarked for the "New Vatican", as they call it. On the banks of the River Po! The trouble is the mayor seems to believe it too.'

'So what do you wish me to do?'

'Why, to call his bluff, that's what!'

'Let me see if I've got this right. You are saying this fiction is influencing the mayor's thinking to the point where he is considering paying off Marchetti?'

'Yes.'

'Absolute nonsense! I'll have a word with the mayor.'

Grossmann's eyes narrowed.

'At this stage, Oreste, I think it would be better if Marchetti were told by someone else. It should come directly from the Prime Minister's Office. Someone of national standing should tell him, "Fine, go right ahead!" It's an utopian dream. My feeling is he knows that too. If his bluff were called, I'm sure he would quickly come to his senses and retreat from the proposal. Being told by someone such as yourself, for example, would have a profound effect.'

Oreste Pacino suddenly saw opportunities. It would be a crowning achievement to be selected mayor of the city. If the present incumbent were seen as ineffectual, and he was able to scotch this ill-considered scheme, it could set up his candidacy nicely.

'Well, if you think that I could help . . .'

Arriving back in Rome after a tiring journey, Lambertini had almost fallen asleep in the taxi. Stripping off his clothes, he had pressed the remote button of the television set in the bedroom and gone to fix himself a well-earned drink.

As he was walking through to the bathroom he heard the newscaster announce:

'Today, a body was found near the popular resort of Lake Bracciano. A walker uncovered the shallow grave of a young woman, after his dog had scratched at a mound of earth. The dead woman is believed to be in her early thirties. Police are treating the discovery with suspicion.'

The call, at such a late hour, irritated him. Who would phone him at this time of the night? He glanced at the clock at his bedside, then lifted the receiver and listened.

'*Ja* . . . *Ja* . . . You have done well. Then we need take no action against those in Venice. *Ja* . . . OK, let me know of the outcome as soon as possible, in case we have to do something in *La Serenissima*. Goodnight!'

The conversation had been guarded – nothing to excite the attention of any eavesdropper, innocent or otherwise – but its import had been clear. Someone at top government level was going to undermine The Plan.

201

If that were the case, there would be little need to get rid of the wayward cleric and the arrogant American journalist. Until that moment, before the call, he had had every intention of eliminating them. Now, as he lay in his bed in the schloss at Klais, his mood was pragmatic. He would stay his hand for the moment, and delay the supreme sanction. If Grossmann could pull it off, so much the better. Why expose himself to scrutiny.

Geri Bellman was also in bed. It had been a good day. In many ways the studios of Brescia had shown more promise than those in Cremona. It would be interesting to see what tomorrow would bring.

The instrument makers had been very forthcoming – explaining their ambitions, showing him their facilities, allowing him to inspect and play their instruments. Of course, they had not appreciated the real reason for his visits. The explanation, which he had given with only minor variations since setting out on the task, had been that he was representing a German investor, a person keen to revitalise the tradition of instrument making in the region, but who first wanted to satisfy himself that his investment, and the publicity it would generate, would be matched by the resident luthiers' abilities.

It was only a hair's breadth from the truth, but kept the real reason safely hidden. Bellman had also taken photographs – not immediately necessary, but they gave credence to his efforts, and satisfaction to the workshops he visited. In a few days' time he would have the results of his investigations ready. When he presented them to Marcus, he would be in for a surprise.

Chapter Forty-Four

Marcus sat on the sofa, nursing a coffee. Lisa and Leonardo had both gone to bed. Leonardo! It seemed strange to use his name. Being known as the 'Messenger' (that damned Messenger!) had made him anonymous – ever-present, but always in the third person.

He reflected on the meeting at Ca' Tomasina smiling to himself when he recalled the look on Granadigli's face.

'What do you mean, Marcus?' Alfredo had asked, mystified by his remark that the proof was there to be had.

'You are testing a violin made in 1742 by Giuseppe Guarneri del Gesù. If there is any truth in what I am saying, Alfredo, your department at Ca' Foscari will come across signs of arsenic residues.'

Granadigli had concurred.

'The electron microscope images wouldn't have shown traces of arsenical compounds. That's why we are subjecting the sample to other tests.'

'Right. But while it might show traces of the deadly poison, who is to say that it was not absorbed by anyone in the workshops?' added Marcus. 'Unless . . .' He looked across at Tomasina. 'Unless, we had the opportunity to discover that the poison was also present in their bones.'

Tomasina had immediately realised where he was heading and looked apprehensive.

'Just supposing, Alfredo,' Marcus had continued, 'that we had the opportunity to analyse the bones of someone who had been working with one of the maestros at the time? If arsenic were found in their remains, might not that be considered conclusive?'

Alfredo had nodded, still not understanding the direction of the conversation.

'I'm not sure I should disturb the relics of my ancestor,' Tomasina had interjected, quietly.

'What does he mean by that?' Granadigli had asked.

'Let me explain, Alfredo. In the casket on the buffet lie the remains of an early member of the Tomasina dynasty – great, great, great, great, grandfather Giovanni Tomasina, an apprentice to Antonio Stradivari. He worked alongside the master in his studio for eleven years, before returning to Venice. Tommaso told me he came back home to this very studio in 1737.'

'I'm sorry, Marcus, Alfredo, I cannot sanction such desecration.'

'I believe we have a very critical situation here, Tommaso,' Granadigli had declared. For once his face was sombre. Gone, the bright remark, the ready humour. 'I appreciate your concern regarding disinterment. But, let me point out, I would need only the merest piece of bone. It would not be noticed. And, as you know, I would treat your grandfather with the utmost respect.'

The debate continued for another hour. Eventually, and with dignified sadness, Signor Tomasina had passed the casket to Grandigli.

'In the circumstances, I think it would be best if I stored this immediately at the university for safe keeping. Do you agree?'

'My only request is that, for protection, Leonardo should accompany you. I trust you have no objection?' Marcus had asked.

'None at all.'

Marcus and Lisa had waited at the studio until the Messenger had returned. It had been an uncomfortable period, for Tommaso had clearly been troubled at relinquishing what, to him, was a most treasured relic.

After sitting in silence for some time, Marcus had wandered across to view the framed selection of instrument makers' labels, exhibited above the spot where the casket had rested. Tommaso had followed him.

'Unfortunately, they are copies. But it is interesting to note the various styles the luthiers adopted and revised during their lifetimes. I was given them by Professor Roberts of Verona.'

They had chatted about the labels and the removal of the casket until the Messenger had returned. Soon afterwards, they had left and taken a water taxi to the hotel.

Marcus got up and poured another coffee. He wasn't tired; there was too much to think about.

There was the burning question, which everyone else had largely ignored, yet which kept coming back to haunt him: why would Pietro of Venice knowingly sell toxic chemicals to the Cremonese? Perhaps the others had baulked at voicing the question until there was proof. He knew Granadigli and Tomasina were sceptical. He wondered if Lisa were wholly convinced.

As Marcus sat back on the sofa his mind turned to the labels produced by Pietro Guarneri in his studio in Venice. In Tommaso's display they had been ranged alongside those of Guarneri del Gesù. It now struck him that the Venetian's labels had been over-ornate compared with those of his brother, and the rest of his family.

Pietro's labels had included decorative borders, while the other Guarneris had declared the maker's references and the instrument's date of production on a slip of plain, unadorned paper. Pietro had gone in for ornamentation – until the 1750s when he had reverted to simple inscriptions without lines or borders. I wonder why he changed them, thought Marcus idly. Unless, of course, it was remorse.

He sat upright.

Perhaps, part of the answer lay in the psychological state of the person. Twenty-five years earlier Pietro had been striving to make his name. Could his high-minded style and temperament have been reflected in the manner in which he presented his labels? When his father and brother were accorded higher recognition, could family rivalry have given way to jealousy, even hatred? That bitterness might even have extended to all the Cremonese. When Pietro was struggling to achieve a standing as an instrument maker in Venice, the epicentre of culture in northern Italy, regard was growing fast for the craftsmen in a nondescript little town in Lombardy.

Could Pietro have thought it unfair, an injustice that had to be corrected?

With the Cremonese disposed of, the path would have been open for Pietro Guarneri to gain the plaudits. Conceivably, though an accomplished luthier, he realised he could never attain the heights of his brother, father or grandfather. Perhaps, when realisation dawned, there just might have been a growing feeling of remorse – an emotion that slowly consumed him, dragging him down from the egotistical heights of his earlier years.

He remembered, once more, that Pietro had fathered ten

children – yet not one of them had been encouraged to train as a luthier. Was this another sign that his passion for instrument making had been soured? Or did he fear that if they took up the profession, his sons might harbour similar jealousies and conspire to do away with him?

He drained the cup and got to his feet. These tangled thoughts were getting him nowhere. All the same, in the morning he would have a word with Alfredo.

'Yes, I do have a university friend who is a psychologist. Why do you ask?'

In the light of day, the idea of getting the labels of Pietro Guarneri analysed by an expert suddenly seemed ridiculous. What had he been thinking of last night?

'Marcus? What's this all about?'

Hesitantly, he told the chemist the conclusion he had come to ten hours earlier.

'It seemed so logical. They often say that how you express yourself, in writing, painting, in most media, is a reflection of the soul. I was taken by the way in which the pattern of Guarneri's labels had changed over twenty-five years. I just wondered if a specialist in the way our minds work could tell something of Pietro's darker side from his changing designs. That's all.'

There was a silence on the other end of the phone.

'His name is Mario Gaudi. He is in the Faculty of Humanities, which is in the Dorsoduro, down by the maritime station. I think this is what you would call *un inseguimento di oca selveggio*! – a wild goose chase – but I'll phone him and ask him to expect your call. *Ciao.*'

The next move was to catch Professor Roberts before he left for the Institute.

'Marcus! How are you? Have you completed your report, yet?'

The voice of Adam Roberts was lively and welcoming.

'Not quite, Adam. Coming on. It's in connection with that, and one of the Guarneris, that I am phoning. I need copies of the labels you have of Pietro of Venice, del Gesù and their father Giuseppe. I won't show them in the report, I just need to study a particular aspect of them. Could you possibly help me?'

'No problem, Marcus. I could E-mail them to you now. They are all on disk.'

'Brilliant!'

'They'll be with you in the next few minutes. What's your E-mail address?'

'It was easier to accompany you than give directions. Also, I can make the introductions – to assure Dr Gaudi that, though you are talking nonsense, you are really quite normal!'

Granadigli laughed as he stood with Marcus and the Messenger in the foyer of the building.

A figure approached, the very antithesis of Granadigli: tall, about the same height as the Messenger, slightly stooped, with a lugubrious, almost hang-dog expression which did not change, even when Alfredo bounded across and grabbed his hand and arm.

'Mario! May I introduce Leonardo? This gentleman, the crazy one I was telling you about, is Marcus.'

Mario did not shake hands but performed something between a nod and a bow.

'Would you care to follow me?' he said briefly, turning on his heel.

They trooped behind him in crocodile as he led them down a corridor, through a door, up a flight of stairs, then into what was clearly Gaudi's private sanctum. The Messenger glanced at Marcus, then went out shutting the door behind him.

'Is he not joining us?'

'No, signore. He will take his ease outside.'

'Would you care to sit down?' There was an assortment of chairs scattered around a desk. Gaudi sat back, tipping his seat onto two legs. It groaned at its misuse.

'Alfredo says you have some documents upon which you would like me to comment.'

Marcus reddened slightly. Is this the moment I make an utter fool of myself? he wondered.

'Dr Gaudi, I am seeking to understand the inner drive of the celebrated luthier, Pietro Guarneri. It's important that I gauge how circumstances may have affected him – if, over a period of time, alterations to his psyche might have manifested themselves in his label designs.'

'An almost impossible task, Signor Danby,' commented the psychologist dryly. 'As Cundick and Weinberg have stated, time and time again in the Mental Measurement Yearbook, such interpretations are rarely supported by empirical evidence.'

Marcus opened his document case, and withdrew six sheets of paper.

'Let me explain. I am not calling for a profound analysis from a few scraps of paper; that would be insulting to your calling. What I am seeking is the merest suggestion that such things might have occurred.'

'I'm glad you appreciate what is involved, signore. As you say, it would be imprudent of me to make a snap judgement. If you are seeking a hint, a suggestion that Pietro of Venice was assaulted by demons, I can tell you without examining any documents – the answer would be "yes". We all are from time to time, are we not?' He relented slightly. 'But come, show me what you have.'

'These are copies of labels for instruments Pietro Guarneri made between 1721 and 1754. Also included are the designs created by his brother and his father.'

Gaudi took hold of the sheets. Pushing aside various items on his desk, he spread them out for comparison. The Pietro labels he placed in the centre, flanked by those of his family.

Silence.

Gaudi sat forward, bunched his hands into fists and leaned his chin on them. Then he opened a drawer and drew out a magnifying glass. He gazed through it, running the glass over several of the sheets. He returned it to the drawer.

'Very interesting, Signor Danby. What do you think we have here?'

Marcus was perplexed. Having expected a curt dismissal, he was now being asked to give his opinion. Or was it a trap, to demonstrate that he was reading too much into the ordinary? He reddened again. Alfredo smiled at his discomfiture.

'I believe, Doctor Gaudi, that in the seventeen-twenties Pietro Guarneri had a high opinion of his talents and assumed a self-importance that was ultimately misplaced. He was at odds with his brother and father, and left Cremona for Venice to make his name. Misfortune befell his family. He felt guilty, and with the gradual acceptance that, although extremely able, he would never achieve the outstanding excellence of the Cremonese instrument workers, he suffered feelings of great remorse.'

There, I've said what I think. Let him do his worst.

'An interesting appraisal, signore,' commented Gaudi. For the first time a slight smile touched his lips. 'I know, of course, the history of Pietro of Venice. I am aware that he was estranged from his family.'

He picked up one of the sheets for a closer inspection.

'I do not know all the finer details of his relationship with his brother and father, so it would be difficult to draw any firm conclusions. But my immediate reaction, though tenuous, is that your conclusion is highly possible. On the minimal evidence before me, I could not transform your assumption into something as strong as fact – although I might possibly deduce that Pietro was a tortured soul, thwarted in his ambitions, and ultimately showing all the classic signs of conformity in order to regain the respect of his family. It is very evident that initially his nature was flamboyant, perhaps even dismissive of others around him. I would also suggest, as you have, that, slowly, he came to realise his limitations. The plainness of design in his last labels is a likely mark of contrition, an acknowledgement of the superior ability of his father and brother.'

The psychologist looked up from the photocopies.

'However, I would strongly warn against reading too much into what I have said. It is only an opinion drawn from the briefest of exposures to a fragment of material. I would want much, much more detail before I dreamt of giving a complete appraisal!'

Marcus breathed out slowly.

'Thank you for your time, Dr Gaudi. I was seeking no more than an indicator of his mindset. By the way, did you know that Guarneri had numerous children? Not one did he encourage to come into his workshop. I wonder if that is also significant.'

This time the psychologist did smile.

'You mean his lack of success, compared with his kin, was too much to bear and he didn't want his children to suffer the same frustrations, the same injustices? Yes, that could well be so!'

They had parted from Granadigli and taken a water taxi back to the Al Ponte Antico. Once in their suite, the Messenger had excused himself, leaving the couple alone.

'So, tell me! What did the expert say?'

'He agreed with my interpretation. Well, he said that no reliance could be placed on it, but the labels could be regarded as the classic symptoms of arrogance, followed by repentance, followed by the need to conform more to the image of those he might have wronged.'

'Phew! Did you tell him who it was?'

'Yes, though not all the details, nor the fact that we think Pietro did away not only with his family but all their contemporaries!'

'Not something you would wish to broadcast – certainly not on the evidence we have. So, what now? After we hear from Alfredo, do we pack up and go back to Cremona?'

'I think so. But if the tests Granadigli is doing are positive, that leads us to another question, to my mind just as vital: if he knowingly sold the materials to the workshops in Cremona, *why* did Pietro Guarneri murder the Cremonese? Was it a strategy he alone contrived, or was he working with someone else?'

Chapter Forty-Five

He slipped out with few noticing his departure, excusing himself on the vague grounds that he had to attend to a minor matter and would be returning in minutes. It was a short step to the Hotel Savoy, further along the Via Vittorio Veneto, from the Palazzo Margherita, the neo-renaissance building housing the American Embassy. A gathering of dignitaries and Church men from the United States was the perfect cover for such a meeting, if he could conclude it quickly. The Cardinal Secretary of State had been called to one side by the ambassador. He would be unlikely to notice his absence.

The door was opened for him by someone who noticed the flash of purple beneath the dark suit. He smiled his gratitude. A brief word with the portiere and he was whisked up to the third floor and shown to a room. He knocked. It was opened by Oreste Pacino, of the Prime Minister's Office.

'My apologies, Signor Pacino for the location of this meeting. Unfortunately, I am much occupied at the moment, and my diary is very full. It was purely fortuitous that I was in the area today, so we could snatch a few minutes together.'

'Thank you for fitting me into your schedule, Your Eminence. It will not take long, I hope. It is more to clear up a misunderstanding.'

The cardinal smiled – a rictus of the lips.

'Please, won't you take a seat. Something to drink, perhaps?'

Thank you, Signor Pacino. Some water, I think.'

The politician moved to a sideboard and poured two glasses of water. They sat opposite each other in comfortable chairs – a small ornamental table between them.

'How can I help, signore?' asked the prelate, knowing the direction the conversation was likely to take.

'I am sure there is nothing in what I am about to say which warrants the slightest credence. However, far from waning, as even the most entertaining rumours eventually do, this one is gaining ground.'

Pacino took up his glass and drank a little from it. Looking over the rim, he added, 'Moreover, there is a growing opinion that it emanated from your office. I wanted to meet with you to give you the chance to deny this. Then I can act to eradicate it.'

The cardinal also picked up his glass, but he did not drink.

'What if I tell you it could be true? That it is not a rumour, but a strongly-held line of thought that the Vatican should consider what best suits its future; that it may be all to the good that the Holy See takes steps now to secure a separate identity, and is no longer regarded as merely an adjunct to this city? What would you say to that?'

The bureaucrat's eyes narrowed.

'My view,' continued Cardinal Marchetti, 'is that we would appeal to a wider audience, ensure more loyalty from our adherents, capture a greater number of converts to the faith. If the Vatican were divorced completely from Rome, it would truly enjoy the status of a separate sovereign state.'

'Do you seriously expect such a mammoth undertaking to work? To recreate the splendour, the history, the physical requirements of a new city, let alone have a site in which to locate it? I might accept your point of view if such a project were feasible but, with all due respect, Your Eminence, it is totally impractical. Not only would it be far too costly, it could just never happen!'

The cardinal smiled again.

'I beg to differ, signore. This is not a fanciful scheme. It has been seriously planned. We have detailed, comprehensive plans of action; surveyors, engineers, architects, town planners – all have made their contributions. We have a model that indicates we could have all the major elements in place within five years, the rest of the state, occupying over a hundred hectares, within ten years.' He leaned forward. 'This is no idle boast! We are committed to the break with Rome. So much so that we would take the Vatican with us, Stone by stone – every palace, museum, church; even the piazzas would be dismantled and rebuilt on the new site! As you said, an immense task, but one we are pledged to undertake.'

He put down the glass and rose.

'Thank you for seeing me, Signor Pacino. I'll see myself out.'

'What do you mean: it is not an idle threat? Didn't you tell him it was beyond logic? It can't be done!'

The voice on the other end was positive and and vehement.

'Damnation! I don't care if he has all these experts working for him, and it appears to be a realistic venture. You should have thought of some way to thwart him!'

Cardinal Grossmann was quiet for a moment whilst the other voice spoke.

'Yes, I suppose the location and the land would be a major issue. Good! Then I suggest you pursue that line of opposition.'

The cardinal returned the phone to its base.

So, Marchetti had declared his hand. He wondered just how committed the Cardinal Secretary would be to this scheme if he knew his deputy was now at odds with both the national and local administrations.

Clearly he had been granted freedom to organise this grandiose project, but did the Cardinal Secretary appreciate all that Marchetti was doing in the name of the Church? He must be told. Such a radical step must not be taken without every member of the Pontifical family expressing an opinion.

His anger blinded him to the key issue, and the demands of the Austrian. Grossmann had agreed to undermine the Plan. That was now forgotten. Of much greater moment was the internecine struggle taking place on the third floor. He would seek an appointment with the Cardinal Secretary of State as soon as possible.

The door was opened for him by a Franciscan.

'Come in, Gustav. Would you care for some coffee?'

'Thank you, no, Your Eminence.'

'Then, take a seat. What can I do for you?'

Grossmann had had time to consider his approach. To accuse his fellow prelate of subversion would be extreme. Marchetti might well be working to further his own ends, but the evidence was circumstantial and likely to be dismissed. The best way was to refer to the rumour, indicate that it was worrying government at every level and disrupting long-held relationships, and recommend that a statement of denial be issued forthwith.

'I'll come straight to the point, Your Eminence. I am concerned about this rumour that is causing agitation among city authorities and national offices. Far from disappearing, it is gaining in strength. Even the Prime Minister is expressing serious concern.'

'Is he indeed?' remarked the Cardinal Secretary. 'Do you know the source of the rumour? Do you know *exactly* what is being said?'

'As I understand it, Your Eminence, it is to the effect that the Holy See will rebuild its city away from Rome.'

The senior cleric laughed.

'And the Prime Minister believes it? Do you seriously think we could re-establish ourselves elsewhere? That we could pick up our metaphorical bed and walk? I am afraid, Gustav, you are the likely victim, as are many others, of a rumour that beggars belief. I am surprised you are being exercised by such a prank.'

'But I have it on good authority that it is true.'

'What? The rumour or the intention?'

'I am told, Your Eminence, that plans have been drawn up in detail for the Vatican to be dismantled stone by stone and rebuilt away from Rome.'

'Who on earth told you this fanciful story?'

'One of the Prime Minister's aides. And Cardinal Marchetti told *him* in great detail at their meeting on Wednesday!'

'This week?'

'Yes.'

'Let me assure you, Gustav, the man is deceiving you. The cardinal and I were at the American Embassy all day. He was by my side throughout the meetings with Church representatives from the United States. An aspect central to those discussions was the catastrophe facing us in Portland and other, as yet, undeclared areas. He would hardly have been absent from such critical exchanges.'

'But, I assure you, a meeting took place.'

'Impossible! Now I forbid you from causing dissension among the Family. Go away – reconsider your attitude towards your brethren.'

Grossmann was taken aback. Was the cardinal covering something up? Was he firmly in favour of Marchetti's activities? If he were, Grossmann would be unable to stop them. He must seek another route.

'Then go to The Holy Father!'

Goehr was furious. Everyone in the Curia was involved, Grossmann had whined. Then go to the top – a simple directive.

As he held the phone to his ear, listening to the convoluted explanation, the meaning hidden under so many layers of circumlocution, he came to a decision. He was not going to sit back and hope the situation would resolve itself. It was time for direct and overwhelming retaliation. He would let loose the dogs of war!

Chapter Forty-Six

The call had startled him. Sifting through his notes and checking facts, he had been totally absorbed in writing the report.

'*Pronto?*'

Marcus, it's me, Alfredo. I was wondering if we could meet this afternoon? I've been speaking with Tommaso and he has agreed we could get together at Ca' Tomasina. Would that be alright with you, Lisa and Leonardo?'

Marcus had been expecting the call from the chemist, but his heart was racing as he put down the receiver. Does he have the answers, he wondered? Am I going to be disappointed if it has been '*un inseguimento di oca selveggio!*' – a wild goose chase – as Granadigli had described it earlier?

Lisa had been packing. She came into the sitting room area.

'Was that Alfredo? What news does he have?'

'He has asked that we meet at Ca' Tomasina after lunch. We can be on the road by four and back in Cremona this evening.'

'Will you be terribly disappointed if your theory falls apart, Marcus?'

She came over and put a hand on his shoulder.

'I suppose when you create a belief, take account of other factors, perhaps bend them to support the assumption, expectations grow. Will I be disheartened? Yes. Quite frankly, I shall be – although, it will mean that I can quickly finish the job the Messenger set me. And the sooner we can get away from it all the better.'

She grinned. 'Where do we go from here?'

He stood up and encircled her with his arms.

'Anywhere you want – As long as it's back to England.'

'Hey! Wait a minute! Why should I want to do that? I'm an American.'

He kissed her.

'Because it's the place for civilised people to live.'

'Are you saying I'm uncivilised? Listen . . .'

But she got no further. The outer door opened and the Messenger entered the suite.

Hurriedly releasing her, Marcus said, 'Alfredo phoned. He wants us to meet at Ca' Tomasina after lunch. Is that OK with you?'

'Of course. Does he want me to escort him to Signor Tomasina's studio?'

'I didn't think to ask. I'll phone him.'

It was arranged that the Messenger would go to the university, collect the violin and accompany Granadigli to the meeting place.

'I presume we'll go on from Ca' Tomasina to the station and head for Cremona, signore? In which case I'll brief my associates,' said the Messenger, making to leave.

He hesitated, then turned back towards the couple.

'I have been told that they are aware of our presence in Venice. What worries me is that they appear to have a great many individuals looking out for us. We have taken precautions, changing taxis, altering our routes, each going in different directions before meeting up. All the time they have been alive to our efforts. Members of their team have been following us everywhere.'

Lisa bit her lip. 'What are we going to do?'

'I am going to increase our numbers. My associates have contacts in the city. I'll ask them to bring in helpers. Leave that to me. My cousins will escort you. I'll see you both later, when I arrive with Signor Granadigli.'

Marcus climbed the stairs behind Lisa and Signor Tomasina.

When they reached the owner's private world, he was relieved to see the casket in its original setting. Catching his glance, Tomasina said, 'It was returned the very next day, Marcus.'

They made themselves comfortable.

'I must confess I am as excited as you are at what Granadigli might tell us.'

'I think, Tommaso, that Marcus is almost dreading the moment,' commented Lisa, glancing across at him. 'Aren't you Marcus?'

He smiled wryly. 'I wouldn't say *dreading* – apprehensive perhaps. If nothing comes from the tests I can get on with the project. However . . .'

He got no further. They heard the distant bell as the studio door was opened, then the troop of footsteps on the stairs. Heads appeared above the ornate banister rail. Alfredo's face was solemn.

Marcus was downcast. Was it bad news?

Granadigli fell back into a seat, taking a moment to recover from the climb. He had a briefcase on his lap and, with deliberation, unhinged the top and delved into its recesses. He withdrew a sheaf of papers. Looking around at the circle of faces, intent on every word, he took spectacles from his pocket and put them on.

Marcus found he was holding his breath.

'My friends, these are the chemical evaluations. I have to tell you that . . .' He glanced down at the top sheet. 'You were absolutely right, Marcus – on both counts.'

Lisa let out a yell, leapt out of the chair, embraced Marcus and kissed him hard. Two spots of colour lit her cheeks as she turned, embarrassed, to look at the others.

'*Eccezionale* Marcus!' cried Tommaso. 'So my ancestor was poisoned too.'

'Yes, though presumably he had not had as much as the others.'

Granadigli stood up to shake his hand. 'So, my crazy friend, your weird ideas were correct. I congratulate you!'

The Messenger also rose and patted him on the shoulder.

'We must drink to the moment. Let me get something suitable,' said Tomasina.

A short time later, glass in hand, Granadigli was explaining to them how the tests were conducted, and the details of the results.

'In this spectrographic analysis you can clearly see the Raman effect. When material is bombarded by a laser, light is scattered, a tiny fraction of which shifts in frequency as atoms in the material vibrate. Analysis of the frequency shifts, or spectrum, of the light reveal the characteristic vibration frequencies of the atoms, and hence the chemical composition and structure of the material. It can pick put particles as small as one micrometre – a millionth of a metre!'

'What was the concentration of arsenic in the remains?' asked Marcus.

'Not sufficient to be lethal in the short term, but continued exposure to the levels that were found in Signor Tomasina would eventually have killed him. He was fortunate to leave when he did. Even so, he would have suffered loss of appetite, stomach cramps, nausea, and other debilitating side effects. It's a wonder he managed to sire any offspring with that amount of poison in his system.'

'That's interesting,' observed Marcus. 'Guarneri del Gesù never sired any children. I wonder if the arsenic affected him that way?'

'Come to that, I'm not sure Omobono and Franceso Stradivari had any children either – although his daughter did,' added Lisa.

'What are you going to do now, Marcus? Will it change your report?' asked Granadigli.

'No, I can't see that it will have any effect on that.' He glanced at the Messenger. 'Although I feel that this discovery has raised further questions.'

'Such as?' enquired Tomasina.

'I just cannot believe Pietro killed all the Cremonese simply because he was jealous of their success. They were recognised and received numerous commissions, but they were not as highly regarded then as they are today.' Marcus paused for a moment and contemplated the floor. 'I think there must have been another motive. A large sum of money, perhaps . . . the predictable thirty pieces of silver . . . an improvement in status, even high office. It's hard to say. Whatever it was, it suggests others were implicated. Pietro may have persuaded the instrument makers to take his materials, but it is more than likely he was influenced by someone with a clear aim in mind. I wonder who it might have been.'

'Are you returning to Cremona?' asked Granadigli. 'If you are, I'll mail copies of these results to your hotel.'

'Yes, we are leaving now. But first, if you agree,' he responded, seeking Lisa's approval. 'I would like to call upon Professor Roberts in Verona. It won't take long, and it's en route.'

The convoy arrived at the Hotel Dogana in the early evening.

Leaving the autostrada at Peschiera, it had made only a minor detour to Sirmione on Lake Garda, which Roberts had suggested would be a more congenial place to dine than Verona.

The departure from Venice had been a major logistical exercise. The Messenger's cousins had recruited three additional guards, making a protective force of seven. Lisa maintained that it was as if they were being chaperoned like Victorian maidens. Surely one or two acting as deterrents would be sufficient!

'Now I know how the President feels!' she had declared hotly.

Surrounded by their bodyguard they had crossed the lagoon by train to Mestre to find that a further Alfa Romeo had been added to the fleet. Their car, driven by the Messenger, had taken up position in the middle of the trio, the cousins leading, the Venetians bringing up the rear. The three black Alfas had travelled the hundred kilometres non-stop in tight formation. Now they were side-by-side in the car park. It had been agreed the cousins would remain in their car while the others went to eat in Sirmione. Afterwards, the Messenger's people would patrol the grounds around the hotel and restaurant, while the new recruits were to look after the cars.

Lisa, Marcus and the Messenger had made their way to the restaurant to find Professor Roberts and his wife already there. Marcus had made the introductions, saying that both Lisa and the Messenger were helping him with the project. They had had an enjoyable meal in the elegant surroundings and Lisa had soon struck up a rapport with the professor's wife, whose name was also Lisa. Marcus noticed that, unlike her husband, she spoke with a soft, Scottish accent.

'Your wife comes from Scotland, Adam. Do I detect an Edinburgh accent?' asked Marcus.

'Yes, we both come from Leith. Sadly, I think I've lost mine, though it soon returns whenever we are back home.'

The Messenger responded politely when questions came his way, but refrained from general conversation.

'Have you recovered from your fall, Marcus?' Roberts questioned, glancing quickly at his wife.

'Yes. Stupid of me! Too much to drink, a desire for fresh air, and a low balcony rail. They all conspired against me! I still have some aches and bruises. Fortunately, the discomfort is disappearing fast.'

'I'm pleased. When Granadigli phoned to say he had seen you in hospital, I was worried.'

Marcus saw the opportunity.

'Thank you, everything is fine. It meant, of course, that we could not complete our researches, so we went back to Venice for a few days and spent some time with Alfredo, and Tommaso Tomasina, whom you also know.'

He glanced at Lisa and the Messenger.

'What I am going to say now may surprise you. You are aware

220

that the Cremonese line of instrument makers died out with the passing of Carlo Bergonzi in 1747?'

Roberts nodded.

'We now have incontrovertible evidence that Pietro Guarneri was trading in materials for Venetian artists, and also supplying the people in Cremona with grounds and varnish ingredients. Among the chemicals he sold to the unsuspecting Cremonese was what Venetian painters knew as "King's Yellow"!'

'That's dangerous. It could have been fatal if used incorrectly.'

'Especially, when combined with highly-irritant propolis, also provided by Pietro.'

Roberts frowned. 'What are you saying?'

'Perhaps you've already guessed. In just a decade, Pietro poisoned all the leading figures in the instrument world. By his hand, the Cremonese literally came to an end!'

'My God! It can't be true!'

'I am afraid it is. Let me tell you what we have discovered.'

There had been little need to follow closely. The transponder on Danby's car had given them a clear indication of their route. Leaving the A4 at Pescheria, they had driven at a leisurely pace towards the signal, stopping well short of the hotel. Soon afterwards, one of them had gone to reconnoitre. In the gathering dusk he had sighted the three Alfas, parked in the order the procession had made its way from Venice, the signal emanating from the middle car. He also noticed that the vehicles were occupied each by a person who was clearly a guard, taking shelter against the cold night air.

He reported to the others. Thirty minutes elapsed, then two of the passengers climbed out and went to the boot. The shorter of the pair dragging a dark hood over his white hair. He unfastened a bag and bent to tinker with its contents. Then, silently, they made their way through the undergrowth towards the hotel car park. They remained watchful for some minutes before the hooded, slightly-built figure opened the bag and, withdrawing its contents, made his crouching way towards the central vehicle. Crawling the last five metres, he stopped briefly when the glow of a cigarette appeared in the driver's window. He would have to be extra vigilant. Slipping beneath the Alfa, he shone a pencil torch on the underside, removed the transponder and selected a spot close to the fuel tank. Then he slipped the cover off the magnet, positioned the unit and slowly offered it up until a secure contact was made. He waited briefly, hoping the occupant had not picked up the faint sound. Gingerly, he flicked a switch. A faint red light shone and the unit emitted a soft buzz. When arming a bomb, there is always that moment of uncertainty. He was less anxious when he pressed another button and a green light appeared. It was now receptive to the radio signal. Just one casual movement of a remote finger would detonate the explosive, sending its occupants and much of the car to kingdom come.

It was then he realised he had been holding his breath. With a low sigh, he edged from beneath the vehicle and crawled back the way he had come.

Throughout the detailed summary of events in Venice Roberts had sat with his eyes fixed on Marcus. Occasionally he nodded. Sometimes his brow compressed in a frown.

'And that's about the size of it, Adam.'

'Unbelievable! An amazing discovery Marcus. I congratulate you. Tell me, are you going to make this public? It would certainly be a turn-up for the music world.'

'Perhaps, but not yet,' Marcus replied. 'You see, the question now is: why did he do it? What had he to gain?'

'Well, it wasn't jealousy. I would find that hard to believe.'

'Interesting you say that. Lisa and I are of the same opinion. We wondered if he had been offered some huge reward, something he could not refuse. Was it to secure a position in Venetian society? Or perhaps even blackmail? We just don't know. But I strongly feel it has to be answered. In my view, it would be wrong to reveal only half the puzzle.'

Roberts stroked his chin.

'What happened after the demise of the Cremonese? Is that not your starting point? Who stood to benefit from their sudden departure? At the moment, I confess I haven't a clue. However, if I can be of help, just let me know, old chap.'

*

The identical red and green lights on the monitor cast an eerie glow in the interior of the car.

'I see that we are able to communicate with our present for Signor Danby and friends. You have done well, Franz. And you, Tomás. I am pleased you spotted the guards; otherwise it could have been difficult.'

Franz grinned, although the flash of teeth went unseen in the dark. He looked across at the new man. He had not met him before. Apparently, he was a Hungarian, forced to leave Budapest in a hurry a few years ago.

When Jozsef had told him Heinz would not be with them he had not asked why. Perhaps it was a sixth sense, concern for his own safety, that had caused him to refrain. But, he had experienced a frisson of fear when Jozsef had calmly mentioned that the big man was no longer part of the team and that two replacements would be coming.

He peered round the seat to catch a glimpse of Akos, another Hungarian. He had come across him before. Physically he was not much taller than Franz, but he always carried an air of brooding menace. Good with weapons, he was a loner. He would respond to authority, but only if the leader were decisive and capable of defending himself in a confrontation.

Where, at first, Franz was content to be part of the team, now he was not so sure. Jozsef was a psychopath, a controlled psychopath, and therefore able to exact the best from those he commanded. But these newcomers seemed to have their own agenda, their own methods. Was it time to disappear, before he disappeared?

Before the end of the meal the Messenger made his farewells and, turning to Lisa and Marcus, mentioned he would join them at the cars.

'A quiet type, Marcus. Do you know him well?' Roberts had enquired.

'I've known him only a few weeks, Adam. But he is very efficient.'

The professor had nodded and the conversation had turned to other, lighter topics. Finally, when they rose to leave, Roberts caught his arm.

'I meant what I said earlier, Marcus. Whatever help you need, come to me. There will be others who might offer the same, but I'm afraid they may be less scrupulous if they knew your story.'

Marcus clasped him by the hand.

'I appreciate what you are saying, Adam. You will be the first I shall turn to if help is needed. Thank you.'

The Roberts waved as they drove away. Lisa and Marcus turned towards the car park. The Messenger materialised out the shadows.

'Dammit! You gave me a start, Leonardo,' Lisa hissed at him.

'He is always doing that,' said Marcus. 'I thought I had got him out of the habit.'

'I've spoken with both teams. No one was anywhere near the restaurant. And the Venetians have not seen a thing.'

As they neared the vehicles, the occupants got out and joined the Messenger's cousins.

'It's too cold to stand around, Marcus,' said Lisa. 'Shall we get in?'

'You go ahead. I just want a word.'

He walked over to their protectors .

'If you wish, I'll drive, Leonardo. It will give you a rest from concentrating on the speed and keeping your distance behind the lead car.'

'Thank you, signore. But it is not necessary. I did not drink anything other than water, whereas you were drinking wine.'

Was that a rebuke thought Marcus. He had drunk only two glasses. He had not wanted more.

'If you are sure? I can navigate then.'

'Thank you, signore.' It was said with an artlessness which implied he knew the route well.

The Messenger paused, then called to one of his cousins.

'Enrico, thinking about it, our Venetian friends do not know the road. It would be advisable for one of you to travel in their car. Just as a precaution.'

'A good idea,' Enrico exclaimed. 'Paulo, you go with them. Make sure they don't get lost.'

The three Alfas drove out the hotel grounds, through the town of Sirmione, and on towards the autostrada, keeping well within the speed limit.

Several hundred metres behind them was another car.

As the signs appeared the leading vehicle's indicator lamp flashed briefly, and took the slip road onto the A4, heading for

Brescia and Milan. The Messenger followed; at the rear came the last of the trio.

They moved into the middle lane, gradually increasing speed until the Messenger clicked on the cruise control and eased his weight back in the driving seat. The car in front was fifty metres ahead, the car behind, the same distance. A kilometre further back another car was also accelerating. It passed the convoy in the outside lane, its tinted windows obscuring the glow from the mechanism held in Jozsef's hands. The red and green lights illuminated his face, giving it a ghostly cast.

'In two kilometres we shall reach a section where the autostrada curves to the right. Slow as you reach the end of the straight.'

Akos, the driver, nodded. Only the hum of the tyres intruded on the silence. They breasted the rise, and began their descent.

Fifteen seconds later Akos said, 'Jozsef, I am now slowing to a hundred kilometres.'

'Look back, everyone. Tell me what you see!'

He pushed the button. Suddenly, a huge ball of flame erupted behind them. It took a moment for the sound to travel. Then they were engulfed in the deafening rumble of a fearsome explosion.

Chapter Forty-Seven

The lift doors opened. Grossmann hesitated. For once, he ignored convention and turned left towards the Pontiff's private quarters. It was too important to let matters rest. He would seek guidance from the Supreme Head. He should be party to what was going on under the very roof of the Apostolic Palace.

Nevertheless, he was nervous. Even though he had known the Pope when he was first a bishop, and, in later years, a cardinal, it was still a breach of protocol to approach him directly.

He neared the desk, and the guards.

Make it appear he has been summoned. Yet there would be no note of his appointment. Be insistent; suggest an error has been made – not an unknown occurrence.

As he was about to announce himself, one side of the tall double doors opened. The guards stood to attention as the Secretary of State walked through.

'Ah, Gustav. Were you looking for me?'

It was said with a certain urbanity. He knew very well why he was there. 'Come, walk with me!'

The two cardinals retraced their steps down the corridor. The Cardinal Secretary glanced at his companion, noting the competing emotions on the other's face.

'His Holiness and I have been meeting a foreign delegation. I brought up this business of the rumour. Surprisingly, his thoughts were that it might not be a bad thing! We were both amused when an American visiting bishop said, "It's like one of our hurricanes – the faster it spins, the more intense it becomes!"'

They halted by Grossmann's door.

'Perhaps we can talk further at lunch, Gustav. For the moment, I have several matters to attend to.'

The cardinal entered the outer office, ignoring the Franciscan, and slammed the door.

He had been thwarted. Now there was no way to turn. If the Primate knew of the situation and had accepted the impression conveyed by the head of the Curia, there was no other route he could take.

'I have just met Cardinal Grossmann, Angelo. Do you know where?'

It was a rhetorical comment. He waited for the Cardinal Secretary to continue.

'Outside the Pontiff's door! If he feels so strongly that he is prepared to ignore all the principles by which this administration works, then there is more to it than you are telling me.'

He stared at the tall man standing before his desk.

'I ask you again: is what you are doing, in any way whatsoever, likely to damage the Church, individuals within our community, relationships with the city, our sovereign status with the national authorities? These are vital questions, Angelo. I need to know the answers.'

The Secretary's voice was raised – a rare event.

Marchetti sat down, waiting for his superior's temper to cool. He looked at the floor and clasped his hands together.

'You have my word, Sylvestre. There will be a few ruffled feathers in the short term, nothing more. I repeat, what I am doing is neither illegal nor corrupt. It is a means of ensuring that we have adequate funds to meet an uncertain future. You have already seen Lord Bishop Marsini's summary and, no doubt, his assessment of our finances in the next decade. It makes for unwelcome reading.'

Marchetti spoke in a monotone. His quiet manner lending emphasis to his words.

'What he has not taken into account are the events in Central and South America. In my view these will exacerbate the situation. If we do not have the funds to counter the problem, we shall witness the disintegration of the largest bastion of the faith. We cannot afford to let that happen.'

The last had been delivered in a rising tone and when he stopped suddenly the words still rang around the room.

The Cardinal Secretary stared at him for some minutes.

'I want nothing to erupt that could cause embarrassment to the Holy Father, Angelo. Do you hear?'

'You have my word, Sylvestre.'

Chapter Forty-Eight

They had been thrown violently sideways by the blast. The rear window had shattered, glass cascading over the passengers. Somehow the Messenger had kept the car upright as it had zig-zagged helplessly across the carriageway.

Deafened, Marcus, who was sitting in the back, had at last managed to turn his head.

'My God!' he exclaimed. 'The car behind has just exploded!'

But no one heard him. He could not even hear himself. He stared at the scene, mesmerised, then realised they were still moving.

'Stop the car! Stop the car!' he shouted, thumping the Messenger on the arm.

He looked at Lisa, who was rigid in the front seat, her eyes closed.

'Are you all right?' he shouted putting his hand on her shoulder.

She neither moved nor replied. She was in shock.

The Messenger stared straight ahead, increasing speed to catch up with the lead car. Marcus slumped back. He could do nothing. What on earth is happening to us? he wondered. The world has gone mad.

Then, they were slowing down. A service station appeared just before the turn-off to Desenzano. The normality of the scene was bizarre, thought Marcus – people chatting, laughing, visiting the restaurant, filling their vehicles with fuel . . .

The Messenger drove to a deserted area and stopped beside the lead car. As soon as it had come to a halt he jumped out. Marcus went to the front passenger door, opened it and took Lisa in his arms. She burst into tears.

The Messenger returned grim-faced.

'We must drive on to Cremona. There is nothing we can do for them!'

At that moment, two fire engines, their sirens wailing raced down the opposite carriageway of the autostrada. The Messenger watched them go by.

'It was a bomb, wasn't it?'

'Yes. A large one. And it was intended for you. If Signora Robards had not objected to the guard's cigarette smoke, if we had not taken one of the other cars . . . we would have ceased to exist.'

'I'm sorry. One of them was your cousin,' said Marcus abjectly.

'When we get back to Cremona, I must return to my home . . . to explain what happened.'

'What about the bodies?'

'In that explosion, Signor Danby, there will be no sign of any bodies. I doubt they will find much of the car!'

Marcus knocked softly on her door.

He did not expect an answer, for Lisa had taken a shower and gone straight to bed.

'Is that you, Marcus?'

He put his head round the door. The drawn curtains shrouded the room in darkness.

'How are you feeling?'

'I didn't really sleep.'

'I'm sorry you had to witness it.'

Marcus edged towards the bed as his eyes adjusted to the gloom.

'One of them was Leonardo's cousin, wasn't he?'

'Yes. He has gone home to report his death. He keeps a stiff upper lip but, now I know him better, I could see he was really cut up.'

'It was meant for us, wasn't it? And to think I actually said we had too many guards.'

'Well, I've made up my mind. You are going back to the States on the next available flight.'

'Are you coming with me?'

'No! I'm not going to let them beat me,' he said fiercely. 'We are so close to the real answers.'

'Then, neither am I.'

'Dammit, Lisa! You are going whether you like it or not.'

'Who says? Who do you think you are, telling me what to do?'

'Have you no sense, woman? They mean business. They were pretty damn close back there! Who's to say how much closer they will get next time? You are going . . . no arguments!'

Lisa jumped up and stood on the end of the bed.

'How dare you tell me what's best? You jumped-up, small-minded, pompous ex-cleric!'

Her hands were on her hips, body angled forward aggressively. She wore not a stitch of clothing.

Marcus crossed his arms.

'Do you realise, my belligerent little lady, that your argument is rendered ludicrous by your lack of dignity? I shall wait outside while you dress, then we'll continue the discussion.'

Lisa grabbed at the duvet cover.

'Oh, Marcus, whatever are we going to do?'

It was said in such a dejected tone of voice that he turned and swept her into his arms.

'Darling, I only want you to be safe. Nothing else matters. But, can't you see, I have to go on. If whoever is behind this savagery wants us out the way, it must be worth a great deal to him. It's my duty to reveal his secrets. If not, he will be quite prepared to do away with whoever gets close next time – and the time after that, and so on!'

'Marcus, I've found you, and I'm not letting you go! If you carry on, so do I – and that's final!'

'Did he suffer?' his aunt asked.

'*No, zia, è stato molto rapido, non ha sentito nulla!*'

It was true. It had been very quick; he would have felt nothing.

His uncle took him by the arm and led him outside.

'What actually happened, Leonardo?'

The Messenger told him. Tears glistened in the older man's eyes.

'Is Mario OK?'

'Yes, uncle, and I shall make sure he is always safe. You have my word!'

His uncle clasped him to his chest. He still bore the memory of his damp cheeks.

'So be it, Leonardo. I thank you.'

He came down the hill from San Fortunato and turned onto the superstrada heading for Rome.

What news do you have?'

The cardinal was standing by a window, his face in shadow.

'The report will be finished very shortly. I shall return to the Vatican next week with the completed document.'

'Splendid! Have you encountered any problems?'

'I am afraid that a bomb intended for Danby and the woman, Robards, killed four other people on our journey to Cremona yesterday.' The Messenger paused. 'Three of them were people I employed in Venice.'

'The other. Who was he?'

'Someone from Umbria I knew well.'

'Never mind. As long as Danby and the girl were unharmed and can continue with the report . . . Do you know the results of his findings?'

The Messenger hesitated.

'I would say that Signor Danby will be able to identify all the factors that will lead to a revival of the Cremonese – provided, of course, the present-day luthiers have the talent and skills.'

'Doesn't he know if they have?'

'I believe he will do so within the next forty-eight hours, Your Eminence. That will be the concluding chapter and the assessment of their abilities, the appropriate appendix in the document.'

'You have done well. Just make sure you keep them alive for another five days. After that, we shall be withdrawing your services.'

Chapter Forty-Nine

A note had been pushed under their door. It triggered a memory. But what was it? Its elusive grip on the edges of his mind drifted away . . . it was gone! He picked it up. In the envelope was a message from Geri.

Marcus,
*   I need to pass over the assessments I have prepared. You*
mentioned you would be back this evening. Hopefully, you will have
returned when I call at ten o'clock tomorrow morning.
*   Geri Bellman*

One of the Messenger's cousins looked up, and smiled. He was sitting in an easy chair, his jacket pushed into a fold. As Marcus passed he saw the butt of a hand pistol in its holster. They really are taking no chances, he thought.

The table was strewn with files, notepads and records. He opened the computer. He had an hour before Geri arrived, time enough to add more material to the document that now comprised well over a hundred pages. He realised the appendices, which contained all the references to published items and the comple-mentary data, would have to be printed separately, otherwise the finished report would be far too bulky.

Within a few minutes he was totally engrossed. So much so that when his mobile phone rang it did not register at first. Lisa, coming from her room, picked it up from a side table.

'*Pronto! Tommaso! Come sta?* . . . Yes, we are alright, thank you. You want to speak with him? . . . Just a moment. I'll pass you over.'

Lisa gave him the phone.

'Tommaso! Good to hear from you.'

'Marcus, I'm glad you're there. I wanted an urgent word with you. Is it alright to speak, discreetly?'

'Of course. You sound concerned. Is something wrong?'

'Marcus, is Leonardo close by?'

He turned his back from the guard.

'No, not at present.'

'Good. It's about the violin he brought to studio, on which Alfredo did the analysis. As you know he took a sliver, and we carefully concealed the place where it had been removed.'

'Yes, that's right.'

'I took a number of photographs of the instrument, for the record, you understand, and to show I had actually held a del Gesù.'

There was a brief silence.

'I would have done the same,' said Marcus, filling the pause.

Tommaso's voice became hesitant. 'It was later, when I was looking at the photos, that something struck me. I went to one of the many reference books we have, and compared it with a photograph. It's the same instrument.'

'How do you mean, the same instrument?'

'Listen to me carefully, Marcus. I even had two of my people check the photos with a number of illustrations we have. There is no doubt.'

'Tommaso, what do you mean, no doubt?' exclaimed Marcus, looking across at Lisa.

'It's the missing "Magnificat", Marcus! Guarneri del Gesù made it in 1742. Similar to the "King". The edges are broad, and the *f* holes more upright, giving it a deeper tone. It was commissioned by the Austrian Empress, Maria Theresa, for her husband, Francis Stephen of Lorraine.'

'Good Lord! Are you sure?'

'Positive,' replied Tomasina. But something in his voice caught at Marcus.

'I have a feeling there is more to come!'

'Marcus, the violin disappeared in 1943. At the time it was owned by Joshua Liebermiers, a Viennese Jew. It was expropriated by the Nazis. I've checked. It's on the list of instruments never returned to their rightful owners or their successors. Where did the Messenger get hold of it?'

*

Geri Bellman had phoned to check they were there. Punctually, at ten, there was a tap on their door. The guard peered through the spy-hole, then stood aside for Marcus.

'It's OK. Let him in.'

The round figure turned in surprise at the man standing menacingly at Marcus' side.

'Have you already got company? Shall I come back later?'

'No need, Geri. I'll explain shortly. Come, sit down. Would you care for some coffee?'

The guard stayed by the door in the small lobby. Lisa and Marcus sat on the sofa. Geri had taken a chair to one side.

'The key question, Geri: do you believe they are up to it? Could we encourage a return to the methods, styles and standards of yesteryear, to bring about a renaissance?'

Geri grinned, sipped from his cup, then unclipped the folder he had in his hand.

'Without any shadow of doubt, Marcus. Here are the individual assessments. There is no question in my mind that, given the necessary impetus and an injection of cash to allow for an initial downturn in income, all the luthiers I have seen could play their part admirably.'

'Brilliant! That really is good news, isn't it Lisa? I am indebted to you, Geri. I couldn't have done it without you.'

'Does that mean that, with the addition of my contribution, your report is almost finished?'

'I need to polish it a bit. Lisa will help me. Then, yes, it will be ready to pass over.'

'I'd like to read a copy when it's finished. Will there be any chance of that?'

'I hope the Messenger's principals will agree, but, I would have to check first.'

'Naturally.' Bellman smiled at the couple. 'Did you have a worthwhile trip to Venice?'

Marcus glanced at Lisa.

'Yes . . . and no!' He leaned forward. 'I must tell you, Geri. Two things have happened in the last twelve hours that have shaken us. I mean really got through to us. On the way back to Cremona one of our cars was blown up. A bomb had been placed underneath it. We would have been travelling in it – if Lisa had not objected to the cigarette smoke – a guard, minding the vehicle, had been

235

smoking, so we swapped cars. On the autostrada it exploded into a thousand pieces.'

'Who would do such a thing? God! You were lucky!'

'Then, this morning, I had a call from Venice. An expert we were using phoned to say an instrument the Messenger has in his possession was stolen. In fact, it's the Magnificat! The instrument expropriated by the Nazis when they were rampaging through Europe, seeking out the finest instruments they could lay their hands on. Where does that put me? Is the Messenger representing a fascist clique from the past? We just don't know what to think, or do.'

'The Magnificat! That's amazing! Everyone has been searching for that violin. We all thought it had been destroyed. It's absolutely priceless!'

'Geri! You are not listening to me. It was stolen. It doesn't belong to the Messenger.'

Marcus was troubled by the look in his eyes. Overcome by the mention of the instrument, it was as though Geri Bellman cared nothing for its true ownership or its history.

Marcus finished the draft that afternoon. Lisa took his seat, and began putting it into a more presentable format. During a short break, he asked how she was faring on her article.

'Like you, I've got to the final draft stage. But I'm not going to submit it until we have a few more answers. There may even be a last chapter for your magnum opus.' She smiled wryly. 'That's if we get through unscathed.'

At eight o'clock there was a knock at the door. Marcus checked the spy-hole. It was Geri. They had arranged to eat together in the hotel. In the restaurant, their two guards took an adjoining table.

'Do they go everywhere?'

'Almost everywhere!'

'Are they really necesary?'

'Geri,' Lisa said, 'someone, though it's probably more than one, is very keen to get rid of us. They attacked me in Milan, but that was more of a deterrent. They tried to run Marcus off the road. When that failed threw him out a fourth floor hotel window. And, as Marcus told you earlier, on the way back from Venice, they tried to blow up our car!'

'Have you told the police? Surely this has gone far enough. You should place the matter in their hands.'

'They would never be able to give us round-the-clock protection. Nor could they react the way our own guards would,' explained Marcus. 'I know it would be logical. But the sooner we can finish the report and clear up several other outstanding items, the sooner we can leave Italy.'

'What is driving this person – or people – to silence you?'

'We just don't know,' replied Lisa. 'However, I think it could be that we are getting closer and closer to something they don't want publicised.'

'Is it to do with your report?' queried Bellman.

'I can't see it. Mind you, we have discovered an interesting fact,' said Marcus, enthusiastically. Out of the corner of his eye, he saw Lisa frowning. She had not wanted any reference to Venice aired until they were sure of their facts. But Geri was a close friend. He saw no reason to hide it from him.

'What's that?'

'Pietro Guarneri was supplying finishing materials to the Cremonese. A number of them were toxic, and I'm convinced he knew the effect they would have. It's our belief he poisoned them!'

'Are you sure?'

I would say 99% certain. We have had tests done that show arsenic was present in the varnishes and in the remains of one of Stradivari's apprentices.'

Bellman was silent for a moment. 'Why on earth would he do that?'

'We don't think it was jealousy. Our thoughts are he was working for someone, He was either paid handsomely, or promised something of consequence. We just don't know . . . yet.'

'How do you mean, "yet"?'

'We are going to get to the bottom of this, Geri,' declared Lisa. 'We are not going to be thwarted. Something seriously big is, or has been, going on. We intend to find out if Pietro was an agent for others, and what the reasons for a grand cover-up might be.'

'Have you looked at this situation logically?' Bellman asked, as the first course of their meal was served.

'Meaning?'

'Meaning, Marcus, using the police dictum: motive, means and opportunity!'

Marcus glanced at Lisa.

'Well ... no. We haven't really come down to earth after the bomb incident.'

'Then let us review the case calmly. For example, who stood to gain from the demise of the Cremonese?'

'The luthiers in Padua, Milan, Bologna, even Rome, perhaps,' suggested Lisa. 'Any one of them could have wanted to bring down Cremona.'

'True, Lisa, but, who *really* profited from their departure?'

'Well, I suppose, the Venetians,' she responded, hesitantly. 'Pietro could have been working for a cabal in Venice. There was a flourishing group of luthiers when he was there – Serafin, Montagnana, Gofriller ...

'What about the Germans?'

'The Germans? Yes ... I suppose so. Or, more exactly, the Austrians,' replied Lisa, thoughtfully. 'They controlled Füssen, Mittenwald and Absam, where the Stainer dynasty was. I recall instrument making in these border towns only got going after Lombardy died out. Are you saying the Austrians were behind it?'

'No,' Bellman laughed. 'You are jumping to conclusions, my dear. Though, on reflection, who is to say that might not be one possibility?' He picked up his glass of wine. 'It could easily have been some high-ranking official of the Empire, close to the Hapsburgs, suggesting it might be useful to have the centre for the world's finest instrument making in Austria, rather than in the tenuously-held lands of Northern Italy. Who is to say the Holy Roman Emperor wouldn't have acted upon it. He would certainly have had a motive and, with his power, the means and opportunity.'

The knock heralded the expected visitor. This time Lisa checked the spy-hole and nodded to the guard.

'Roberto! Come in, please.'

The bookseller came hesitantly into the suite. when he saw Marcus his face lit up.

'Fra' Marcus, how are you? It's good to see you again! So, do I now presume you are friends?'

Lisa smiled. 'You could say that. One thing I should clear up. Marcus has relinquished his position in the Church.'

The older man's eyebrows came together questioningly.

'Let me explain,' said Lisa hurriedly. 'Unbeknown to me, Marcus had decided to give up his vocation before we met. He had already applied for his release from the Xaverian Order. He is a free man. He has his own room over there.'

Lisa was making a hash of it, Marcus thought. He came to the rescue.

'Signor Marciano, have you had breakfast? Would you care for some coffee? Something to eat, perhaps?'

'Coffee would be fine, er . . . Signor Danby.' He turned to Lisa, who was still discomfited by her garbled explanation. 'Cara, why did you want to see me so urgently? It sounded like the end of the world!'

'Sit down, signore. I'll bring you your coffee,' said Marcus.

Lisa led him to one of the sofas, and they sat together.

'Roberto, we have known each other a long time, have we not?'

'Since you were a little girl, cara!'

'I know I can trust you. But, now you are here, I feel a little nervous – for two reasons: I need to have your absolute assurance that what we say will go no further, and my fear is that speaking with you might be putting you in danger.'

'Lisa, who would want to do anything to a harmless old man? Tell me what you want, it will be in complete confidence.'

Lisa looked up at Marcus. breathed deeply, and began.

'You've got an extensive knowledge of the Cremonese, and you know the effect it had on instrument making when the last of them, Carlo Bergonzi, died in 1747. If I tell you we can prove their deaths were premeditated, can you think of any good reason why? Can you think who could possibly have benefited from their cold-blooded extermination?'

'You say you have proof of their murder? All of them?' Marciano sat there in silence for a moment. 'Do you know, it does not surprise me! I have always thought it strange – no, suspicious more like – that seven eminent luthiers should pass away in such a short space of time. One of those eternal questions I have often asked myself.' He gave a half-smile. 'So, you think they were dispatched for a reason? Now that raises any number of questions. Rivalry gone too far? Another city coveting Cremona's pre-eminence? A group of individuals happening upon a scheme to undermine the Cremonese? Someone sees an opportunity to improve his lot by their disappearance? The reasons could be legion.'

239

Marciano drank more of his coffee.

'Such an enterprise would take planning, and considerable patience. To wait a decade for the moment would be beyond the patience of most men. Therefore, it would have to be a sizeable power, one capable of employing individuals who could be persuaded to do its dirty work and keep quiet. And for what? A gift, a bribe, blackmail, whatever – it doesn't matter. But powerful inducements would have been necessary.'

He sat back on the sofa, and closed his eyes.

'So, logically, let us examine the likely contenders. In Northern Europe there were those emerging as capable, though not distinguished, instrument makers. For example, the French, headed by the Vuillaume family, are possibles. In fact, Jean Vuillaume was, supposedly, an apprentice of Stradivari's. Jean Baptiste, the family's shining light, used to make precise replicas of Guarneri del Gesù's violins; few could tell the difference. So he must have had access to his designs.'

He paused.

'There again, Gagliano of Naples was also an apprentice of Stradivari's. He, and his sons, were the acknowledged founders of the Neapolitan School. They, too, could produce Stradivari lookalikes.'

Marciano crossed his arms, and rested his chin on his chest.

'Of course, there's Venice. Probably the greatest of them was Matteo Gofriller. Though thought of as a Venetian, he was actually Tyrolean – like David Tecchler. Now he was a wild man of the times! He eventually moved to Rome, but frequently came back to Venice.'

Marciano continued to muse.

'Domenico Montagnana was a pupil of Gofriller's and Pietro Guarneri worked for him for a while, before starting up on his own. Yes, it could certainly have been the Venetians; there was no love lost between Cremona and *La Serennisma*!'

'Signor Marciano, it is our belief Pietro Guarneri was the one responsible for the deaths of the Cremonese. We have discovered he supplied arsenic in the materials they bought from him.' declared Marcus.

Marciano did not seem surprised by the revelation.

'A likely possibility, my friend.'

'Do you think he could have been influenced by Gofriller or Tecchler?'

'In what way? Style, do you mean?'

'That. Perhaps political allegiance? Could he have been motivated by their ties to Austria?'

'He could easily have been. They were ardent Hapsburgians, even though their calling took them away from their fatherland.'

'A close friend of Marcus has suggested,' said Lisa, 'that the Austrians might have been behind the murder of the Cremonese.'

The bookseller studied the pair.

'I must admit, I hadn't really thought beyond our boundaries. But then Lombardy wasn't part of Italy, was it? It had been annexed by the Austrian Empire. It's an entertaining idea. Instrument making certainly took off in Austria and Germany after they died. Tell me more about this theory.'

Lisa cleared her throat.

'It was no more than a surmise, you understand. However, just imagine if the Hapsburg monarchs, Charles Vl, then his daughter, Maria-Theresa, wanted to take the Italian jewel in the crown away from Cremona, to re-locate it in Austria. Not in the centre – that would have been too obvious. Somewhere in the border towns, where they could have made good use of the Cremonese patterns – like Mittenwald and Füssen. Stainer had his empire in Absam, no great distance away. They would certainly have enjoyed a freer run at all the European markets. I'm almost convinced that's what happened.'

Marciano raised an eyebrow. 'Intriguing, my dear. If Pietro Guarneri were the one supplying the toxic substances, it could well have been the Tyroleans who hatched the idea of wresting the title away, blending their ambition with Pietro's antipathy towards his family and others in the Piazza di San Domenico. They could easily have persuaded him to poison them.'

He looked up at Marcus.

'Do you think I might be permitted something stronger than coffee, Signor Danby? It's early, I know, but I think I need something to fortify me after what Lisa has suggested.'

'Of course, Signor Marciano!'

Marcus found a bottle of Pomace in the mini-bar.

'An interesting supposition, cara – one that should not be

discounted. If, as you say, you now know Pietro was responsible for the deaths of the Cremonese . . . then I would also go along with your comment that he must have been influenced by others. From what I have read, he was a vain man, angered by the fact that his talents, which he rated highly, did not enjoy wider recognition. Presumably, you have no proof he worked for the Austrians?'

Lisa shook her head.

'Not yet! But, if it's there, we intend to find it,' declared Marcus.

'By going back to Venice?' the bookseller enquired.

'No. I think we should go to Austria.'

It was then a thought struck him.

'Tell me, Signor Marciano, what do you know of the instruments expropriated by the Nazis during World War Two?'

'Why do you ask?'

'Someone was telling me about the hoard of violins and other instruments gathered up by the Germans during the war.'

'It is true,' he said simply. 'My family lost a violin made by Giacomo Cordano. I remember it well. I was occasionally allowed to play it. Not that I was really interested at the time. But then, it did not have the value such instruments have today.'

Marciano smiled at the recollection. He looked across at Lisa.

'That's when I met your father, cara. He and his father introduced me to their synagogue. Our families were living in Trieste at the time. As Jews, we thought we were free from persecution. But, in 1943, when the Germans put Mussolini back in power, that's when the witch hunts began.'

He looked into the depths of the glass, seeing again the past.

'They began rounding us up. Their troops systematically cleared Jews from Milan, Genoa . . . right across northern Italy.'

Marciano paused at the memory.

'My family remained. Lorenzo, Lisa's father, and I were taken by his people to Fiume, across the Croatian peninsula. Rijeka, I believe it's called now. But the Germans came there as well. Fortunately, we were given false documents by Giovanni Palatucci, the policeman who saved hundreds of Jews. The Nazis, or, to be precise, one particular group, was led by a man called Alfred Rosenberg. Under Hitler's instructions he put together a team of musicologists whose job it was to evaluate, catalogue and transport the best instruments in occupied Europe back to the Music Office in Berlin. Known as the *Sonderstab Musik*, Rosenberg's task force collected our prized violins, violas, and cellos. Their aim? To use them in a university to be founded in Linz, Hitler's home town, after Germany had won the war.'

'I didn't know any of this!' said Marcus, shocked by Marciano's revelations.

'Well, I knew something about what happened from my father – but not the expropriation of instruments or the proposed university,' said Lisa.

'Actually, it's noted in recently declassified US military war records. They hold captured German documents and post-holocaust claims. There's also material about the seizure in the Centre de Documentation in Paris – and even Nazi and private documents in Cambridge University in England, Marcus. All substantiate what Rosenberg did on behalf of his Fuhrer. There is even a database of confiscated Jewish property, listing the instruments stolen, in the State Archives in Vienna.'

Chapter Fifty

'Welcome, Your Eminence. I believe you know many of us here. They all certainly know of you!'

Marchetti smiled – his customary smile that failed to ease the tensions felt by everyone seated at the large oval table.

The limousine had pulled up outside the Campidoglio, and had immediately been attended by the mayor. The cardinal, accompanied by his secretary, had been courteously ushered through the foyer of the building and onwards to the meeting room. Following behind were Lord Bishop Marsini and two of the Vatican's lawyers. Brother Felipé carried numerous folders and the cardinal's briefcase.

Marchetti entered the opulently furnished salon, and was presented to the Deputy Prime Minister, who had made the opening remark:

'Thank you for the opportunity to discuss our position. Where would you like us to sit?'

They were led to one end of the oval. Around them were representatives of the mayor's office, people from the Ministry of the Interior, and several faces Marchetti did not recognise.

He immediately took the initiative.

'I do not know everyone here, Mr Mayor. Perhaps you would be so good as to introduce the gentlemen on my left.'

'They are from our legal department, Your Eminence. Signori Fiaschini and Matreleo.' They nodded towards the prelate. 'The two people next to them are from the law firm we use. Signor Francchini and Signor Bottolini.'

Marchetti bowed his head in acknowledgement.

The Deputy saw his chance and opened the discussion.

'I am told, Your Eminence, that you are in the final stages of a plan to relocate the Vatican. Perhaps, like others, I have been

misled. Could you correct me if I have been given false information? Or confirm, at this table, that the Holy See is about to
move its entire city to another site?'

Let the game begin, thought Marchetti.

'As ever, Mr Deputy Prime Minister, there are truths in both
assertions. I, too, was apprised of this rumour. Clearly, someone
party to the many discussions which take place in the Vatican has
revealed what I would term a random idea cast at an internal
meeting.'

He scanned those sitting around him.

'In fact, I can recall offering the notion perhaps a year or so
ago. Anyway, it doesn't matter. Subsequently, I have heard it on
the lips of others. Several people have even suggested it emanated
from my own office. A fanciful insinuation! But, as we are all aware,
it has gained momentum. Why? Because, logically, it is not without
merit. So much so that I initiated a number of research projects. I
employed organisations to consider the feasibility of such a move,
and they have worked long hours assessing the "rumour" as a
sound proposal. That explains how we became involved – and what
has occurred as a result.'

'Really?' The Deputy's response was sceptical. 'So, am I to believe
that the scheme is not yet finalised?'

'Let me put it into it context. Theoretically, were we to take the
decision now, the civil and structural engineers, architects, surveyors, town planners, utility service providers, all are adamant we
could create a new Vatican City within five years. They have even
produced a visual guide to demonstrate how it could be effected.'
Marchetti placed both hands on the table, and surveyed his audience. 'Brother Felipé has spoken with one of the mayor's people
about disk transmission, I believe. We can show you something of
their proposal, and the cultural aims we have in mind.'

It was a brief but encompassing presentation, graphically portray-
ing the preparation of the site on the river, the dismantling of the
major buildings in the Vatican, their re-erection, the creation of
numerous facilities within a walled enclave and, importantly, the
resurrection of the Cremonese tradition.

When it ended, the Deputy remarked dryly, 'Your people have
done their homework well, Your Eminence. However, I would be
interested to learn why you have assumed that the city might be
located on the banks of the Po. Equally, that you have such firm

ideas about how such a plan would work, given the short amount of time you have had at your disposal.'

The cardinal's lips parted in the semblance of a smile.

'We own one hundred hectares of land on the banks of the Po, between Cremona and Mantua – an ideal position.'

'Really? May I enquire how you came to possess this land?'

'From the Holy Roman Emperor himself, Joseph II. He gave it as an unfettered gift to the Pontiff, Pius VI, in 1785.'

'But is that not land in Italy? The Vatican may have rights of tenure but, if memory serves me correctly, not absolute rights of ownership of a foreign soil. Perhaps the mayor's lawyers could answer this point?'

They had obviously been primed. Documents were pored over: whispered discussion took place.

'You are right, sir. Another country or state may have dominion over part, or the whole, of an area of land only with the express permission of the resident sovereign state.'

'I do not refute it,' replied Marchetti calmly. 'My lawyers have told me the same, Mr Deputy. Though you will appreciate that, at the time, the land was gifted by the Austrians who were the ruling power in Lombardy. As many of the statutes pertaining to their governance are still observed, our legal interpretation is that our dominion is indisputable.'

'I am afraid you have been misled, Cardinal Marchetti,' said the Deputy, a half-smile playing at the corners of his mouth.

'Perhaps, Mr Deputy.' Marchetti was all cordial urbanity. 'Naturally, it would not have been wise to rely absolutely on such a lawful and binding agreement because of its age. That is why we had the authorities' legal department in Milan, the capital of the region, assess the deed. They indicated it could be brought into question. That's why they recommended that, as an Italian citizen, I acquire the land from the Vatican for a nominal sum, and become the rightful owner. This I did, and have now legally given the Vatican free and full use of all those lands I own, for as long as they shall be required.'

'That cannot be done, Mr Deputy. That is an unlawful act!' shouted one of the lawyers.

'Not according to the Milanese,' stated Marchetti. 'I would add that the plan I personally presented to the various official departments, indicating my wish to build a small township, was welcomed.

It promises much work for the local people and would undoubtedly encourage further development in the area. They readily agreed to endorse the building project.'

Marchetti turned to Brother Felipé, who removed a copy of the relevant document from the briefcase and passed it across the table.

The Deputy nodded.

'How would you finance the move, Your Eminence?'

'Again, I have consulted with experts. I am informed that the sale of the land occupied by the Holy See in Rome would fetch up to seven billion Euros – more than enough to cover our costs.'

'It would if the privileges of sale were yours. But they are not. The Vatican may be a sovereign state, but if it were to leave its location it would cede all rights of entitlement.'

He looked across at the lawyers for affirmation. They nodded. Another orchestrated move, thought Marchetti.

'As you might expect, Mr Deputy, my people have examined the documents relating to the agreement signed in 1929 most assiduously. As with any embassy, office or department housed in a building in a foreign country, the occupants benefit from the deeds and titles. Invariably they were purchased for that particular use, and the occupiers have the facility to sell at the price they nominate if they choose to leave such premises.'

The cardinal was enjoying himself. This time the ghost of a smile even reached his eyes.

'I will ask my colleague, Brother Felipé, to show you one of the documents your legal advisers may have missed. It is a bill of sale, signed by Monsignor Pacelli on 11th February, 1930. It clearly shows that the forty-five hectares were purchased by the Church.'

Once more a sheet of paper moved between the two parties. The Deputy was tight-lipped.

'This move could still be blighted, Cardinal Marchetti,' declared the mayor, rising to his feet. 'All the contractors you would use might suddenly find their order books full – committed to other projects, unable to meet your schedule; the whole project could be jeopardised. One should never overestimate one's workforce! If they are not prepared to work at the speed you require, or within the constraints you impose, the move could easily founder.'

The cardinal recognised they had reached the threatening stage.

Clearly, the legal tactics they had hoped to employ were not going to work.

'True, Mr Mayor. But I can tell you with absolute certainty that there are many who would work to whatever demands we placed upon them. And those that would not . . . well, we have contracting companies standing by within neighbouring EU countries who would gladly take their place.'

The mayor sat down abruptly. This time Marchetti got to his feet.

'I must tell you, gentlemen, this whole project, which has grown from an idle comment to occupy the centre of our minds, is one that would revitalise the Church and all its members. It is an inspirational concept and I am proud to be a part of it.'

He surveyed the upturned faces.

'We shall also revitalise the region of Lombardy. Even as we speak my people are assessing how we can bring about the resorgimento of Cremona; resurrect the skills and talents of the Cremonese. Just think . . . the revival of the town as the centre of the world's instrument-making! The Milan authorities are prepared to invest in such a magnificent venture. They are not casting doubt on the projected move; they applaud the scheme and all it will entail. I believe the national government should do the same. Thank you, gentlemen.'

The Lord Bishop Marsini, the two lawyers and Brother Felipé followed in his wake as the cardinal swept from the room.

Chapter Fifty-One

'It was not your fault, Jozsef. Do not keep apologising.'

They were in their customary meeting place, the stube at the Altenburg Hotel on the outskirts of Innsbruck.

'It would appear they changed cars on a whim. You cannot allow for that.'

So that's what happened. But he is being far too tolerant. Is there something else on his mind? wondered Jozsef. It's not in his nature to forgive, even when a course of action is thwarted by the unexpected.

'So, Herr Goehr, what do you want me to do?' Jozsef drank his beer. 'Shall I finish the job? I could use the Steyr 50HS, with the scope, from a distance of several hundred metres. They wouldn't get near me!'

'No. You might get one, but not both. Anyway, they are so well protected even that would be risky. I have a different plan.' Goehr marshalled his thoughts. 'Firstly, we should do nothing more in Italy. To continue there will only alert the authorities. I want them here, in Austria, where I can be satisfied of their removal.'

Goehr finished his drink.

'Get rid of the others. They are no longer needed. Just keep a watchful eye on the couple, and report their movements. I believe they will soon be heading in this direction.'

The news bulletin mentioned that a van had been seen in the vicinity of Canale Monterano. As yet, there was no evidence to connect the dead body with the vehicle. However, the police would like to interview the driver, merely to exclude him from their inquiries.

Lambertini switched off the car radio. He was finding it difficult to concentrate these days. Several of his clients were considering the appointment of another lobbyist.

I must pull myself together, get back on track, he rationalised. But the image of the body in the shallow grave occupied his thoughts. It was even haunting him at night. Not only was he not sleeping, Lambertini had lost interest in his food. Drink, and plenty of it, seemed to bring the only solace.

The cardinal's secretary called down for a Messenger.

As had happened so many times recently, a sealed envelope was handed to him with instructions to travel to Mittenwald. The despatcher noted that he was travelling to the German border town with a package weighing less than fifty grams.

He looked back through his records.

While the Messengers had varied, the cardinal had sent someone on this route nine times during the past month. Sometimes that person had returned with an envelope of the same weight. The cardinal was evidently exchanging correspondence with someone in Mittenwald – correspondence important enough for it to be delivered by hand. The despatcher went about his business. Nothing would be said, but the question of why such secrecy was necessary kept recurring in his mind.

Franz was worried. Jozsef had been called away – no doubt to be rebuked by their employer. He sat in the room, watching television with the two Hungarians. Cans cluttered the table, unwashed dishes lay in the kitchen sink.

What was he doing here? More critically, what would Jozsef do when he returned? Franz had been responsible for placing the bomb under the car. He had been convinced it had been the right one. He could not understand what had gone wrong. Was he just to sit and await judgement? Might he disappear, as Heinz had disappeared?

I don't think so, he concluded. When these two finally drink themselves stupid and pass out, I'll make other arrangements. In the meantime I'll slip out and pack. When they are asleep I'll even relieve them of their money. It will help fund my exit.

Chapter Fifty-Two

The Messenger returned just before lunch. As he came silently through the door, Marcus leapt up from his chair and strode towards him.

'I've got one question for you, my friend. Who really owns the violin?'

'Signor Danby, do I presume you are upset over something?'

'Too right, he's upset!' cried Lisa. 'He took a call from Signor Tomasina yesterday morning. Do you know what he said? He said your violin was stolen Jewish property. Stolen by the Nazis in 1943. What do you have to say to that?'

The Messenger sat down. His features gave nothing away.

After a moment's silence, he said, 'I cannot tell you who the owners are, Signora Robards. But I am positive they are above suspicion. I am confident they would have been unaware, as were you, of the previous owner.'

'Is that all you can say!' retorted Marcus. 'Frankly, it's unconvincing! Do you realise that what you were offering me is not only priceless, it has on it the blood of countless thousands who have perished? I want no part of it . . . of all this research.' He flung an arm in the direction of the table. 'Or of your masters. We are finished, do you hear? Finished!'

The Messenger stared at him. When he spoke his voice was chilling.

'Signor Danby, as I have said several times, you have a contract. And I repeat, I cannot allow you to break it. If you attempt to do so, at my word, your protectors will become your executioners.'

Lisa and Marcus were dumbfounded.

'You will complete the document as agreed. Just remind yourself, from time to time, of the dual role my cousins can play. It might help focus your thoughts.'

251

Marcus could hardly believe his ears. This man was no friend. He had been lulled into thinking so, but the Messenger represented a higher, dispassionate authority – one, it seemed, that would not be deflected from its aims.

'How dare you talk to us in this manner,' Lisa exploded. 'Come on, Marcus, we're out of here.'

'Signora, I wouldn't risk it. You have too much to lose.'

'Let's go, Marcus. This guy's too much! Who does he think he is?'

'Giancarlo! Remove your pistol from its holster and aim first at Signora Robards. When I give the signal, shoot her, then Signor Danby.'

'You wouldn't dare.'

'Signora, who would take notice of the sound of a bottle being opened? No one! Disposing of your bodies might present a problem, but not an insurmountable one. I mean what I say. You would never walk through that door!'

'Even if we don't leave now, there will be other opportunities,' said Lisa defiantly. 'I will not tolerate being told what we can and cannot do by you, or anyone.'

'Perhaps you should listen to Signor Danby. What do you say, signore? Shall I kill your lady friend? I will have no hesitation in shooting her, so do not try to leave, or destroy the material on your computer.'

Angry as he was, Marcus knew they had little choice.

'Lisa, we cannot argue with a loaded gun,' he said. Then, turning to the Messenger, 'But beware, my friend! I shall remember this.'

He subsided into the chair and stared at the piles of papers and records, representing the sum of their many hours researching the Cremonese. It was a tangible mark of his efforts. Could he simply abandon it?

Lisa went into her bedroom and slammed the door.

Marcus added several paragraphs to the report, then began annotating the appendices. He had been sickened by the Messenger's readiness to shoot them, and his heartless exploitation of Marcus' attachment to Lisa. Leonardo knew there was no way he would allow harm to come to her.

The Messenger lounged on a sofa. For all his apparent detachment, he was disquieted by the threat he had issued. Abruptly, he rose, strode to his room and locked the door. Uncertainty was growing about the strength of his allegiance to his masters. In the past, in moments of doubt, it had been convenient to incline to the view they could do no wrong. They were at the pinnacle of the faith; they should be above suspicion. But the chinks in their ideological armour were growing wider and deeper.

Much troubled, the Messenger picked up the phone.

'*Pronto!*'

'*Papà, ho besogno del tuo aiuto!*'

He had again turned to his father for advice.

Twenty minutes later he re-entered the sitting room. Telling his cousin he was no longer needed, he turned to Marcus.

'Signor Danby, please be so kind as to ask Signora Robards to join us.'

Marcus did as requested.

There was a knock at the door and two waiters were ushered in with a large lunch trolley.

Lisa glared furiously at the tall figure when she came out.

'Please sit with me, Signora Robards, Signor Danby.'

They sat away from the Messenger. He rose and poured white wine into their glasses, then resumed his chair.

'I have been considering your discovery, and what you said.' He paused. 'I am sorry for my attitude earlier. I want you to know that, personally, I am not involved in anything illegal, nor, for that matter, I hope, are the people I represent. But you are right. Because of what has come to light you should know who they are, if only to understand that they are probably innocent of any wrong-doing.

The plane's wheels scuffed the runway, picking up speed to cushion the landing of the Tyrolean Airways flight from Milan to Vienna. A short while later Lisa, and two of the cousins, joined the queue at the taxi rank and climbed into one vehicle. Marcus and the Messenger rode in another.

Having checked in at the Intercontinental by the park, they booked a junior suite and an adjoining room. Even after the Messenger's apology Lisa had been distant. On one hand, her anger was mollified somewhat by his explanation, yet, on the other, she was less than happy to be venturing into Austria.

Marcus had won her over.

'If you think the Austrians were behind it, that they manipulated Pietro Guarneri, then where else do we check? We both agreed we have to go on while we still have protection. Frankly, the sooner we clear up the matter, the better. In my opinion, if you are right, it would also offer the clearest possible explanation of why Italian instrument-making went into decline after the Cremonese.'

Marcus had hesitated.

'Actually, there are two strands to this research. If we think the poisoning was prompted by the companies themselves, then we have to go across the border into Germany. The local records are bound to give us a clue, some indication of what happened all those years ago! If you believe what you said, so vehemently, last night and this morning, that the Hapsburgs were behind it, we must explore the Austrian State Archives.'

Five tickets had been purchased for an evening flight to Vienna. With a few hours to spare, Marcus had made further additions to the report. These included a reference to instruments missing since World War Two, and how they were now appearing for sale on the international market, often with a dubious provenance. In some cases, instruments were being discovered in the hands of organisations or individuals who could not fail to be aware of their original ownership.

Chapter Fifty-Three

'There's a policeman to see you, Signor Lambertini.'

'Oh!'

The statement shocked him. Why on earth were they here? He had left nothing that could connect him to Angelina.

'Tell him I'll be right out!'

In the reception area he found two police officers. One, clearly the more senior, stepped forward.

'Good morning, signore. I am sorry to trouble you. I am Inspector Leoni. Could you spare my colleague and I a few minutes?' He thrust out a warrant card.

Lambertini hesitated. It would not be appropriate to hold a conversation here, it was too public.

'Of course. Why don't you come through to my office.'

When the lobbyist closed the door, the officer got straight to the point.

'Signor Lambertini, do you know a woman called Angelina Scacchi?'

'No.'

'Are you sure, signore?'

He appeared to ponder on the question.

'I do not know anyone of the name of Scacchi. The only person I know called Angelina is the receptionist at the Town Hall. She wears a badge with her name on it.'

'Ah! I see. Then you have met her?'

'Well, in my business, I regularly visit the Campidoglio. She often greets me. Why do you ask?'

'We have found her body, signore,' answered the other policeman. 'What is more, she had your visiting card in her handbag.'

'That's possible, I suppose. As I say, I am often at the Town Hall.'

255

'But, why would you give her your card, signore? Surely, if you are a frequent visitor, she would not need it? Wouldn't you give it to the person you were seeing rather than a receptionist?'

He was being persistent. Lambertini shrugged his shoulders. 'I really cannot say why she had it. Obviously, I passed them to the receptionists some time ago so that they might remember my name. But I haven't given them cards in recent times. As you say, there's been no need.'

There was a slight pause. Then Leoni said, 'Well, I think that clears the matter up. It's merely a routine enquiry, you understand, tying up any loose ends. Thank you for your time, signore.'

'They're in Vienna. I managed to buy a ticket at the airport and followed them. They are staying at the Intercontinental Hotel. They've got two rooms on the fourth floor.'

Goehr let out a sigh. He had got them this far. Should he arrange something in Vienna?

'How many are there?'

'Five.'

'Continue to observe. Keep me posted of their movements.'

'What are they doing there?'

'Because I want them there. Quite literally, it is a step in the right direction.'

'But that means they are unearthing things. They are getting closer. You must stop this game, Martin. Now!'

'We both know the need for silence. You haven't been able to handle it, so I will. *My* way!'

The phone went dead.

Cardinal Grossmann folded his arms across his chest. Then, lifting a hand, he pulled it hard down his face. It was becoming complicated. His past was rising to haunt him. If the real story were to emerge . . . Those teenage years in Vienna were not something he wished to have made public. Obviously, they would be searching in the State Archives. What if they came upon any incriminating documents?

The memories flooded back: he had been a key assistant to the Former Hitler Youth leader, Baldur von Schirach, when he was

Gauleiter of Vienna. Baldur had liked young men around him. He had encouraged Gustav to help the Vugesta, an agency of the Gestapo, to confiscate Jewish property. Grossmann recalled the zeal he had shown, how proud he had been to bring to von Schirach expensive jewellery, valuable books, paintings – and musical instruments.

At the time, he had not cared what happened to the owners, nor what they thought of him: the notes they scribbled down of his atrocities. However, he knew that damning evidence was there somewhere – buried deep no doubt, but extant in the files stored in the Austrian capital.

Chapter Fifty-Four

The Messenger had apologised, but Marcus was still wary. It was clear he had a strong commitment to the Pontifical Family, an attachment as elemental as the umbilical cord.

When Marcus emerged from his room for breakfast, the Messenger was finishing a conversation on his mobile.

'*Si . . . Si . . . molto bene . . . et cum spiritu tuo!*'

There it was again! 'And with thy spirit'. The response to a number of Latin phrases, particularly '*Pax vobiscum*' – peace be with you. The Messenger looked up.

'It is all arranged. We are expected at the State Archives in Minoritenplatz at eleven o'clock. We shall be met by Herr Schoenen, who will take us to the Hapsburg Family records. Perhaps you would inform Signora Robards.'

'Thank you. I have been thinking about that. The problem for us will be that all the documents and files will be in German. How do we go about obtaining a translator?'

'There will be no need. I speak German. I shall translate for you.'

'Excellent! I'll tell Lisa.'

They were led through the building to the Hapsburg Collection.

Herr Schoenen was an earnest young man who spoke English with a lilting accent. He was anxious to please: if they needed the slightest help, they should call him. He gave them his internal phone number, all the time his eyes straying to the Messenger, deferring to him as leader of the trio.

When he had gone, the Messenger said, 'It appears, there are four sections relating to the Hapsburgs. The *Habsburgisch-lothringis-che Familienarchive*, which covers family correspondence, records,

258

and details of baptisms, marriages and deaths, travel and property matters; the *Kabinettsarchiv*, which comprises papers relating to the administration of the Hapsburg lands, the documents which the emperors always kept close at hand, and those dealing with ecclesiastical matters; the *Hofarchive*, which hold the records of the many judicial, ceremonial and administrative duties at the imperial court; and finally, the *Ah. Privat- und Familienfonde* – these relate to the history of the royal family, the administration of their domains, and the management of their many palaces.' He shrugged. 'I cannot suggest where you start. References to Venice or Cremona could be in any of them.'

Marcus looked at Lisa, and raised his eyebrows.

'This is going to take longer than I thought. I suppose we could do it by a simple process of elimination, in order of possibility. For example, I don't think there would be anything in the last section, their family history and the maintenance of the palaces. Almost on a par would be the third. You say this section deals with the judiciary and ceremony? An unlikely repository for whatever we are seeking. What do you say we start with the second one, the Cabinet Archives. I'm intrigued that the documents here are those which the various emperors wanted by their side.'

Lisa had a smattering of German and was able to pick up the gist of many documents. Marcus, who had no understanding of the language, had the Messenger by his side reading the pages he turned. When required, the Messenger, who was seated in the middle, swung to his left to translate an item for Lisa.

Two hours later they decided to halt for lunch. Looking at the tomes in the first section, Marcus realised the enormity of their task. They had ploughed through eleven volumes, but this constituted merely one small part of the first section. He said nothing to the others.

After a brief meal, they again set to. They had almost finished the *Kabinettsarchiv*, but for two volumes, when Herr Schoenen came to tell them the Archive building was about to close for the day.

The next morning, the same format was adopted when they moved on to the family records and correspondence. By midafternoon, nothing of any relevance had appeared. They had worked straight through and Marcus was beginning to wonder if they were wasting their time. Lisa had finished her volumes and now selected several relating to the *Hofarchive*, the administrative aspects of judicial and ceremonial duties and the work of the Supreme Master of the Hunt, the *Oberstjägermeister*. Marcus was still turning the pages of a tome concerning the Hapsburg's personal correspondence.

'This is interesting! Have a look at this.' Lisa said to the Messenger. 'Look at this. In 1785, Emperor Joseph made a bequest of 100 hectares of hunting land to the Church. Have I got that right?'

The Messenger studied the document. 'Intriguing! I must have a copy of this. Well done, Lisa!'

He forgot himself, she thought. It obviously means something to him, he called me by my first name.

Twisting in his chair, the Messenger glanced at the next document Marcus had turned to.

'Stop!'

His shout echoed throughout the book-lined room. Marcus leaned forward. Lisa jumped to her feet. They both peered over the Messenger's shoulder.

Oktober 1765

Ihre Majeſtät,

Wenn Herr Goehr Schwerigkeiten hat, dürfte er vielleicht auf die Stradivari Geige zugreifen, die für Ihren Ehemann erworben wurde? Dieſ könnte ihm helfen, seine Fähigkeiten zu perfektionieren.

Ihr demütiger Diener,
Joachim Schneider

'Well, what does it say?' asked Marcus, anxiously.

'My friend, you have uncovered a piece of the jigsaw!' exclaimed Leonardo. 'I'll read it to him, shall I, Lisa? It's dated October, 1765.'

"Your Majesty,
If Herr Goehr is having difficulties, perhaps he might be permitted access to the Stradivarius violin, acquired for your husband. It might help him perfect his skills. Signed, your obedient servant, Joachim Schneider."

'Confirmation of the intrigue! After Maria Theresa's husband died earlier that year, presumably the violin found its way into the Goehr family. We must have a copy of this letter as well.'

Herr Schoenen came into the salon, an apprehensive look on his face.

'I heard shouting. Is anything wrong?' he enquired anxiously.

'Far from it, Heinrich . . . far from it! Would you be so kind as to make three copies each of these two documents?'

Marcus was surprised the Messenger knew him by his first name, and noticed the request for the copies was given more as an order.

He turned back to the large, leather-covered file on the table, intending to close it and remove his cotton gloves. In his excitement, he nudged the heavily-bound volume, and the inserts started to roll forward, before coming to a halt at another page. It meant nothing to him; but something caught Lisa's eye.

'Wait a minute, Marcus! What's this? Leonardo, quickly – see what Marcus has turned up. I think it could be important.'

The messenger leaned over and studied the document carefully.

Marcus looked at Lisa quizzically.

'What is it?'

'It looks like a handwritten note about Mateo Gofriller. Whoever the author was, he wrote it as Gofrieller. And Venedig in German is Venice.'

The Messenger looked up, a smile on his face.

'You are right, my dear. You found it, now tell us what you make of it.'

He stood up, and Lisa took his seat. She stared at the single page in its transparent sleeve, for several minutes.

261

Venedig, den 23. April, 1733 im zweiundzwanzigsten Jahr der Herrschaft unseren teueren Kaisers

Zu den Händen von Herrn Reidseck, dem kaiserlichen Stallmeister

Sehr geehrter Hans,

Matteo Gofrieller hat mir bestätitgt, daß ein Mitglied der Familie Guernieri ein Mittel ausgedacht hat, womit er ihre Arbeit erschüttern und ihren Ruf schmälern kann.

Wir schauen in die Zukunft, und wenn alles gemäß nach seinem Plan läuft, werden unsere Instrumentenherstellern in 25 Jahren die Interesse auf sich ziehen und durch ganz Europa unglaublich wohlbekannt und berühmt sein.

Bitte übergeben Sie diese Nachricht Seinem Majestät und Ihrer Kaiserlichen Prinzessin, Maria-Theresa.

Ihr untertänigster Diener,

Martin Schaffer

'Venice, 1733. It looks like it's addressed to the Emperor's Stallmeister. What's that?' she asked.

'I would translate that as "equerry",' answered Leonardo.

'Right. It's signed by someone . . . I can't make out his name.'

'My dear Hans, having spoken with Matteo Gofriller, he declares . . . no, confirms . . . that a member of the Guarneri family, has created . . . devised . . . a means of . . . undermining their work and acclaim. It will take time, but we are looking to the future. If all goes according to plan, within the next twenty-five years, our instrument makers will be renowned throughout Europe . . . Please pass on this message to His Majesty and to the Princess Imperial, Maria-Theresa.'

We've done it, Marcus! We've done it!'

She rose from the chair, hugged him tightly, and kissed him long and loudly. Then she rounded on the Messenger, and did the same to him.

The Messenger was grinning broadly.

'Well done, Marcus,' he said fervently.

'We must have a copy . . . no – plenty of copies!' she cried. 'This is confirmation absolute of the conspiracy!'

When they were walking down the corridor to the exit, Marcus turned to the archivist. 'Tell me, Herr Schoenen, I understand the State Archives house a database of confiscated Jewish property. Is it in this building?'

'No Mein Herr. You will find it at the *Kriegsarchiv* in Nottendorfergasse. It's about three kilometres away, close to the river.'
'Thank you.'

When they left the building, Lisa said, 'What are you up to, Marcus? Why did you ask him that?'

'Because, my dear, that's our next port of call.'

'I'm going to need your help again,' Marcus said to Lisa and the Messenger as they followed yet another archivist down another corridor. The young lady, smiling at them through large-windowed glasses, was only too eager to help.

263

'Here we are!'

She led them into a compact room. On a desk, occupying much of the space, stood a computer.

'Allow me to open the file for you.'

She sat at one of the chairs. A few minutes later: 'Here we are. *"Recht Als Unrecht – Die Akte Beschlagnahmten Jüdischen Eigentums: 1942–1944"* It means "Right as Wrong! The File of Confiscated Jewish Property". Beside each of the items there are the names of the owners and, where possible, it shows from where the item was stolen, and the date. The file also contains the names of those responsible for the thefts and the atrocities they committed. It is quite a comprehensive record, listing the works of art and items of value taken from more than fifty thousand Viennese Jews!'

The trio took their seats in front of the monitor.

'What exactly are we looking for, Marcus?'

'I know for a fact that the Magnificat, the Guarneri del Gesù violin that Leonardo has in his possession, was last seen in Vienna. I was hoping to verify that, and confirm the name of the last owner, in case it had changed from Joshua Liebermiers. If Leonardo gives it to me when he receives the report, I am going to see the violin is returned to its rightful owner – or his heirs. And that's not the Goehrs!'

They spent several hours scanning the database, looking under instruments, then by owner's name, then randomly – but it was not shown.

Marcus' heart sank. It was a priceless instrument, and the thought of it having been so cruelly snatched from the true owner was hard to bear, particularly when Herr Liebermiers had probably been taken, with so many others, to Dachau – his final destination.

Marcus asked the Messenger to open the file of those responsible for the mass expropriation. The document on the screen dispassionately outlined the aims of the Third Reich, dwelling on the future creation of a magnificent music centre in Linz.

It clearly identified Alfred Rosenberg's role as the supremo of the grand confiscation, as he swept through Germany, Austria and Italy. In Vienna he called upon the services of an élite group, knowledgeable in their field of culture, aware of the locations of all the prime objects of value in private hands.

Under the heading of *Seltene und Wertvolle Musikalische Instrumente*

– Rare and Valuable Musical Instruments – were the names of six men:

Karl Rutgers
Fritz Abelmann
Julius Friedmann
Achim Goehr
Dietrich Rubcke
Otto Schumann

There was a sharp intake of breath from the Messenger.
'What is it, Leonardo?'
'Nothing . . . it is nothing!'
The Messenger quickly scrolled to the next page.
This identified the unit working in support of the élite forces. Headed by Baldur von Schirach, the Gauleiter of Vienna was shown not only to be collecting for the Reich, but also trading priceless manuscripts, works of art and numerous musical instruments.
The research had been thorough. Also listed were the names of his enforcers and collectors – his six lieutenants, recruited in the city:

Johann Slieman
Robert Greiser
Adolf Kaufmann
Hans Myers
Gustav Grossmann – Hitler Youth
Sylvester Ottomeyer – Hitler Youth

'Shall we move on, Leonardo?' said Lisa, after a moment.
But the Messenger's gaze was fixed on the screen. With a sudden gesture he turned off the computer.
'We must leave!' he said, rising abruptly.
Puzzled, they followed him from the building. In the taxi he was silent. In their suite, he went straight to his room and shut the door firmly behind him.

Chapter Fifty-Five

At eleven o'clock the limousine drew up in front of the Town Hall. Once again, the cardinal was shown every courtesy as he was ushered through the building to the mayor's quarters. The door was opened for him and Cardinal Marchetti strode into the room. From chairs either side of the elegant Emperador marble fireplace two men rose to greet him.

'Good morning, Your Eminence. I'm delighted you could join us at such short notice. Please, take this seat,' said the mayor, moving to one side. 'May I offer you anything?'

'Thank you, no Signor Mayor,' answered the cardinal, taking the seat proffered. He glanced across at the other man, who had also sat down and nodded in his direction.

'Signor Deputy!'

The mayor drew up another of the Genoese rococo chairs. He rubbed his hands together. A tell-tale sign they have made a decision, thought the cardinal. I wonder who will declare it.

'Your Eminence,' began the Deputy, 'we congratulate you on your thorough application to the project you outlined for us recently. Considering how much you accomplished in so short a time, it does you, and your people, much credit.'

The cardinal inclined his head a fraction.

'As you might expect, we reviewed the substance of your ideas. Frankly, I have to tell you, there are parts of the proposal that would either be in contravention of State and Regional Laws, or would take so much time for agreement to be obtained in all the many departments that serious delays could interrupt your well-conceived plans.'

The cardinal did not comment. Silence prevailed.

Eventually, the Deputy broke it.

'You see, I was wondering if your declared intention to remove the Vatican might be tempered by all the many, unfortunate, bureaucratic problems that might arise; and if, in the circumstances, we might reach a compromise. What do you think?'

The cardinal measured the time to remain silent.

'I don't quite understand you, signore. Are you suggesting we drop the idea?'

'Well . . . yes.' He glanced at the mayor. 'We would like to persuade you that the Holy See should remain here, in Rome.'

'But we have a carefully conceived notion of what we want and what we shall achieve. I don't feel that we can alter our commitment to the project at this stage.' He paused. 'Not without careful consideration.'

The mayor and the Deputy exchanged another glance.

'When you say "consideration" are we, perhaps, talking financially, Your Eminence?'

'Not necessarily. However, it does seem to be the benchmark, these days, for any form of understanding between two parties.'

'If we were to evaluate a change of policy in monetary terms, Your Eminence, what would one be thinking of?'

The moment had arrived. All these months of planning, scheming and other unstated activities had been edging their way towards this confrontation. He appeared to ponder the question.

'If we were to alter our position radically; to dismantle all the many aspects of the move from Rome that are in place; to realise, even in part, by staying, what we would achieve by moving . . .' He paused. 'I would say that ten billion Euros would seem an adequate sum!'

'Good morning. My name is Leoni. I am with the Rome police. I came to see Signor Lambertini a few days ago. Tell me, have you worked with the company for long?'

The receptionist was flustered. Michelo Lambertini was not in the office. She could not ask him how she should respond.

'Er . . . two years, signore.'

'So, you were with the company at its previous address?'

'Yes.'

'When did you move to this present location?'

The questions seemed innocuous.

'In June this year, signore.'

'Thank you for your time.'

The connection was cut. Replacing the receiver, she frowned slightly. Then she dismissed the call as irrelevant and went on with what she was doing.

Chapter Fifty-Six

They had had a hurried, early breakfast, then dashed by taxi to the airport.

The Messenger was still tense from the discussion which had taken place the previous evening. He had joined Lisa and Marcus for dinner in the suite but, apart from the occasional monosyllabic response, had remained silent through much of the meal. Eventually, exasperated by this morose attitude, so markedly different from his earlier cheerfulness, Marcus had demanded to know the cause.

'I cannot tell you, Signor Danby.'

'For goodness' sake, Leonardo! We have shared much together – some bad, some very good. If you are concerned about something that also affects us, you should tell us. I was hoping it would be something of a celebration. I don't enjoy you sitting there with a miserable face, not saying a word.'

Lisa was kinder.

'You can tell us, Leonardo. Perhaps, we can help?'

He glanced down at his hands.

'Yesterday, I believe I had a glimpse of some disturbing connections with certain of my masters – long-forged alliances that may account for our current predicament.'

'I'm not sure I understand you, Leonardo,' said Marcus quietly.

'No, I don't suppose you do. And because of what I do, and for whom, I cannot give you a fuller explanation. I hope you will trust me on this; I need to go to Innsbruck immediately to check some details. That is the first step. I can find out about another matter here in Vienna when I return.'

'In your present frame of mind, Leonardo, I don't think you should go alone. Do you, Marcus?'

'No, we'll all go. I'll make the arrangements now. How long do you think it will take, your search?'

269

'Just a few hours. But there is no need for you to come.'

The statement lacked conviction. Leonardo had lost his customary assertive manner.

Marcus picked up the phone and made five reservations for an early flight to Innsbruck.

'I didn't realise you already had them running in your direction. They've just gone into the departure lounge bound for Innsbruck.'

'What? They're actually en route? But I haven't done anything!'

'Well, the flight takes off in fifteen minutes, so they'll be in Innsbruck in an hour and a half.'

'How many of them?'

'All of them. Five. If you wish, I'll get the next plane.'

'Do that – and liaise with Schumann.'

'A call for you, Your Eminence.'

It had come through on the Curia's main switchboard.

'Who is it?'

'He didn't say. But he said it was a matter of the greatest urgency.'

'I don't speak with anyone who does not reveal his name. Is he Italian?'

'No, Your Eminence. He has a German accent.'

'Put him through.'

'Gustav, it's Martin.'

Grossmann was beside himself with anger. 'Why did you phone me on this number? You know it can be intercepted.'

'Because, my friend, your private line was busy, and this was important enough for me to interrupt.'

His anger was replaced by anxiety.

'What has happened? Has someone got hold of . . .?'

'I don't know. Phone me straight back.'

The line went dead. Twice he fumbled with the numbers before the connection was made.

'Gustav! I have just learnt they are flying to Innsbruck.'

He was marginally relieved. If they had uncovered a reference to himself, surely they would be returning to Italy.

'What has prompted them to go there?'

'At the moment I don't know. However, it has saved me the bother of drawing them in this direction, which I was planning to do.'

Grossmann refrained from asking why.

'Let me know when you manage to solve the problem. Goodbye, Martin.'

He sat back in his chair and wondered why, at his age, when most cardinals had retired, he should be subjected to such concerns. What had happened should have been buried so deeply it could never surface. In all probability his youthful actions would not come to light. And what were they really? Slight indiscretions, committed over sixty years ago. These days, no one attached blame to what teenagers got up to. Their activities were regarded as part of the exuberant process of growing up.

The trouble is, he thought, I hold an elevated position in an organisation preaching love for one's neighbour, an organisation which professes to help the needy and the dispossessed, irrespective of background, and holds all human life sacred. It must never, never come to light!

At the Europa Tyrol hotel they booked a suite for the day. Shortly afterwards, Lisa, Marcus and Leonardo left and walked the short distance to the Records Office, the *Tiroler Landesarchiv*, in Michael Gaismairstrasse. They arrived as the doors were opening. Behind them strolled the other two members of the team.

Further back, a tall, suited gentleman, casually window shopping, noted their movements.

Slipping the mobile from his pocket, he made a brief call.

'The three principals have gone into the *Tiroler Landesarchiv*. Their two bodyguards have taken up positions outside the main entrance.'

'Excellent! I should have everything ready very, very soon. Jozsef will be joining you shortly. You can work out the signals between you. Was the tall one carrying an instrument case?'

'No.'

'OK. Then we shall have to continue with what we planned.'

*

271

After two hours the Messenger had the information. He shut the bulky volume with a thud.

'Thank you. It is now clear to me. I think we should collect our things from the hotel and take the first available flight back to Vienna, then to Rome.'

'OK. But it sure is a brief visit! I thought we would be here a little longer,' said Lisa.

'It is too dangerous. Every minute we remain we are vulnerable to attack.'

As they were walking through the building the Messenger used his mobile to speak with the cousins outside.

'We are leaving now. Organise two taxis while we wait inside the entrance.'

As they neared the main door two taxis drew up. The cousins jumped out of the one behind and peered around in readiness while Lisa, Marcus and the Messenger climbed into the first.

'*Wo wollen Sie hin?*' The driver turned to the Messenger, who was sitting beside him.

'*Hotel Europa Tirol, bitte.*'

They entered the Südtiroler Platz at speed and were unprepared for the jerking slide as the taxi came to a sudden halt. The passenger doors were wrenched open and a man stood in front of each of them with a gun.

Not again! This is not happening, thought Marcus – it's an impossible dream!

'*Sie zwei, gehen Sie raus! Schnell! Sie bieiden hier!*'

'He wants us to get out,' said Leonardo. 'Do as he says!'

'*Nicht Sie!*' said the gunman, pointing at Lisa.

'What's he saying, Leonardo?'

'Just get out of the car, Marcus.'

He was slow to react, and the man pulled him roughly by the shoulder, spinning him to the ground. They jumped in. Doors slammed and the taxi accelerated away, its tyres squealing.

Still on the ground, Marcus looked up.

'My God! Where's Lisa? They've taken Lisa! Quickly! We must phone the police.'

He staggered to his feet, his mind whirling. They are going to kill her! We must do something – anything! Just get her back. He found himself gripping the Messenger's jacket, yelling loudly. Hotel staff were running towards them.

'Marcus, Marcus! Listen to me! Not a word of what has happened! Do you hear? Not a word! Whoever has done this wants something, otherwise they would have taken us all. Now, tell them you fell from the taxi when it pulled away.'

Over Marcus' shoulder the Messenger noticed his two cousins walking uncertainly towards them.

'Well done! . . . They have already changed vehicles, you say . . . In about an hour? Excellent! You have done a good job, Felix . . . No, tell them to go to the schloss at Klais.'

'I believe it is Martin Goehr. If I am right, he is almost certainly the one behind the attempts on your life.'

They had been in the third floor suite for two hours. The waiting was more than Marcus could bear. He paced the floor, then dropped into a chair, then walked to each of the windows in turn, staring out without seeing. He could not settle, or think straight.

Leonardo and his cousins sat in a huddle discussing the situation.

'Who do you think it is?'

The same question had been asked twice before. Leonardo gave the same answer.

'Who is this Martin Goehr you keep referring to?' asked Marcus.

Leonardo rose and joined him at the window overlooking the Platz.

'There are a number of elements to this rather complicated jigsaw. Goehr is key to a significant part.' He put his arm on Marcus' shoulder and lowered his voice so that it did not carry. 'I want to tell you a few things about myself, Marcus. Firstly, my role in the Curia demands unswerving loyalty. I am a member of *I Messagieri*: twelve men who undertake special work for the Curia. Mostly, we are what the name suggests, messengers, taking documents, letters, parcels to individuals and organisations around the world on behalf of the administration. I have been to Mittenwald on a number of occasions for one of them, Cardinal Grossmann. Always to the same person, Martin Goehr.'

'Tell me about him.'

'He and his family own Instrumente Tiroler Gmbh, a prominent company making stringed instruments in Mittenwald. This company, and a number of others at the time, were formed by special charter in the reign of Empress Maria-Theresa. To be precise, in 1748 – one year after the last of the Cremonese died! In Innsbruck, I found the date of that charter, and the signatories.'

'So, the Hapsburgs were behind it,' murmured Marcus through clenched teeth. 'Even more proof! But who would go to such lengths to protect their name? It was more than two hundred and fifty years ago! Many more atrocities have taken place in Europe since then.'

'True! But perhaps it's not just an attempt to hide an unpleasant historical incident. If the names of the families linked to the death of the Cremonese, and who still prosper by it, were threatened with exposure, they would surely want to suppress it. It may well have begun with the Hapsburgs, but it was engineered by individuals who took full advantage of the relocation of instrument making to the Austro-German border towns.'

'Surely, that's not enough to kill for?'

'It is if a member of one of those families is tipped to be the next Pope,' declared Leonardo. 'In 1748, I'll wager the Austrian instrument makers were just as keen as the Empress, and the Goehrs were probably the sovereign's strongest supporters. I checked the family records of the Goehr family in the *Tiroler Landesarchiv*. I discovered that Martin, the present chief executive of the leading company in Mittenwald, is the brother of Cardinal Vincent Goehr – the strongest contender for the papal throne! I strongly believe he would not allow anyone, or anything, to stand in the way of his brother's elevation.'

'But what does kidnapping Lisa achieve? He'll kill her, won't he?' said Marcus, turning pale-faced towards Leonardo.

The Messenger dropped his gaze. 'Eventually, yes . . .'

Before he could say more, the phone rang.

Marcus rushed to pick it up.

'Yes?' The caller was speaking German. 'Leonardo, quickly, take it!'

'*Hallo! Wer spricht? . . . Jawohl . . . Ja . . . Ja . . . OK!*'

Marcus stood at his side, anxiously trying to read some sort of message from his replies. He put the receiver slowly back on its rest.

'Well! What did they say? They haven't hurt Lisa, have they?'

The words tumbled out.

'She is all right, Marcus. They are holding her safe for the moment.' Leonardo paused. 'They want a ransom. They will exchange Signora Robards for the Guarneri del Gesù. They want the "Magnificat" in return for her life.'

Chapter Fifty-Seven

Franz had caught sight of Jozsef at the airport in Vienna. He had dodged back quickly, taking advantage of a pillar to peer at his erstwhile leader. He was in the line for the flight to Innsbruck. No one was at the check-in desk; he was too early. He is always too early, thought Franz. The flight was not for another seventy-five minutes.

Why is he going into the Tyrol, not to Munich? he wondered. Probably still pursuing the cleric and the American woman, wherever they are. Despite his fear of the man, Franz was intrigued. Jozsef was wearing his clerical garb – his assassination mode. He was probably about to close on the unsuspecting couple. On a whim, he went to the Tyrolean Airlines counter and bought a ticket to Innsbruck. No loss, he thought. The money acquired from the Hungarians would cover the cost. The trick, now, was to avoid meeting Jozsef.

'Your Eminence, thank you for seeing me at short notice.'

'Mr Deputy, I happened to be free at this particular time.'

'Well, I shall not keep you long. As you might have expected the amount you indicated at our meeting received the fullest discussion. After that, I took your proposal to the Prime Minister, who also gave it much consideration. As a consequence, I have been requested to make an offer to you.' The Deputy eased forward in his chair. 'The Prime Minister, the national administration, the city authorities, all want to avoid a rift in our relationship. They feel it would be detrimental to both our interests. Accordingly, I have been authorised to submit a figure of five billion Euros for your maintaining the status quo – doing nothing, other than to foster mutual co-existence'

The cardinal stared at the official.

'Clearly, Signor Gordino, I did not convey our intentions as precisely as I had hoped. The sum I declared was not the opening gambit in a game of negotiation. It was a realistic statement on my part of the figure we might, and I emphasise, *might* consider. It was not open to interpretation. Do you think for one minute that we would go to all this trouble and expense, if we were prepared to involve ourselves in some sort of sordid horse-trading? I would suggest you go back and tell your principals the matter is closed. We are now resolute in our determination to bring about the new Vatican in Lombardy.'

Martin Goehr pulled into the tree-lined drive to the mansion. It was not obvious from the road, and thus afforded the perfect place for his activities, from assignations with his mistress – a woman well-known in the social circles of Mittenwald – to business meetings away from the prying eyes of his work colleagues, and other nefarious pursuits.

He drove to the rear of the building, where several cars were already parked. Entering by the rear door, he ushered his visitor into a room before descending the stairs to the basement, where four men were waiting. One of them advanced to greet him.

'Sorry, Felix! I expected to be here sooner, but his plane was delayed. Where is the woman?'

'At the moment, Martin, she is behind that door,' he replied with a twist of his head. 'She is sleeping. I had to inject her. She was making far too much noise.'

'Good. Let us go upstairs and be more comfortable. I want to discuss our next move.'

They trooped up the stairs behind Goehr and entered a large, well-furnished room with a view of the lawns and drive. Felix Schumann shook hands with the new arrival.

'Please help yourselves to drinks,' said Goehr expansively. He looked out of the window. At last, he thought, I am manipulating the final stage. It had been an uncertain period – sitting in his office in Mittenwald, issuing commands to minions who did not have the capacity to do a job effectively, or the ability to implement alternatives if problems arose. Yes, a very disturbing time. Still, it would all soon come to an end. He would be rid of the meddlesome trio, and would have the 'Magnificat' back, at long last. Very satisfactory!

'Gentlemen, I wish to discuss what will take place within the next few hours. Please be seated and give me your full attention.'

Passing through Mittenwald, they turned onto the S2542, the minor road to Klais.

After Leonardo had told him of the ransom demand, a strange calm had enveloped Marcus. He had stopped wandering around the suite and begun to think rationally.

Observing Marcus slumped in a chair, his head in his hands, Leonardo's first thoughts were that he had surrendered to the inevitable. But some minutes later Marcus had been galvanised into action.

'Right, this is what we must do! I want you, Leonardo, to hire a large, sturdy car. Tell them we shall be returning it in Vienna. In the meantime, I'm going shopping. We shall meet here in half an hour; then we shall discuss what I have in mind. After that, we shall drive to the rendezvous.'

They still had another nine or ten kilometres to go. According to the instructions they were to arrive at the house on the outskirts of Klais at four o'clock. Marcus looked across at Leonardo. As ever, his features were inscrutable.

The suggestion of a ransom had been a thin disguise. It was clear that Goehr would not release any of them. Once he had his hands on the Magnificat, they were doomed – unless his idea worked. In the afternoon, it had all seemed very plausible. Now, as they drew closer and closer, doubts crept in. Perhaps they should have gone to the police, told them everything and appealed for their help. The trouble was they had had so little time.

'I've been thinking, Leonardo. There's no need for you to be involved in this. Stop the car! I'll go on my own.'

'Marcus, do you think they will allow me to live? I know too much. We are in this together. Now keep your eyes on the road, and tell me when we come to the house.'

The doubts grew. I've let Lisa down, he thought. I'm sure I could have saved her some way. My defences were down in Innsbruck. I should have been ready for anything, and I wasn't.

'Is that the road to Kranzbach, Marcus?'

'Yes. Sorry!'

278

Chapter Fifty-Eight

'A call from the Prime Minister's Office, Your Eminence.'

'Be kind enough to put it through, Felipé.'

'Cardinal Marchetti? It's the Prime Minister here. Our weekly cabinet meeting of ministers is tomorrow morning. Would you please indulge me, personally, by attending? I would welcome my colleagues hearing your proposal.'

'I have appointments, as you will appreciate Prime Minister. However, your summons takes precedence. What time do you wish me to be present?'

'Shall we say eleven o'clock?'

'I shall be there. *Arriverderci!*'

Jozsef turned into the drive as the brake lights of the car ahead glowed briefly. It came to a halt in front of the house. He observed the occupants as he drove around to the rear. They've arrived, like lambs to the slaughter!

He had followed them from Innsbruck, checking if they stopped anywhere to confer with others, in case they had travelled in convoy with their protectors. But it was obvious they were alone. He had seen the taller of the two go to a nearby car rental. He had not seen the other slip out of a side entrance and return with a bag a short time later.

Now they were here, without back-up and without anyone knowing their whereabouts. In an hour or so, all three would cease to exist.

Chapter Fifty-Nine

They walked up the stone steps to the front door, which was opened by a tall, elegantly dressed man. Marcus took careful note of his demeanour.

'*Meine Herren! Kommen Sie bitte herein.*' He stood to one side to allow them to pass. 'My apologies. It would be better if we were to speak English, would it not? This way, gentlemen.'

He walked with a slight limp. Marcus was sure he had seen the man before, but at that moment there were other things to think about. The man knocked on a door of sturdy, dark wood, simply panelled, with an ornate handle.

'*Treten Sie ein!*'

Turning the handle, he pushed it open, again stepping to one side.

'Gentlemen! Thank you for coming.'

The unnecessary welcome came from a well-fed individual seated in a high-backed chair. He was holding a glass in his hand, with which, somewhat theatrically, he waved them in.

'Come, come! Don't be shy!' He smiled warmly. Marcus and Leonardo came slowly into the room and stood to one side, their backs to a flamboyantly-papered wall.

'We *are* being cautious! No matter. This should not take long. You have the instrument, I presume?'

'Yes. But first I should like Mrs Robards here.'

'Of course! Felix, bring her in.'

Again the slight-framed man limped from the room.

Silence.

Marcus looked around, taking note of the furniture, the space it occupied, the full-length windows. He also took in the backs of two men seated in front of the white, marble fireplace. Neither had turned during the opening exchange.

Lisa was half carried into the room.

'Are you all right, Lisa?' he enquired anxiously.

She looked up but her eyes were not focusing properly.

'M . . . M . . . Marcus . . . they have drugged me.'

The two men dropped her unceremoniously into a chair.

'As you see, gentlemen, none the worse for wear. She will soon recover. Just a little something to calm her down.'

Marcus knelt beside her and took her hand.

'Darling, I'm here. You'll be all right now.'

'Will she, Marcus? That rather depends on you,' said one of the men who had their backs to him.

He knew that voice. His heart lurched. The figure rose, and walked towards him.

'Hello again, my dear fellow!'

It was Geri Bellman.

'What are you doing here? My God! You're not caught up with these people, are you?'

'Marcus, I have always been with these people, as you call them. Where do you think I was born? In Innsbruck. Martin Goehr and I grew up together. We are soulmates, as our fathers were years before. Austria is my homeland. Mittenwald was where I worked in my youth.'

'Isn't that a delightful surprise, Herr Danby? All this time your mentor in England has been directing your progress. And, of course, reporting it to me,' sneered Goehr.

'How can that be, Geri? I asked you to come to Italy to help me.'

'Let me tell you his real name,' smiled Goehr. 'Your friend is Gerhardt Abelmann! He chose "Bellman" because it sounded more English.'

Abelmann looked at Marcus. 'I would have come anyway on some pretext or other – especially when Martin told me how close you were getting. Who do you think recommended you in the first place? Your name was passed, by various means, to those in the Vatican.'

Marcus was devastated. His friend, ally, confidant, for so many years; the man he had turned to for guidance – it had all been a charade. He shook his head. He must pull himself together, otherwise they were doomed.

Leonardo's face showed nothing as the truth dawned of the conspiracy perpetrated by the successors of those named on the database: Achim Goehr, Fritz Abelmann, Otto Schumann and their young friend, Gustav Grossmann. The last piece of the puzzle had fallen into place. Our only hope, he thought, is that they will be greedy enough to make the plan succeed.

Marcus retreated to stand alongside Leonardo.

'Enough! The moment for the exchange,' declared Goehr. 'I trust the Magnificat is in that case?' He looked across at Abelmann. 'Gerhardt and I have been seeking it for years, but we could find no trace of it. Now, at last, we can add it to the collection.'

'What collection?' asked Marcus, wanting to discover whether his answer to why they had not been killed in Innsbruck was correct. Just how highly did they prize the Guarneri del Gesù?'

'Our fathers were the original collectors,' said Goehr with a smile. 'A great many instruments were shipped back to Berlin during the war, but not the important ones from Vienna. They are in Innsbruck. Three Stradivaris, four Amatis, two Pietro Guarneri cellos, a Bergonzi viola, two da Salos, a Montagnana, and many more. But the one you have in your hands will be the real prize of the collection. Once, it was briefly in my family. Now it's back where it rightfully belongs. You two!' he called to his henchmen standing in the background. 'Help Mrs Robards to her feet. Come, my friends, the violin!'

Marcus took the instrument case from Leonardo. He placed it, almost reverently, on a small side table and unclipped the lid. Slowly, he turned the case at an angle, removing an object as he did so.

There it was. Its soft, lustrous finish shone out from its velvet-lined compartment. The incredible workmanship glowed for all to see.

Goehr gasped. Abelmann's eyes stared fixedly.

'Quick, Gerhardt! Bring it to me.'

As he lunged forward, Marcus shouted.

'Stop! No one move! You see this hammer? If anyone dares come near us, I shall smash the instrument to pieces. All you have desired will be lost, Goehr – so much matchwood ... just fragments, splinters ... This tribute to the craftsmanship of the Cremonese will be gone forever, if you do not allow us to leave. Believe me, I mean what I say! We've nothing to lose. But you ... you will have your dream of a lifetime shattered.'

Leonardo took hold of Lisa. To emphasise his words, Marcus

removed the violin from the case and held it out, the hammer ready to descend.

Goehr's jaw dropped. This was not how it was meant to be. The demands were to have come from him. Yet *they* were dictating events! Let them smash it. Did he care? Of course he did! So did Gerhardt! How could anyone destroy such a priceless object of such beauty? What do I do?

One of his men stepped forward. Marcus raised the hammer.

'No!' shouted Goehr and Abelmann in unison.

'Give them room,' said Goehr hoarsely.

Marcus and Leonardo, supporting Lisa, backed to the door, out into the hall and slowly down the steps.

'Take Lisa and get the car started,' said Marcus calmly. 'Then open the front passenger door.'

The Mercedes swung to a halt behind him. Features frozen, uncomprehending and impotent, Goehr and Abelmann looked on. Marcus slammed the door. The car accelerated towards the gates, throwing up a shower of gravel. It had been that simple.

Chapter Sixty

The limousine stopped in the Piazza Colonna. An official opened the door.

'Welcome, Your Eminence. Let me escort you to the meeting.'

Another expanse of carpet; a wide, over-decorated corridor; the hesitation outside a salon. Thereafter, events moved quickly. The Prime Minister appeared and threw open the tall double doors.

'I am delighted to see you, Your Eminence. Come! Meet my fellow ministers.'

He was shown into an imposing assembly room. Around the table were seated a body of people, representing the many ministries in Rome. A chair was proffered. He sat down.

'Ladies and gentlemen, as I informed you earlier, we have had a number of discussions with the Pontiff's delegate, Cardinal Marchetti. I have kept you briefed on the progress of such meetings. However, to my regret, we have reached an impasse in our deliberations. I thought, as representatives of the people, we had made a fair and reasonable offer. This has been rejected. Consequently, I think it appropriate that you hear what His Eminence has to say. Cardinal Marchetti.'

A fascinating opener, thought the cardinal. He is clearly implying that we are to blame in rejecting a most respectable offer. No doubt, they will agree with this viewpoint, and no amount of persuasive talk will alter their feelings. Therefore, I shall adjust my approach.

'Ladies and gentlemen, the inevitable problems and numerous irritants which result from the cheek by jowl existence of the city and the Vatican should, perhaps, have been tackled long ago. We are an autonomous country, yet live within the thrall of the nation's capital. For the country's sake, if not for those who inhabit Rome, the many who find the proximity of the walled enclave a burden, it might be prudent for all, if we were to move. There is a site available to us. What is more, as someone has probably explained to you, our removal would coincide with a 'resorgimento' of the skills of the luthiers of Lombardy. It would be our express aim to rekindle the lost talents of the Cremonese, and thus regain for our eminent instrument-makers the recognition of the world.'

He looked at their faces. There it was, that predictable heightening of interest.

'The trouble is,' the Prime Minister interjected, 'I am still not sure that you have an entitlement to the land, particularly for building purposes. According to the EU constitution, it is deemed for agricultural use only. The legal arguments could rage for years on that one aspect alone, Your Eminence. In my opinion, it might not be the logistical problems that would confound you. I am informed you have investigated the whole matter most thoroughly. But you would . . .' He laid stress on the last word, '. . . without doubt, find yourselves embroiled in any number of courts for a great many years. That's why I would strongly urge you to consider the sum we would offer – six billion Euros!'

He has shown his hand, thought the cardinal. One billion more than on the previous occasion. But it is not enough.

'May I show a DVD to your ministers, Prime Minister? It would not occupy more than a few minutes of their time?'

'I have seen it before, Your Eminence.' Gordino, the Deputy, was on his feet. 'I relayed to the cabinet every aspect of what was portrayed. It would be a waste of time to show it again.'

'I think everyone should scc it, Prime Minister,' declared Marchetti in a steely tone. 'It might better illustrate our purpose.'

'Waste of time!' sneered the Deputy to those around him.

The Prime Minister pondered the request.

'Very well. If it doesn't take too long!' The cardinal nodded. He had already primed one of the secretaries to be ready for the PM's agreement. The room darkened and a screen dropped from the ceiling.

The opening showed a river scene. Then, as before, the progressive development of the surrounding area, colourfully presented in graphic form. The site was cleared, the existing Vatican buildings appeared, and over one hundred hectares were filled with hotels, museums, gardens, piazzas, and people – multitudes of people.

The blinds covering the windows opened; the room returned to normality.

'As I said, Your Eminence, the same presentation. I gave the members here full details of what you envisaged. The only difference, perhaps, was the view of the river. I didn't recognise it.'

The cardinal stood up and began collecting his documents.

'That, Mr Deputy, is because it is not the River Po. It is the Rhône, on the outskirts of Avignon. The national authorities and the Département of Vaucluse, have invited the Papacy to return to France after an absence of six hundred years. It is a very tempting offer. They are prepared to install the Vatican, pay all the costs, and provide us with a contribution of ten billion Euros. Good morning, ladies and gentlemen!'

Chapter Sixty-One

'How is she?'

'Coming round slowly. I'll make her more comfortable.'

Marcus leaned round the seat and tugged Lisa onto her back, swinging her legs into the well. He struggled out his jacket. Rolling it up, he tucked it beneath her neck.

'Are they still following, Leonardo?'

'Yes! They're in two cars, staying back about half a kilometre. Not getting too close – just keeping watch.'

As the car accelerated onto the autobahn, Marcus came to a decision.

'Leonardo, let's forget Vienna. Come off at the next junction and take the A13. We'll head south for the Brenner Pass. We'll drive all the way.'

'It could be congested at this time of year. People are still on holiday.'

'At this time of year, most of them will be returning to Northern Europe, not heading south – I hope!'

For the next hour Marcus sat beside Leonardo in silence. Reflecting on Geri Bellman's betrayal and his callous disregard for him and his companions. How could the fellow ignore all that had passed between them? The hours spent in each other's company; the innermost thoughts and feelings Marcus had revealed to him; the advice and help he had so readily provided. All that had evaporated in a second when Geri – Gerhardt – had shown himself indifferent to their imminent death. His friendship with Bellman had meant a lot to him – and he had betrayed every word that had passed between them these past weeks, having first identified him as the intended victim. Cold rage seized Marcus. He would be damned if they were going to succeed! Now he knew who and what they were up against, he was going to take the fight to Goehr,

Abelmann and all the others who were out to ensure their dark secrets would never be revealed.

'The toll, Marcus. Have you got ten Euros?'

Franz had tailed Jozsef out of the airport, hoping to follow him in the next taxi, but a car had pulled up at the kerb and they were gone. As quickly as that! Irritated, he had made his way to the Altenburg, knowing this was his usual stopover when in Innsbruck. He had waited around the hotel, eaten a meal, and thought about what he would do when Jozsef appeared. With his lunch he had enjoyed a bottle of wine, followed by four glasses of schnapps, then some beer. Over the course of several hours, his annoyance developed into belligerence.

What right has Jozsef not to pay me what I'm owed? I did a good job. It wasn't my fault. They told me what car to attach it to. I risked my life placing that bomb. I could easily have been caught. It was risky. What did he care? Just because he got a rocket doesn't mean he should take it out on me. I want my money!

The little man was working himself into a temper. Fuelled by the drink, he was ready to tackle anyone.

Only one car followed them over the Pass. That was all that was needed. It was clear they were heading back to Cremona, taking the main road south through Bolzano and Verona. The driver of the second car took the exit to Mutters, just south of Innsbruck.

'Why are there so many people, about?' asked Jozsef.

'It's the day of the cattle drive,' explained one of Goehr's men, a local from Innsbruck. 'Traditionally, this time of year, they round them up from the hills. Now it's more an opportunity to party. A few token cattle, decked out in flowers are paraded through the streets. There are stalls and dancing. Everyone has a good time.'

'They're blocking the road,' muttered Jozsef.

He was upset by all that had happened, and furious that the two men and the woman had escaped their clutches yet again.

'I don't know why we didn't shoot them there and then,' he declared angrily to the others in the car. 'They were standing there, armed with nothing more than an old violin! I went forward, but what did he say? "No one lift a finger, let them go." Bloody

fool! They threatened to break it into pieces, and we were power-
less. I've never seen such stupidity!'

The others were silent. They knew his role and reputation. he
was not someone you would wish to cross.

'Come on! Come on! Clear out of the way!' he shouted.

As if he had been heard, the road opened up and they drove to
the hotel.

'What do you mean had to let them go? . . . I thought you had
everything under control. How could you let this happen?'

He was shouting, he realised. His hands were shaking, beads
of sweat breaking out on his forehead. The worst possible thing
had occurred – they were free. He couldn't bring himself to do
it because of a damn violin! All was lost for the sake of an old
fiddle!

'I will not permit you to ignore your duty, Martin. To me as well
as yourself. Terminate them now, or your brother is finished!'

Grossmann slammed down the phone.

Jozsef led the others through the door and turned towards the
stube. He was to wait there until Goehr arrived. Then, they would
discuss the next move. Whatever it was, he was going to ignore the
protection this violin afforded. When he caught up with them he
would kill all three without caring about the niceties. He would
destroy the violin as well. It had become an irritation.

The waiter brought the drinks. He had requested a large whisky,
but this had been doubled by one of his travelling companions,
who hoped to ease his mounting frustration, and thus defuse the
growing resentment of those around him.

Jozsef appeared not to notice the amount in the glass. His mind
was elsewhere and he drank it quickly. He was still dressed as a
priest and looked out of place in such a group. But this was a day
for partying, few in the hotel took notice.

'So you've finally decided to show up, have you?'

Franz was standing at his shoulder, swaying slightly.

'I've been waiting hours for you to appear – to pay me what you
owe!'

The little man's voice was raised and carried to others close by.

It was a peculiar scene. There was somebody shouting at a man of the cloth, demanding money. Was it part of the festivities?

Jozsef was perplexed. What was Franz doing here? He had cut and run in Cremona. He got to his feet, rocking slightly as the alcohol hit him. This was the last straw.

'You left me in the lurch, Franz. No one does that and gets away with it!'

He bunched his fist and, spinning round, hit him full in the face. Propelled backwards, Franz crashed into a waiter carrying a full tray. Food and cutlery fell everywhere with a resounding clatter. For a moment he lay there dazed. Jozsef looked on contemptuously, then resumed his seat.

Franz picked himself up. His clothes were splattered with food and sodden with spilled drinks. Humiliated, enraged by the laughter of those sitting with the fake priest, he bent down and picked up a steak knife. With a murderous roar he ran full tilt at Jozsef, burying the knife up to the handle in his neck.

A moment's stunned silence was followed by people screaming and rushing for the door. The men with Jozsef backed away. He sat there quite still, the blade planted in his neck. Then he rose slowly and started to turn towards the diminutive figure who stood frozen, aghast at what he had done. But, in turning, something was severed. A gush of blood erupted from the wound, spraying those standing before him. Jozsef reached out, then toppled to the floor.

It was the spur to action. Franz ran for the door and sprinted away, not knowing in which direction – anywhere from the nightmare unfolding behind him.

Goehr approached the hotel from the south. It was all going wrong. He must brief Jozsef quickly. If he had to sacrifice the del Gesù, Abelmann would surely understand. Whether he did or not, his brother's ascendancy was imperative. Why had he been so blind to what was truly important? This time his executioner would complete the task. There would be no more delays, no more vacillating about the course of action. It would be done within the next twenty-four hours. Then he would phone Grossmann and ensure he gave his brother maximum support.

As he turned into the car park outside the hotel, two police cars arrived from the opposite direction, their sirens slowing as they came to a halt. Why had they been called? Nothing to do with his people, he hoped. Goehr followed them into the lobby. It was crowded. One of his men sidled over.

'I suggest you leave. Jozsef has been stabbed. He's dead – a knife in the throat! Don't get involved.'

In a daze he retreated to his car. My God! Who could he turn to now? It would take time to get someone else. Just how long have I got, he wondered.

'Forgive my calling at such a late hour, Signor Lambertini. There were a few things I needed to clear up.'

'Not at all, inspector. Come in.'

He was shown into a wide hallway; illuminated bronze-framed paintings lined the walls. Inside the door stood a circular rustic grotto table. Passing into a sitting room he saw the theme continued with two rustic sofas either side of a small table.

'Nineteenth century, Signor Lambertini? I've always favoured this style of furniture.'

'Yes, inspector, it's a favourite of mine.' He was surprised the policeman had knowledge of period furniture. 'How can I help?'

'Well, signor, the other day, when asked how she came by it, you said the visiting card found in Angelina Scacchi's bag was probably given to her when she first joined the staff at the Town Hall – to remind her of your name in the future.'

'That's right.'

'What I find odd, signor, is that the card shows your current business address. You only moved your offices three months ago.'

Lambertini frowned.

'I have no answer, inspector. I know I gave her a card a long time ago. Where she got the new one from I have no idea.'

'I see, signore. I was also intrigued when a cat was found outside the deceased's apartment. It was scratching at the door. The neighbour who took it in, said that it was Signorina Scacchi's cat – a white-haired animal.'

The policeman sat down uninvited and looked up at the man before him.

'We have found white cat's hairs in your car, signore. They could have got there when Angelina Scacchi was a passenger, or from your clothing when you visited her at her apartment. Which would it be, Signor Lambertini?'

Chapter Sixty-Two

On the outskirts of Trento, just north of Lake Garda, Lisa sat up.

'Where are we? How long have I been out?'

Marcus swivelled round.

'That depends what you remember, Lisa. Can you recall the house outside Klais? What Martin Goehr was trying to do? Getting into the car?'

She was silent for a moment, collecting her thoughts.

'My God! That awful man! He drugged me. I can't recall much else, except being held up by Leonardo, and lots of people shouting.'

Leonardo interrupted.

'Lisa, thanks to Marcus' ingenuity, we all got out the house in one piece. It was touch and go for a while.'

'I can remember being thrown into this car, but not much else. How did you manage it, Marcus? I knew you would come after me, but I really thought we'd had it this time.'

Leonardo answered again.

'Marcus played on their greed. He threatened to smash the violin in front of them if they didn't release you. It's a long story. Marcus will tell you when we reach Cremona.'

'There's one thing I have to tell you, Lisa. You were right to be suspicious about Geri Bellman,' admitted Marcus, sadness in his voice. 'His real name is Gerhardt Abelmann – a close friend of Martin Goehr, and a spy; he was telling him our every move.'

'Oh, Marcus, I'm so sorry. I know he meant a great deal to you.'

Marcus nodded dumbly. There were no words to express what he felt.

'How long before we arrive in Cremona?' she asked.

'At this rate, about another two hours,' replied Leonardo.

'What do we do when we get there?'

Leonardo glanced at Marcus. It had been on both their minds but, until that moment, had gone unvoiced.

'I shall pass the report to Leonardo. He will take it to his principals. I hope he will not give them back the Guarneri, but will ensure it is returned to its rightful owner. You, Lisa will pack; so shall I. We shall then get to Milan airport as fast as the car will carry us.'

She leaned forward in the seat and kissed him on the cheek.

'There is just one little thing I have to do,' declared Marcus. 'Do you realise that, in all our searches, we have never found any documents belonging to the Cremonese? We have come across references, sketches, working drawings, but, invariably, they've been copies. Over the past weeks, we have travelled far and wide and not seen a sign of them. I've been giving the matter a lot of thought these past few days. I believe they still exist, and I'm convinced they are in Cremona, somewhere.'

There was a sense of coming home when they walked through the door of their suite. Marcus had not noticed Leonardo pick up the violin case during their departure from Klais and was relieved to place the instrument back in its protective cover.

'I'm going for a bath, Marcus,' announced Lisa. 'Then, can we have something to eat, I'm starving?'

'It's best we eat in. I'll order a meal for the three of us.'

Leonardo had gone to make some calls and to refresh himself after having driven for five hours.

It was close to nine o'clock in the evening when they emerged from their rooms. The food trolley arrived on the hour and they were served by two waiters. Marcus poured the wine.

'I hope it's to your liking' he said, looking at his two companions.

'Now, a toast – to friendship! Especially friendship in adversity.'

They clinked glasses.

Conversation was sporadic. Each of them savoured the moment, realising that they might not have been dining in comfort, but mouldering in a hastily-dug grave in some remote part of Austria.

'What do you want to do then, Marcus?' asked Leonardo.

'If everyone agrees, I want to go back to the Records Office in the town to have another word with our archivist. I think, if he were pushed, he could be helpful. If you remember, Lisa, it was he who directed me to the Stati dell'Anime which, in turn, led you to uncover the information about the Stradivari household. I must admit, I could never understand his change of heart.'

Leonardo lowered his eyes to the table.

'You know why, don't you, Leonardo? As I recall it was you who engineered me out of the Archives to let Marcus in. How did you accomplish that?'

'I cannot reveal how, signora,' he said softly. 'It is not a subject I am free to discuss.'

Her eyebrows twitched.

'Leonardo, you risked your life for me. You faced terrifying dangers to secure my release. If it were in my power, I would tell you anything you wanted to know.' She paused. Then, more quietly, she said, 'Despite our occasional differences, I truly regard you as a friend – an ally, a confidant. Are you sure you cannot tell me? You have my word, it will never go beyond these four walls.'

'I owe you both a great deal,' said Leonardo. 'We came together at first through necessity, then as colleagues. Gradually, we became companions. Now we are friends.' He paused. 'Have you heard of . . .'

His mobile phone interrupted. He took it from his pocket, saw the number, and rose saying, 'It is important. Please excuse me.'

The door of his room was shut firmly.

Chapter Sixty-Three

He had taken the call in the evening, as the offices were emptying and the building was growing quiet after the day's activities.

'Your Eminence, Signor Gordino, the Deputy Prime Minister, wishes to speak with you. Shall I say you are here?'

Cardinal Marchetti smiled. Of course I'm here, he thought. 'I've been awaiting his call all day. You had better put him through, Felipé.'

The Deputy came on the line.

'Your Eminence?'

'Mr Deputy. You have just caught me. I was about to attend a meeting with the Holy Father. What can I do for you?'

'Your Eminence, after your departure yesterday, there was considerable debate about your project. I argued most strongly that we should meet your request. In fact, some hours were spent on the matter, and I stood firmly by my opinion that the Vatican should receive the just sum.' He paused for a moment. 'As a result, I have persuaded all the Ministers to support the payment of ten billion Euros to the Vatican's account. It will be paid tomorrow. Can I, therefore, inform the Prime Minister and the Cabinet that the plan to remove the Holy See from Rome will be dropped?'

Marchetti held his silence, letting the tension build.

'You have my word on the matter, Mr Deputy. The status quo will be maintained.'

He sat with his hand resting on the receiver. He had done it! All those months of planning, persuading, cajoling others to support him – it had been well worthwhile. The smile reached his eyes. There were still some loose ends to tie up, but first he must formally break the news. He called in his secretary.

'Felipé, go at once to these offices and give these notes to the named recipients. Then arrange for me to speak with the Secretary of State.'

'Thank you for coming at, undoubtedly, short notice. However, it was important for this committee, the working group that has masterminded the Plan, to learn of the outcome.'

The assembled company listened expectantly.

'Today, at a little after four o'clock, the Deputy Prime Minister phoned me. He confirmed that the city and national administrations will pay us ten billion Euros to remain. They are of the opinion that Rome and the Vatican are inseparable, and are willing to share the income they mutually attract. My friends, we have done it! There is the small matter of expenses incurred by some of the services we have employed – trifling sums. You can leave that to me to clear up, and to ensure that nothing of our efforts will ever be known to anyone outside this room.'

As ever, Cardinal Temple was the first to react.

'My congratulations, Your Eminence. Your tactics have been bold and masterly. As you know, I cannot but feel it was a sordid affair – our holding them to ransom.' He nodded thoughtfully. 'However, I also accept that we have long been ignored where the income from tourists is concerned. You are, I trust, convinced that knowledge of the Plan will never come to light?'

'Absolutely, Your Eminence.'

Other voices were heard; all the comments were congratulatory. Within fifteen minutes the outer doors closed on the last of them. He was alone. Now for the Cardinal Secretary of State. He would still be in his suite, even at this hour. Before he went along the corridor, there was one urgent call he must make.

'The first thing we must do, Leonardo, is to present ourselves at the Records Office, when they open at ten.'

'I'm afraid that will not be the case, Signor Danby. I must ask you to accompany me on a short trip. You too, Signora Robards.'

'What are you talking about, Leonardo? Have you forgotten what we need to do?' asked Marcus, perplexed.

'You've got something on your mind, haven't you, Leonardo?' said Lisa. 'It was that phone call last night, wasn't it?'

He nodded. 'We must leave immediately. There is no time to waste.'

Lisa's face had changed. Gone the vivacious, dreamy look; now it was wary and calculating.

'And what if we don't obey?'

The Messenger pulled back his coat. In a shoulder holster nestled an automatic gun, its shiny, metallic blue finish contrasting with the paleness of his shirt.

They rose from the table, the Messenger walking behind them, took the lift to the lobby and went out to the car park.'

'You will drive, Signor Danby. You, signora, will sit in the front with him. Take the Mantua road, and do exactly as I tell you.'

They passed through San Felice, continuing westwards.

After five minutes of silence, he said, 'Turn left here, through Vescovato.'

They drove another three kilometres.

'This will do. Pull off the road and head for those trees.'

The car stopped with a jerk.

'Now, both of you, out!'

The Messenger was carrying a canvas bag. He drew the gun from its holster.

'Let us walk over towards those pines.'

'Where did you get the gun, Leonardo? You didn't have it yesterday – more's the pity!' said Marcus as he stumbled along the track.

'I met with my cousins last night, my friend – whilst you were both occupied.'

Marcus suddenly halted.

'OK . . . this charade has gone far enough! What's this all about, Leonardo? We are not going a step further until you tell us.'

'I am completing the task my principals set me, Signor Danby. Getting rid of any loose ends. They regard you and Signora Robards as loose ends, to be removed.'

'Now wait a minute! This can't be happening. You were with us last night. Was that to soften us up? To make sure we fell in with your wishes? Was that it?' Turning, he made to step towards the Messenger.

'I should not do that, signore! It might be the last thing you ever do. Now, face the trees.' They were helpless. After surviving all that had befallen them, they now faced an ignominious death on a piece of scrubland in Northern Italy. And no one would ever know.

He was behind them. They heard the zip of the bag being unfastened.

'I think it would be better if you were to lie on the ground,' he said in an even voice.

Slowly, they knelt before him, then stretched out on the thin, undernourished grass, their hands seeking each other's. They closed their eyes.

He aimed carefully, and squeezed.

Chapter Sixty-Four

'That was not funny, Leonardo,' said Lisa.

'It was the only way I could ensure you would come with me. It also demonstrated to those watching that you were being taken against your will. They would not have been deceived if you were acting. It would also have shown in your faces as you were lying there.'

'Do you mean to say that your own people are following you?'

'My cousins told me we are under surveillance, not only from Goehr's team, but others as well. My principals need to be satisfied you no longer constitute a threat.'

'But you've got the report they requested. Why should they want us dead?'

'Because now you know too much.'

Lisa shivered.

'Wait a minute! Are you saying there are two factions after us? The sooner we are out of here the better.'

'How many shots did you take, Leonardo?' enquired Marcus.

'Eight or nine. Let me show you.'

He lifted the digital camera so they could see the viewer. The first few photos showed the couple lying on the ground, eyes closed, distress evident on their faces.

'That's gruesome, looking at your own execution!' remarked Marcus. 'It's too realistic – especially with all that stage blood! I'm pleased you brought us a change of clothes.'

'Let us return to the hotel.'

'But if we are being watched we can't use it anymore, can we?' exclaimed Lisa.

'Yes, you can, provided you don't go through the main entrance,' said Leonardo. 'My cousins have arranged for you to come and go through the service area. We shall meet them in town

300

shortly, and they will take over my duties and my room. Our first visit must be to an instrument maker. You take the real violin. Hold on to your insurance! I shall return a suitable copy to my master.'

They got into the car.

'While you are exploring the archives, I'll book my flight. All being well, I should be back tomorrow night. However, if by chance I don't make it, I want to tell you some things about myself and my work. We can do that over lunch.'

'Something strange happened earlier! The tall one escorted the man and the woman to the car. They looked worried, and he made no attempt to disguise the fact that he was applying force. He sat in the back: they were in the front. The man drove. When we tried to follow a truck blocked our way, so we don't know where they went. They haven't come back.'

Goehr listened intently. What was happening now? By tomorrow he would have someone to do the deed, and retrieve the violin. Unless, of course, the Messenger had already taken care of them. If so, it should be even easier to retrieve his prize.

'Just stay where you are. I'll speak with you tomorrow. Someone will be joining you. I shall want you to brief him.'

'Brother Felipé, the three of them left the hotel together. It was clear the couple was being compelled to walk in front of him to the car. When they passed me, the man was driving; she was sitting beside him. The Messenger was in the rear. That was three hours ago.'

He was speaking on a mobile. As he turned, something caught his eye.

'Wait a minute! The Messenger has returned. He is alone.'

In the event they bought two violins. Leonardo took them to the hotel, concealed in a holdall, while Lisa and Marcus made their way to the Records Office. The archivist was there to greet them. This time they knew his name.

'Signor Bandalotti, it is good to see you again.'

301

As they shook hands, the bespectacled, young man whispered.

'*Pax vobiscum.*'

'*Et cum spiritu tuo.*' It was a conditioned response.

'Come! We shall talk in my office. You must tell me how I can be of service.'

They followed him down a narrow corridor.

'Please take a seat,' said Bandalotti. 'Would you care for some coffee?'

Both declined. Seated behind the desk, he leaned forward in anticipation. He really is keen to help, thought Marcus. I wonder what Leonardo said to him when he phoned to make the appointment.

'Signor Bandalotti, you gave us a great deal of help on the last occasion we called upon your services. Our research was much improved as a result. However,' added Marcus, conspiratorially, 'we need one further favour from you. I'm sure you will be able to point us in the right direction.'

'As you know, Fra' Marcus, I shall do whatever is in my power. As an associate . . .' He glanced at Lisa, 'You have only to ask.'

'Let me explain how far we have got, signore. We have studied the Cremonese in detail, learning about their commissions, studios, materials, techniques and about those who were apprenticed to, or worked with them. But much of the written word and drawings are not original. In our searches we have come across few of their actual documents. Perhaps they don't exist. They may have been destroyed. Or have they? If they still survive, they are somewhere here, in Cremona. Where do you think they might be?'

The archivist pondered the question.

'No one has ever queried the documents we hold in our records. I would disagree, and say that a great many originate from the eighteenth century. But I know what you mean. For all their work, the length of time they occupied the Piazza of San Domenico, there should have been more. I have never considered it in terms of quantity before.' He became more animated. 'I wonder if there could be a cache of their material lurking somewhere?'

Suddenly, he grinned.

'How exciting! I suppose the best way to assess the problem is to review what has happened over the centuries. Firstly, we know they spent their lives around the Church of San Domenico. The Cremonese all lived within metres of its front door. The parish priests

302

were authorised to conduct their Stati dell'Anime every year at Easter-time. These records were stored by the church, as were the birth, death and marriage certificates. They were also the repositories for numerous other records, especially the personal documents of notable parishioners. Such archival material would have been taken to the church for safe keeping. There would not have been enough room in a household to keep papers and memorabilia. In those days, conditions were cramped; space was at a premium.'

Bandalotti went to a book shelf, and removed a thin volume.

'Let us presume that each time one of the Cremonese died their documents were placed in the crypt of San Domenico. Now we know that in 1869 a so-called developer tore down the piazza, many of the houses and the church, to make way for new buildings. According to a reference here, the Stati dell'Anime papers were taken to Milan – at least most of them. Many items, and conceivably a great number of the Cremonese documents, were removed for storage to Sant'Agata, the main diocesan church in the Corso Garibaldi.'

He went back to his chair.

'I know for a fact that Stradivari sent some of his own records there. That was where he married his first wife, Francesca. He had a special affinity for the church. No doubt, he checked to see if the crypt was less damp than many others at the time. There the trail seems to disappear, I'm afraid. Sant'Agata no longer houses any records of former times!'

However, he was clearly enthused, keen to push forward and solve a mystery.

'Look, I won't keep you. Let me continue my searches. Give me a number where I can reach you.'

Marcus wrote down his mobile number. 'Signor Bandalotti, we are leaving Cremona tomorrow. It would be our dearest wish to solve the mystery. Phone me, please, whatever the time.'

They were escorted to the rear of the building by a circuitous route. The taxi had dropped them and the two cousins four hundred metres from the hotel. Cutting through the back of the car park they had entered a door leading to an unauthorised section where the boiler plant and storage facilities were housed. They went up several flights of stairs, along dark, unpainted corridors, until they emerged by a service lift. It took them swiftly to the fourth floor, away from prying eyes.

Leonardo arrived as lunch was wheeled into the suite. He poured them both a glass of wine.

'Was our friendly archivist able to help you?'

'I think so. Again I got the distinct impression he was treating me as a fellow conspirator. His manner was odd, but he went out of his way to be helpful. What did you say to him that made our Signor Bandalotti so anxious to please? Come to think of it, he was like it the last time we met.'

'I noticed he said "Pax" then something or other, Marcus,' Lisa frowned, recalling the conversation. Leonardo looked slightly abashed.

'He said "*Pax vobiscum*" and I responded with "*Et cum spiritu tuo*". That's a bit unusual outside the confines of the liturgy, but . . .'

'Normally, there's more to it,' interrupted Leonardo. 'We add "*Pax et Bonum, Residuum revertur*!" Peace and Goodness, the Remnant shall return! This last phrase applies to the Truth throughout history. A remnant has always remained faithful to God, despite the corruption and lapses of their leaders. It is the opening gambit among members of a Catholic Group of which I am a member.'

'Like Opus Dei?' asked Lisa, her interest quickening

'Not exactly. We believe in the evolution of the Church, albeit as a gradual process. Members of Opus Dei are staunchly conservative.'

'And, presumably, Signor Bandalotti is a member?'

'Yes.'

'Someone told me he was an unfrocked priest. Is that right?' asked Lisa.

'Not quite,' Leonardo smiled. 'He was an acolyte in Rome, but he flew too close to the sun!'

As they ate, Marcus asked if he had made his reservation.

'Yes, an early evening flight from Milan. If all goes well, I should be back late tomorrow night.'

He picked up his glass, and drank deeply.

'As I said earlier, before I go, I want to tell you something about myself. I have told you that I am a Messenger for the principal cardinals in the Curia. In many respects that's a misnomer. We do convey messages but, as you will have realised, our remit is much wider. We undertake the work the cardinals can trust to no one else.'

Over the next hour, Leonardo took them through every facet of how *I Messagieri* operated: the briefing he had been given on how to secure Marcus' allegiance to the project, the need to protect him until the report was finished, and the duties as intermediary between Marcus and the Vatican.

'But it was always intended to be an exercise in futility. To Cardinal Marchetti it was just another means of turning the screw on the administration, to reinforce the ransom demand when he revealed the Grand Plan – to pay the Church a great deal of money or the Vatican City would be removed in its entirety, and relocated on the banks of the Po.'

'My God, Marcus! What have we got ourselves into?' cried Lisa.

'You mean to say, all the hours we spent researching the Cremonese, fending off assaults, driving all over the countryside, Lisa being kidnapped . . . all of us nearly being killed! That was for nothing?'

'If the City had not succumbed to the Plan, then no, it would not have been for nothing. There were others, like yourselves, taking part. In fact, I believe Marchetti, who masterminded the whole exercise, would have been pleased if they had rejected the demand. But it's too late. They are about to receive the ransom.'

'How much?' asked Lisa.

'Ten billion Euros.'

'Good grief! That's almost twelve billion dollars!'

Leonardo continued. He related how Goehr and other Austrians wanted to suppress revelations about the deaths of the Cremonese. How, while the Empress Maria Theresa was technically responsible, the involvement of the Goehr family in the wanton destruction of the Cremonese would have harmed the chances of the Austrian papal candididate, Cardinal Vincent Goehr, Martin's brother.

'If the truth came out that the Austrian Hapsburgs and their leading instrument makers had colluded to bring down such a revered Italian institution, the fall-out, in this country and the rest of the world, would have killed Cardinal Goehr's chances of the Papacy.'

'And the illicit instrument collection,' added Lisa.

'Yes, there was much more to it than I suspected. The discovery that Goehr's and Abelmann's fathers were part of the Nazi drive to strip the Jews of their precious instruments would also have had an unwelcome effect. Just imagine if *that* came to light! Plus siphoning off of a considerable collection of violins, violas and cellos for themselves, it would have cancelled forever any likelihood of his accession to the Papal Throne.'

He emptied his glass.

'There is one other thing I must tell you. During World War Two, their fathers were abetted in Vienna by a leading member of the Hitler Youth. That man is now a cardinal. It is my belief he is trying to liberate the instruments held by the Vatican, using the services of his friends in Mittenwald.'

'How did the instruments reach the Vatican in the first place?' asked Marcus.

'It is my understanding that they were some form of payment, or gift, from the Fuhrer to Pope Pius XII. There have always been rumours about their close association – the Pontiff's failure to condemn the atrocities; the questions about the Vatican's role in sequestering gold seized from the Jews in Eastern Europe; the ratlines, supposedly run by the Vatican, which helped many of the Nazis to evade capture. There were many such signals of their relationship. Conceivably, this was yet another manifestation of the bond that existed between them.'

'It's going to be dangerous going back, isn't it Leonardo?' said Lisa quietly.

'Perhaps. I should be able to satisfy Cardinal Marchetti. I'm not so sure how Cardinal Grossmann will react. By now, he will know of my role in this venture, and things could be difficult.'

She rose to her feet again and walked round the table.

'Be careful Leonardo. Come back safely.'

Chapter Sixty-Five

'Someone is on their way to Cremona . . . Yes, he should be there by midday. When we speak again, this time tomorrow, it will all be over. Finished! Nothing, and no one will exist that could lead to any unwelcome disclosures . . . Then we can get back to discussing our arrangement. Yes, continue with what we first arranged . . . Agreed, in my official capacity, I shall call upon you in the Vatican . . . I'll write that in my diary . . . Good . . . Then we can organise their complete purchase and transfer. Goodnight, Your Eminence.'

A phone was ringing. Disorientated – somehow there were too many arms – he eventually put out a hand in the direction of his mobile.

'Fra' Marcus? It's Bandalotti.'

He was suddenly wide awake.

'Sorry to ring you at this hour, but I think I've found something. Before San Domenico was razed to the ground, I was right, the documents were transferred to Sant'Agata's. Anyway, I contacted the priest, who knew nothing about it. But he directed me to a church historian in Cremona. Do you know what he told me? In 1901, a great many records were taken to the vaults of San Luca. It's a church within the diocese of Sant'Agata. Its vaults were used as overflow storage.'

'That's fantastic, Signor Bandalotti! What do we do? Go to the church tomorrow morning? Where is it?'

'Close to Sant'Agata in the Corso Garibaldi. Let us meet there, say, at eight o'clock, after the first morning service. We can then check their existence with the priest.'

Marcus switched off the phone and sank back.

'Was that our friendly archivist?' asked Lisa drowsily.

'Yes. He may have picked up the trail of the missing Cremonese documents.'

'*Pax vobiscum.*'

'*Et cum spiritu tuo.*'

Brother Felipé smiled at Leonardo. 'He is waiting for you. I am to send you straight in. Did you have a good trip?'

Leonardo nodded. 'Everything has turned out well, Felipé.'

The Franciscan tapped at the door and, opening it, ushered in the Messenger. The cardinal turned from his usual place at the window and walked towards him.

'Do you have the report?'

He opened his case and removed the two spiral-bound manuscripts.

'It's quite substantial, I see. Have you read it?'

'No, not the entire document. But it is a well-considered, carefully constructed appraisal. It confirms that the instrument-making talents are available, and that the methods, techniques and materials could be replicated.'

'Excellent! However, for the moment it will not be needed. What of this fellow Danby, and the woman, Robards? Did you do as I asked?'

'I was about to. I took them out of the town to a quiet spot, but we were followed. The Austrians shot them. Fortunately, I managed to escape.'

Marchetti's eyes narrowed.

'You managed to escape. How?'

'I had the violin. Were you aware, Your Eminence, it was the "Magnificat"? One of the masterpieces created by Guarneri del Gesù? I was carrying it, and threatened to destroy it if I were not released. Goehr and his companion, Abelmann, are avid collectors. They stopped their men from launching themselves at me. I walked away holding the violin aloft, ready to dash it to pieces. Later, when I returned to the scene on the outskirts of Cremona, I found the two bodies.'

He drew the photographs from his pocket and placed them on a buffet table. Marchetti peered at them for some time, then raised his head.

'That completes the matter. Most satisfactory! One last detail, then you can go. The violin, if you please?'

'I left it with Brother Felipé.'

'Then be so kind as to bring it to me. I need it here.'

The violin case was opened. The cardinal looked at it for some time.

'It was not damaged, I hope?'

'No, Your Eminence. It is as good as new.'

'One last thing. I need you to take a message – to Mittenwald.'

In another part of Rome, Michelo Lambertini was savouring his morning coffee, enjoying the start of a new day. A new beginning, he thought. An hour earlier he had taken a call from the cardinal.

'I shall no longer be requiring your services, Signor Lambertini. You did well, very well! Everything has worked out most satisfactorily. I doubt that we shall be speaking again, so listen carefully to my parting comment. Remember just how fragile your future would be were you to utter one word of our little venture. I shall be watching, Signor Lambertini. Goodbye.'

He could live with that. He would tell no one – *tutto quello che sai morrira con me*! He grinned to himself. At last, I can relax.

The telephone startled him. It was the portiere in the lobby of the apartment block.

'I have two men here, Signor Lambertini. They wish to speak with you urgently.'

'Who are they? I'm not expecting visitors.'

There was a muffled exchange.

'He says his name is Leoni – Inspector Leoni.'

He wasn't sure he wanted to see him. But what choice did he have?

'Send him up, please.'

He was standing at his front door when the lift arrived.

'Good morning, Signor Lambertini. I believe you know my assistant. May we come in? I have something I wish to ask you, signore.'

He led them into the sitting room.

'Yes?'

'You could not give me an explanation of the cat's hairs found in your car the other day, signore. Have you thought any more about how they could have got there?'

'No, inspector, I haven't. Is it important?'

'On its own, no, Signor Lambertini. But we also found the same hairs in a white van – a van you hired, apparently. They were close to some other marks we discovered. The DNA tests show they were from Signorina Scacchi's body. Signor Lambertini, I am arresting you for the murder of Angelina Scacchi. You do not have to say . . .'

A cool wind seemed to blow into Marcus' face whichever way he turned. It was just before eight o'clock in the morning, and he stood on the steps of the church of San Luca. He had been smuggled out of the hotel and was again accompanied by a member of Leonardo's family.

Bandalotti appeared on the hour, as the distant peal of bells gently faded away.

'Fra' Marcus.'

'Signor Bandalotti. You worked late last night.'

'My interest is as keen as yours. It will be a fascinating story if we discover the missing papers. Clearly, many believe that the documents currently available are all that were stored at the time of their deaths. It would be marvellous to uncover more.'

The archivist was obviously excited. They stopped one of the altar boys who was about to rush past, and he showed them to the sacristy.

'Father Tantini? Do you have a moment?'

The priest looked round enquiringly. 'Good morning! I can't recall seeing you at the service?'

'No, father, we were not,' said Bandalotti. 'I should explain. I am the Chief Archivist at the Town's Record Office. My colleague . . .' He indicated Marcus. '. . . is conducting an official research programme of the document files and records of eighteenth century life in Lombardy and Piedmont. He was wondering if he might inspect what is stored in your crypt?'

The cleric finished putting away his chasuble.

'He could if they were there! We are clearing out the crypt at the moment – clearing away what has rotted, burning what is indecipherable.'

Marcus' heart sank. Another dead end!

'Most of what's left has been moved to that room through there.' He gestured towards a door.

'Would you mind if we looked at what remains, father?'

'Help yourselves. I'm going for breakfast, but you can have the key. Call me when you have finished.'

Bandalotti took it almost reverently. As the priest walked out he inserted the key in the lock and turned the handle.

Before them were mounds of paper, and the pervasive stench of dampness.

'Where do we begin?' asked Marcus, overwhelmed by the huge volume they would have to search through. 'It's a hopeless task!'

'No, it's not,' insisted Bandalotti. 'Look for anything tied with green ribbons. As I recall from previous research, the Cremonese always tied their records in that manner.'

'OK,' said Marcus dubiously. 'Shall we start at opposite ends?'

'I think so. You go down the room and work your way towards me!'

Two hours later – when they were hot, sweaty, and tired – the priest returned with bottles of water.

'I could hear the noise you were making. Judging by the effort you are putting into it, I thought you might be thirsty.'

Marcus and the archivist had ploughed through about a quarter of the pile.

At this rate, he thought, I could be here for days!

'Father, tell me,' said the archivist. 'Have you come across any old records tied with green ribbon?'

The priest thought for a moment.

'Yes. I believe there are some around here.' He walked down the room, peering amongst the mounds, pulling out occasional armfuls of documents. 'Yes, I thought so. Are these what you are looking for?'

There, at the foot of a mound were sheaves of papers tied together in the Cremonese green ribbon.

'That's it! Father, you are wonderful!' cried Bandalotti. 'Marcus, help me free them.'

They set to with renewed enthusiasm. Even the priest helped.

Eventually, they were extricated and carried to the table near the door. Marcus and Bandalotti each took a pile and began the slow task of sifting through them. They were clearly the Cremonese papers and related specifically to the period from 1700 to the deaths of the last instrument workers.

Another three hours were spent reading and interpreting the many documents that referred to household purchases, materials for the workshops, letters of commission, bills, and numerous drawings and designs.

The archivist was in his element, delighting in every word, sentence and signature.

'This is outstanding, Marcus! The library will be immeasurably enhanced by all this. I owe you a deep debt of gratitude.'

'Enrico, as far as I am concerned, you are the rightful finder, not I. It is you who should receive any public acclaim for such a find.'

'No! That cannot be possible.'

'I insist!'

It was at that moment he turned over a faded sheet and a signature caught his eye – Carlo Bergonzi.

Marcus gasped.

'I believe I've got what I am looking for.'

'What is it?'

'A letter written by Carlo Bergonzi. Read it.'

Like the others, I will soon depart this world. I fear my affliction, and despair it has caught me at a moment when I have still much to offer.

I shall join my peers long before my time is due and, because of this, will stand unfulfilled and ever in their shadows.

Why, and who has done this to me?

Signed this day – 17th September 1747

Carlo Bergonzi – Instrument Maker

'Fascinating! What does he mean by affliction?'

'It's a long story, Enrico,' responded Marcus, contentedly. 'Look, you wanted to share the discovery with me. But as I said, it's all yours. Just let me keep this slip of paper.'

'If that's all you want, take it.'

'Damn you, Marcus! Why didn't you ring? I've been sitting here all day, worried out of my mind they might have caught you. In fact, I

312

phoned the Records Office, and they told me Signor Bandalotti hadn't been in all day.'

Marcus was suddenly contrite. In searching through the mountain of papers, he had forgotten everything else.

'I'm truly sorry, Lisa. Please forgive me. You will when you read this.'

From a padded envelope, he carefully withdrew the sheet of paper, and passed it to her. As she read, Lisa's mouth dropped open.

'This is it! The final item of proof that they were murdered by poison! Did it come from the archives of San Luca?'

He told her how they had come across it after being faced with a daunting task; that Bandalotti was still there, reading every last word, totally delighted with the find that Marcus had declared should be his.

'Absolutely right! We don't want your name broadcast. It could put us in even greater danger.'

The executioner met with the lookout.

'I think your job has been done for you!'

'What do you mean?'

'I believe the tall one in your photograph,' he said, pointing at the figure, 'got rid of the other two. They all went out in their car yesterday morning. He was sitting in the back, the others in the front seats. When he returned, he was alone.'

'It could mean, of course, that they are getting into the hotel another way,' commented the assassin. 'Have you checked their room? Have you spoken with any of the staff?'

'Well, no! I thought I'd wait until you arrived. After all, I was only supposed to watch them. Nothing more.'

'Hm . . . I'll enter their room tonight. If they are there, I shall attend to them!'

Chapter Sixty-Six

'Gustav, come in! Come in! I'll be with you in a moment.'

It was said in a half-whisper, the mouthpiece of the phone covered by his hand. The conversation lasted only a few minutes longer.

'How are you, Gustav? Well, I hope!'

The Cardinal Secretary of State was being solicitous, thought Grossmann. Should I be concerned?

'Well enough, Sylvestre. You wanted to tell me something?'

'Yes, my old friend, I did want to speak with you. Tell me, how are things going with our charity, Cor Unum? Is the liaison with Caritas Italia working smoothly?'

He is prevaricating. Why doesn't he get to the point?

'Everything is working well, Sylvestre – as I wrote in my report.'

'Good! Good! By the way, I've been thinking . . . Cardinal Goehr speaks Spanish and Portugese, does he not? . . . Perhaps he ought to spend some time away from the Vatican. Somewhere less warm, for a couple of years. If they come to light, his brother's exploits could have a damaging effect on his future. In three years or so, he could return, and have a year to organise his campaign.'

'What, for the Pontiff's Chair?'

'Of course.'

'But he could go on for years!'

The Cardinal Secretary said in a low voice, 'Believe me, he will not.' He smiled disarmingly. 'In four years time we shall be holding an election for a new Pope.'

The Cardinal Secretary rose and came to stand at Grossmann's shoulder.

'I have come to a decision, Gustav. I am appointing Cardinal Marchetti to oversee the sale of our treasured instruments. I know you were going to organise it but, frankly, he has been so successful in bringing funds into the Holy See I feel he is the one for the task.'

'Do you, Sylvestre?' snarled Grossmann. 'You don't realise that, as a result of his meddling, our names are close to being made public. There is every chance details of our backgrounds will be spread throughout the world's press. Then where will we be?'

'Yes, I know,' said the Cardinal Secretary, blithely. 'You should have changed your name, as I did mine sixty years ago. I've forgotten everything about Sylvester Ottomeyer, I've been Sylvestre Cantoni for so long!'

He put his hand on Grossmann's shoulder.

'The trouble is, Gustav, you are a prominent figure in the Papal charities. If it came out, it wouldn't be viewed favourably that a Prince of the Church had been a vigorous member of the Hitler Youth ... running roughshod over the Jews in Vienna during World War Two. You'll have to resign your chairmanship of these as well.'

Responsible for his parents being shipped off to Dachau, Grossmann had retained his full name as a belated mark of conscience. He had not given the reason to Cantoni all those years ago: he was not about to do so now.

'So, Marchetti will take over the sale of our cache of instruments, will he?' Grossmann sneered. 'What does he know about such things? To whom will he sell them?'

'I rather thought he would use your friends in Austria. As you have said yourself, they know what they're about.' The Secretary smiled wryly. 'And a great deal more about collecting and trading. I've already instructed Cardinal Marchetti to contact them.'

Grossmann rose unsteadily to his feet, bowed to the Secretary of State and walked from the room.

Chapter Sixty-Seven

'When he asked me to deliver a package to someone in Mittenwald, I'm sure he saw my surprise. It wasn't until later that his secretary . . .' He noted their looks. 'Yes, he is also a member of "Pax vobiscum" . . . told me that the cardinal had been asked to sell the Vatican's horde of instruments, including, of course, the Magnificat or what he believes is the "Magnificat".'

'How long do we have before they come after us?' interrupted Marcus.

'Three days at least,' replied Leonardo. 'I told him that I had been instructed by the administrator to take the customary break in duties. I asked if he wanted another Messenger, but he said it could wait until I returned.'

'But you are not going back, I hope, Leonardo? It would be too dangerous.'

'What else can I do? I have a family tradition to maintain.'

'You have no children, Leonardo. You are already breaking the mould,' said Lisa fiercely. 'No, there is no other option. You will have to come with us.'

'She's right,' said Marcus. 'You can't go back. Anyway, we need your protection.'

Leonardo was silent, contemplating the radical change being forced upon him. Until now, he had considered no other alternative to his work. It had become a vocation, a commitment. But, the man standing next to him had adjusted to a new way of life. Why couldn't he? Lisa was right, the line of patrimony was already at an end.

'Yes, I now believe my days as a Messenger are finished. I'll think about what to do after we have sorted out our current problems – if ever we can, for now we have two enemies.'

'Once Marchetti learns the truth, he will be as dangerous as Goehr. From that moment we shall never be safe, wherever we go!'

'Even if they believe we've still got the Guarneri del Gesù?'

'Marchetti will ignore Goehr's greed. He will make every effort to ensure we are removed.'

'What do we do?' said Lisa.

'The first step is to put as much distance between us and them as possible. I should imagine Goehr still believes we are all here. If Marchetti has watchers, they are probably inexperienced and will conclude I've got rid of you. But Goehr's people will want to be sure. They are going to come looking very, very soon.'

'Do we leave now?'

'First, let's order dinner!'

The executioner walked along the corridor towards the waiter pushing a food trolley.

'Is that my order for room four-four-eight?'

'No sir, this is for room four-one-two.'

As he thought – their room.

They passed each other; then the executioner pivoted round and followed him. As they neared the service area, he quickly closed the distance and in one motion propelled the waiter through the swing door. Drawing a pistol, he levelled it at the man's head.

'Strip!'

Minutes later, a waiter resumed his journey.

At 412 he knocked lightly and called 'Room service!' Not waiting for a reply, he used the pass-key. He pushed open the door and wheeled the trolley into the middle of the sitting area.

They must all be in their bedrooms, he thought. Even easier. He could take them out one at a time. Stealthily, he moved to the door on the right. With his back to the wall, his gun arm vertical, he eased the handle down with his left hand. Spinning round, he pitched into the bedroom, knees relaxed, swinging the gun in a stiff-armed arc. No one was there!

Slowly, he moved forward towards the bathroom and kicked open the door. No one was there, either.

Swiftly, he tried the other two bedrooms. They had gone. Nothing was left of their occupation, except a violin case lying on a sofa.

He freed the catches. The instrument nestled in its velvet lining.

'I can take that back to Mittenwald,' he muttered to himself. 'At least Herr Goehr will have part of what he was seeking.'

They waited in Barcelona forty-five minutes before the next leg of the journey.

Leonardo had paid the bill at the hotel in Cremona. Then, giving the suite some semblance of occupation, they had slipped out of the now familiar exit, across the car park and into a car with one of his cousins at the wheel. They had made good time to Milan, booking in at the Montini Hotel, four kilometres from the airport. Early next morning they had boarded an Iberia Airlines flight which landed briefly at the Spanish airport before flying on to Chicago.

After eating a light meal and dozing briefly, Marcus awoke somewhere over the Atlantic.

Lisa saw his eyes open. She leaned against him

'What are we going to do, Marcus?'

'I'm not sure.' He yawned. 'I suppose it would help if people were aware of what has happened, Lisa. Publicising all that we know, all that we have encountered, might reduce the danger.'

He turned his head sideways to look at the sleeping Leonardo.

'The trouble is I shouldn't think any newspaper would want to print the story. It would appear an unwarranted attack on the Church, one they could easily refute. How could we prove they ever had the Magnificat in the first place? If Leonardo declared it were true, he would be seen merely as a disgruntled ex-employee. And how could we convince anyone that a leading Curialist was holding the local and national governments to ransom? Or that the civil authorities paid the Vatican a vast sum of money? Marchetti was keen to ensure no loose ends existed.'

He took hold of her hand.

'Then there's Martin Goehr. He deliberately tried to stop us finding out about the deaths of the Cremonese and his family's ties with the Nazis. There is nothing to connect him with the assaults we suffered. I suppose we could show his father helped pillage Vienna – that might scupper his brother's chances. But all that happened over half a century ago. What journalist would be interested in old news? Life moves on. We are in a serious situation, Lisa. How do we get what we know into the public domain without one iota of proof?'

She was silent for a long time. Marcus thought she had dozed off. Then she nudged his arm.

'After a few days, Marcus, can we go to Los Angeles?'

'Why? Do you fancy finishing your article on some Pacific shore?'

She smiled up at him, and lifted the arm between their seats.

'I'll tell you later. I've had an idea. It's a long shot, but it just might work.'

The plane touched down at O'Hare after a fifteen hour flight. Marcus hired a car, and they drove out on the Interstate towards the town of Rockford, a hundred miles west of Chicago. Lisa used her mobile to book Marcus and Leonardo into the Residence Inn, just off the main highway.

'It's not in the centre of Rockford, but it's easier to get to my parents' place,' explained Lisa. 'They live near the Country Club towards Loves Park. I can take a cab from the hotel.'

Tired after their journey, Marcus saw Lisa into a cab, kissed her, and went to his room. He didn't bother to eat. Falling into bed, he was asleep in minutes.

Two days later they were en route to Los Angeles.

The time spent in up-state Illinois had been hectic. The day following their arrival, Marcus and Leonardo had joined Lisa and her parents for lunch. They were an engaging couple, but naturally protective of their daughter. Marcus found each of them frequently gazing at him. When he did so, they had the grace to smile and look away. However, it was evident that they were seeking to discover what he might have to offer their precious off-spring. Following the meal, they had been invited to the family house in Loves Park for the evening.

'Come early, Marcus! I want to discuss a proposition with you. If you agree, we've got to move fast.'

The cab dropped them at Lisa's parents' house. She came out to greet them and led Marcus and Leonardo to a shaded verandah. She was alone. A bottle of white wine stood on a small table. Lisa poured, and passed round the glasses.

'I told you I've been married, Marcus, At the time, my husband was a struggling screen writer, and a workaholic. The marriage was OK, at first. He was a nice guy, but I rarely saw him. When I did,

319

he was never really with me. He was always thinking of his next project.'

She looked away briefly.

'It's what drove us apart. I was devastated. I don't think he even realised what he had done! Still, his commitment paid off: from writer to assistant producer, assistant director, then to director. Now he is one of the principals at Warner Brothers.'

She smiled at them both.

'I couldn't reach him yesterday. However, I managed to have a word with him this afternoon. I presented him with an outline for a movie. It revolves around the instrument makers of Cremona, and how, several centuries later, their deaths affected two people bent on discovering if the glory of the golden age of the Cremonese could be rekindled. I also introduced the Vatican into the whole affair, particularly their ploy to move to Northern Italy if the government didn't pay them handsomely to stay.'

Her smile broadened. 'How am I doing? At first he thought it was a bit far-fetched. Nevertheless, he wants a synopsis on his desk the day after tomorrow.'

Lisa wrote the synopsis, discussing each aspect with Marcus and Leonardo. Eventually she produced a document that combined brevity in its telling with continuity in the extraordinary sequence of events.

At the given hour the three of them presented themselves at the studios.

Chapter Sixty-Eight

Margarit Brandt had nearly finished her packing. Just the last few items, then she would check, yet again, to make sure the spare strings, rosin and shoulder rest were in the instrument case. She would dearly have loved to purchase a new bow, but she would have to wait a little longer before she had sufficient funds for that.

This was her first tour outside Switzerland. What would make it even more memorable was the fact it was to Vienna. Margarit played for the Zurich Tonhalle Orchestra, which had been engaged to play at the Auersperg Palace, a concert hall much loved by her Viennese grandfather.

She had never met him, of course: he had been taken off to Dachau. But her elderly mother still talked fondly of him, his passion for music and of his collection of prized instruments that had disappeared when expropriated by the Nazis in 1942. Conveniently, her mother had been a student at the University of Zurich at the time, and events in Austria had encouraged her to remain. Later she had got married there.

Musicianship had skipped a generation. Though her mother had had no particular talents, Margarit was recognised as a future leader of the orchestra and she hoped that, during the tour, the coveted role might, occasionally, be conferred upon her. If only grandpa Liebermiers could be there to witness it, she thought wistfully.

The bell startled her. Was it the taxi? If so, it was far too early.

'Fraulein Margarit Brandt? Sign here.'

The courier thrust a long box into her hands.

It was not heavy, but it was extremely well wrapped.

Mystified, she forgot time as she gradually removed the layers. Whatever was in there was decidedly smaller than the package. The final protective sheath was a soft bandage, which she began to unwind. As she did so, the first suspicions of what it might be took root. With just a few twists left, an envelope fell to the floor. On it was written: 'The Property of Margarit Brandt'.

She put it to one side and undid the final wrapping. Freeing the clips, she raised the lid. Its beauty caught her breath. Its workmanship overwhelmed her. She sat down quickly, before her legs gave way, staring at the violin in awe and amazement.

It seemed an eternity before she recollected the envelope and put out a hand to retrieve it. Inside was a gold-rimmed, white card, bearing the words:

THE MAGNIFICAT
CREATED BY
GIUSEPPE GUARNERI 'DEL GESU' – 1742
*The rightful property of Joshua Liebermiers
and his heirs*

Chapter Sixty-Nine

The limousine glided up to the marker. The rear doors were opened and Lisa, Marcus and Leonardo stepped onto the red carpet. Although unknown to many in the crowd, as the stars of the film clustered around them, they were given generous applause.

Since the film's premier six months earlier, they had slowly emerged from their reclusive existence. Several attempts had been made on their lives. A bomb under their car had been quickly detected by one of Leonardo's cousins – even in America he seemed to have no lack of cousins! On another occasion their pool had been contaminated with a highly toxic chemical. Once more, it had been discovered and the problem dealt with.

Then, suddenly it was over.

Leonardo received the news via the "Pax Vobiscum" network. The Cardinal Secretary of State, Sylvestre Cantoni, and Cardinal Grossmann had relinquished their responsibilities within the Curia, withdrawing to their original dioceses where they would play supporting roles to the resident bishops. Both were beyond the normal age of retirement, and, in each case, this was considered sufficient reason.

Cardinal Marchetti had been promoted to Cardinal Secretary of State.

Nothing much was said about Cardinal Vincent Goehr. He was somewhere in South America, attempting to resolve a number of difficult issues. Privately, it was thought, the Cardinal Secretary would be in no hurry to bring about his return to Rome.

The sidelong glances cast at the instrument makers in the border towns of southern Germany forced them, much against the vociferous protests of one manufacturer, to restrict sales activities for fear of possible customer backlash. Further objections from this sector became muted when the chairman of the leading instrument company in Mittenwald was struck down in a hit-and-run accident in Klais. Neither the driver nor the car were ever found, despite the detailed description of the incident provided by a number of witnesses. The vehicle had been driven by a small man with a distinctive shock of white hair.

The film was called *The Messenger Shoots Back*. It was a fascinating tale of eighteenth century mass murder, the nefarious activities of the Hapsburgs, intrigue and corruption within the Curia, and the many problems that beset the hero and heroine before they finally win through. It received worldwide coverage in the media, for the story seemed to embody a number of inherent truths. In Italy and Austria, the film raised enormous controversy. It was revealed that the Mayor of Rome had quietly resigned. But the quickening interest in the ramblings of a life-serving inmate in the Novara maximum security prison, once a leading political lobbyist, came to nothing when he was found dead in his cell.

Nominated for five Oscars, it was widely predicted that the well-crafted screenplay by the husband and wife team, Mr and Mrs Sam Lucas, would scoop major honours. The generally held opinion was given succinct expression by the reviewer of the *New York Times*, who concluded a probing article with the statement: 'It is so incredible it has to be true.'